THE PLAYERS

ALSO BY STEPHANIE COWELL

Nicholas Cooke

The Physician of London

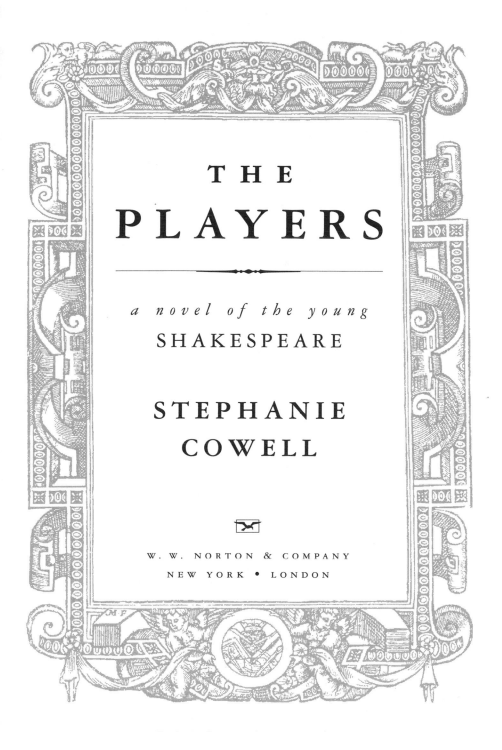

THE
PLAYERS

a novel of the young
SHAKESPEARE

STEPHANIE
COWELL

W. W. NORTON & COMPANY
NEW YORK • LONDON

For information about permission to reproduce selections from this book,
write to Permissions, W. W. Norton & Company, Inc.,
500 Fifth Avenue, New York, NY 10110.

The text of this book is composed in 11/14.5 Garamond No. 3
with the display set in Garamond No. 3 Bold
Composition by Tom Ernst
Manufacturing by The Maple-Vail Book Manufacturing Group.
Book design by JAM Design

Library of Congress Cataloging-in-Publication Data

Cowell, Stephanie.
The players : a novel of the young Shakespeare / by Stephanie Cowell.
p.   cm.
ISBN 0-393-04060-7
1. Shakespeare, William, 1564–1616—Childhood and youth—Fiction.
2. Great Britain—History—Elizabeth, 1558–1603—Fiction.
I. Title.
PS3553.0898P53   1997

813'.54—dc20   96-34987
CIP

W. W. Norton & Company, Inc., 500 Fifth Avenue, New York, NY 10110
http://www.wwnorton.com

W. W. Norton & Company Ltd., 10 Coptic Street, London WC1A 1PU

2 3 4 5 6 7 8 9 0

for
my husband, Russell,
and
A. L. Rowse

THE PLAYERS

I do remember this day, Emilia, as I have not done in a very long time. There were those moments when the evening candles burned low, and we had sung all the songs we knew, and sat about some common room (you perhaps as you once did on the floor beside his chair, while he stroked your hair). We spoke in those hours of our hopes, and indeed they seemed to linger among the floor rushes and cling to the wall hangings. Then we found perfect love, and nothing mattered for that time but that we all be together.

We heard the chimes at midnight, and after a time stretched, and found our legs aching from sitting so long. A flea had bitten my arm, and the dog smelling so heartily of itself rubbed its nose against my worn shoe. You had your head against his knee, your hand girlishly on your cheek. A book you had been reading had dropped to the floor, and in the dimness of the parlor your eyes shone. And you both always wanted to know why I was a player and a writer, how it had come to be. That, though I was uncertain of it myself, I tried to answer.

It hath rung the late hour, you said.

And we stood at last with some discomfort and stiffness, reluctant to leave the last crumbs of this night which seemed a part of all such nights which might ever have been. Oh the lute! you said, looking to see if it had been put into its case. I do not recall me what happened next, if he mounted the creaking stairs with you or if I did or if we indeed, as had occurred once or twice or maybe more that I have put from me, mounted up together.

When was the last evening? . . . the last quarrel, the dregs of the wine, the last rind of cheese, the last creak of the shutters? Did they cease or did they fade? And why did I cherish them so, imperfect as they were? Because I think, my dear, I truly believed in those moments that none of us would ever grow weary of the other or grow older. I truly believed it.

It was not so and the fault was mine. I grew weary, I grew older. I grew from both of you, and then in consequence as it was I who held you together, you fell from each other. Ah God's mercy! Why do I even now recall a thing of such uncertainty, pain, and unfulfillment as the most perfect thing I have ever known? And yet and yet it is so. I should not care for it ever to come again, but I shall never entirely put away its memory.

PART ONE

THE GLOVER'S SON

HE TOWN OF Stratford was not small: you could not call two thousand people a small place. It extended from Clopton Bridge (which spanned the glittering river Avon) through Rother Market and then out to the meadows. All around were elm trees, and by the Avon's mossy banks in spring grew wild heartsease, daffodils, and rosemary, whose fragrance was carried on the wind. But for a long time the small child's world was the kitchen, where he was bade not to go too close to the fire but did once, and stood shocked and weeping, though not greatly hurt. Behind the house was a garden. The world was hearth, steps, the creak of the upper floor, the sounds of horses and carts from the street, and the rich soil which he bent to touch and for a long time after could smell on his fingers, moist and greeny.

On the parlor table was an English Bible, and a candle holder whose edges were thickly clogged with wax. Above the garden hung a dipping clothesline where great rough linen sheets and chemises and shirts of inordinate proportion blew in the light summer wind. Wind came, stirring the heavy branches of the trees, and all was mystery, most of all himself.

The world was big to William. Even the infant dress he wore, which had been his father's, hung to the floor, and the cradle in which he was rocked so solemnly to his mother's sweet low voice seemed a great thing until one day he clambered to the side of it and fell to the floor rushes. Another time he managed to reach the latch which opened to his father's glover's shop, and yet the world beyond these counters was so vast he could not begin to comprehend it but sometimes stood listening towards where he knew the street ran ever on.

On the shop table were creamy calf skins which his father would bend to cut, a frown on his handsome, long face. Bits of lace, escaped from the trimming which would be sewn to the finished gloves, fell under the table. The small child knew that something beautiful and individualistic could somehow be made from a plainer, more humble substance.

Yet there was something beyond all this, and the first of these beyonds was indeed the river Avon which flowed under Clopton Bridge. His mother, who under her plain white cap was the most beautiful woman in the world, held him over the bridge's railing to carefully drop pebbles in the glistening stream far below. The second beyond was Rother Market, where she took him when she went to buy cheeses and butter, spices, and bloody, uncomforting meats: dead fowls with their heads hanging down as if in shame. All of these were tucked into her cavernous basket. He followed her gravely among these great tables whose tops he could barely see, wearing a now larger creamy linen dress, which was the garb of all little boys before they obtained the dignity of breeches.

Then he was older, and the world began to be his own. He could go as far as the street, and cross it carefully looking out for the carters and flocks of sheep sometimes driven through the town. Everyone knew his family, and subsequently himself, the oldest son. They called out for him to mind his way, or pressed a sweet into his hand. Thus the market became his to understand, and the voices and faces of the merchants. And all outside the town, the fields and trees, and what beyond that?

He was climbing the apple tree in their garden in October, for the one fruit he coveted was very high, but once it lay within his palm, he was apprehensive of climbing down again. His little brother Gilbert, nappie half undone, ran below him round the knobby trunk, every now and then glancing doubtfully up at the branches, a jam smear about his mouth. His knees were dirty. The boy in the apple tree held his breath. To see and not be seen!

Where are you, William?

That was his mother's voice: he had heard the creak of the door which went from kitchen to garden. From his place he could just see her, hands on her hips over the apron, and for a long moment he made no reply.

OH ENGLAND, GREEN and glorious land, and the little town of Stratford on the sleepy river nestled between fields and woods! Above him the sky with its lazy white clouds, and the sun so bright that he did not dare look at it. Once he did, and had a headache for the afternoon and could not see the letters on his hornbook which spelled out Our Lord's Prayer. That was crucial: he must know these things. He learned so fast, they said. By this time it was all quite clear. The town was the center of the world, and he was in the very middle of that.

He ran. He ran every day up and down the steps of the house, jubilant with the creaking of them. Every day his legs grew stronger. How strange was memory, and how vastly different he seemed to himself each season! The world expanded. For an inexplicably long time he was seven, and life nothing but seasons ever turning. He looked back in scorn at the infant he had been. They said he was like his father. He learned dignity, at least the importance of having his own, and what it was to be honest; he learned to look about him. Then the world shuddered, and grew once more.

HE WAS NINE years old, walking by his father on a dark road some few hours from the town. They had gone to visit friends and stayed overlong, and now somewhat tired had started for home. The way was familiar to them both, for they had often traveled it by cart with wool or fine leather for gloves, and the boy recollected some of the trees well; there was one in particular when the road turned that was so gnarled and old that he felt some spirit must be caught within it. Now as their footsteps sounded as one on the soft dirt, he took his father's hand, feeling the broad scar which had been made one day by a slip of the knife he used for tooling.

Above them the stars were flung over the sky as far as they could see. He had been reciting bits of his lessons, and every now and then his father's deep voice would murmur a reply from far above him. Gradually, though, he had the sense that John Shakespeare had ceased to listen, but heard instead some stern voice of his own thoughts.

They had a faintly lit lantern between them, the flame kept low that it might last, for the moon had not yet risen. Things appeared strange in darkness. The boy glanced about at the shapes of the trees, the walls of heavy stone, and then at what seemed to be a hut.

At last his father began to speak in the soft voice he had used to tell bedtime stories. "Some say the stars are where men's fortunes lie. They hold all that will happen to us: even now, they know."

"'Tis passing strange, Father."

"Aye, but so men have always believed."

The boy was silent with awe in the contemplation of it, and they walked for a time more hand in hand. Ever so faintly the lantern cast its light on the dirt before them. The spring had been dry, and dust rose from the declivities of carts. They said if rain did not come, there would be a food shortage again, nor would there be fodder for the sheep.

"There's Shottery, lad," said John. "Canst not smell the animals?"

Indeed it was, the faintest shapes, the faintest residue of roof, of yard, of barn, of steeple. How could he explain his deep, intense curiosity? Even more than the stars, William was drawn to the houses of the village they were passing. Behind almost every window a candle or lantern burned, lighting . . . what? Did whoever was within read, or whittle, or talk of this or that? Were there babes in cradles and old men by the fire? So many houses, of both the poor and the rich, and within each buried an incomprehensible vastness of dreams, each private and fervent. Did they wish to ride to battle, or did the girls dream of wreaths of flowers and a wedding day? What were men's dreams? For each man, no matter how humble or exalted, desired something.

The boy's heart arose to encompass them all. He felt he was the only one who could know as he walked, a stranger in the night. It was not an arrogance, for he was a simple boy, but a quiet certainty. Each house with a light or two which would, as the hours of the night progressed, be gradually extinguished; then all the world would be lost in dreams.

Now the village was behind them, and he craned his neck once to look back. "Knew a lass there once," John said softly.

"Did you, Father!"

"Loved her, or thought I did—I was a scrap of a lad."

"What, don't you love Mother truly and only?"

"Why, sweeting, of course I do." William felt the great warmth of this large man gazing down at him with a tenderness so palpable that he did not need to see it. He longed for another village, but there would not be one this way.

"Weary?" said his father.

"Some."

They came over the bridge with the water rushing below, and down Henley Street, and the nightwatch tipped his cap to John Shakespeare, who was, after all, Lord Bailiff. All along the houses of his schoolfellows not one light burned, but when he approached his own he saw a candle in the window, and his heart leapt. There was warm broth and bread, and he climbed the stairs peacefully and fell asleep to the sound of his mother's low voice.

HE LOVED THE night owl's hoots, rushing water ever going onward, flowering herbs by the garden wall. The world was strangely alive to him, but there were two worlds: one inside his head and the other without. He lived in both, and it was so natural that it did not occur to him that most men did not. Sometimes the energy within him sprang up so hot and fast he did not know what to do with himself. Running amid the calves in the field with weeds for a switch, singing bits of songs, climbing on things, tumbling down, feeling the roughening of his body.

The singing in the church on Sunday. "Oh God whose grace we do embrace!" He had come with his family once more to gravely hear words so old that it did not occur to them that there was a time in which they did not exist. ". . . by whom, and with whom, and in whom in the unity of the Holy Ghost . . ." A sparrow had somehow flown into the church and was hopping about the pews. William and his younger brother began to laugh, and then controlled themselves. The officious church warden, his heavy buttocks wriggling with indignation, came with a staff to poke it out. Here now, cheeky! Put thee in stocks I will. . . .

The bird darted, rushed up with a flurry of humble brown feather, rose like an arc in the air, and was gone. Later when service was done the boy walked between his elders, their best padded clothing stiffly creaking, their manners dusted and polished (his uncle would not blow his nose in the dirt nor swear by the devil until they came home to dine). He felt his younger brother smiling mischievously at him, and had to look away not to laugh again. Headstones stretched over the sweet spring grass of the graveyard. He walked about respectfully, sometimes tracing the weather-worn letters with his fingers. *To the memory of that most excellent and sweet lady, my wife Rosalind.* . . . What a lot of writing! Still he could not but hope there would be more. He could read anything, English and even a little Latin.

> *Magnae copiae hostium Romam oppugnabant.*
> (Large forces of the enemy were attacking Rome.)

A sparrow fluttered in the trees; he shaded his face against the sun, searching for it. Was it the very same one? Had it in some strange way a message for him? And if he fell, would God know it and bless its resting place among the leaves? He ran down the path until he was recalled to march decorously with his family once more past the shops of the town. "A blessed Sabbath, my lord Bailiff!"

Oh light!

He shaped his life to its ever-renewing presence, leaving at dawn for school when it hung wet and grey like old soaked linen in a pan, scrambling in the fields of a Saturday afternoon when it drifted like gold over the heavy trees, walking solemnly down the town street of a long summer twilight with his father in his alderman's robes. Light flung itself over the furrowed fields and glistened on the tops of trees. He was the eldest son, the next being Gilbert, who followed him everywhere, and then Richard, who was too small to be considered. His sisters, Joan and Anne, clambered after them petulantly. He barely tolerated them at times.

His closest friend was the son of a tanner—round-faced, magisterial Dickie Field with his blotched, freckled face, scabby knees, and sense of propriety. With short sharp knives nestled in scuffed sheaths at their belts, they tramped together miles and miles over the countryside; on long summer evenings when school was done, they often sat crosslegged in the yard of the tanner's shop, whittling ships for themselves and their younger siblings, who hung open-mouthed over their shoulders and wanted to know where the ships would go. "This one is going to fight the French!" William would exclaim. Before the sun set they would run down to sail their craft in the Avon, where the miniature vessels sometimes got caught in the leaves near the bank. Dickie had seven brothers, and there was always one about somewhere. William with his lively imagination decided the games, and the other boy organized them.

For his sister he whittled a doll which they clothed in bits of tawny velvet and called Eleanor of Aquitaine; he made up stories for her of lovers run away to a forest where imps and sprites hid under the ivy. She breathed noisily through her mouth, and he had to shake her lightly to bring her back to the earth.

"Silly dolt!"

"Thou!"

She bragged, "Will can make up anything."

Once, when the day was fine, the boys could not bear to go to school, but stayed in the fields, and the next day they were beaten for it by the master. William felt the light strokes of the switch with both shame and curiosity . . . pain did come, invading one: a bloodied knuckle in a fight, a split lip, a bruised knee. A forsaken girl had been found drowned in the stream with flowers bound about her hair, and was refused a churchyard burial but laid to rest outside the wall. A crazed woman lost her only child to a sudden summer fever, and crawled about hedges in a torn skirt looking for her. Pain came to himself and to others—sharp voices which answered his most tender moments, and his mother shouting from behind the bedchamber door, "But John, why!" Then his peace was broken by parental quarreling, and the sound of her sobs which he heard standing on the stair below.

To escape such things he retreated to the tanner's house with its eight raucous sons clambering up the stairs and elbowing for room at the table, and the heavy scent of leather which came from the shop and the skins hung to dry in the muddy yard like the partially whitewashed scene of a crucifixion in a church he had looked into one day. The hot scent of too many young males penned together, and he both of them and apart. Running about the muddy yard, splattered and sweaty, they were indivisible.

There were school plays in Latin, and now and then strolling players. Once when a few came with a tragedy, he and Field squeezed into an inn-yard to watch it in a cold rain amid the farmers and tradesmen, and then walked home shivering. The tanner's son declared, "The one who played the father spoke poorly; still, though he had a mouth of wool he looked a fine fellow."

William leaned against a tree. "The fellow who played the Queen had but few teeth!" he howled. "But oh, Field, to act such parts! It cannot be a bad thing!" They went home discussing the heavenly and baser natures of man, the higher being the duty of all Christians and yet the lower of sometimes far greatest interest: an old woman suspected of being a witch, an idiot boy who, it was whispered, had spilled his seed into the woolly hindquarters of a large sheep. Things spoken of behind the hands of matrons: sin in all its fascinating aspect, and death. Death not laid to earth with sanctimonious prayers, but that of terrified rabbits trapped illicitly on someone else's land. He was fourteen when he went with some older boys to poach a deer and felt the blood of it on his hands when they felled it. The gamekeeper after them, they ran crashing through the woods, and he jumped in a stream with Field for safety. One of the oldest boys was caught and whipped; remembering it, William woke up with his heart racing and bolted his door, but no constable came through their garden.

There was always Field. Sometimes they climbed an elm in a wooded area beyond the churchyard and looked down at the world through its branches. No one below could see them, and if they rustled the leaves, maids below glanced about puzzled; sometimes they whistled low like the nightingale. Once they pretended to be ghosts and sent a matron shrieking from the wood, only to have her husband and brothers return with cudgels later, angrily stalking the bushes. There they exchanged secrets, and William poured out how he had pushed his sister into the table in a quarrel, and another time yanked a clothesline to the mud in a moment of rage; how he sometimes did not know how he belonged within the neat rooms of his house.

He fought for words. "Everything there's perfect except me, but thine . . ."

Field turned his head. "What, do you think my house is better?" he demanded in his stern, boyish way.

"Is it not? Your dad's not somber."

"Oh is he not. Listen!" The older boy wet his lips, and lowered his head, and there was the longest silence that had ever been between them. "There's things that happens there . . ." he whispered, but would say no more.

Taking arms, they moved closer to each other's warmth as the night began to fall over the fields and cottages. "What do you want, Will?" Dick Field whispered, as they turned towards the town.

"I don't know." William was impatient with himself, feeling that he should. The high grass whispered past his wool hose, the trees stirred, the air was sweet, and they paused to turn their jackets inside out so that no ghosts should harm them. William said, "I think I would like to see the world."

"Dost remember the deer?"

"Aye."

"Wouldst do it again?"

"Wouldst thou?"

"Aye."

They were fourteen and fifteen years in the spring when they sat yet again facing each other on the branches, and Field said casually, "Dad's sending me to London to apprentice under a Flemish master in printing. There are fifty-three presses in the city, people are that eager to read books. Here they have only use for Bibles and books of metric hymns, but in London they buy *everything*. I'm off week next."

He swung his scuffed knee and added, "I shall miss thee sorely!"

Some days later, William stood on the hill to watch his friend and the tanner ride off on one horse and thus became acquainted with that loneliness which does not go away. For months after on market days he thought to see a lad who looked like him. They wrote to each other as often as they had the penny for post.

Sweet Will,

Marry you would not believe such a place could exist as this great city of one hundred thousand souls! Thank our sweet Savior I arrived with but two shillings in my wallet, for that was lifted from me somewhere about the churchyard of St. Paul's when I was perusing a book on becoming a gentleman. Then some fellow, hearing my country accent, wanted me to exchange my father's ring for what he said was London coin, and later I found it to be but glossed tin. How any Christian soul lives in this muckheap of sin and later finds heaven, I do not know! However, I have found my own earthly heaven in the presses, am inked to my elbows, and do not care a wit for anything else.

I have very much laughed at the ballad of your making which you sent me. You ask, do people pay for such things here? By my faith they do! As for us, we are forever buying religious pamphlets and others that make great fun of any foreigner (foreigners are here despised, though they come in such prodigious quantities from the Netherlands, France, the Baltic—steelwork-ers—and all set up signs to give lessons in their horrible tongues).

So I am a member of that most honorable group of lads the London apprentices, who know everything, and cannot be fooled. I am no longer a Stratford bumpkin, but a true Londoner: I modify my speech, wear my hair as long as the guild allows it, know how much to pay a ferryman, and will never again have my coins taken. More, I intend to be a rich man!

It is the sadness of life that we have partings, yet ours need not be for-ever. My master says you may have a pallet in our rooms when you come, and I shall show you the beasts in the Tower and how the whores are whipped at Bridewell, a merry sight I can tell thee. Only plan to do so, sweet friend, for art too loving and impetuous.

We have bad tidings of your family. My brother wrote to say your pretty sister Anne who was sickly so long has died and been buried with much grief. He also said your dad does not come to council meetings and his friends fear there is some trouble. Any words you write will be respected with the greatest confidence. Believe me, I have kept your family in my prayers.

JOHN SHAKESPEARE of Henley Street had not for some time been the punctual alderman in red-trimmed gown sweeping to gatherings in the guildhall, nor the generous friend of all within the town who would not judge his neighbor, nor even the man who rolled out a barrel of ale at the end of every harvest to drink and dance with the farmers in the feast of Harvest Home. Sometimes he sat for hours alone in his locked, dark shop, whose bell had inexplicably begun to ring less frequently, as if customers feared some vague contagion within. One time William found the glover with his hands over his face crouched down in the wood shed, the ax beside him.

He had been mending a shutter in an upper chamber on a November day, and bending to retrieve a dropped nail, he felt his hand pass over one board which seemed loose. Lifting the corner and staring down into the darkness of beam and the cold smell of a space which has been long secret, he was drawn to the flicker of the early sunlight on white paper. Curi-ously he pulled up what seemed to be a document carefully bound in old ribbon. At first he was puzzled by the religious tone of the writing, until it came to him that what he had spread on the floor was a Catholic testa-ment of faith.

He knew enough of the rumor of the county to understand that Jesuits came through illegally, spreading these documents and leaving in each several blank spaces for the supplicant who hoped for heaven to write his name. Everyone knew that those who favored this Catholicism most likely also wished to murder their precious Queen, and that a man who followed Romish practices could never be trusted by his fellows. Leaning over the document, William made out the signature of his father. The boy moved his lips into the words "Oh Christ." What was a good, ordinary tradesman, whose very hard-earned position of honor in his town depended on having the proper, Protestant faith, doing with this thing? The more orthodox a man's outer faith the better, and the less one thought about it inwardly, when surely there were richer matters to turn over in the mind, the more contented one would be.

The boy leapt to his feet, and in a moment was hurrying down the steps, papers held against his chest so that if his sister Joan or his brothers rushed up again they would not notice it. Naught!—a bill for wool, a list of fabric to be made into sheets. It seemed forever until he came to the shop door.

John Shakespeare the glover was facing away from him, the broad shoulders under the old, shiny leather jerkin bent as he counted a new delivery of skins. When he saw the paper clutched against William's chest, he pushed aside his work and bolted the door. Taking the boy by the arms and looking into his eyes, he said seriously, "Dost know what this containeth? Hast read it?"

"Some!" blurted William. "I can't help but read what I find, Father!"

The older man nodded, wetting his lips with his tongue. "Thou canst not help it," he murmured unhappily. "Bless thy sharp mind and wit. Ah, Christ's love, I am glad somehow hast found it, Will, for the secret's so heavy I cannot bear it—even thy mother doesn't know! I'm haunted at times, boy, for fear of my salvation. Sometimes devils come to me and seem to dance about my bed, showing me hellfire."

William's narrow chest under the white shirt heaved impatiently. "Why hellfire?" he cried. "There's not a better man than thee!"

"Ah, I am not a good man!" groaned the glover, shaking his head as if to deny himself. "I deserve punishment, I am not good! We do not know how we sin!"

"This doubt itself is the only wickedness hast ever committed, that I know upon my soul!" replied the boy passionately. "God loves thee, 'tis said in service He loves us all. These doubts come insidiously somehow of thy mind alone, believe me!" Impulsively he pressed the palm of his hand to his father's forehead as if to locate and then wipe away the sickness. Something was there beneath the bone, something dark and terrible, and yet he could not touch it. Perhaps it was grief for the dead daughter, over which William had also wept hoarse, youthful tears.

Pushing his son away with embarrassed clumsiness, the glover murmured, "Why do you question me and speak of what you cannot know? I am your father. We won't talk of it further! Return the papers and nail the board, and let's forget them. I cannot say from whence the darkness of my mind comes—and to whom can I speak it? The deepest longings of the heart must always remain silent and go to the grave with us. Never mind, sweet heart. Put back the papers, nail the boards over, but do not burn them. God knoweth—" He turned his dank face.

William whispered, "Father, Father!"

"Do as I say. Obey me."

The boy nodded gruffly. Taking the papers, he hurried up the stairs to bury them again, hammering down the boards with fierce, angry strokes. For some time he knelt with his hands clasped over his face, praying both with great passion that his father should be healed and that things should be restored to what they had been.

He knew then he must never leave Stratford.

THE YOUNG MAN

HEN WILLIAM WAS fifteen, having learned all that
there was to teach him, he left school. Money was a lit-
tle short, and he did not press to be sent on to university. Each day he took his place beside his father in the
shop. Sometimes they stood so close his slender shoulder touched John
Shakespeare's, who would turn and gaze at him with a weary smile. In his
free hours he would run, flinging himself into the grass, and up the
branches of trees, scraping his knees, tearing his clothes, running down the
streets. He did not know where his strength came from, and he had no
words for all that he desired.

He learned how to tool fine leather, and sew on a border of lace to a
glove; the needle left small marks on his finger, which faded slowly. He
was changing; soft brown hair gathered in the crevice above his upper lip
and on his chin. He passed his hand over them, satisfied.

One day when walking at the edge of town he looked through an open
cottage window and saw that the burly, muscular blacksmith was making
love with his wife. Her pale naked leg rested on her husband's back, and
she arched up until her hair fell in loose waves down the side of the bed.
They moaned and grunted, she seeming both to pull her husband towards

her and push him away. Her arching, her arching up! William stood there for seconds, yet it seemed years, and then hurried on.

Later he found a hill and rolled down it, the rocky earth knocking his slender body until he came to a heap on his stomach on flat ground amid the weedy daisies. Lying there, he felt as if he had gathered to himself wild grass, daisies, trees, river, air, and sun. His body hardened within his breeches; he was angry, excited, and cursing beneath his breath.

There was this now: rough, unpremeditated, imbedded within him, and yet an imposition. Was it he or did it really have nothing to do with him at all? What had it to do with the richness of the variant feelings of which he seldom spoke? Was it sin? This was one sensation and longing, riding over all others, sometimes encompassing them, sometimes suffocating them. It spoke, I am myself, am human, must love, must grasp. Oh this strange, brutal, shouting individuality! His sensuality found release against the hard earth: he tumbled to himself, bruised with its being done. He crept back past the smith's house, sullenly averting his eyes from the wife who was hanging wet clothes in the yard and singing under her breath. He dreamed of her pale flesh.

HE LOVED HIS family so, he could not stop loving them, though at times it seemed as if they would choke him and he had to rush away from the supper table to stand by a tree looking down towards the Avon. Sometimes while working by his father he felt he could not breathe, and after a time he accepted other employment in the form of a clerkship for a barrister. His father, though disappointed, did not reproach him. He knew his son had come to be the necessary consoler and mender of all that was broken within the house.

Sometimes the young man still thought to make the long journey of a hundred miles to visit Field, and at the last moment gave some excuse. Growing up consisted of putting aside silly dreams, which were, in the end, no more than the fancies he felt when running about the fields in the sun. The glittering of the water was that, no more . . . there were no ghosts in the churchyard. There was only the scratch of his pen as he wrote out the last will and testament of a dying townsman by his bedside and held the man's trembling hand to make his mark in the proper place. So there was the scratch of the pen, and the sound of the knife cutting glove leather, and the creak of the great iron soup pot as his brother cranked it away from the fire. His mother's back often ached, and she said she was growing old. At night the silver hairs from under her cap shone in the firelight. He still felt she was beautiful.

He borrowed books of the neighbors: books of war, sailing, discovery, other countries, cities. He saved Dick's letters and read them until he knew them. With other boys he took a deer again, and ran home in the darkness with only the sound of his beating heart to accuse him. Nothing happened, though he heard the gamekeeper and master of the land murmuring angrily about it in the churchyard. William looked at them innocently, pushing back his hair; they would not suspect that the alderman's son, who had a reputation for scholarship, yet bore the taste of half-roasted deer meat in his mouth. They also did not understand his unspoken depth of rage.

The years passed until he was eighteen, and while poaching wild hare with friends from a neighbor's land he saw a young woman walking under the trees. She was like a vision passing below the elms with her arms full of white cloth, and when he followed her she was gone.

HER NAME WAS Anne Hathaway, and the next he saw her was outside their church, where she had come with her brothers, her father being dead. She was standing by the gate, and the sun came through the branches and made a coppery gold of her hair. Her cap blew away, and he scampered after it for her. As she waited for her brothers to finish some farmer's business with a colleague by the church wall, he walked up and down the path at her side, his hands behind his back.

She had been promised to another, she told him at last with sadness, and then abandoned. William swore softly, searched for his handkerchief, but could not find it. He murmured things in consolation, for he felt at once he must help her; he was, after all, the fellow who mended spindles, dolls, tables, and he felt himself destined to mend her. She flung herself against him behind the church; he comforted with clucking noises under his breath, and she pressed her breasts against him until he felt he would catch fire.

Each day they wandered farther; they found scarce-trampled paths, a deserted broken chapel, a barn whose slats had half fallen away and through which the sun came, an empty cottage. She held her skirt primly above the sheep dung of the fields. Each day he touched something new of her: once her naked breast, once reaching lower her warm belly, once feeling up her leg under the hose gartering her soft thigh. Each day he gathered her more to him. The moon waned and grew great again; the clouds were harvested in the night sky. He had her almost all, and bayed like a dog who suffers in his longing.

And then she gave herself to him.

It was in a garden grown wild amid camomile which made a carpet. She had little breasts with dark, round nipples and a flat belly, and the crevice of her buttocks was a mystery. Still so full of passion was he that he did not see her, as you sometimes cannot make out objects when you come first into the brilliant sun but only the shape of them. His head ached trying to focus.

"Oh sweet!" she said. "Oh sweet, art mine!"

"Aye, by my faith!" he swore, reaching for her again.

THUS THEY BECAME lovers as any others who wandered secretly in the forests and fields of Stratford that season. At times he was blissfully happy with her; the aching of his body satisfied, he quieted the doubts of his mind. He could not speak to her of what lay within his heart, especially if it was contrary to her own wishes, but what could one expect? The problem was that when very young you expected everything. For each man everything was possible. Should he go to war, become an alderman, accumulate property and goods, travel foreign lands, become supremely wise? Perhaps growing up was learning not to expect too much, to be content with little. A place had been created for each man, and he must only live contently in it, fall at night into clean sheets and count his blessings.

Thus he lay in a field with Anne, looking up through the branches of the trees at the glittering sun and the very ephemeral air which seemed to dance before them, and she scolded, "Art thinking again, William! I wish you would not do so—I hate it, by God's grace!"

"How can I not think?"

"Sometimes I don't know thee a whit," she answered with pouting lips. "Thinkst, but whatever 'tis, dost not think of me . . . oh no. And I wish you would not do it, at least not silently, when with me." And as she said these things she seemed to change: he saw her as one of the town matrons folding sheets in lavender, walking to church with platitudes on her lips and he ever by her side. He saw himself suddenly as old before he had ever been young, and his heart was heavy within him.

THE YOUNG MAN

FROM THAT MOMENT on he knew that he did not love her; he had only been curious. There was a difference. Curiosity, as his father said, often brought a man into terrible trouble. Keep hands on work and mind on God, and forget the rest. Oh, such stuff to catch a man! After it was done with her he sometimes wanted to thank her politely and be off, yet could not by any means do that. He knew in these moments when he was sated that he found her tedious, and that to couple himself with her for a life-time would be a disaster. In reaching out to grasp the world swollen with life, he had pushed it away from him.

He made up his mind to avoid her.

Weeks passed. Once he slipped early from church to escape her before the congregants drifted sanctimoniously away down the path under the elms, the music of the last-sung psalm on their lips. Another time he climbed from his window when she and her friend came knocking at his door. He blessed the fortune that she could not write and could send him no chastising notes, and hoped with all his heart that she would forget him.

Then when hurrying to his office on a lovely morning, he felt her behind him. I must tell her the truth now, he said, gathering his courage, and turning with the packet of copied documents under his arm, he began with some kindness, "Dear Anne . . ."

"I'm with child," she replied miserably, as if the fault had all been his. "You've had your way with me, and now we must marry."

Those were the darkest days of his life. A play had come to town, and he stood in the innyard to see it, hands in his belt, moodily leaning against the wall. He walked to the hill to watch the little pack of actors and their cart going off in the dust, singing and talking. To go off around the world like that and never stop—to be not one thing, but something else every day. He would be an actor.

For two weeks he ran off with them, and then in a clumsy fall he injured his knee. When he returned shamefaced and limping to his father's house, he found the glover stern. "Mistress Anne's brothers have been at my door!" he said. "What shame will you bring upon us in your lust? Now you must marry her and make the best of it." His sister and three broth-ers gazed at him with sympathy, and the youngest, Edmund, who was just two years old, hurled himself against William's leg and clung there.

* * *

THE BRIDE WORE a pale linen dress embroidered with yellow flowers, and many people came heartily to wish them well and dance to the music of the town band. When they were alone at last that night he fell upon her pregnant body greedily and buried his despair in his embraces. The little girl Susanna was born, and then the twins Hamnet and Judith; three years passed.

He had become the teacher in the grammar school. "Lads, we will read Caesar's account of the Gallic Wars." He liked lads very much, but hated to discipline them. Sometimes he was so deep in his thoughts that he looked up to find the schoolboy had finished his recitation long before and was staring at him.

Through this time he continued to write his friend in London. Field's letters were full of news, and he pressed them to his face to inhale the strangeness of the city, to sense if he could breathe the words of parlors where men conversed of the new sciences and lands, booksellers, taverns, all those things of which he was beginning to make a castle and a refuge in his head. Field's master had died, and the young printer had cleverly married the widow and become the new owner of the shop.

A DECISION WAS forming in William so deeply, so subtly, that he could not recall its beginnings. He began to save his money, putting the spare penny away under the very same board in which lay his father's secret papers. For the first time he earned a little by his pen. He wrote funeral orations and once even some sermons, and actually, on behalf of some merchants, courting letters.

Each night, after the boys had joyfully rushed home with scarcely a bow in his direction, he remained in the schoolroom. There he also wrote verses and sometimes bits of a play until the candle made strange shadows of the empty desks with their deeply carved names of boys who had long ago sat here and since grown old. Often the whole house was asleep when he returned, and he drew in his breath at the thought of how once more his wife's silent little shoulders would reproach him. Why did he not love her more? Why did he not attend her? What was the matter with him? Sometimes when he made love to her he felt emptier than ever before. He could have beat his head against the bedposts in his rage, and once did so, to her terror. He was twenty-three years old.

She wept, "You don't love me."

"I do as I can."

"You're strange! You don't walk the ways of godly marriage." Tearing her handkerchief, she stared at him in accusation. "You never told me you were like this when you took me lustfully in the green."

"But I do not know what I am like," he murmured.

"Then you are . . . bad!"

"Oh, Christ's mercy!" he shouted, so that the very soot in the chimney seemed to tremble and he knew he would soon hear his father's accusatory soft slippered step, and the righteous knock upon the door. Then the lecture would come. You have too much imagination! 'Tis grievous as bile, my son. Hast work, wife, and home . . . what can you want? Ah, Christ's mercy, you know my troubles and now you grieve me more! (The last spoken with bitter mouth.)

On the night of the last quarrel he waited until she had cried herself to sleep, and then, finding paper and pen, hunched over the kitchen table by the last small light of fire. Several times he began, scratched it out, and ground his teeth.

Dear wife,

I must follow my heart for a year and go off to London to make something of myself in the world. These coins should sustain thee. If I cannot earn far more there within that time, I will return to teach again. I will remain faithful to our marriage vows. God knoweth it grieves me that I have made thee unhappy. I never meant to make any woman so.

I will go to my own friend Field, and see if he can help me.

Thy husband, Will

The house was asleep when he came home, pried up the board, and divided the coins, taking only a small amount for himself, and thus set out on foot the hundred miles to London.

THE PRINTER'S SHOP

 T WAS A warm day in early October when William,
coming up the road from Warwickshire on foot, first
saw in the distance the spires of London rising before
him—old Roman town that it was, old fortress town,
full of wood houses and thatched roofs and a hundred churches with an
ancient stone wall about it all.

He had worn for his long journey plain brown breeches, doublet and
heavy white shirt, and sturdy shoes of the country, and over his shoulder
carried a satchel which he shifted now and then for the weight of the books
within it. His large, brown, slightly protuberant eyes were tired; the modest beard needed trimming, and he longed for a clean bed and pillow. At
the same time he looked about with the greatest curiosity, composing letters in his mind to his family on all he saw.

Approaching from the west, he lost himself two or three times in the
streets off the Strand before passing at last through Temple Bar to Fleet
Street, and from there into the city itself. The burnt spire of St. Paul's
Cathedral rose on his left, and the streets to his right swept steeply down
to the Thames River, which wafted a scent of fish, boats, and putrefying
sewage. Each alley he peered into led to another, and sometimes it was all

so tangled that he could no longer tell which direction he was going. The central streets were cobbled, but the little ones were muddy and full of puddles from the recent rain. All about him were cries of costers and lads bawling oysters, mussels, hot buns, cesspit cleaning, footpath sweeping, and ballad sheets for sale.

He looked up. Above him swooped great grayish-white gulls, dipping and shrieking and hurling themselves ever upward again. They had come from the sea far away, traveling on wing or ship up the river. Some perched on the thatch roofs and blinked down at him with hooded, critical eyes. He gazed at them with lips parted in a peculiar joy. Then he went on, shifting the satchel, and beginning ever so slightly to limp, which occurred now and then when he was weary since his fall.

At last he came to the gates of the neighborhood which had risen over the past half century from the ruins of the Blackfriars Priory, and after being roughly regarded by the sentry, hurried down the streets towards where he understood the printer shop of Richard Field to be. It was set back on the first floor of a half-timbered house whose upper stories extended farther into the street than the ones below them. Yet William saw at once that the printer's sign did not hang; the door was also locked and the shutters fastened closed, nor could he hear the sound of the presses or anything else from within.

Passing his hand over his forehead, he looked up and down the street. He should have written beforehand that he was coming. As he stood there, a matron with flour all over her arms hurried from the next doorway to throw a pail of slops into the gutter. Tipping his hat to her, he asked if she knew the whereabouts of the printer and his family who lived within.

"Why, they went away of a sudden this morning!" she exclaimed. "'Tis an apprentice holiday today, knowst not that? 'Tis the Lord Mayor's Show, when he processes with all of London on the water with a boat with silver oars. Good Queen Bess floats as well on her barge with banners flying, ladies close about her, save her virtuous virgin Protestant soul! And later they will all to Guildhall to dine on many meats." She blinked her eyes piously and folded her hands over her stomach.

"I have just come to the city and know not of such things," he replied. "But of the printer, do you know, dame, where he traveled?"

"Why, to a wedding!"

"When to return?"

"I know naught of the matter."

"Then, dame, where may Cheapside be?"

"The great market street! Why, go that way, and ask any Christian soul!"

Come to the Bear and Bull on Cheapside if you are ever about London streets, lad! the actors had told him when he had run off with them for the few weeks years before upon understanding that Anne was with child. Now as he turned the avenue of many shops and stalls, broader than he could have ever imagined, he formed his plans more clearly. If Field was not home, he would perhaps find news of the convivial men he remembered so well from those brief days, and announce to them that he had finally made his decision and come away to the city. Jenkins . . . he recalled the leader with his rough curling red hair and rotting teeth, who had let the eager lad from Stratford follow them though he had been but of perfunctory use to the four or five vagabond players who seemed to have no past or future but the performance of the very same tragedy in different innyards or country fairs under trees day after day. The story had been wretched, and he had cleverly made a few suggestions to improve it, which were greedily accepted and then forgotten as the men made up the drama extempore each time.

The tavern, when he found it at last, was furnished with a few long tables and benches crowded under the fire-blackened beams of the central room, with more private booths and chambers seen in the hall beyond. Over the bar hung a chalkboard for the writing of purchases, and a collection of wood and pottery mugs dangled from hooks along the wall. By the door were posted many papers of apprentices wanted, books printed, ships bound for foreign lands, and rags for sale.

The sharp-chinned barkeep looked up from the book he was perusing. "God's greetings, and what is thy pleasure?"

"I'm told actors come here."

"Actors, writers, tumblers, and bear-baiters," responded the keeper. "Look at the signs hung there! A play to be given and a poem to Harry Hunks the blind bear. Do you seek one in particular? Does he owe you money? You shall whistle for it, by my faith! From whence have you come?"

"Stratford."

"Where by Christ's sweet mother is that, goodman?"

"By the Avon to the north. The man I seek is red-haired, called Jenkins."

The keeper leaned back against the bar with its chalkboard listing monies owned for provender. "Oh, Jenkins!" he spat. "I tell thee where canst find him—churchyard of Lawrence Jewry, six feet under and not so lively as he has been. Some scurvy pox took him, and he died owing me two crowns."

"That's bad fortune!" William cried. "I knew only two men here, and one's gone the Lord knoweth where, and the other's dead! But first I'm famished! Let me have a penny plate of beef and bread and small beer."

He ate hungrily, using the knife at his side, ignoring the pleasant stare of the taverner. All the time no more than two or three men came through the door, for it was indeed the day of the Lord Mayor's procession and all were down by the riverside watching the ceremonial barges.

Then the taverner said, "I can tell at once art country-bred and know nothing of city life. Art honest? Then you can come to no good! Now let us suppose," he continued more kindly, "let us suppose you cannot find your friend! What will you do? Men are no angels here."

Then the young man burst out, "Neither are they in the country. Angels live in heaven—why should they consort in such streets? But we are fit to do it, being between angels and demons, being men. . . ." The small beer, drunk hastily in his thirst, made him heady.

Once more, the keeper shook his head. "I advise you to stay away from actors and acrobats and the like. They are a sorry lot."

WILLIAM HEARD THE noise of the procession up the water as he left, and making his way down the steep unpaved streets which led to the river, he stood for a time listening to the music and watching the silken banners of the boats go by, beneath them the lacy ladies and somewhere in the midst, he supposed, the Queen. About him the town seemed yet sunk in the medieval world of warring kings. He could almost feel the dust of dead princes gathering on his shoes as he walked back up the streets: that dust mingled with the flutter of fading silk banners from even more ancient pageants upon the royal river barges, with the haunting sound of the haut-boys carrying over the water and echoing against the stones of the bridge. His fancy throbbed . . . for a time he trembled with excitement, until it gave way to weariness and discouragement. He did not know when Field might return, and he had only one penny and no idea what to do, and when he returned to the tavern he found that none of the actors had come.

A penny could not even buy a night's flea-ridden lodging in a brothel, that much the keeper had usefully informed him.

Dusk came and settled over the roofs and spires of the city, and one by one the lanterns or candles behind closed shutters were quenched, and after at time there was little sound of anything but the wind knocking a shop sign which had been forgotten on its chains, or a baby crying, or down an alley a rough clatter where a few men were tossing dice on a barrel top. From behind one window above the street he heard the high feminine voice of a young wife cry out sweetly, "Harry, nay . . ." and the insistent murmur of her husband and then his low contented laugh.

The bells sounded from St. Paul's Cathedral and yet again, and streets away he heard the growled warning of the constable: "Twelve o'clock, and God's blessing be upon thee, good people!

> "Look well to your locks,
> Fire and your light,
> And God give you good night
> For now the bell ringeth."

William hesitated as an animal does in fear, sniffing the air with its mixture of mud and muck, the thick dust of coal fires, rot, horse dung, old stone, dried wood, dried thatch. His own town and house seemed to call him as a whisper in the wind, and with it came as in a dream the more wholesome scent of the sweet elm trees which filled his own streets. Then as he stood there not knowing which way to turn, he seemed to feel most intimately against his chest the malleable, soft bodies of his very young children, and how he rocked them in his arms in the darkness when they were troubled, and kissed their hair, and told them stories. Judith, Susanna, Hamnet his son whose little nose was always snuffly. Back and forth he had walked countless nights holding them close against his long linen sleeping shirt, while outside the streets of the little town drifted away to the enclosed pastureland.

A pang of homesickness came over him so intense, that he put his hand on a wall to steady himself. What on earth would he do here? What did any honest man do here? Despondent, he walked slower, feeling indifferent to the hundreds of houses and whoever might bide inside them, wanting only what was known.

A few hours past midnight he stumbled once more to Blackfriars, and this time as he came about the corner, he saw two horses and several people before the printer's door.

RICHARD FIELD'S BODY was heavier, and he wore a thick, dark beard. Yet even so, William saw only the boy he had been. Sending the weary family up to bed, they took food and light into the printer's shop. Eagerly William hurried about in the shadows with his candle to make out the stacks of paper, and thin rope stretched across the room where sheets printed the night before had been hung to dry. He had already noticed that unbound books, roughly sewn together, were piled on the edge of every stair and crates of unused paper filled the parlor. Bottles of ink and boxes of typefaces were meticulously arranged on shelves, and towards the center of the room stood the press itself. Further stocks of books filled boxes; there were many small pamphlets, and several gorgeously engraved expensive volumes of the classics. On a high desk a herbal lay open near an assortment of jars of paint and brushes; someone was coloring the flowers by hand.

It was that peculiar hour some while before dawn when, as boys, they had crept out to the churchyard on All Hallows' Eve and seen a ghost sitting on the churchyard wall. Now gazing at his friend's solid form in the shadows of the London printer's shop, William embraced him once more.

"Ah, eat, eat!" the printer murmured, embarrassed, rubbing his hands and once wiping tears from his eyes. "Hast not changed—still slender and eager—but I have much."

"'Tis more within than without. So you married old farmer Hathaway's lass and it did not suit you!" The printer shook his head and pushed the plate of meat towards the traveler. "Unwise, yet . . . once done, perhaps better preserved. I would have told thee not to come, I think, to leave her thus, if had written me."

"Then you are sorry I am here!"

"No, Christ's mercy, Will!" said the printer in his deep voice, which seemed to reverberate in his full chest. "I have longed to see thee. . . ." Carefully, ever adjusting printer trays or paper stacks near him, he began to speak of all that had occurred. He had stepchildren, and his work was more prosperous every day. William, in turn, told of his few professions, adding much of what he had not said in letters, and described his three children with much love.

He could hear his friend smile in the darkness, "You are as I always thought you'd be, Shakespeare! "I do not know if I have ever talked to anyone as I did to you . . . and here you are again. Yet I have changed! I was a sinful man, and now have found God. There are many temptations in this city, and it is best to avoid them. . . ."

William replied honestly, "I must work so much to send money home that I will not have time for temptation." Leaning forward and cracking his knuckles, he said, "What work can I find?"

"Let me think! You're a clever man with a pen. The best would be a secretaryship to some lord, to wear his livery! That's the way of this city; without the protection of powerful men it is hard to get on. But until then, I may have work for you myself."

Rising with a candle, Field rummaged in a box on a shelf and came back with several slender pamphlets, moving the light so William could read the covers. "We print treatises—little books on such matters as gardening, travel, how to find wedded happiness—and sell them at our stall in St. Paul's Churchyard. If you can write such for me until you are better situated, I will pay you for them so you may have money to send home."

"Can a living be made with this?" asked the Stratford man.

"Even so! Everyone's eager to quickly improve himself."

For a moment Richard Field was silent, and then his voice darkened with anger. "As for Stratford," he said suddenly, "it's not at all as fine as I'd like to recall it! Fair meadows, fair morals. My father used my brothers lewdly: I kept it from you. He would have done the same to me had I not fought him with all my strength. Remember the heart of man is a dark thing, and we must turn from it and keep our thoughts on heaven."

"Ah, the old goat!" William cried, his eyes filling with tears. By this time the faintest dawn was seeping under the cracks of the shutters, and Field rose resolutely and, unbolting the shop door, breathed deeply of the air of the old priory streets.

SPACE WAS FOUND for William in the garret with the apprentice lad: there was a low cot, a chest for clothing, some hooks placed in the wall, and a table for his writing. On this sat a lantern with glass slats. The roof looked out over the city down to the river, and sometimes gulls perched on the tiled roof and cawed lustily out to the tides. He could see the tops of ships' masts, and a sea of laundry hung on lines from house to house. Through the window came the smell of sewage and river, old horse dung, boats, and coal fire.

A canon of the cathedral had committed to gather a book of popular Latin quotations, but had been stricken ill when it was half done. William spread the notes for the work before him and began to make a pamphlet from them. *Dura lex sed lex*, he wrote . . . law is hard, but law it is. *Per angusta ad augusta* . . . from difficulties to honors. *Abyssus abyssum invocat* . . . one misstep leads to another.

For the next week he wrote steadily from dawn to dusk at the table in the garret by the window. Only at twilight did he take time to walk about the Blackfriars Liberty, which had once belonged to a monastery. Like other city liberties, it was a small district exempt from the jurisdiction of the sherriff, and was presently home to many fashionable people, tradesmen, and artists. Returning to the shop at dark, he fell to work again until bedtime. As soon as the pamphlet was done, Field whisked it away and gave him in its place some badly written pages by an apothecary on beautification for woman. The Stratford man learned that hair could be dyed chestnut by mixing lead, sulphur, quicklime, and water, and that skin could be whitened with egg white, vinegar, and white lead. By this time his head ached, and at one point he threw the pen across the room, where it left an inky mark on the newly whitewashed walls. Still, he had earned enough to send something home.

Yet when he went into the streets to buy bread or fetch water, all the faces were strange to him. He did not understand that the joy in his heart with which he had come had dissipated a little, and that the enterprise he had begun so jubilantly left him wanting somewhat he could not define.

On one particular morning, Field said to him, "Take these pamphlets over to my seller, who hath a bookstall in St. Paul's Churchyard. Mind your purse and watch, for there are those who'd take them from you. If you do not return by dusk, we'll send the constable for you, for the city's a wild place."

"Why, I can watch for myself," answered William with an irritability which surprised him.

Still, he was so curious about the alleys and streets that he lost his way a few times, for though he could see the huge cathedral looming over the whole of the city, he could not find the street to approach it. At last he came through the gate and found himself in the churchyard crammed with the striped, brilliantly colored awnings and painted stalls of booksellers, and more volumes than he had ever dreamed of in his life. Where there had at one time been bones, now there were books. Leaving the pamphlets, he looked about him.

Death was still here amid the crowd, for to one side of the doors was a gallows, and from it, like a shadow over the bustling merchants, hung a wretch with a blackened, strangled face. It left a sudden sickening emptiness in William's stomach, as if his muscles would push up and away the herring and bread he had consumed but shortly before. Even as he stood there the corpse moved as if it would approach him. Some dirty boy had thrown a stone at it, and for some time it continued to sway back and forth with a terrible dignity and a kind of reproach. William could not turn his eyes away, as if he had some personal responsibility for the stranger's terrible end.

"What did he do?" he asked a peddler.

"Beat a maid to death for tenpence, but there's one other we know of did the same for a copper penny."

Feeling something tugging at his side, William turned to see two ragged women about to cut his purse. Laughing like geese, they pushed their way into the crowd and were lost to his sight.

The shouting of carters and costers, the ringing of bells, the noise of a raucous puppetry show hammered against his mind; surrounding him and thrusting rudely against his body from every direction were foreigners, thieves, courtiers, carters, merchants, whores, and rich, fragrant, saintly-looking women followed by their desirable plump maids. He was offered gold, cakes, lottery tickets, flowers, treatises, mummy powder, and two sparrows for a penny. A preacher from the outdoor pulpit pounded on the railing and shouted of hellfire. Turning suddenly, William began to hurry towards the city gates, yet even as he went he was followed by the bawling of balladeers and a herd of cattle driven towards the shambles to meet their end.

On he ran, men turning to shout angrily at him, a wild dog yelping between his legs when he collided with it to avoid a carriage. He would at that moment have given his soul to be in the fields outside Stratford, with only the sound of his own breath and the rustle of high grass as it bent before him and the wind which fluttered about the drying leaves of the trees.

> In a herber green asleep whereas I lay,
> The birds sang sweet in the middes of the day . . .

Towards Aldersgate he went, fleeing out past the city ditch with its ordure and filth, its dead animals and ghosts. Still, when he looked back he made out the houses built into and over the city wall, the brilliant sun on the homely reddish brick, and the flutter of pure clean wash which hung in lines from the windows over the golden yellow trees, it seemed nothing more than a decent city of the ambitious merchant and good husbandman, tending his garden and saving his coins. Turning, he walked more slowly onwards past the ancient medieval Charterhouse, and St. Giles in the Fields.

Here the world was more quiet; the protests of the herded cattle faded far off towards Smithfield, the mixture of the sensuous and the sour which had sickened him was left behind. Cool winds of autumn stirred the hairs of his chest under his open shirt. Birds sang. He sat down on a tree stump, and looked back at it all. Then he understood what troubled him was that Dick Field, but for the conversation of their first evening, no longer spoke to him but on matters of business. Still, he murmured, perhaps it is just that we have been apart so long. I must be patient.

Picking up falling leaves as he went, he began to walk back towards the shop.

WILLIAM INQUIRED ABOUT the city for the few actors he had known, but he was told they had scattered or found other work. That was the way with provincial strollers, the taverner on Cheapside told him one morning. "Still, there are other players enough within the city walls!" he added, wiping clean a tray of clay mugs. "London's the place for them, and many's the young fellow turns his sight to that work, for surely it must be a fine matter not to be plain John Barleycorn but to play an emperor in the best of silk to the cheering of the crowd!"

As soon as he had sent his first money home, William walked over to the Theater outside the walls of the city on a Thursday afternoon dressed warmly against the early winter day to see his first London play. The singing of the little boys who played the maidens was delicate, and the band of instruments rang up to the two galleries which rose above the stage and the orchestra where the ordinary people crowded, and stirred the old thatch of the roof through whose opening he could glimpse the windy sky. Occasionally he could hear the blast of muskets as the volunteer military bands of the city practiced target shooting in the field beyond. The platform stage was draped in black cloth to delineate that a tragedy was being given. Gold thread glittered in the padded velvet costumes; swords flashed, love was thwarted, and a general amount of the cast was murdered before all the players returned, marvelously resurrected, to make the last dance and bow to the shivering audience, crying, "Give us your hands! Adieu, gentles all!" William left so possessed with what he had seen that he hardly knew which way he walked and did not look up until he had gone half a mile past the printing shop.

Shortly after her Majesty Elizabeth had ascended the throne some thirty years before, actors had begun to appear on the London scene—not simply guild players on holiday, but tumblers, acrobats, and fire eaters who had fallen into this profession for want of a better one. Some sober citizens considered them little more than mountebanks; indeed, some actors were that (as the taverner confessed), but others were as hardworking a group of men as could be found in any trade. In fact, they were almost respectable, and a few even possessed houses of their own, and went to church of a Sabbath with beards perfumed.

There were a few men at the time in London who had a vision that the theater could be more than a few shouting churls barking out bad lines. One was James Burbage, who had at first been a carpenter and then an actor with one of the new groups of players called Lord Leicester's Men which was more or less in that lord's protection. He had gathered capital and leased land north of Bishopsgate on which he built the polygonal, galleried playhouse with a raised stage which he called the Theater. The land stood outside the domain of the city government, whose Puritans would have forbidden the structure. Burbage had two sons, the younger of whom, Richard, was then nineteen years old and already one of the most popular young actors around the city. Men wept to see him play.

The second man who believed a good living could be had from the theater was the loud, coarse Philip Henslowe. Born the son of a gamekeeper, he had risen steadily as a dyer and a dealer in land in the southern parts of the city. He owned a pawnbroker's shop there as well into which all manner of men and women crept with goods to pawn: cloaks, pewter plate, lutes, stolen gloves, rings, watches, astrolabes, and chamber pots. Thieving boys were said to dispose here of their ill-got gain. He was also building a theater on the south side, which he called the Rose, for it was on the site of a former rose garden in the Liberty of the Clink. Neighbors reported he could be seen at night coming home with a cart which he'd wheeled across the bridge heaped with soiled secondhand clothes he'd bought in the evening clothing markets at Cheapside. These his wife and serving maid remade into the costumes of kings and queens, and dyed in a great vat in his yard at night into peaspod green or periwinkle blue. He presented plays in all the theaters of the city.

During his third month in the city, William made up his mind to try a speech before Henslowe who was now at the Theater, to see if he could be hired for work which he perceived as far more interesting than writing treatises on preparing marmalades. "Henslowe's looking for actors," a man told him one day as they conversed by a tavern door. "He'll have you by the day to play smaller parts for a shilling—bishops, peasants, comic servants, hapless lovers. Canst handle a sword? Canst sing? These things are needed to be a player."

Printed playscripts were sold among the many other books in St. Paul's Churchyard, and for sixpence he bought one of the great old tragedy *Gorboduc*, loosely sewn together and wanting binding, and wearing his best brown doublet, which he had bought secondhand the week before, he walked over to the Theater beyond the city walls. He found himself in a chamber behind the stage cluttered with costumes and props, trunks, swords, painted trees, a bed, an execution block, some royal chairs, and banners of every description and color. An old man who did not bother to raise his head was gluing curls to a woman's wig, and the floor was covered with scraps of fabric and feathers. A few other men with speeches written on loose paper, or holding musical instruments, were already waiting. William looked about: here was fantasy made.

"Idiot! Pisspot! Turd!" shrieked the old man. "Do not lean against the costumes, you in brown! They are worth more than your sorry arse!"

Through the door from the direction of the stage he heard a great shout and a stream of profanity which bellowed so to make the shields on the wall tremble. "A fart of my arse! Never come here more to wound my ears with such speeches. Cut purses if you will, rob the dead, scratch for the Queen's fleas, but do not think to be an actor!"

Moments later a lad in a wool cap hurried through the door muttering furiously, with his face burning in shame. Triumphantly, the old man rose to his toes and pounded the table after the boy had gone. "Master Henslowe hath put him right . . . the scullion, the flea-bit hedgehog! Do not lean near the wigs, idiot, scoundrel!"

Standing by the door, William heard each of the speeches. One applicant had a burly Welsh accent, and an Italian musician did not speak but played several instruments, and explained himself with wild gesticulation. Then there was no one left but himself. Sun glittered on the straw-thatched roof above the top gallery as he walked carefully to the edge of the stage. Below him standing in the yard with his arms crossed and a scowl on his lined face was a very small man with large ears and a deep, startling voice. Bowing slightly, William looked about at the galleries and began a speech from the tragedy in his slightly rolling Warwickshire speech.

Almost at once Henslowe began to shout. "Must stand as saints do stiffly to receive the arrows of sorrow? Look to the top gallery and let them see your face! Shake your fist at the heavens. Grind your teeth in rage. Who recommends you? How do I know you are honest, trustworthy, sober? So many men fancy to play upon the stage! They do not know the difficulties of it! You are given your part with your cues on a sheet and have a day or two to memorize them; we rehearse once, perhaps twice, especially the swordplay and the dance. No craftsman or tradesman in the city works harder than the actors, sixteen hours a day at times!"

Having exhausted himself with his speech, he waved the young man off and muttered, "There may be work in spring when we have new plays. Leave word where you can be found."

"Sir, have you need of a writer? I would remake any play you like for very little payment."

"Hast done this work? I see not! Art a university man? Then by Christ's nose, nay! Why, every man who hath writ a love letter to a milkmaid thinks he can write."

WILLIAM WALKED ALL the way to the river before deciding to turn into a tavern and find something to drink. He could not bear to show his face at any man who knew him, for he felt it to be swollen with dreaminess, disappointment, and yet not entirely extinguished hope. The face of sensuality . . . he felt a man should not have such a face, but one that conceals, and yet he hardly knew how to begin to do it.

This was a boatmen's tavern, frequented by those who ferried passengers across the Thames. Because it was the middle of the afternoon, the room was not crowded, though one boatman had rested his oars by the door to keep an eye on them lest they be stolen. They were weather-worn, rough men who felt they knew the city better than any others. A seagull hopped near the open door, the wind blew but sparsely cold, and the red lattice rattled. William called for buttered eggs and was soon lost in a translation of Boccaccio's sensual stories with their willing women which he had bought torn for two pennies.

After a time he noticed that a heavy man of great height with a broad chest over a stained jerkin and the innocent countenance of a farmer was taking a place on the bench beside him. Even in his absorption of the tale of plump unclothed damsels, he recalled this fellow from the theater's tiring room, and for one moment hoped that Henslowe had sent him with the good news that William Shakespeare should be hired at once and given a role to play.

No such news came, and when they had nodded formally to each other and sugared wine had been brought with a dish of stewed eels, the bulky newcomer paused with his knife above the fragrant mess and spoke in a reverberating, resonant voice. "So you would be a player! I myself played in one bawdy comedy from the Italian, but the audience despised it and it played no more. I am John Heminges—or Jack as they call me—of the grocers' guild, but I love the theater with the passion of any honest London man who's not a Puritan—and those I spit upon." Turning his face, he spat contemptuously into the floor rushes, which were so old that they might have been laid in the days of the earliest kings.

"Ah well, I am not overly fond of Puritans myself!" rejoined William, remembering the three-hour sermon to which his friend Richard Field had taken him last Sabbath, during which he had fallen asleep. In the printer's house William could more and more sense the presence of a patriarchal God prowling about the stairs to protect the morals of all within, and, like the mortal master of the house, disapproving of much He saw about the city.

Wiping his knife clean on the table's edge, Heminges with a great broad smile held its handle first to the Stratford man. "Will you eat!" he burst out. "I do not fancy to dine alone this day."

With scrupulous politeness, William answered, "I had thought to call for mutton as well."

"Well, call for it, and let's feast. I believe you are an honest man and I like your ways! Still, you must not trust every London man—I sense you country-born."

They began to speak with some reticence, leaning arms on the table, and after a time William sighed, fetched his own knife from his belt, and loosened the buttons of his brown doublet. The sliced mutton was brought and some of an oyster pie, and amid the shouting of the boatmen they bent their heads and began to eat. William called for bread, which the server marked on the board. The voices of the boatmen rose excitedly over the allowed price of a ride which they wished to raise, and he looked up several times at the wide, good-natured face of this lumbering grocer, and smiled. He judged him about thirty, and felt a strange innocence about him which he trusted, and his chest softened, as happens when you discover among strangers someone whom you like very much though you do not at first know why.

Made passionate by the wine and the hostess whose full breasts swept his shoulders each time she squeezed past him, and with his ears full of the shouting for claret and the squawking of gulls which perched on the open windows, William began to talk more rapidly, waving his free hand about as he ate. "'Tis not as if I have never acted before! Why, I have spoken some fair parts in Latin at Christmas in my school at home."

"But that, as he says, is not London theater," replied John Heminges, shaking his head as a master might at a pupil who has made a slight error. "Why, this is the greatest city in the world, and as Henslowe says, we must have the best, the best, for the citizens will stand for naught else!" He began to laugh, took a slab of eel on his knife, and concluded simply, "Now, I am not a great actor, but I do well enough. . . . You will also when he tries thee."

With the sugared wine racing through his body, William let his thoughts wander. "I could perhaps also remake a play or two," he muttered almost to himself.

John Heminges gazed at him reflectively. "Most playmakers fail, which is why he's loath to trust another. But even though a man hath a great desire to do a thing, and even much skill, he may yet fail . . . aye." His broad face darkened, and he took a deep resentful breath. "To think a man could work with skill and strength and fail!"

After a time he took some of the tougher bits of mutton and flung them with some tenderness to the excitable dogs who had been hurrying about from table to table. Then with his beautiful eyes darkening, he said, "My father and grandfather were grocers before me in our family shop, which I inherited, on the north side on Bread Street just off of Fish Street." Breathing deeply as if the story pained him, he began to carve something on the table. "'Twas this way. Heavy rains came one night when I was away with my poor wife at her mother's house in Hampstead; there was a flood, and when I arrived back at the shop I found most of my stock ruined. Shortly thereafter my wife died, may she rest in peace and sing with the angels! So now I live on the south side, one of the worse neighborhoods in a far smaller store, with my little girl, Susan. Look here, I have made her name . . . strange to make the name of a child in this place! But she waits for me with the old woman who cares for her, and loves me more than I deserve. Mayhap I am not as good a man as I think and God has found some fault with me . . . but I so love life. Do you think it sin to love it so?"

"No," answered William, "for then I would be damned. Yet did I love it less I might please better those who are dearest to me . . . and yet some of the dearest are strangers, and sometimes a stranger comes closest." Then he spoke of his marriage and his children, and pushed away the scraps of food, rubbing at a grease spot in his jerkin.

They talked so long that many boatmen left, and more came in to drink and sup. At last they emerged as well, walking even deeper in conversation along the rough streets that lay behind the Tower of London. The night was dark, for there was no moon. It was when they had come to an alley which reeked of old fish and dung that they heard the muffled footsteps and voices. Before he could reach for his dagger, William was seized from behind. Rough hands felt lasciviously for his purse. Struggling free, he grappled with the man, was held again, felt his face in some rotten cloth that covered a foul-smelling body; his nose dilated, and a fist fell against his back.

With a shout of rage, he broke free, lifted the man, and hurled him several feet away to the dirt. He leapt at him and began to throttle him. The fellow's terrible cries of "Ah! Ah!" broke through to him, and he punched him several times and rolled him away. He was then aware that there was a second man, who ran, and John was after him, hurling him to the filth of the gutter. The grocer's heavy fist struck the thief's bone with a sharp sound and brought a groan. Crying, "Worms! Stinking gentry worms! May your pricks rot and turn to pickles!" the two thieves stumbled down the alley, knocking down something iron which crashed against something else. Then there was only the crying of the gulls.

Panting for his breath, John Heminges cried in a voice of scorn, "I lift bags of flour and sugar with one arm such as they could not move with both, and do they think to play with me?" Wiping his mouth, he staggered over to William to see if he had escaped harm. "Christ's mercy, we routed them well," he shouted. "The Lord in His heaven be praised! We could have lost our lives this night, but He favors me, though He provokes me sore. . . . Gentry, they thought us gentry! With eight pennies to my name they called me so. . . . Seest the virtue of costume and darkness? In darkness or on the stage even a beggar bears a coat of arms!"

With a shout, William placed his hands on the dirt path, flung up his legs, and balanced there with great delicacy and skill, his shoe buckles glistening in the light of a wick candle over someone's door while his ragged hair fell down.

The grocer put his fists on his hips. "That's fairly done!" he cried. "Such a gift is well in a man of the theater, almost better than one from memorization! What other gifts hast, merry fool?"

"Why, fellow!" replied William through his hanging hair. "Can you not tell to look at me? I can play the lute. I can sing the bawdiest of songs. What, shall hear it now?"

"Nay, the watch will come with his stave."

"I care not! Why, all things that can be done in this world I can do, by Our Lord's mercy!" Panting, he rose to his feet again, smelled his hands, and with a gesture of disgust, sought for his handkerchief to wipe them. "I can hunt a deer, make a lady's glove. Why, I write pamphlets on how to do anything which a man cannot do, even those things which he ought not do. I can eulogize and make epitaphs on any man, especially those I have never known or seen and have not heard of before yesterday. I sing to make wise men weep, and can find the lass who's worst for me in all the country and make her mine."

"Christ's mother, you make me laugh! God's mercy, my stomach aches!

No more tonight!" Heminges fought to control himself, and then, remembering what had occurred, brought his swollen, bruised knuckles to his lips. "I like thee well," he said thoughtfully. "I do not decide such things easily, but 'tis resolute with me that I like thee well. Aye, should I be made to declare it before all the barristers in Chancery Court, I like thee fair. Let us make a pact then that we will play upon the boards together come spring."

"The pact is made! Here's my hand. I will do much for it: serenade this Henslowe, or bed his ugly wife."

"Christ's wounds! What is thy family name once more, you merry fellow?"

"Shakespeare."

"Leave word for me at the Mermaid and Boar's Head. A good night, friend! I must make my way over the bridge now, for my little one does not sleep well until I come!"

William stood by the bridgepath as the grocer mounted, turning before he came to the first houses above the water, and waved once more. Then with a shout of joy the Stratford man stood again on his hands and balanced between alleys and bridge in the almost perfect darkness of the city which smelled of sewage and the sea.

THE FRIENDS

S HONEST JOHN Heminges had stoutly sworn, both he and William were called for one play in the spring, a revival of the ancient *Castle of Perseverance* rewritten to include clowns commenting on city inflation and four madrigals (a part of which Jack sang in his sweet bass voice, but which showed William to sing but poorly). With a cast of ten men and four boys, they crowded into the tiring room and clothed themselves in silks and glittery brocade, sweeping hats with audaciously dyed feathers which swooped and drooped and spoke of prosperity, to strut before the crowd. The audience, however, was bored, and *Castle* was played but twice before being hustled off the boards, leaving a great debt for the expense of refurbishing costumes.

"Such is life," said Jack Heminges philosophically, stripping off the sweaty lacy shirt of his character, and pulling on his plain linen laced one, which had assumed over much time the shape of his full chest. "This play was poor one hundred years ago, and not even dancing can make it better. Still, we'll be called again. But you must come dine with my friends! They've asked who's the nimble lad of such wit who sings like a frog in heat."

"Oh, me!" answered William with a smile, putting off the borrowed velvet feathered hat in which he had played a Virtue, and buttoning his brown doublet once again. Carefully he replaced his sides, the sheets with his part alone written on them and only a line of two of others' speeches, on the table; he suspected they would be used in the future to wrap wet fish in a woman's basket on market day. This production should not be mounted again.

After that for as many hours a week as he could manage away from his writing of treatises, he would slip from the printer's house and hurry over to Eastcheap to meet Jack and some of the other actors, writers, and musicians whose worlds centered about both court and theater. Everyone was fond of the big, good-natured grocer who stammered when he was troubled, even on the stage itself when for a moment he was flustered and could not recall his move.

They went first to the Boar's Head Tavern on an early summer day, when such a sticky warmth hung over the city that even the flies seemed to sleep in corners of the woodwork, and stagger over the great drying round cheese that was placed in the center of the table. The tavern was in a cellar down worn stone steps, and voices hurled themselves to the rough, low ceiling beams and down to the kitchen, where a fat, sweaty girl rushed back and forth to serve them and answered to bawdy names with a sweet smile. From behind, when the door opened briefly, came a rush of heat from the roaring fire, whose flames leapt up in a frenzy of grease like the much-reported flames of hell so fondly spoken of by preachers from his childhood.

William gazed at the men who had squeezed about the table, on which burned a smoky wicklight, for the one small window of the Boar's Head was broken, covered with waxed paper, and admitted almost no light. He turned his face somewhat shyly at the speaker, who was the most beautiful young fellow he had ever seen, and as William soon learned, was a scholar down from Cambridge. Christopher Marlowe was held in amazement in literary circles for his translation of Ovid. They said he knew Raleigh, the explorer and Queen's favorite who had journeyed across the ocean to attempt to colonize a place he called Virginia in her honor, and at whose house the poet had stayed for a time. He always had money, though no one knew where he got it.

To his right and almost squeezing him from the bench with the generous, heedless wild gestures of his arm was a stocky, gruff young man with large shoulders, a squarish face, and brilliant small, accusing eyes. This was Benjamin Jonson, who was not yet twenty and was now in the fourth year of apprenticeship to the bricklaying trade under his father. It was poverty alone which had put him to this work, for he made plain to tell them between shouting for more beer and eggs that he had studied under the renowned scholar Camden at Westminster, and knew his Latin and Greek.

They were discussing theater, for two of the other men were presently playwrights of the town. "I tell you!" Benjamin shouted, banging his enormous fist on the table. "What's writ for the stage these present days is swine's flesh. Classical drama must place all action in one day! No more than three characters may appear on the stage. Why, I shall beat any of you once my start's given, with my hands tied behind my back. I shall write with my teeth, I shall do better than all!"

The pounding shook the table; William felt it shake through him as if he had been taken by the shoulders and awaked from a long sleep. He gazed at them all greedily. Half-conversations began here and there, and then were drowned out in others.

Ben Jonson turned to him. "The theater's a pissing sickness, but life's naught without it!" he challenged. "Come, share my food! Yet by Christ's good mother, if you are dull I shall dunk you in the Thames, for I can bear dishonesty in a man, but not dullness. There is no sin greater than this, thus saith the Lord! What, can you not curse, fellow? Thou country lad, thou moldy cheese."

"Swine's buttocks!" said William. "A fart on thy grandfather." The fat sweaty girl hurried towards them, the firelight glinting on her plump, naked neck, winking and showing the red hose above her shoe. He sat back with a smile against the worn wall, flushed and happy with drink and the company; the desire for life rushing through him until he felt almost faint, he wanted to gather the room and the city against his swelling chest.

THERE WAS NOT then a new or revised play given but that they had to see it. There was *The Troublesome Reign of King John*, and *Galathea*, set in the English countryside, in which each year a virgin must be sacrificed to a sea monster under an old curse of Neptune. It was full of goddesses and shipwrecks and dismayed virgins. John Heminges appeared now and then in smaller parts; he sputtered with emotion as one of the virgins' fathers, and once or twice broke into a stammer, for which he bitterly cursed himself. William began to know several of the actors. He woke before dawn to write his treatises by candle so that his afternoons would be free to go to the plays and then to eat with the theater men and writers, and often did not come home again until the whole of the diligent printer's family were asleep.

Gradually thus his life began to divide, like two continents which split apart and drift in their own directions. There was the wholesome world of the shop, its punctual meals and polished brick kitchen floor, and this new one with its smell of stale beer, easy language, and meat heavily spiced to disguise its quality. The actors were fallible, like himself; he could feel their life as he could feel the wind, and he sometimes unlaced his collar to have it blow against the fine hairs of his chest.

Benjamin Jonson was almost always there. Sometimes it seemed as if he slept in that poor tavern on Eastcheap, down worn stone steps, which was so dark and smelled of tallow candles and stale wine and greasy mutton and hard bread. Jonson would come in shouting, "A light, a light— thieves, scoundrels, a light for my mind that I may search this cellar in every corner and find me an honest man." He had begun several drafts of his first play and often left his mortar, trowel, and cart of bricks unattended to rush off and join the men, for he could not bear to keep his thoughts to himself. He knew what everyone should do, and ranted that they did not listen to him. Generally he wore a workman's blue smock much stained with bits of mortar. His large hands were rough, the nails cracked. On and off he fought violently with his stepfather and left home, and then slept in so many places he could not remember where he had been the night before. He said he was writing a nonsense play for Henslowe, and could not recall at what address he had left it. Never mind, he said, he could write it again. He only regretted the waste of the paper, which he could ill afford. He borrowed a pen of William, and forgot to give it back. The next time he saw him he could not recall William's name. When he had not one penny left he finished the play on the back of ballad sheets, and when paid went round to the taverns seriously paying his debts.

He swore once a sentence, and wept when drunk of his love of God. He bragged he knew half the doxies in the Southwark brothels by name, though perhaps their names were not right, yet still he called them some-

thing. He had been thrice in jail for brawling, and claimed the lice he had
adopted in the Fleet remained yet loyal to him. He could pick a pocket
better than any man, though he was too honest to do it.

"I will educate the audiences," he cried.

"But the audience does not wish to be educated."

"A quill pen up their asses, I shall do it anyway. Why, I shall make a
scholar of every London cutpurse!"

Christopher Marlowe would fold his arms across his chest, surveying the
lot of them, biting on a chunk of tobacco and spitting it out, as if he knew
better. He might have been a baron come slumming for his exquisite
clothes, which were, when you looked closer, dirty. The brown, almond-
shaped eyes glittered. He also could not be found for days, but it was said
he was at the home of his patron Sir Francis Walsingham. He was writing
a play from Fortescue's *Collection of Histories* on the life of Timur, the
Scythian conqueror, whom he called Tamburlaine. William borrowed the
Ovid translation from a friend and found several unfinished pages of *Tamburlaine* which were left in an alehouse. He read them by rushlight, astonished at the swelling of the verse.

By this time he had also met a brilliant Italian translator called John
Florio, who had in turn introduced him to the courtly Sir Fulke Greville,
for whom the Stratford man now occasionally wrote letters in his great
library. This was the first splendid house to which he was admitted, and
he had stood for a time caressing the library latch, made in brass with
the face of an angel, with the palm of his hand. On the freestanding
shelves were all the books of literature, the Greeks, Romans, and men of
the Renaissance. This was great poetry, and next to it there was the
young Christopher Marlowe, who it was said would rise in London as a
flame. William thought heavily of his own poor pamphlets, and flushed
that anyone might see them. He was a plodding writer with some inclination to comedy, but no university education, and Christopher Marlowe's verses inclined you to think that their author had sprung
full-grown as from the sea. Sometimes he wondered what would ever
become of him; he was at times stricken with great shyness, and other
moments burst out with audacity of the things he could like to accom-
plish. Life rushed by as quickly as a procession beneath the window when
you lean out and see all the gaudy colors, and reach out your hands as far
as they can go.

Yet even when these thoughts were most melancholy upon him, he did not return to Stratford.

Mine own brother Gilbert,

To the good one who hath stayed, from the prodigal who hath gone far away. Well, dullard, what dost? Here I have been making a fine treatise on distance in my mind: a fine place to make such a thing, for the mind is the only whereabout where distance can be folded like a cloth, and is as naught. This instance for example I pummel your arm, sheep's ass. But oh when I come from my mind it expands an impossible great length, near one hundred miles. How much shoe leather is that to walk, how wearing on the knee, how taking from the time I need here to earn and earn and earn. Do not marry young, pig's ear! I dare not express to Mother and Father how bitterly I long for the sight of my little ones, how I pray for them each night. Can it be they speak so well and are so clever!

Everyone here is concerned that the Spanish will invade us and the country will be brought down with war.

Understand I do not tell them at home quite the truth of my life here but when the truth's a less shabby thing to tell, I shall say more of it.

To his wife, Anne, he wrote passionate letters of his experiences and did not send them. She could not read, and would not have understood. Still he sent all the money he had, and once a gift of cloth.

IT WAS ON a day in August when shouting from the streets carried through William's window in the garret; barely lacing his breeches, he ran barefoot down the steps. The whole town seemed to be tumbling from its bed, and every bell in the city rang out, while above them, driven from a somnolent night in belfry and on high gargoyle of church roof, pigeons and sparrows whirled into the sky. A burly fellow who mended shoes rushed towards him, caught him about the arms. "Hast not heard!" he shouted. "The Armada's routed . . . driven away, sunken, the Spanish damned down to hell, which is pleased to have them!"

"What, have we driven away the invaders?" William cried.

"Aye, by Christ! They shall pluck their bones from the mouth of fishes. Let them try themselves against Francis Drake and the English sailors!"

Later that day the announcement was read from Paul's Cross at the cathedral. The war was done, the invasion deflected, and the infidel had been roundly defeated. Everyone was running to the water, men with their swords not yet buckled on. Women hung from the window, their bodices half laced and bosoms showing almost to the nipple. They paused in awe for the sound of cannons over the river and then the bells that joined them once again. Men wept in joy, embracing each other. Bonfires blazed on almost every street, and the Spanish king was burned again and again in an effigy of straw with a paper crown upon his wispy head.

God save the gracious queen, Gloriana!

Long live fair Gloriana!

He shouted himself hoarse.

In the days that followed, the city seemed to be on endless holiday. He and John ferried to see the great *Golden Hind*, Francis Drake's ship, which had circumnavigated the globe a few years before, and was now decked with banners and flowers as it lay at dock in Greenwich. The city bands played their instruments outside Drake's city house, and an inordinate number of ballads were printed in his honor, most exaggerating, all extolling him near sainthood. But nothing in the city was still anyway, for it was a hot, oppressive August where men suffered from lice and a rapacious desire for life, and the theaters were full and girls could be had for tenpence behind warehouses and brick kilns. It was the time of the annual Bartholomew Fair in Smithfield, the great, most dishonest, most splendid, rascal-infested, cheerful fair in all of England, perhaps in all the world. No bazaar of the East, or so those said who had been there, could hold a candle to the magnificent squalor and crowds of this annual London event, for there was gambling of every sort, animals and every good sold from pottery to pins, feats of balance and strength, music and dancing and food from the civilized world. Every pickpocket and liar prepared to make his fortune there that day.

As agreed, the friends met by the gingerbread tent with its hot, spicy fragrance and tattered flag. John Heminges, who had left the grocery in the hands of the halfwitted boy who helped him, was the first to arrive, and William came second, for he could not walk quickly when there was so much to look at. His soft face was flushed from an argument with Field, who had said he should not go, and they had parted with coldness.

Ben Jonson appeared as if from behind the trees, wearing neither doublet nor smock and his shirt plastered against his chest and back in the heat of the day. At his side trotted a finely built, boyish man with hair of a shocking burnt orange like an artist's spillage upon a pallet. His beard, which was trimmed to such a point that it seemed to be made of some hard substance and sharpened with a knife, was of the same color. Jonson introduced him as a treasure: a new writer, a university man, so gifted that he was able to author anything which needed to be authored in a matter of minutes. He already had a play submitted to Henslowe, though he had just arrived a fortnight since in London. Before that he had been the vicar of a parsonage in Tollesbury, Essex, but of that the small man declared he would not speak, and his mouth trembled with rage. His name was Robin Greene.

He was not alone, for a fragile girl great with child clung to his side, whom he paused thoughtfully to kiss every few minutes. Several times he pointedly referred to her as his wife, and then she looked about with some interest and smiled shyly. All the time they walked he kept her arm in his as if she were a possession he might lose.

"Let me tell you my story!" he cried as they walked about eating hot gingerbread and cream. "Bess was betrothed to another, but he was a wife beater, had done his first to the grave, and she was frighted—weren't you, Bess? So I left my vicarage and we came away together, sleeping in barns. God watched over us. We were married by the waterfront, where they do it quickly without questions. They don't care about the banns, and who should care, for love must speak for itself. Love of all things must be, is without doubt, free." His sharp face wavered between the crafty and the innocent.

"Ah!" he cried, waving his arm at a muscular depiction of a half-naked man on a large wood board before a tent. "The strongman! I will contend with him," and he pompously began to roll up his shirt over a sinewy arm.

"Oh, shall you?" said Ben Jonson, raising his upper lip.

"Why, there is naught I cannot do if my mind's set to it!" cried little Robin Greene furiously. His red beard sharp as a dagger, and dragging the girl at his side, he led them into the tent to confront a beast of a man, far older than his portrait, who rose to his great height and belched. He turned to Jonson, from whom he had supposed the challenge had come, and then, bored, to the husky frame of the grocer Heminges. When he was directed to delicate Greene, his mouth broadened with a sneer.

With a yawn he engaged Greene's hand on his, yet it was a while before the red-bearded writer would allow his arm to be forced down, though he grimaced in pain and bit his lip. "The dog!" he murmured furiously as they emerged.

Jonson cleared his throat and frowned in sympathy. Then, looming over the delicate writer, he said with much empathy, "In a contest of wits with thee he would be a dead man."

"Ah, that's so!" muttered Greene, and after a time began to smile. Looking up, they gazed past a tightrope where stood a foreign lass with bare legs. William clapped and whistled, and threw roasted nuts into the air, first to her, and then when she paid him no attention, catching them in his open mouth. By this time Christopher Marlowe, perfumed to his beard, had found them and was also introduced.

Greene threw his arms about them all in turn. "Give us good wishes, gentles!" he murmured. "Give us good wishes for our happiness, for we love much, she and I! Can a clever man do well here with his pen? Shall we be friends and always together, the five of us . . . even thou, sweet Will, who hath a good heart though it's said you cannot sing."

THEY STAYED AT the fair until some time after the dinner hour of eleven, when Jonson suggested they go to the bear garden on the south side, for the great blind bear Harry Hunks was to defend himself against four dogs that day.

The bear garden was a polygonal structure whose smutty exterior walls were covered by crude markings in charcoal, some with the names of dead bears who had fallen for the citizens' pleasure over the years. Other scribbling referred to women in the Liberty of the Clink, and their various talents. Lovers had scrawled their names roughly surrounded by flowers and a heart, and messages had been left as well: "Mark thou turd, I awaited thee here since four hours past dawn and comst not. Be thou damned." There was also a tribute to one memorable beast who had escaped and lumbered through an innyard south of the city with its neck chain clanking on the cobbles, and stopped by a pastrymaker and consumed a dozen meat pies before his agitated owner ran up with whip and sticks shouting, "Jacob! Jacob! Dried pizzle! Stinking turd!" The great creature was a favorite of the town from that time on; dubbed Meat Pie, it had more coins bet upon it than any other of its species.

The friends found their way into the arena, which smelled of the beasts and excrement, of the sweat and thick hair of excited dogs, of old wood, sweet warm strawberries for sale, and frothy ale. So hot was the day that the rough wood of the galleries seemed to splinter to the touch, and the

drying boards of the steps groaned as they mounted up. The place was full
of foreigners as well as townsmen, each crawling over a friend to make a
bet with still another fellow as to which dog and which bear in whatever
match should prove victorious. There were papers passed about of other
matches.

Four bears were set to contest that day, but two had already done so, to
their disappointment. The third, called Apollo, was now brought into the
arena in his wheeled cage, roaring bitterly. The smell of his thick brown
fur made the dogs strain wildly at their leashes and snarl until the boy who
held them smacked them on the noses with a small whip, and still they
groaned and growled and slunk to the earth and then reared up on hind
legs, tongues out, panting violently, salivating.

"Here's tuppence for blind Harry," Jonson shouted to his friends. "I
know not this Apollo, for he's hardly tried. Who'll speak for the dogs in
this match?"

"Aye . . . a groat . . ."

"A fart on thy groat! Wilt insult me with a groatsworth of wager?"

Greene bought a pennysworth of strawberries wrapped in an old paper,
fragrant and sweet amid their green leaves, and the others called for nuts
and cakes, all full of cinders.

Now the door of the cage creaked open, and the beast was driven out
with a whip and a stick and made fast with chains to a heavy stake. On all
fours, he looked about as if he could not judge his circumstances, for it was
only his second match. Seeming confused for what he should do, he gazed
silently up and about at the crowd, whose shouts began to rise. "Loose the
dogs!" "Let's see how he fights. . . ." "Last one owned by Martin was the
great one . . . for the days of old Meat Pie! Come!"

The dogs were straining and salivating, and then barking so that the
voices could hardly be heard above them. Three strong men held them
back, letting them come almost within tasting distance of the bear, who
had begun to growl and whose chains yet held him. In a circle they went,
stalking each other. One of the dogs had a great scar on his back. A clown
came out on stilts, shouting insults to the audience. "Pricklice! Pisspots!
A fart of my ass to you! Marry, let him that's fainthearted crawl away. . . .
What, art ashamed to lay wages?"

"Oh dull!" shouted the crowd.

Two Italian acrobats with flowing dark hair and spangled soiled dress flew through the air in each other's arms. A boy came out and also tumbled and stood on his hands and taunted both dogs and bear. Another smaller lad of perhaps ten years, scantily dressed as a mermaid and naked to his navel, was wheeled on a cart singing to a lute which he played with scrawny arms, yet in the noise hardly a note of strings nor piping voice could be heard.

The men in the galleries shouted back at the clown, who had returned to incite them, and began to pelt him with eggs and fruit. The cracked rotten eggs fell over the dogs, and the tumbling boy walked about on his hands and stood and bowed to the audience, and the other lad who played the mermaid was taken away by the man who drew his cart, and who began to slap him before they had left the arena.

A strong man came and broke his chains, and above the shouting the bear bellowed louder and louder in confusion. At last with a great cry the men loosed the dogs, kicking them to go forward. The bear, however, was yet held. Still he rose to a great height and opening his mouth, roared to the walls of the garden and to the river and across it to palaces and beyond. He had been bitten, and was angry, and the keeper laid a whip across his back to make him angrier still. He rose in a frenzy and broke from his chains.

The crowd leapt to their feet, cheering.

The beast reared up again and then dropped to his forelegs, seizing one dog in his mouth. Back and forth he shook him, eliciting a terrified whining from the captured canine. Ignoring the other dogs which bit into his back, he rose up again and hurled the now limp, bloody creature across the arena. Then the great beast rose up again and roared, and blood dribbled between his teeth and down the fur. From across the theater men groaned with pleasure, leaning forward, clutching the railing or each other's shoulders, almost climbing over the barriers. Across the arena staggered the bear, now on all fours, roaring to shake the dogs who clung with their teeth. Again he rose up taller than before, bellowing to the heavens. "Kill the bastard!" someone yelled. "Two shillings for Master Henley's dogs!" "Kill the bear!" They began to howl and beat with their boots on the gallery floor, and bang with their fists on the railing. Someone hurled a bottle, and another a stick. Men rose to their feet shouting for the bear's blood.

Round in circles staggered the screaming beast, a dog still clinging to his back, blood now pouring from his gaping mouth. Jonson had risen to the rail itself, his great arms holding to the roof above for balance. "Do not die, brave Apollo!" he shouted. "Yet as thou dost, thy soul shall surely find revenge and peace!"

Christopher folded his arms across his chest and, appalled, murmured, "Bricklayer's son, have done!" He rose to his feet and, with William at his heels, pushed his way through the chanting, rocking men to the doors, out past the little boy who had played the mermaid and was now weeping, to the yard. Meticulously crossing to the muckheap, Christopher vomited.

Slowly Greene with his pale, fragile wife and Jack Heminges emerged, shamefaced, shaking their heads as if to push away the dust and stink of the place. "They like it better than plays," John said. "Thine have as much blood, we hear, Christopher."

"Be still."

"Ah, he's touchy today!"

Jonson was the last to emerge, walking slowly as if he had to coax his heavy body to move. Taking a bit of coal, he wrote in great letters on the side of the theater, *May his soul rest in peace.* "They had him, but he gave a fight, gentleman! Oh, he gave a brave fight. . . . Come, to the taverns. *Requiescat in pace, in nomine Patris et Filii et Spiritus Sancti!* Come, let's away. I cannot bear to see his corpse drawn by!"

They found a booth in one of the many low-lying south side taverns which were built up on raised platforms in the uneven, marshy earth, and called for hot buttered beer, wine, and sliced mutton from the kitchen below. A great rough loaf of yellow-brown bread arrived as well, which they tore apart with their hands. Soon the tavern was full of men from the match, all debating what they had seen, and cursing the neophyte bear who had fallen so peremptorily while the blind one, Harry Hunks, his old fur fleabitten and his thick flesh scored with whip marks, had philosophically triumphed once more. They cursed the money they had lost.

Robin Greene, with a shy smile, looked about at them all and said softly, "I shall read my play to you. Hear and tell me thy thoughts, for I must sell it this week if we are to eat." Then, opening the rolled loose pages which he had carried within his jerkin, he began to read his comedy in a melodic voice. Worn with the heat and heavy food, the friends leaned upon the table to listen. "Oh, poet!" said John. His eyes were soft and tender. "There is a poet, gentles."

As Robin Greene read on and on, his wife leaned further against him as if she would all but slide under the table. "Oh, Robin, have done," she whispered grievously. "I'm weary—take me home!" Because he did not listen to her she ate more of the strawberries which they had bought at the match, their juice staining her narrow mouth like blood. Tears filled her eyes.

Greene turned to her at last. "She wants to return to Tollesbury," he said sadly, "where we can never go. I shall never be a vicar more. Be patient, sweet Bess, for I must sell these pages if we are to eat."

The hours moved on, and many of the men who'd come from the fight rose with a grunt and reluctantly bid each other a good eve. Darkness slowly came through the few windows and they called for candles, and checking their pockets, found that only Christopher had coins to pay for them. The death they had witnessed of the beast mingled with the pretty lines of the verses had made them all uncertain of where they wished to be and where they might think to go, and reluctant therefore to rise and depart. John Heminges, moved by the verses, was increasingly quiet, as he rubbed his great fingers on the mug's edge. He thought of his little girl, curled with her doll on her cot, with the old woman muttering about her. A love for her, and an anger he had not done better by her, filled him. He resolved in his soul this moment to get up and go away, and found himself unwilling to do so.

The bells rang the hour of ten, and the barboy was washing the glasses in a large basin of water fetched from the pump. The young wife had slumped into a sullen sleep, her head on the table and her golden hair half loose from her cap. William gently began to stroke it; his whole soul was filled with tenderness for the girl, who had run away from a brutal marriage, run away with this unthinking, chattering young poet who was just now triumphantly reading the last of his play.

Ben Jonson made a choking sound and began to weep. They turned to see the tears running down his face as he cried, helplessly and openly, like a small boy. "He was a good bear," he murmured, "the best . . . and men repel me, and yet and yet I am one of them. Dost know what it's like to be repelled by men, and yet be irrevocably one of their members? I shall kill my stepfather, or he me, before my apprenticeship's done! For each day it's the same, brick after brick, in the same manner . . . and so *ad infinitum, ad nauseam*, for all my life. Christ's wounds! Christ's mercy! To look down the long path of life and see this . . . and know I'll to my grave one day with nothing more!"

Stumbling he rose, his shirt half from his breeches, looking about incoherently as if for a place to piss. John leaned back and said with a frown, "Ben, whither?"

"To the garden," was the half-coherent answer. "To free old blind Harry."

"Art in thy cups."

"But not from my mind. I'll free old blind Harry, and the man who makes to stop me will be corpse himself ere the hour's done." Pushing his hand through his wild thick hair, he gazed at them all with a kind of despair and crashed out through the tavern doors.

The men looked about at each other. "Surely he's not in reason!"

"He'll be back."

"What o'clock 'tis?"

"Nay, my watch doth not run." They fell more silent, every now and then consulting the clock near the bar.

"He's not returned," Greene said anxiously, after over half an hour had passed. "Wilt find him, friends? I myself must see this lass to home." He glanced at her with some distaste, his beautiful upper lip raised, as if she were suddenly between him and all he wanted. Then his great tenderness returned, and he shook her gently. "Good night, gentles!" he said as they parted in the tavern yard, the poet with his wife leaning heavily against him and the others towards the bear garden.

Above them purple clouds drifted across the moon, and below both the Rose and the Hope theaters stood in silhouette. From the tavern as they left it they could hear the host's wife quarreling with a drunken customer. Most lights behind shutters in ordinary houses had been doused. It was that peculiar hour when they felt that all the world slept but themselves, that they alone had consciousness of the city and somehow guarded it.

The bear garden rose before them, with its remembered odors of foul clothing, oranges, and the heated sweaty fur of beasts. John squinted and stuck his hands in his belt. "Ben cannot be within, for I hear naught, and he won't get through the watchman on the bridge, for he hath no penny. Where's he gone? I must return to my little one."

As they stood there they heard the growling of one of the beasts who lodged there and, from cages on the other side of the arena, the returned warning of a few of the dogs who were kept to tantalize them within odorous distance of their opponent, driven into a frustration of violence by the inaccessibility.

The moon shone on the grave faces of the men. "Well," said William uncomfortably, "he's not within, that's plain! And we might as well go home to bed before thieves fall on us instead." He had thought of the books he was reading which lay neatly by his bed in the upper chamber of Field's house, the candle beside them, with some longing.

At that moment they heard a low whistle, and looking at each other, moved softly to the door, which creaked open to their touch. The great amphitheater rose above them in its emptiness, and the dirt smelled of beast and blood. Something was lying by the door, and when they knelt they discovered the guard, moaning softly. "Ben's here then," William said, biting his lip. "Heaven refuse me if he hath not struck this fellow unconscious and gone on! This is not good work. We shall have the devil to pay."

As they approached the cages they heard the muttering of the beasts, and then the growl and the roar. Many were lodged elsewhere by their keepers, but Blind Harry's home for some time had been here. All the city knew him and, for all that they tormented him with the sport at which he was now unchallenged and yet which bored him, loved him. Some men felt he had lived forever, for he was a very old bear and wise, if one can be said to be wise, and often sat in the corner when he was tired of going round and round the small space three hundred times and more.

By the moonlight they made out that the cage door had indeed been opened, and that young Jonson, with his burly shape and wild hair, was within, brandishing a heavy stick with which he now and then prodded the great lethargic beast. "Rise, Harry!" he cried. "Get up and take thy freedom like a true Englishman. Do not wait to be trampled down by life, but seize it, seize it, Harry! Make me an example of thy beastly wisdom! Behold the bear of God that taketh away the sins of the world. Go in peace—*Ite, missa est!* The mass hath ended!"

The beast cocked his head, raised his paw, and then with one blow sent the bricklayer's apprentice sprawling and gasping on the cage floor. John Heminges seized a whip which he found outside the door and approached, knees trembling and breathing in a heavy, concentrated way. "Jonson, come!" he said steadily. "Come, lad, do not tarry—he wilt not long play with thee, Ben."

Stumbling to his feet, the poet cried, "Sayst I should go without this worthy creature's freedom which mayhap I must persuade him of? Nay, brave friends! I do not fear him, for I live among men and men are worse . . . far worse."

"Jonson, dost bleed!"

"Hath not my heart bled?" he roared. "And why should I not do this one, great thing? What other worthiness shall I do? No one will weep for me, I have no one!"

"Christ's love, be still! The constable will come."

"Nay, I shall not go! Brave Harry, go thy way! Sweet Harry, lumber off to ancient English woods where once bold men stole from the rich to give to the poor! Touch neither widows nor orphans, Harry, for the love of Ben Jonson, who hath so praised thee as only a poet can! Go, Harry!"

The large bear gazed at him with mild, unseeing eyes. Then he came forward, sniffed, rose on his hind legs, and swatted hard. John snapped the whip and the beast stumbled back, roaring. Beyond, the dogs in their cages barked ferociously. William and Christopher had seized the bricklayer, who struggled with them. "I cannot leave him!" he shouted. "He doth not know friend from foe, for he hath been so long without human charity that he doth not recognize it. I can yet tame him with my words! Give me leisure to do it. . . . Await my leisure, good bear, and the songs of the one, the unmatchable Ben of Westminster!"

At that moment they heard voices and footsteps, and the door was thrust open at the other end. "Oh, Christ's breath!" John whispered. "Mark me for a sinner if not 'tis Harry's owner, who liveth hard by, for the neighbors must have warned him. Now art betwixt bear and bully, lad, and will have the worst of it from one. Where's the key, in Christ's name, Benjamin? Benjamin, thou turd of turds, where's the pissing key?"

They dared not search a second later but leaving the cage swinging open and the bear of whose next action they were unsure, they ran for their lives to the boxes and fell over the wood stands as the torches came towards them. Lying on their bellies amid the nutshells and apple cores, they heard the running feet and cries. Soundlessly William rolled to his back. Above him rose the ghostly galleries as once had risen the ancient Colosseum of Rome, and above it, pale and placid, the full summer moon. He thought, Oh goddess!

"Come," Christopher said abruptly when at last they understood that the others had ceased to look for them and the beast was once more secured, "these revels are ended! Forsooth, let us take our bricklayer home."

"A piss on thee, Christopher."

"Twice on thee."

They stumbled in the darkness as silently as they could to the last forbidding roars of the blinded beast and out a small broken window, each dropping to the muddy earth. William heard his shirt sleeve tear and swore under his breath. Through the dark streets they went, the moon now hidden behind clouds, their hearts beating anxiously under their jerkins as they approached the bridge. There in one of the few openings which overlooked the city, Jonson broke from them and clambered to the railing high above the water.

Expansively he cried, "Oh city, here is thy son who shall make thee immortal! Whore, wilt love me as I have loved you? Or wilt betray me sore?

> "I will fetch thee a leap
> From the top of Paul's steeple to the standard in Cheap
> And lead thee a dance through the streets without fail
> Like a needle of Spain, with a thread at my tail . . .

"The poem's mine."

Then more reflectively he added, "I think the beast hath broken my arm, or sprained it sore. They are no better than men I think, in the end. Alas, I believe in nothing anymore. Do not mind it; I am going home." Shaking them off, he lumbered between the houses in the narrow walkway of the bridge, hunched and hugging his hurt arm with his good one, round-shouldered and shaking his great head.

John, Christopher, and William stood on the bridge. "God knoweth," Jack Heminges said regretfully, "what my lass might think hath become of me if she wakes, for she has bad dreams sometimes and creeps into my bed and puts her arms about me. Life's a sorry thing since I lost my wife. A good night, friends! It has been a full one." He shook their hands and hurried off at once by the moonlight which now again lit the houses and steeples towards his shop and rooms behind. Christopher reached in his pockets and found pennies for the bridge fee, and the two last friends made their way across.

As they mounted up towards Eastcheap their walk became slower and more reflective. Christopher bent forward slightly, his arms clasped protectively across his jerkin. After a time, William asked, "Where dost lodge?"

"To say the very truth, I do not know. I quarreled with the fellow whose room I shared and cannot go there."

"Then come with me this night, Kit! Only we must be still, for my cousin won't be happy I've stayed abroad this late hour!" William answered. Even as he spoke they heard the solemn chimes of midnight, and they stopped and smiled at each other before going on. There was such a strange sweetness to be abroad this hour with none but cutthroats and ghosts and the beggars who huddled about and gritted their teeth against bad dreams in the endless darkness of small alleys, as if they were alone alive of all men.

The streets were deserted, and littered with papers, apple cores, bones as they always were on the weeks of the fair. Once they whistled to a dog who came to sniff hungrily at them. Within four hours, carts from the farms which surrounded the city would begin to creak through the gates, and at the first light of dawn maidservants would hurry to Cheapside market, carrying baskets on their arms and rubbing the sleep from their eyes. The whole day would begin again, bringing what things they could not say.

Christopher said suddenly with some darkness, "Ben won't live to be thirty, but mayhap neither shall I. Some tavern quarrel will end it all, methinks, or I'll be found out in my work."

"What work can that be?"

"I may not tell thee."

"Do," said William, "for I feel far from sleep." In the printer's house he entered with his key, and moved as softly as he could up the stairs, where he indicated in whispers that he would bring a lamp and some pure rainwater from the kitchen, for they both were again thirsty. In the darkness he knocked over a box of type, which clattered to the bare brick floor. He swore, removed his shoes, and when he had shut his door again, carefully set the mugs down on the table. The apprentice was snoring, his face turned to the wall.

"Not even the Resurrection could wake him," William said.

"But some of the things I say might."

"Then prithee, say them quietly! How didst find Cambridge, Kit? I should have gone myself, and then would not have landed in the trouble I did! How didst find it?"

Christopher smiled, looking at the water as if he had never seen such a thing before. "We should drink more of this, but then we might be sober and I do not know then if I could face the world."

"Findst it such a dark place?"

"Those men who screamed for the bear to kill the dogs or the dogs to kill the bear are much of humanity; worse, I myself know something of that violence. Didst not feel the bitter stirrings of sexual excitement, of pity, of tears, of love, all mixed as it came towards the end . . . we could have gone sooner but we remained. Why? I ask my heart and it gives me but coy answers—ah, I was aroused to sex and pity. We are a breath away from beasts, my friend, only we have wit to say it."

William nodded: shame suddenly filled him. The day passed by him in a hot flash of sensuality, depravity, useless conversation. He did not feel proud to be himself, or hold his convictions—indeed, he did not know what convictions he held. Totally was he dishonest, and this had been revealed to him by the handsome, half-shaven poet who in one moment seemed an angel of truth, and in the next something far darker.

Christopher leaned back and narrowing his eyes said, "Art witty enough, could write thyself! You could do many things, William, and yet you stand apart observing it all. . . . For myself I feel I have done so much so far that I cannot believe I am but three and twenty. I came from a small cathedral town and entered into the world . . . but I speak in riddles and you do not understand. Do you believe in God?"

"Aye!" was the surprised answer.

"I do not—when I am frightened I do, but otherwise no. I say this simply to you, but I could be brought to task for it, mayhap tortured for heresy. How strange that two thousand years after the Periclean age we still torture a man for what he thinks or what he doth not think in the privacy of his understanding! No, I cannot drink this water but have sack of my own in the satchel. Christ's love, the bricklayer's son hath driven all sleep from me! Sometimes I am awake until dawn and never think to sleep for two nights more. Life rushes by so quickly, and one is struck down and all is over—I love a great deal, or I think I do. I can't say. Drink with me."

"Aye, gladly!"

"I am not a man like thee, Will. I fancy boys—I want them until I am sick with wanting, and then having had them, I am sick with that too and go into my mind. If only we could love without knowing the other's name, without having to look into the eyes—to spend oneself, take a kiss, and forget about everything. But you have a conscience, my friend! For all that you left your wife you are good, moral, steady—all the things I both admire and despise. I should not have come here."

William took the poet's arm. "Nay, Kit, stay!" he cried eagerly, forgetting to whisper. "Why did I travel to London? Because I need to know things that I have no words for—and where I have come from, they are contented to pull the centuries over themselves like quilting and sleep. That is mayhap why I left, that and—fear, I think, that things would not remain the same way. Christ's wounds, we are driven up like birds in a rush of wind, we hardly know where, and land on strange continents."

"Then you do not object if I say, God's damned?"

"I do not believe it but I do not object."

"Hast been with whores since here?"

"Aye."

"Likst it best to mount above them or lie beneath their weight?"

"Marry, both in their turn."

"Strange, good boy! I see myself in thee as I was, and we will travel I think a time along the path together until we find each other tedious and part!" The brown eyes were slightly glazed from drunkenness, but the voice deliberate and steady. "I think mayhap of all of them thou art sensible enough to know," he said. "We have a decent Protestant queen on the throne, and everywhere are Catholic conspiracies to unseat her, assassinate her . . . the country's a web of spies and counterspies, those against the Queen, those against the conspirators. And which Catholics are decent, which traitorous? So many men employed in finding out we do not even know each other. So nothing's as it seems, nor am I."

"This is why you have coins in your pocket?"

"One reason. My patron is generous. Wouldst join us? Art a clever fellow, and there's always such needed."

"Marry, what would they say at home?"

"Why that the devil hath blown such a fart as hast sent thee into his camp for a merry time."

They began to laugh and their voices grew louder. Two or three times the sleeping apprentice stirred, and they looked over with some apprehension. They both slept, and before dawn Christopher shook William, bid him goodbye, and made the sign of the cross on his forehead. "Where dost go?" William murmured.

"To make up with him with whom I quarreled, for he hath my heart! God bless thee, darling."

When William awoke again, the sun was pouring through the window and he could tell from the sounds of costers in the street and wagons that the day was already old.

When he had dressed and come down the steps, he saw Richard Field standing below, his face quivering with resentment. Pulling William into the shop, he closed the door behind them both and turning to him, whispered furiously, "Who was the fellow lodged with thee this night? In the name of all that's holy, do I run a bawdy house? My lad heard many of the words you spoke, and so did I and my wife lying in our chamber below, for it carried through the windows! Do you keep these hours and come home with an atheist, a sodomite?"

William picked up a pile of lightly sewn pamphlets and then threw them down again. "He had nowhere to lodge," he answered passionately. "I could not leave him in the street."

"By Our Lord's suffering, Shakespeare! What I have heard—conspiracies, spying, and whores and your use of them. Your use of whores while you stay under this good, Christian roof." Field hurled himself onto a stool and covered his face.

His own face suddenly burning, William muttered, "On that I told him false, this I swear!" Thrusting his fingers in his sword belt, he walked to the window to look down the street.

Slowly Richard Field looked up with much grief in his eyes. "Nay, you tell me but half of it. . . . I was the older when we were young, and am still, so mayhap for old love you will be led by me. London is no place for a man who is not willing to lock his doors and heart to most of what it contains. You will come to trouble. It is best you return to Stratford."

"Sweet Christ, wouldst wish this to me!" William leapt across the room. "Harken to me! I'm not entirely merry here . . . I weep, yes I weep, for my children! Yet Anne and I are bitterly different, for my heart's open to so much, and hers is closed. Would you send me back? Do you think I don't suffer? And you have no power to do so," he added haughtily. "Do you think I would consent?"

"The city is not so large that word does not come to me of where you go and with whom. And now whores!"

"I have not touched them," shouted the Stratford man. "I have said I did not do it! Do you say I lie to you? Yet if I did, were it not better than to have nothing?" He broke away with trembling lips, and passing his hand over them, glanced back at his friend in a supplicating way. "I must stay here a time longer, I must on my soul! So far I have done little, but will find my way. I think I am meant for something which must bring a sort of dignity . . . don't you know how I long for it?"

Then Field began to shout as well. "We have been sworn friends since I could remember! Dost not think I recall when you talked of the heavenly and baser natures of man? It kept me in my senses when I saw things in my boyhood which I could not say even to you. Hence I know, I know we must live as pure men, and I say if you are to remain under this roof you must cease to consort with these wastrels."

"That I will not do."

"Then must go and live among them!"

William said nothing but climbed the steps and packed his few possessions. Still, when he came down again and saw Field standing angrily looking into the street, his heart relented and he touched his friend's sleeve. "'Tis the way of men," he murmured. "Even sworn friends change, for no man can tell how he will be tomorrow. It breaks my heart, Dick, for my old love of you. Still, I have not come here to be less than I am." Then he cried out, "How you have disappointed me! My God, it grieves me so."

Two gentlemen were coming through the shop door for their work, and with his head down William bowed stiffly to his friend and went out the door and away towards the river.

P A R T  W O

THE GROCERY SHOP

HE NEIGHBORHOOD IN which the grocer John Heminges lived was called the Liberty of the Clink.

About the waterfront were shops and stalls devoted to the needs of the innumerable boatmen who ferried travelers up and down the great river and, most often, across it. At the suburb's edges here on the south side were farms which rolled in green abundance away from the city towards the county of Kent. That was admirable country. However, Heminges's grocery was not there, but wedged tightly in the thick gathering by the waterside of houses, brothels, cockpits, gambling dens, and bearbaiting arenas. It was a swampy area largely owned by the Bishop of Winchester, whose palace was hard by, and by enterprising investors in new real estate such as the theater builder Henslowe, whose very first property hereabouts was said to be a brothel.

William was mounting the steep path from the water when he made out Heminges's stout, broad-shouldered figure, emptying a chamber pot on the muckheap at the end of the street. He blurted forth his predicament, and the grocer thrust down the pot, wiped his hands on his breeches, and embraced the Stratford man. "Bide with me!" he cried. "We shall live a life of poetry, work, and friendship."

Two rooms were tucked behind the shop. In the one that served as kitchen was a very small hearth with several old pots for cooking, so that it was cozy and warm this late-summer day. William deposited his few articles of clothing on pegs and looked about. Hung here and there were the garments of a little girl; though they had once been periwinkle blue or other exquisite colors, they were now faded, and he supposed they had belonged to other children before coming much used to their present owner. There was also a small garland made of roses to be worn on the brow, perhaps from a midsummer festivity of a year ago or more, for the flowers were fragile and brown, and the leaves rustled to his touch. On a low cot in the second room was a neatly folded coverlet, and on it several solemn rag dolls lay limply against each other.

He walked to the back to see if there was a garden, and found a rich and fertile one. As he knelt to touch the soil, he saw a round-faced, solemn little girl of about six years old looking eagerly at him from a corner.

That very day she was taken with fever. The doctor arrived, pompous in his rusty black coat and breeches, and proclaimed at once, "'Tis the pox! Keep her warm by a fire so it will rise to the face, for better a pox in the flesh than in the heart, where it can kill a lass." For this he charged three shillings, and the men had to put their coins together to pay it.

William said simply, "I have had the pox, and can nurse her."

"How grateful I am to thee!" was the grocer's passionate reply, squeezing his friend's hands again and again. So for the next three days William kept the hearth warm and sat by the child, catching her fingers so she would not scratch and dabbing the festering sores with distilled cucumber water.

"I'll tell thee a story of fairies," he said, "in a place where I live called the Arden forest. 'Twas named for my mother's family generations back, and they say the fairies live there in trees, and under flowers. Hast never seen them?" He wove a tale for her of lovers and enchantment, and when she was tired of it he stood on his hands and described how the room looked when upside down. Later she fell asleep in his arms.

All the day Jack had stood behind the counter of his store with his dull-witted assistant, and when at last he put up the shutters, he sat for a time beside his child. "I'll make a dowry for her," he vowed solemnly, his large arms folded across his smock. "That at least I can do. I pray to Our Lord each night to grant me this. I also would like to marry again, if ever I could afford it, for I am far from an old man. Ah how I long for that!"

THE GROCERY SHOP

*　　*　　*

FALL CREPT INTO the city, and in the ancient ritual as old as the earth, the leaves began to turn yellow, the ones nearest the river going first. William saw them with some heaviness of heart, for he felt uncertain to which direction he should now turn his life, and once more had little money to send home.

The grocery was so close to the water that he could look down the street towards the docks and boats which seemed ever to be sailing past. All about them were shops for the ferrymen, and gulls and red kites strutted about before the door. William gathered herbs and fruits from the garden, and dried or preserved them; he made a conserve of pears with sugar, the recipe of an uncle on his mother's side. John in his blunt generous way at once insisted they share everything. There was not a great deal of work to be had that season in the theater, but if one man had a part or two in a play, the other would mind the shop.

Still, as much as Heminges was drawn to playgiving, he did not conceive that it could be a life; though he was fond of the men who came and went, the tradesman in his soul scoffed slightly at them. Writers and players—what were these? To spend one's days wresting coins from scribbling words, or wearing a wig and shouting speeches to the galleries, seemed but a poor thing to recite at judgment day when each man must proclaim what he has done with his life. Besides, he did not doubt but that such a living must end in the poorhouse. Heminges's father had been a grocer and his grandfather the very same. The old shop within the city walls, a commodious one in a house with a red tile roof, had been his inheritance, and having lost it through ill fortune, he wanted nothing more but to find a way to make it his again.

The Worshipful Company of Grocers was one of the twelve great livery companies whose principal functionaries walked in all great processions, and its guildhall was one of the prides of the city. Two hundred years before at its inception its members had been known as the Pepperers for their enthusiastic contracting in that spice, but they were renamed Grocers or Grossers, because they dealt in bulk, shortly thereafter. Their hall also encompassed the London apothecaries, who sometimes chafed and muttered that they wished a hall of their own.

Heminges's shop was small, damp, and neat. Bags and jars filled with both spices and the common herbs such as rosemary and sweet mustard lay on shelves and in cupboards; there were potatoes and several grades of flour from rich yellow to a greeny-brown mixture with peas, dried fruits of all sorts, and heavy, crystally blocks of sugar, which, when cut, left a crunchy dust in the floor rushes. At times he sold golden glittery thick honey on the comb, and in harvest months had a small supply of fresh vegetables. He sold oil pressed and imported for dressing salads, hard salt, and a biscuit which had to be soaked in water to be edible, and was especially useful for taking on long voyages, though few men in Southwark went farther away than the fields of Kent in their leisure hours, and the great explorer Raleigh purchased his seagoing biscuits elsewhere.

A few mornings a week he bought his produce from the Cheapside stalls or climbed directly onto the merchant boats which docked in the city. He had a personal interest in explorers' finding a direct path to the Indies and thus giving him a more reliable, cheaper supply of commodities. He had heard, when about his company hall, of the Italian Columbus, who had nearly a hundred years before been determined to find such a route, and landed instead in a savage, enormous land far off. Jack Heminges felt the Italian had done a poor job and shook his head. Had an Englishman made the voyage, he would have managed it better. He often talked to William of these things.

William listened patiently. He craved not nutmegs and dried biscuits, but experience and adventure. A few mornings a week he walked over to Florio's house to write letters for him in French, English, and Latin; the scholar was compiling an Italian dictionary as well, with the widowed Countess of Southampton, it was said, as sponsor.

Florio's house was small but respectable, an anteroom to the larger mansions which were spread on the long road between the city gates and the palaces and courts of Westminster. In Catholic days many of these dwellings had been ecclesiastical palaces, but since the confiscation of church property by the crown some half a century before, they had been disbursed among the great men of the land. In Florio's house there was but one servant to walk over the plaited-straw mats in soft shoes, but the halls were hung with a few threadbare tapestries which the translator had inherited from grateful patrons. Now and then William saw men at dinner of whom everyone spoke: Walter Raleigh himself, and much of the intellectual circle which moved freely about Europe and talked of science and geography and the New World by candlelight until all the rest of the city was asleep.

One day when crossing the Strand between the carts, peddlers, and mountebanks who were juggling for coins, he was hailed by a friend. An elderly Jew was dining that moment at Florio's table, the man exclaimed excitedly, and there had been none of the Hebrew race living within London these three hundred years since they had been made to go. William hurried to the house and through the kitchen, but though dishes still lay about with their fragments of fish and meat, the old man had gone. He picked up a cup. "How did he look?" he asked of the servant. "I would have given much to see him!" The following day when he arrived he saw the Jew mounting his horse; the dark eyes were tired, wise, and resentful. Months after, William found a Hebrew book in a secondhand shop, and stood for a time running his hand lightly over the shapes of the letters.

There were many people who came to Florio's, some to discuss a wide-seeking religious faith that was so near heresy that no word of it must, by unspoken agreement, pass beyond the wall hangings and portiere curtains which closed off drafts from the doors. William thought of his father's secret spiritual questioning, how conceivable it was to find a place to express it in the vastness of this city, and how impossible within the narrow mental confines of their town.

Some men and women also came to Florio's for Italian lessons, and there was a dark-haired, gruff musician called Bassano whose heavy-handed playing of the virginals rang through the wainscoted rooms. William always borrowed books, for he could not afford to buy them, and once was given a water-stained copy of Holinshed's *Chronicles of England, Scotland, and Ireland* to keep.

It was a long walk back home across the bridge, but the warden there let him cross without the penny, for he liked him. Below him the water flowed against the starlings, the wood casing which was built about the foundations sunk deep into the Thames from before the memory of man, and innumerable small craft and swans floated away towards their destinations. He passed the gorgeous Chapel of St. Thomas, which was now a storage house for some merchant's goods. He was sending almost all his money home, and if there was anything left he bought a ribbon for Heminges's daughter, Susan. He also brought her cakes from Florio's kitchen with their sweet fragrance of other lands.

Gulls cried, sparrows came; the leaves had now turned brown and fell in profusion down the unpaved street. William read his borrowed books as he minded the shop; sometimes he was so deep into his reading that he did not know for some minutes that he was wanted by a customer. Sailors stopped to purchase sugar, spices, and dried fruit for their wives' kitchens and sometimes lingered to recollect the endlessness of the sea at night when they seemed to be the only living men upon earth with nothing but the stars to know it. An elderly soldier stood proudly with his market basket on his arms to recall how he had searched the dead on a battlefield to find the body of his boyhood friend, and had taken from his shattered torso a sacred amulet. Watermen who lived about these streets came with their rich language, including one who claimed his true vocation was poet and proceeded to declaim his doggerel amid the bags of spices and sugar.

> "Wer't not for the Thames (as heaven's high hand doth bless it),
> We neither could have fish nor fire to dress it,
> The very brewers would be at fault,
> And buy their water dearer than their malt."

Sometimes boys hurried in from the Bishop of Winchester's kitchen, for his lordship was to have a supper party and there was not a fig or raisin in the larder, and surely the cook would beat them if they did not procure them straightway. Sometimes the men saw the bishop himself, a small angular man in his middle years, shooing a wild pig from his garden, crying angrily, "Is this a pig of thine?" He had inherited with his bishopric the property on which much of the whorehouses stood, and the doxies who worked therein were called Winchester geese.

These lovely young creatures also came into the grocery of a late morning, pale with heavy lines beneath their eyes after a night's work, paying for their dried fruits and such sometimes with foreign coins which some traveler who had stopped to shake the sheets with them had left. Sitting on a barrel, the remainder of their rouge like the last of modesty on their pale, sleepy faces, they would tell stories of the darker side of lust. They told of the men they loved, the ones who cheated them, or idolized them or beat them. All of this the countryman heard, and he dreamed of them. Jack was scandalized.

"Art a Puritan," William said stoutly.

"Nay," the grocer replied, "'tis only that I'm saddened by my lust and that of others! Ah that God had not created mankind so weak of flesh! As for me, I am ashamed of mine own. I want love if anything, William! I want a wife."

SCARCELY TWO DAYS passed that the writers and friends did not come to sup, and to speak of everything new in the world, in the court, on the stage, and across the seas. Benjamin Jonson would bang on the door with his heavy fist, hurl himself into the rooms with mortar crumbling from his boot edges to the rushes. Once he came sick with remorse, having knocked down his father, and remained for the evening with his head buried in his rough hands. Greene would invariably arrive near dinnertime wearing a dainty doublet with great gooseberry-green sleeves so fantastical in expense that they could not help but wonder how he came by it. He would throw himself down near the hearth, for he was always cold, and burst out the troubles of married life: his wife was even more swollen of belly and yet she did not bring forth the babe, they could not find a place to live they could afford, he could not write fast enough to please himself and his creditors. He sometimes took a bit of bread or cheese from the dinner, carefully wrapped it in a discarded sheet of manuscript, and took it away in his pocket.

The exquisite Christopher was more elusive. Still, now and then he knocked upon their door past midnight, full of bragging words about his first play, which was a success, and of someone he loved; only by looking directly into the brown eyes could they see he was drunk.

When they had no money to fetch food from the ordinary at the end of their street where the boatmen bought their dinner, they searched the grocery sacks and jars and one winter's night had to made do with hard bread soaked for hours in water and wine, and spread with lard. Then Greene would stand up unsteadily and say, "When I have come into my fortune, I shall take care of you all." He hinted he had a rich relative somewhere who would leave much to him, but smiling coyly, would say no more. Once he took his knife and carved upon the inner door the names of the five of them. He also carved his name in a heart with that of his wife, and the night she gave birth he pridefully sent a boy to tell them.

They knew each other's ways, or they thought they did; they had opinions of each other which they held as true, one such being that bad times would pass. At times they were hungry, and more often skeptical. They felt bound together against a world which tossed them, as the sea tosses all manner of things onto the shore and then scoops them up again next tide and bears them away. Sometimes when they talked to the point where they were too tired to rise, they felt there was no one left but themselves in all the world, and if they went out to the silent streets they would find all the houses deserted and empty as if the householders had fled before a plague or a war. They spoke then of the fear of what lay both without the doors and within their own souls: cruelty, fury, pride, devotion, a but scant faith in God, and the need of beauty and of love.

Darkness enveloped the neighborhood at night: there were things done in alleys, bodies sometimes of men or newborn children found wrapped in burlap when dawn came, or a cat slain and disemboweled in some ritualistic attempt to arouse the spirits of hell. The stink of foul water lay about everywhere after householders had put up their shutters and thrice bolted their doors.

On such a winter's night, John and William were awakened by a violent banging upon the grocery portal. Stumbling from their beds, they found Christopher in the lane, a low-burning lantern glistening on the gold-embroidered brown doublet; he stood like a messenger from the gods in his faintly wrinkled, mended white silk hose, one who had mistook the centuries, and somehow walked long enough to come into their own.

With his upper lip raised haughtily under the small mustache, he surveyed the uncombed hair and rumpled nightshirts of his sleepy friends. "'Tis but gone ten!" he said. "I'm to the cockpits, for I have a fair wager on one bird called Lucifer, and will have ten gold harrys before I see my bed. Wilt come?"

Waving him away, John said stoutly, "A piss on thee, thy bird Lucifer, and thy harrys! I must rise at dawn to go to market."

"Then, William—thou!" came the supplicating response.

William craned his neck and ran his hand through his wild hair. "Nay," he muttered, with a shy smile; he would have liked to go, but felt he should stand by John.

Christopher burst into laughter. "Dost desire it!" he cried. "Oh, good lad! Do not dress too finely, for I'm off to the Winchester stews later. 'Twoud be a shame to truss too many points and have to undo them again as well."

"The stews . . . whores!" said John, expanding his broad chest. He looked aside, coughed, and frowned, passing his big hand over his mouth.

"Nay, come!" cried Christopher. He glanced down the shadowy street. "We die too young! Shall we not take pleasure while we may?"

William threw back his head. "Well," he said, "I will come."

And John raised his hands and followed reluctantly, saying, "I must perforce go also, for Kit hast damned sleep for me. Well then, I will go." He breathed heavily as if he had been racing. They dressed, made sure the child was sleeping soundly, and then, taking lanterns, followed their friend to the streets.

Under the shadows of the overhanging upper stories of buildings they went, past the warehouses and boat shops, past the ghostly shapes of upturned boats with heaps of rough cloth piled on them. John stumbled into a pile of lumber and cursed loudly. A sleeping dog roused itself at their approach, and wagging its tail, trotted hopefully after them until Christopher gave it a sudden blow to the snout and sent it howling away into the dusk.

"Satan's messenger," William said wistfully.

"Nay, the Fallen One himself."

"Then how came he to run?"

"Because I am here, and I am more wicked than ever he proposes to be. . . . Come, shall we rouse the dead? Shall we kick up the soil and stones of charnel houses and speak with bones?" As they passed the graveyard of the church of Mary Overy, he untrussed his breeches and let his water splash languidly against the wall. "Ah, this untrussing and trussing," he muttered scornfully. "Better a man go naked like the savages, for we are savages at heart, than disguise ourselves in silk and gold. We are savages, all, all." He picked up a broken pot and hurled it across the path.

Men passed in cloaks as they made their way down the muddy lanes which were here and there forded with boards; mud squashed under their soft shoes. Water trickled from a stream, and the street was so narrow that they had to proceed one behind the other. The cockpit was hidden away in a warehouse cellar, and from the subterranean chambers they could hear the cries of pleasure and the frantic squawking of contending birds. The back of the structure let out on another stream, which made its mucky way towards the great river, sometimes under the earth and sometimes emerging. Pushing open the thick door, the three men descended the slippery steps, the snorting and shouts coming ever closer.

Soft hairs stirred on the back of William's neck.

The large cellar was so thick with the smoke of burning torches that the many men within it seemed as indistinct as if he had wandered somehow into the legendary inferno and would hear momentarily the wailing of the damned. Pushing closer, they were shoved against the railing of the pit where the birds contested, and by the flames saw the great torn crests of one massive cock, glittering razors strapped to its claws. The large stupid eyes caught the firelight; feathers flew, and the room smelled of blood.

William gazed about him, feeling once and again the peculiar excitement within his body that violence evoked. It was longer than he could understand between this place and the days when he had walked down the neat, tree-lined paths leading to the Stratford church of a Sunday in his clean shirt which smelled of summer wind. The words of the setting of the psalm he had sung as a boy came to him.

> God grant we grace, he us embrace,
> In gentle part, bless he our heart.

The garments of the men who pushed about him stank of farm and market, of court and dock and butchery, of the pen and ink of scriveners. Inhaling, he thrust up his nostrils until he felt a part of all of the others. Yet what did he here? He had been reading by a candle some tender romance and now was in this subterranean chamber, shivering with uncouth excitement, having come of his own free will. Once more he looked about him, taking in the fat cellarer who passed with a tray of glasses, the greedy faces, the shouts for bets placed, and the rapid flutter of the struggling birds' wings like his own heart. Drink was passed in a bottle, and he took it and felt it fill him until he no longer knew himself. Duty be damned, he thought. Honor be damned . . . let me live, for soon I will die.

The thought astonished him. Was this himself, his father's son, who sang so charitably the psalms of a summer morn? Craning his neck, he glanced at Jack, who stood beside him, unhappiness on his broad face and arms crossed tightly over his jerkin. A dead bird, carried past them by its feet, brushed his hand; moments later an old man, crouched by the door, began to cut away the razors and strip off the feathers. William's head began to ache. The men about him did not astound him as much as himself. How strange the variety of sensations in one person's breast! Confused, he drank more of the foul bottle which once more had been passed to him and began to push his way towards Christopher.

A man in a farmer's smock snarled at him, the rough face uplifted. "Watch!" he snapped, and lifted his arm to strike.

William answered thickly, "What, fellow!"

"Countryman! Dung choke thee!"

"Will you quarrel?" the countryman said, raising his voice. "Well, I will have at thee!" It would have come to blows had not several newcomers parted them. William made his way about the cockpit, and in a moment had reached Christopher and was speaking feverishly of everything he saw and felt.

The poet's small mustache quivered. "Art drunk!" he mocked.

"Say it on thy life," was the sullen answer.

"Wilt fight me, Will? I say it again: art drunk!" Christopher's hose drooped over his ankles, and the embroidery no longer seemed to glitter. Taking William roughly by the arm, he whispered, "Never mind, you country lad! This place hath sickened me and my money's lost. Let's to the whores."

Heminges, who had made his way beside them, now planted his heavy feet in the rushes. "Nay," he declared stoutly.

"Ah, come."

"Hast coins?"

"More than I need but less than I like! Wilt come, or shall I leave thee here amid the feathers?"

"Ah, do not leave me," muttered the great, honest grocer, fumbling for his hat. "Then let's away."

With their arms about each other, the three men stumbled down the street towards the water. Small waves lapped against the docks in the darkness, and the place smelled of far voyages and the sea. They lifted their lanterns to discover a rough portrait of a bare-breasted woman etched on the door, faded from the river damp. It wavered into darkness as they lowered the lights and pushed inside.

Up the steps they went, finding themselves in rooms which had one time belonged to some minor bishop, and now were crowded with sailors, and merchants from the city pompously dressed with their stuffed doublets and breeches, their fashionable neck ruffs limp with sweat. The same lad whom the men had seen clad as a mermaid at the bearbaiting sang to a lute. He was now dressed as Cupid, and the eyes, yet terrified, seemed to plead, oh, do not beat me, do not ravish me. . . .

Jack had gone, he knew not where, nor did he see Christopher. An old woman took William's hand and pushed him up another set of steps to a room with a low ceiling, whose tiny windows looked out over the houses and warehouses near the docks. There on a sagging bed, behind frayed hangings, sat a girl, brownish, wide breasts exposed. She sat with one leg under her and her hose rolled to her ankles. Under her eyes were dark circles as if she had not slept in a long time.

He came clumsily to the bedside, and sitting beside her with one foot on the floor, he allowed her to unlace his shirt with cold, chafed little fingers. But this is not me, he thought as he bent to kiss her breasts; as his mouth closed over her nipple he thought of his wife with a spasm of confusion that left him exhausted and angry. Anne seemed at that moment holy and removed, and in a place which at that moment he knew he would never see again.

After a time he raised his head and recalled the stranger with indifferent eyes whose body he had kissed. Then he pushed her back and mounted her. He saw the frayed hangings, and her breasts now flatter as she lay there with one arm above her head almost as if sleeping, and one thigh up for him to thrust inside the nest of matted hair between her legs. After his seed had burst within her, he pitied her.

Gently he asked, "What's thy name?"

"Katie, but I'm christened Katherine."

"Where was that, the christening?"

"I don't recall, neither does my mother. I was abandoned and they took me in here, where I'm fed."

Nodding, he sank back on his belly, and after a time he felt her stroking his back, closed his eyes, and seemed to drift off to sleep. The first dim light was creeping through the window, grey as something older than the hills, when he knew himself again. She was asleep beside him, snoring lightly. Curiously he touched the hair between her legs, sensing in it the stickiness of his own life. She shivered, and he covered her with the blanket; she murmured something, rubbed her eyes in her sleep, and curled very small.

As softly as he could he felt for his shoes and his clothing, and taking the now extinguished lantern, went into the hall. From one room he heard snoring and far below a snort of laughter. There was a bad taste in his mouth, and his body ached.

Passing the kitchen, he paused. Christopher was lying half dressed asleep on the rushes beside the hearth boy, his arm protectively circling the lad's naked shoulder. With a kind of pain, he hurried to him, knelt, and whispered, "Kit! Kit! Where's Jack?"

"Devil . . . do I care. . . ."

"Has he left?"

"Aye . . . angry with himself. . . . Let me sleep . . . I have not done so in these many years . . . darlings, I'm sorry."

Dawn was just beginning to rise over the water as William walked towards the heavy, broad-shouldered figure which stood on the dock gazing at the ghostly figures of the still boats. John Heminges's face, older and somehow ravaged, turned mournfully towards him. "Snow will come," he said hoarsely. Joining arms, they walked down the paths they had come with the light rising over the white sails in the river, the brick warehouses, and beyond, the bishop's palace, the gardens, fields, orchards, and countryside.

HE WROTE SOLEMNLY home each month.

Most beloved father and mother,

I send you here my most respectful greetings and prayers for your health, and that of my brothers and sister. Greet my wife Anne for me, and embrace a thousand times my beloved beloved children.

I have but little employment, so the money I can send for Anne and my sweet little ones is scarce, but I do send it by a friend who is traveling that way. If I cannot manage things better after a time I will come home.

His father answered.

Mine own William!

The trouble and heaviness of heart I have endured is known to you alone and to you alone can I look to remedy it. You are no longer young and have not yet settled into a profession. Will you not come and work by my side in my old age? I wait breathless to hear your answer, sweet heart. Your wife weeps.

To that he could not reply, but wrote more letters of the sights and sounds of the city. He told them nothing of importance, for he understood that much of what moved him most would be beyond their comprehension. They mistrusted all he cherished, nor would they understand how much he grieved for them.

WINTER CONTINUED, AND with it bitter cold.

Greene and his wife and baby had found a room on the east side behind the Tower, a bad neighborhood where thieves trained orphaned boys to cut purses, and stale or maggoty food was sold against the law. The houses were old and stank of sewage, and the gutters ran with ordure. Upper stories had their access by outer stairs whose wood had in places given way; one of these William and John grimly mounted with a basket full of bread, eggs, and meats.

They squinted for a moment in the dim light before making out Greene's wife kneeling in the middle of the floor, dipping one of her husband's shirts in a bowl of water, her head bent over her work. She seemed so small and, without the bulk of the child within her, weightless.

But Greene himself with a happy cry leapt up from the bed on which he had been indolently stretched. "Christ to see thee!" he cried. "Fatherhood's not all merriment! I work and work on this play and some stories which must sell if we are to eat, and have not been out in a time." He nodded at the babe, who mewed on a blanket on the floor in a sickly way. "He doth demand much," he said with some sadness.

As if at that word the fragile girl took the child to her and, with a furtive look, loosed her bodice and exposed her small, flat breast. Greene at once dropped to his knees before his family, drawing both child and mother against his shirt as if to shelter them from everything. Then he saw the basket. "Why Will!" he muttered softly. "What are these things!"

"For the babe and Bess."

"Art good men! Ah, how I love thee!"

William burst out, "Darst not say it . . . I'm not good! I have not seen mine own wife and babes these two years. Word comes she weeps for me."

"Nay, nay!" Greene answered. "Be of good cheer! The river hath frozen, so let us do what all merry men may and walk out on the ice to see the fair! Jonson's sworn to be here this very hour. Life groweth too serious! Even he thinks to write a Latin tragedy between laying of bricks for a wine cellar. Come!"

THE SKY WAS a thick white, and all the city seemed grey stone and here and there the red tile of a roof. Before them stretched the majestic Thames, frozen as far as the eye could see, and over this the snow began slowly to drift from above. William's breath made a delicate smoke before him on the air as if his soul preceded his body. The four men at first stepped carefully on the ice, Jack balancing on the others' shoulders. Soon they began to slide and shout, pushing to see if they could make the other man lose his balance.

"A staff up thine arse!" cried Jonson, his great bulk falling; he lay on his shoulder and slid. The brown wool hose which warmed his thick legs was torn behind one thigh, and the heavy knit double jerkin full of moth holes. Scrambling to his feet, he chased after Greene, swatting at him with his great paws. Loose papers and writing implements fell from his pocket to the ice.

"Christ's mercy, there's the pen I lent thee!" cried William.

"'Tis a faulty one; all my bad lines I can attribute solely to it. I would be a wealthy man were not for that pen of thine, for it writes only sad letters saying 'dear my wife' and knowst *I* have no wife but am bachelor."

"Oh come and be hanged!" laughed William. For a moment he balanced on his hands, his legs kicking boyishly in the air, and somersaulted and fell gracefully on his back, his arms spread out in surrender. His small gold earring, which he had recently acquired, glistened.

"Behold the fellow!" Jonson cried in delight.

Greene was faster than the rest, slipping behind tents and narrowly missing the ropes which held them. "Watch!" cried an old woman. Turning nimbly, he bowed. The smell of ginger and of wood fire rose into the cold air with their echoing voices as they slid westward on the frozen river, the heavy bridge retreating from them as they went. Greene could slip and slide about the smallest corners, almost fall and then recover his balance with a sweet smile. A man with a flageolet piped close, and the writer danced about him, his red beard quivering in his joy.

Jack struggled diligently onward. "He who pushes me down shall not rise again," he muttered darkly for the third time. "Thee, Will, as well.

Knowst I could break any lad here over my knee with one hand."

"Pray, try . . ."

"Nay, I am otherwise occupied to keep my balance."

Then Jonson caught their arms and with his breath floating into the cold air cried reverently, "Stop, lads, salute! There's the bear garden, and near by it the Rose!"

They turned at once to the south side with its warehouses and brick tenements, and the two great polygonal wood structures with their galleries rising into the sky. Jonson made a trumpet from his hands. "Long live the whoremonger's theater!" he shouted through it. "Long live Henslowe to recognize my superior, undeniable, God-given worth! And long life to all playhouses!"

Already at the hour of four the February-afternoon dusk was falling. They went as far as they wished past the western gates of the city and turned back, and then made their way noisily eastward towards the bridge once more past the rough wood wharfs and now useless wherries which were tied beside them. Lights began to glisten from the houses which lined the bank on both sides. The air smelled sweetly of wood fire, burning leaves, cold wood, and snow. Before them once more loomed the great bridge which spanned the frozen river, the tops of its tiled roofs and steeples now dusted with snow. Here and there below, boats, stripped of sail, were caught in the ice like captured birds.

William looked towards the north bank. In one window a woman stood surveying the scene, her hands arranging the pins of her cap. All about them were dully striped tents, smoke rising from the braziers. Boys slid by, followed by a wagon with its goods covered by burlap.

A cold night, master!

Look to your fires!

Greene said, "Why, where's Christopher? Say why he is not here this day."

William shook his head. "His patron's sent him to France, I know not on what business. We said goodbye, and I called him my friend, and he said nay . . . I'm no one's friend, least of all mine own. Damn him then, as he will."

The snow was now coming faster, and in the dusky light the whole of the world seemed to glisten like silver. Then as he stood there a great love in William's heart arose for all men he knew, and those he did not. Suddenly he was happy to the point of tears. He felt he touched a purity in himself he had not experienced since childhood.

Dusk had fallen over the bridge when they reached it once more, and they slid under, balancing on the massive stone pilings, past a peddler with his legs wrapped in rags who had fallen asleep near his low fire. As the four of them stood looking out towards the great frozen river to where it turned and eventually led to the sea, William's heart expanded with happiness again. He thought, Ah God, God, could this go on forever! That this one moment linger so that no other lesser moment could in any way ever obscure its intensity! And even as he felt it, the last light slid away, and it was gone.

FIRST PERFORMANCES

———•·◦·•———

N THESE EARLY days, William found the theater a
great joy. He knew by then that this was the work he
wished to do, but he did not know how he should ever
succeed in it. He had so much life inside himself he
did not know what to do with it all; he caught, passionately, all that was
on the surface of him like a river when one is only aware of the upper layer
of the waters and not much of that which lies beneath. Christopher Marlowe had once said clearly that William was afraid of much that was
within him. He had put his hand on William's chest, and the Stratford
man had remained quite still for some seconds as if something angelic or
a higher being had revealed his nature to him in those harsh yet delicate
fingers; then he had shaken him off and turned away. The words Christopher had spoken—*I am no one's friend*—still stung him, and he put them
from his mind.

Winter retreated slowly, leaving ice in the water which caught against
the bridge. The sun came pale from the eastern end of the earth and
climbed as if aged and stiff with frost into the height of the sky. Bare trees
stretched up their branches and runty brown sparrows hopped hungrily
about the cold earth of the garden behind the grocery between the neat,

brick-enclosed herbal beds. Slowly the earth began to thaw. From those bare trees buffeted by the river wind, new life came slowly, but the ones that lounged in stiller, sunnier places began to bud at once.

One or another of the theater companies had use for the young William Shakespeare a few days a week now, sometimes more. The world seemed to glitter as he hurried to the playhouse, sometimes the one near their house and other times the one more than a mile away across the bridge and up Bishopsgate Road to the fields outside the city. Sun glittered off muck-heaps still edged with ice as he went, and off the old tenement brick and the one or two fragile daffodils which huddled against tavern walls. Sometimes when he came close he began to run. At times his body burst with such vigor that he swore he would live forever.

Playing a soldier felled in battle, he lay one warm spring afternoon on the stage with his yet combatant fellows still leaping about him. About and above him he could hear the clunk of boots as the other men took stances to declaim their lines, or thrust with their swords, counting under their breath in the choreographed movement. The wood planks reverberated with their leaping and falling, and far off he could feel the stirring of the audience as they listened rapt to the last words of the play.

Opening his eyes slightly, he beheld far above him the ragged straw roofing, and beyond a perfectly blue sky across which floated one or two small white clouds. In that moment he felt that his life had achieved perfection, and all that he desired was that it should remain this way forever. He felt himself pure, for in those hours he had escaped from the one thing most difficult, and that was to be Will Shakespeare. That's what they called him—*Will*. He felt sometimes he could do anything in the world if he had not to manage to be himself.

FOR A TIME he was most fond of Benjamin. He admired the prodigiousness of the undeveloped talent, was in awe of the fellow who could not write ten pages without tearing up fifty. That Ben seldom finished anything did not disturb William, nor did his obsession with the Roman Empire. For hours, Ben would talk of nothing but his passionate desire to return to those days, which he insisted were a more rational time.

But lately the bricklayer's son, who sometimes did not know truth from tales, exhausted him, as did likewise the ebullient Robin Greene, who had now begun to quarrel bitterly with his wife and was said to have struck her more than once. Marlowe was not about, and only good-natured, practical John Heminges remained. William had seen him little for the glimmer of the others; now he had the leisure to do so.

There was no more honest man in the city than this enormous, broad-chested grocer. Though many girls thought him comely, his serious nature frightened them. A religious man, he knew the scriptures and prayer book well, and never failed on a Sabbath to walk off to the parish church hand in hand with his little girl. One night a month he was volunteer constable for the parish, and walked the whole night, peering in alleys and down cellar steps to make sure all was well for his neighbors. A deeply sensual man, he was troubled by his desires, but then they both were . . . if they loved anything more than the theater, they confessed to each other, it was women.

John wished with all his heart to take a second wife; still, he was convinced that his first wife had died because his shop had failed, and would have no woman marry into his poverty. Until he could afford a lace collar, a servant, and a hired horse every now and then, he would not ask any woman to join her life to his.

The two men continued to share the work of the shop, but William found it so tedious that he spent his hours behind the counter reading and sometimes did not know when people came and went. On a late-summer day John hurried off to meet with the priest on behalf of the relief of the parish poor, and William was left alone. He had performed twice the day before, and very tired, he put his head down on the counter and fell asleep.

He woke with a start some hours later in the strange state where you do not know if minutes or days have passed, if you are yet in the same part of the earth, if the monarchy has changed or any other momentous public event occurred. The day was very warm, and he heard birds from the garden, and yet something seemed different. Rising up with a yawn, he began to look around, and then noticed that the door which was generally locked between shop and private rooms stood open. He could not recall that he had opened it himself, and lazily called up, "Jack, art within? Pisspot, hast come home and said no word?"

No reply came, and, puzzled, he walked through the two small back rooms, the first with its hearth and cooking implements and their cots pushed away, and the second in which the rich late-afternoon summer sun came through the small waxed-paper window, through which he could see the shadows of the pear tree. His heart began to beat a little faster, for everything was in slight disarray. The rag dolls had half fallen to their sides upon the bed, a few of the little girl's garments were scattered about the floor, and her hat, which always sat upon the chest, had been knocked to the rushes. Returning to the kitchen, he now saw that their own beds were rumpled, and his box of letters from home was thrown open as if someone had been searching for something.

The latch was unfastened on the back door, which led to the garden; he pushed the door wide and stood stupidly gazing at the pear tree, herb beds, and cabbages and flowers. Someone had come indeed through the front of the shop past him while he slept and gone out through the garden. By the side wall he could see a bit of broken vine lattice which someone's hand had grasped in climbing over.

He thought, Oh Christ's wounds! There was a sense of violation that someone had touched his letters, and he did not know for what they had been searching or if they had found it. Thus he was still walking about puzzled when Jack came home whistling towards the hour of six. "Put up the shutters," he said happily. "Let's have a game of bowls across the bridge, and sup somewhere, for my cooking is thrice worse thine and the lass is hungry."

"Jack," murmured his friend unhappily, "someone's been about."

John's nostrils widened, and a faintly dangerous look came into his dark eyes. Shrugging slightly, he began to look about. Almost at once his eyes went to the hearth, and dropping to his knees, he pulled out a loose brick. A deep cry left him and he gasped, "Ah, the pricklouse! Ah, someone's been here, Will, and taken all! Someone's taken all I have this day."

"What had you?"

"Forty pounds and a little gold."

"That much!" cried William, aghast. "'Tis a fortune. Why did you keep it here? I never knew you had saved so much and had it here."

"I saved it over a time. 'Twas with the goldsmith's until last week, but I did not trust him."

"You brought it here . . ."

"Aye, in a small locked box."

"Perhaps to put it elsewhere. Think, Jack!"

John pressed his hands to his head and muttered desperately, "Nay, 'twas there indeed. . . ." But still they searched the rooms on their hands and knees, or reaching up to shelves into boxes in dusty corners, looking in empty canisters and cooking pots. John ran out to survey the broken trellis, and pulling himself up, looked over the wall. "Ah, ah!" he cried. "He ran this way to the river . . . we shall not find him! It took me three years to put away so much! I will never have my father's shop again now." He sank to a pile of bricks which he had been intending these past three years to use to heighten the wall and moaned.

Standing over this large, grieving man, William could find no words, and then finally, clasping his arms about his jerkin, he muttered, "Well, the fault is mine, Jack, for I fell asleep and some fellow came past me."

"You fell asleep . . ."

"He took perchance the key of our rooms from the shelf behind the counter."

John Heminges sprang up to his full height, his nostrils quivering and dark eyes sparkling in fury. "How could you do this?" he shouted. "What have you brought upon me and my little girl? Ah, you are no better than the rest of them. Madness to have anything to do with any of you, madness, madness! I am a God-fearing, Christian man!"

William was so overcome that he could only blurt, "I swear I shall one day make it up to you . . . I do not know how ever I can . . ." He had started to weep, and wiped his face on his sleeve, and stumbling inside the rooms, began to pack his things. From the garden he could hear the angry words, and could only repeat through his tears, "Well, I will go away from you, for I don't deserve any better." Then he was so grieved that he sat on the low cot and buried his head on his knees.

After a time he heard John come in and walk back and forth.

"Nay, do not go," the grocer muttered. "Art a good man and my true friend if ever I had one. I do not know how much I care for the others these days, but you are in my heart. To lose you would be to lose most everything, for I'm lonely with the child. Will, don't go! Come, let's think as God hath given us minds to reason! I should not have taken the money from the goldsmith's, but now we must understand how to manage! My half-year rent's due for the shop, ten pounds, and I can't think where to get so great a sum!"

"Henslowe will lend it," William said dully, wiping his face again.

"No, he's tired of lending, and the season does not do well! We must go to my brother in Kent and beg him, but I dread it. He disapproves of all

I am and thinks I lost our father's shop from carelessness, for I was with my sick wife at her own father's when the flood came and not at home."

In the morning they set off with the child between them, past the printing shops and inns of the Old Kent Road, which wound through Kent and eventually came to Canterbury, Dover, and the high white cliffs above the sea. Susan ran about gathering flowers, and when she had more than she could carry they set off again, coming with mud on their shoes and quite tired to the door of the farmhouse four hours later.

John Heminges's brother was some years his senior but looked much older. Though they were both large men, where John's face was wistful, the other man's was stern. Still, it was an excellent house full of every provision, of pewter, of a little silver. With the money went a lecture, which the grocer bore in silence with lowered head, and afterwards he went for a walk down to the mill with his brother, while William received a packet of food from the kitchen girl, who kissed him behind the door.

In the late afternoon they set back again, Jack somewhat silent and every now and then moving his lips, and William holding the child by the hand, with the packet of food wrapped in a cloth and hung on a stick over his shoulder. At a stream they stopped to rest, unpacking the bread and meat pie, and drinking water from a little wood cup. Then John Heminges lay back on the bank, with his arms beneath his head, and frowned up at the heavy trees. "Shakespeare," he said wistfully.

"Aye, my friend."

"I think myself grown older this past year! I look back at some of the things I have done and places I've gone, and think it a kind of madness! My father was much the Puritan, you know, and forbade me any joy. I was beaten too much—it came of all this, I think. I have run between his strictures for me and something else, particularly since Beth died, but I think today I know that though I have not succeeded like him, I am yet a good man and myself and that is all I can be. There comes a time when you must know what you are at heart, and return to it."

Sitting crosslegged beside, William began to strip the leaves off a slender shoot. He gazed with misty eyes to the child Susan, who waded in the stream with small shrieks of delight.

John continued. "I must be honest, not for his memory but for myself . . . and I do believe in a merciful God who mayhap by the trials He hath sent me has made me stronger. I cannot say." Then very quietly he added,

"I will tell you what news my brother had for me." His voice was trembling slightly. "A great-uncle of ours in the city who has not spoken to me since I failed my father's shop is very old and ill, and thought not to live long. When he dies we shall have some money from him, and then I will have my father's shop again."

"And what will I do then, Jack?"

"Why, stay with me as long as I live," replied the grocer. "Don't you know we are friends? We're much alike, I do believe me, William. And I must prosper, I must die a prosperous man."

"Ah, I should like that well!" said William wistfully.

Darkness had almost fallen when they walked slowly by the very same printing shops they had passed that morning. The dank sewage scent of their own neighborhood rose to meet them, the vague smell in the soft wind of bears and dogs.

THEN HE WAS touring again. A regular man had canceled, and one of the sharers of the Queen's Men, a respectable troupe which had once been about the court a great deal and now made a poor living on the fringes of the city and in the provinces, sent his apprentice to call upon the two men who lived behind the grocery on the south side. John could not go for his work, so William packed all he had into a satchel within an hour and met the respectable ensemble of six men and two lads at the White Horse Inn. A cart was loaded with props, scenery, and such personal belongings as they had. Even as they moved slowly from the city, walking beside the heavily laden vehicle, he opened the new pages of plays which had been thrust into his hands and began to memorize them. The dust of the road settled on his hair and clothing, and still he walked on, murmuring the words.

When he did not memorize, he played, and then memorized again, and somewhere while resting under a tree with the boys and men stripped to bathe in a stream in a lovely patch of countryside, in sight of an abandoned and broken monastery so ancient no one in the neighborhood knew its history, his own words began to form. They were not only in the letters which he wrote home, enclosing within each flowers, coins, sketches of the things which delighted him, but balancing the back of a sheet of playscript on his knee, he had begun to rework an old play. Each day he listened to the words being flung out by his fellows in innyards: the glistening speeches of Marlowe, who now had two or three plays on the boards, the lyrical sweep of Greene, the efforts of many others. The loneliness for his children and the caring for his fellows and the passion he felt for the physical world about him compressed inside him until they could no longer be contained, and formed into dialogue. Under a tree with the voices of the bathing players seeming far off, he began to write. Then he brought his work late at night to the kitchen of some inn, and stretched before the dulled fire, the last of its light casting in dark shadows upon his page and his fingers which grasped the pen, shaping and reshaping the old scenes of blood and vengeance. He also was beginning a comedy on the old theme of twins separated at birth.

He did not tell anyone of these things. Still, standing at dawn in the innyard with carters and ostlers, laughing and cursing, drinking warm ale, with the knowledge of his fellows yet asleep in the rooms above, two or three to a bed, he had a strange sense that though he was six and twenty years old, life was just beginning for him.

Through Christmastide and the windiest months of winter he continued. He wrote quietly, tore up what he had, and began again, and then sometimes days went by and he did not work because he was too discouraged, or too busy. At one point he showed what he had written to Greene, who looked it over, smiled quietly, and made no comment. William was annoyed, for he knew the words had some merit. Then he added lines and speeches to a few old plays in repertoire, and to another a sequence of clowns, and was asked to write a whole scene in still one more. It was also a time when he was inconsistently in love, sighing a week or two over this girl or that one. Women faded in and out about him: there was the creak of farthingale and crinkle of the overdress of another, and then for weeks he was haunted by the memory of a girl bending over to retrieve her wash basket on a warm winter day, whose pinned dress had revealed dark, bare thighs. Bosoms swelled behind the tight lacing of blouse and bodice; he stroked the velvet fabric of one of the dresses used in *The Jew of Malta*, imagining soft flesh beneath his hands. John Heminges had seen a girl he fancied, and talked endlessly of her, but by then William had pushed such things aside. He returned compulsively to his work desk, where even as he came home the cheap paper seemed to glisten dully on the table and say, Write—fill us with words.

Words were more than themselves; they were everything. He was both drunk and sober with these words which could hold both all the world and himself, all he had known and all he could ever hope to be.

THE WINTER LEFT behind small drafts of money sent home to Stratford through friends going that way, little profit for the shop, and no sign of John's inheritance. Pestilence and political intrigue had closed the theaters now and then, and he had begun to wonder why he had set his life in this direction. On an April evening he found himself on Bishopsgate, and on a whim turned up the outer stair to the rooms where Christopher Marlowe lived above a wax chandler's shop in a house some century or two old.

Marlowe had come and gone that year, leaving behind him a scattering of fierce, brilliant poetry like jewels which are flung across a floor when a bag has broken; he cared little for it, sometimes leaving scenes barely finished before he was off again. Some said he disdained what he did, or despised those for whom he did it. The remoteness between him and the others was now complete; it was as if he had never come banging on the grocery door long after dark like some messenger of the gods, so completely had he removed himself from the world which they had all shared together. William, disgusted at this betrayal, almost hurried from the alley to more constant friends he knew would be waiting. He did not know why he did not.

He had little expected the poet home, but when he pushed open the door, saw him bent over some papers on the floor, which he was turning with his delicate fingers. Even by the dull yellowish taper candle he could perceive that Kit Marlowe had changed since they had last met. The face was as beautiful, yet somehow slightly worn as the painting on the door of the house of the doxies by the river, washed by wind and rain. The garments, however, were new and costly.

Leaping up with a crooked smile, Christopher came towards him at once. "How fares it with thee, darling?" he cried. "And how come you to hurry up the steps this moment when you have just been in my thoughts! How's old Jack? I saw you both play in my *Dr. Faustus*—you're both pissing actors. We hear Jonson, the fool, has gone to the Lowlands for the wars."

William observed that the poet had been packing as if for a long journey: two large leather satchels held shirts, hose, books, papers. "How have I been in your thoughts?" he asked.

"'There's work for thee."

"What manner of work?"

"The making of plays. My patron's rushing me to some business, and I must to Scadbury in all haste! Come with me to Master Henslowe and we will arrange it."

Hurrying along through the sweet and sour smells of the afternoon market, the wilting vegetables and dully glinting silks set out for sale, they made their way to the Boar's Head. In the room where Henslowe was holding court, the walls were painted with dingy flowers, a bed was upended against one wall, saffron-colored curtains barely covering it, and the remains of a feast of pigeon and beef were pushed to the table's side. A water bowl with a few violet petals and a napkin lay hard by, for the theater manager had washed his hands meticulously before opening his accounting book. He sat at it even now, scratching with his pen the employment record of actors, the cost of wigs refurbished, the estimate of a secondhand lute and a fool to play it.

William forced himself to stand with modest decorum, though his breath was high in his throat, and everything in the room from the shabby draperies to the curled, poorly set wig of the theater manager appeared in such brilliant clarity in his mind that he made silent verses from it. Even the laughter of a barmaid some rooms away rang like bells across a country field.

"God give you a good day, Marlowe," said the manager.

"He may give me one, but not thee, Henslowe."

"And why not, prithee, eh?" said the theater manager, one elfin ear twitching under his wig.

"For thy miser's heart."

"And are you an honest judge of men, seeking whores and cutpurses as you do?" screamed Henslowe, his voice scratching with irritation. "'T'were not for thy art I would not piss on the corner of thy street! Where's the play of King Harry the saintly which you promised this week?"

"I've not got it."

"Thy meaning, prick?"

Dumping the packet carelessly by the wine bottle, Marlowe bent over, selected a capon leg from the table, and began to tear at it with his teeth. "The matter's this, Henslowe," he said, shaking the bone in the direction of the manager, who huddled nervously over his accounting book. "I've scratched a few hours on this old pitiful *Reign of Harry Sixth*; I gave it then to Greene for a week, but he's so busy with his whores and thieves since his wife left him that he has not put a drop of ink to it. Here I return the scribbles; 'tis yours."

Henslowe slammed his small hands to the table so that the flower petals in the water quivered and his great account book stirred. "Marlowe, you whoreson!" he shouted, almost rising from his seat. "Do you mean to go off without completing it after thy promises?"

Marlowe yawned and began to pick at his teeth with his knife. "No matter: here's Shakespeare, who will write it."

"Impossible! He's done no more than augment a scene or two."

"Nevertheless, I swear to him."

"Oh, swearst to him!" said the theater manager bitterly. "Naught's cheaper these days than an oath! What will we do if he fails?"

William looked at them both with a slight, disdainful smile. Already he heard speeches, contention, the clash of weapons of a war on French soil which could go into the drama; they sounded so loudly in his mind he did not quite understand why the others did not hear them. He knew at once what must be done, and he cried passionately, "Master Henslowe, I shall not fail." His voice rose against the tavern walls, and then again was wistful. The dark soft eyes blinked, and the candle caught the glitter of his one round earring.

Henslowe stared at him for a moment, and then shook his head. "Well, what shall I do but trust thee?" he murmured, his sharp face softening for a moment. "Though I shall pay you a little, only a little, because I do not know, though I trust thee, how much that trust should be, and that trust is born out of necessity, not wisdom. A piss on that! I must have it within four weeks. Why do you stand there? Go and begin!"

Clasping the small amount of pages bound in a stained vellum wrapper against his chest, William bowed to them both and then hurried from the tavern into the brilliance of the spring afternoon. By the time he came to the bridge he was ravenous, and bought a small pie and drank a bottle of warm ale. When he reached the other side, he threw himself down on an upturned wherry near a shop of boatmen's supplies, untied the packet, and eagerly began to read.

With the scent of the sea, old fish, and sun-baked wood about him, he skimmed the scene with its many patched, inserted pages, now and then stopping to study the few lines in Christopher's scrawling pen. With that exception, it was as poor and silly a work as ever he had seen, with little consistent in character or history. Greene had not so much as touched the pages. Still, as he hunched over the papers his mind began to have its way with the fragmented ideas and directions: a field of battle . . . just those words alone evoked much in him. Though he did not move, his heart was beating rapidly as if to find a way without his ribs. A field of battle. . . . He raised his face, hardly seeing the glitter of the Thames as the day moved in its ordinary way to twilight. Instead he seemed to sense the contending noblemen of the houses of York and Lancaster rising like ghosts from the dripping river, coming towards him with hands extended: adulterous Margaret the Queen, and poor Harry himself, who was better at telling his beads than the foul hearts of all the men around him.

A field of battle . . . the King's court . . . *Hung be the heavens with black, yield day to night.*

Scene after scene began to build in his mind, fragments of lines, some tender, some martial, and with it the voices of dispute, disloyalty, aggression. That witch the maid of Orleans whom they called Joan La Pucelle coming to aid the French Dauphin to regain his country's precious towns. *Glory is like a circle in the water, which never ceaseth to enlarge itself, till by broad spreading it disperse to naught. . . .*

Leaping up, he hurried home, spread the sheets and some clean ones on the grocery counter, and finding that excellent book of English history by Holinshed among his clothes for reference of battles and contenders, began to compose. When John came home hours later he discovered the soup burned in the pot, and William with fingers stained with ink, and four pages of original writing which he had already begun to remake anew once more.

THE HISTORY HAD been announced in two dozen printed flyers nailed to posts in Paul's Churchyard, on the back of tavern doors, and in one or two guildhalls. Rumor spread quickly, for the events of the contention between the houses of York and Lancaster were not so far removed, and that some old men remembered talk of it in their childhoods. The name of the writer did not appear, for no one knew him anyway.

The history was given for the first time on a hot June day, when perspiration ran down the actors' backs under the thick, refurbished costumes lavishly stuffed with bombast to give them extravagant shape. Shoes were dyed a dozen colors like a field of flowers. It was the third play given that week, with nothing distinct about it but for the inordinate number of characters, which made the actors hurtle into each other in the tiring room in an attempt to find their new wigs and coats, cursing, jesting, inquiring about each other's love affairs, discussing where extra money could be made. Talk was of a lutenist who had been found in the bed of an actor's wife.

Henslowe stomped through the tiring rooms. Passing William, he muttered from the side of his mouth, "'Tis too long! Too many battles, too many actors . . . nay, nay." Yet as reports came that the galleries and ground space were filling, he actually began to smile.

William hurried through his own roles, hardly hearing the compliments from his fellows, and yet at the same time meticulously aware of everything—a slip in a speech, a pigeon which landed on the throne and then squawking hurled itself up into the air again, the two trumpets which did not come in at the same moment, one lagging a fragment of the second behind the other and then making a vague medieval discord. At the scene of the useless death in battle against the French of great Talbot in the arms of his son, he stood by a curtain which hung at the back of the stage and looked out. Several of the apprentices at the platform's edge silently bit their fingers, and somewhere from the galleries he heard a woman sobbing.

He was one of the last to leave the theater. As he gathered his things, he saw Henslowe coming towards him with a pleased, greedy look on his face and a thin packet of paper bound in twine in his arms. These the theater manager threw to the table, dusting his hands of the shavings. "Some scenes and bits from an older play to continue the story of Henry," he said. "With all the battles and rebellions and murders we should have two more plays from it. I will need the first to rehearse end summer for Michaelmas."

All summer he wrote fervently, surrounded sometimes by several versions of the same speech, trying to make a fair copy from them. These early-morning hours of solitude were the most intense he had ever known. There were only the squawking of gulls and the smell of ships and the river as he sat hunched above his paper. Ideas woke him hours before dawn and left him stumbling through the rest of his day. Overhearing some words or a bit of humor in the marketplace, he rushed home to turn it into characters and scenes. When words did not come, he sketched his friends, ship masts, and house chimneys in the margins. He drew Heminges devouring his accounting book, and John laughed so hard to see it that he fell from his stool to the floor.

Afternoons he was thrust together with his fellows in a close, sweat-smelling tiring room, remembering his lines, finding his boots, emotions and characters and time and place rushing by him so fast that whoever he was himself was carried away as if in a flood, yet even with that he knew that he was yet stronger than it, and guided it though it seemed to hurl him here and there. His mind rose above his emotions as if he stood outside his body, watching himself.

And at the end of all this there were the long hours stretching past darkness with friends, always hungry for food and talk. How had it gone? Could it have been better? Red lattice marked the alehouses where they met when thirsty, and bush or vine leaves the taverns where they ate famished meals. Lutenists and singing boys went from room to room hoping for coins, and sometimes the tapster dressed in a bearskin.

Hundreds of taverns lay within the city walls, many more stretching on the dusty way of the Strand from Temple Gate through the little clustered village of Charing, and on to the courts and palaces of Westminster or the Swan near the dissolute waterside ward of Dowgate. The actors and writers met most often at the Boar's Head in Eastcheap. There they left messages for one another pinned to the wall, or insulting slogans or love emblems carved in the tables. When there was money they had beef, mutton, chicken, bacon, pigeon, bread, and beer; on Fridays green fish and whiting and salad, white wine and claret. Talk clattered against the dingy hangings and old painted wallpaper of the yellow room.

It was here in the private room with its painted flowers and upended bed that they first read the second play of Henry and the continuing contention between the houses of York and Lancaster. Some of the men listened with their feet on the table, others bent forward with their heads in their arms. At first William read alone, but then other players, gathering close to him, shared the manuscript and sang out the roles. They read of the rebel Jack Cade whose men propose to begin by killing all the lawyers, and the nobles who pulled, stretched, distorted, and cracked the fabric of the government in their passion to control the weak King and gain the crown. *It is reported, mighty sovereign, that good Duke Humphrey traitorously is murdered. . . .*

Later he walked home with John Heminges across the bridge, hands clasped behind their backs, ignoring the push of carts and donkeys, the shouting of merchants, and the white bird droppings that flecked the paving stones of this roadway high above river and boats. It was in those hours that John first told him that he had found a girl he fancied more than his life, and that as soon as he should come into money he should speak for her. William smiled kindly, but could never remember her name for the story which continued in his mind. He did not notice the streets, nor hear the roars of beasts from the bear garden, for looking away to the south and the lands that led to the sea he seemed to see King Henry, sixth of that name, alone and disguised, crouched on a hill overlooking a battlefield where the subjects of his country contended unto death.

FRIENDS AND RIVALS

RELIABLE SOURCE OF income for players was to process before some noble personage dressed in his livery and bearing his banner. Sometimes upon the death of a man of wealth and prestige, word came to the actors that recompense could be had for a few hours' march bearing a canopy over that elevated soul's remains or marching mournfully before his coffin dressed all in darkest black. Other times they walked in the train of some foreign dignitary who wished to make an expensive show of himself. But the tournaments held now and then for the pleasure of the Queen and her subjects were the most sparkling of these occasions, and William, John Heminges, and several of their friends were for this particular one engaged to march in the livery of the young Robert Devereux, Lord Essex, who was much regarded by her Majesty.

England in the past several years had been suffused with heavily illustrated volumes of the Arthurian legends of chivalry and fair ladies, hero and villain. Gallants from the court and knights from about the country who were already past their prime but yearned to summon up some of the spirit of their great-grandfathers came yearly to try this ancient skill of jousting; they brought heavy armor long displayed in their ancestral halls, employed skilled men to hammer out dents, restore leather fastenings, and polish engraved steel. Others sought the skills of the Greenwich armorers to forge new breastplates and bucklers in a heat of golden sparks.

William, who was standing in orange and silver livery outside Whitehall Palace, looked all about. Though the procession was almost ready to begin, the grocer John Heminges was nowhere to be found.

Grasping one of the poles of the canopy which he would carry over the lord, he turned this way and that, momentarily expecting to see his friend hurrying breathlessly between the tents. Gaudily clad horses, almost blinded for their fringed thick draping, stomped and snorted and flung up their heads while the squires for the day grasped the reins of their masters' mounts. Turning, he glimpsed some hundreds of spectators crammed into the tiltyard, whose balconies and windows once again this October were hung with brilliant soft banners bearing the crests of the knights and the royal arms.

"Hast seen Heminges!" he shouted to the man who held another of the four poles, but the answer was lost above the sounding trumpets.

Dust arose as they began to move forward across the yard. Elongated banners, held aloft on elevated poles, swept over his face. In the distance he could just make out the stand decked with late flowers at the end of the yard where stood their most dread sovereign, Elizabeth, and her virgin ladies. Slowly they approached until he could almost put out his hand and touch the powder gathered in the wrinkles of her bare neck and the jewels which hung in the aged crevices. Each unmounted man fell for one moment to his knee in the dust, and those who rode horses bowed their heads and held their helmets against their hearts in reverence. The dust flew up into his nostrils, and thus they processed out again.

In the squires' tent, William hastily unbuttoned his finery, handed it to a steward, pulled on his own plain clothes, and ran down to the river. Sun glittered on the water so that he could hardly see to hail a wherry, and when he had secured one, he turned about to scan the approaching south side with its theaters, palaces, and hovels. He paid no attention to his shoes as he hurried up the water steps but ran rapidly up the wharf and to the streets he knew so well towards the grocery store.

The sign had not been hung, but the door was unlocked. Hurrying through the rooms calling out Heminges's name, he came to the last one near the garden and saw that the grocer was sprawled facedown and silent in bed, with one hand dangling to the floor. "Oh Christ's mercy!" William murmured, throwing off his hat. "Hast some sickness?" He knelt beside his friend, feeling him for fever, and in a moment's terrible supposition for blood or broken bones. "I saw the Queen closer than you, and she's three hundred years old and doth not like it a whit! Jack, Jack—what dost? Oh Christ, naught has happened to the child?" By this time he was shaking the great grocer.

Slowly John Heminges rolled over and looked up at him with stricken eyes; then, fumbling, he felt for a wrinkled paper under his body and pulled it out. "It hath come," he murmured. "I am a wealthy man, for my great-uncle's died. I can have my shop again." His body shook, and he wept.

Astonished, William chafed his hand. "Well then!" he murmured between embarrassment and affection. "'Tis a great and fine thing, Jack! Why do you grieve?"

"'Tis such a great change and a long time coming. I cannot believe that it will not be taken from me again."

"No, by God's mercy," said William. They sat talking for some time and then walked over the bridge to find friends with whom to celebrate until the chimes rang midnight, and then went home singing through the streets the ditty of three merry men, and the poor maid singing Willow, willow, willow.

AT THE END of October William and John left the south side of the city. They hired carts and came across by ferry with the stock of the shop, and the child's dresses and toys; the little girl's delicate fingers clung to the ferry rail, her mouth parted in joy and the long, uncapped hair come loose and blowing in the wind. She clung close to both her father and William as the ferry neared the wharf on the north side.

The familial grocery shop which was now regained was on Bread Street, some steps away from St. Thomas Lane, just streets off both from the river docks and the ebullient Cheapside with its taverns and market stalls. A great oak tree stood between the houses, and many of the windows were decorated with flower boxes. William unpacked his two boxes of clothing, books, and writing, his bound packet of letters from home, and the prayer book which he had seldom opened since coming to the city. There were commodious rooms above the shop where they would live.

John Heminges hurried to the church of St. Mary Aldermanbury each Sabbath morn, and stared over his psalter at the dark-haired alderman's daughter who lived in Huggin's Lane. She was indeed an enchanting girl whose full lips moved as she praised God and all the things He had made. William was working one evening on the last play of the saintly King Harry and those who sought to depose him when Heminges rushed in from a supper at the grocers' hall. Rubbing his wide hands together as he did when agitated, he began to prowl up and down the shop past the bags and jars of spices, now and then pausing to chip at the sugar block with his fingernails.

"What dost?" asked William.

"You know it well!" came the anguished reply.

"Marry, can it be love?"

"I don't sleep for wanting her, I groan and dream, and every place she's not seems but dull!" Heminges threw his large body down on a stool and rested his fingers against his dark beard. "You must listen to me, my friend!" Reaching over, he tugged at William's sleeve, then sighed and looked away towards the dark street. "Rebecca Knell," he muttered. "I must speak of her or go mad. Ask her age!"

"Well then, I ask it."

"Pisspot! Dullard! Fart! Cannot you feign some interest, eh? She's but nineteen years and a widow; her husband was an actor in the provinces." Rising, hugging his chest, he addressed the floor rushes as if to expect from them some intelligent response. "They all love her—a lad carved her name on the horsepost before the vintners on Stayning Lane: I'd have the beating of him should I find him! William, William! What is she like beneath her beauty? Will she make a sober wife? Will she love my daughter? I want a dozen children, but will she?" Then he added with an angry shrug, "I am mayhap too old for her and not a handsome fellow, and mayhap when I court her, I'll stutter, and that will be the end of all, the end of all!"

Up and down he walked, until William closed his books with a sigh, stood up, and said, "Well, let us go see her, this beauty."

Heminges wrung his large hands. "But what excuse shall we make for the visit!" he muttered, his face contorted with anxiety.

"Tell them you wish to ravish the damsel."

"Thou merciless man, leave off for I suffer."

"Nay, nay, good Jack!" said William in a consoling voice. "Nay, I will speak with a clear mind. Is her father not of this parish? May not one good Christian merchant in good standing with his guild and Savior visit another in friendship?"

"Ah, thou hast it!" returned the grocer. "I must bring a present from my stock. Peppercorns!"

"Nay, nutmeg and sugar to sweeten him."

"Your thoughts are gifted by the gods!" was the reply, and they wrapped the gift in a bit of grass-green velvet left from the cutting of a new costume for a comedy, and tied it with a fragment of gilt ribbon from the same five-act entertainment.

The cold, still night was full of the scent of fires as they walked towards Huggin's Lane, where, with much encouragement from William, honest Jack Heminges knocked upon the door. It was pulled open by a sour-faced matron. Behind her they beheld the parlor with several young men and women sitting about. The women were sewing, and one boy who had been singing to the lute broke off. Coming towards them in the haze of fire smoke, the master of the house greeted them.

"Masters, welcome," he said, recognizing them.

Heminges said gruffly, "I bring an unworthy gift, neighbor, for your generous welcome of myself to the parish." Asked to be seated, the two actors found themselves drawn into conversation and music making. As William played a dance upon the lute, and then sang a song not well to his own accompaniment, he was aware of the beautiful girl who listened intently, her hands tightly wound in her lap, and masses of reddish brown hair not quite covered by a modest embroidered cap.

John nudged his foot gently.

Buttered ale, warmed and sweetened with sugar, was drunk and after half an hour the talk grew duller, and William, whose last song had not been listened to, put aside the lute. Then the girl's father stretched forth his belly against his clasped hands and said with a knowing smile, "And which one of your goodmen hath come for my daughter Becky?"

William threw back his head in amazement, and John, clearing his throat and suddenly pale, rose and bowed with all his dignity and said in a deep voice from his broad chest, "I would visit her now and then of an evening if I might, good master."

"For a purpose honorable which will bring no shame?"

"Aye, being too long a bachelor, I have lately thought . . . and having seen the lass . . . it hath occurred to me . . ."

Rebecca had lowered her head to bury her smiles, glancing up only for a moment with a mischievous look. Rising, she curtseyed to the two visitors and with enviable youth and grace swept up the steps.

The father said pompously, "Well and when I have inquired into your good name and fortune, Master Heminges, and the honesty of your purpose, you may come of an evening and sit in the window there for a time with my poor widowed girl!"

The visitors bowed graciously, gave thanks for the hospitality, and emerged to the rising wind of the January evening. There they took arms and broke into a half run until they came to an alley where a carpenter had left a chest half unfinished, its fragrant carved chips littering the dirt path. They fell laughing into each other's arms, shaking and punching each other.

"Say she's fair and true, Will!"

"Ah, thou pig's gizzard, fair . . ."

"And true, say it, man!"

"Well, marry, I think it! By our lady, wouldst embrace the breath from me?" the Stratford man cried. Their voices lowered as the constable passed swinging his stick, and recognizing the men as worthy citizens, bade them a solemn good night. William dusted the wood chips from his clothing and said in a softer, more reflective way, "Then you'll be happy, for that I'm glad! But at times I do wonder for myself. . . ." His voice trailed away in the light summer wind, and the sound of bells ringing from Cheapside.

"Why, you shall be as fine a playmaker as Marlowe!" pronounced the grocer. "Finer, mayhap!" They turned once to blow kisses in the direction of Huggin's Lane, and then, arm in arm, walked home to the grocery shop.

THE GIRL'S FATHER, only happy enough to have her married once more, gave his consent. A courtship ensued with the giving of many small presents, and the betrothal party was arranged for the last week of winter.

William woke that day on his cot above the grocery, somewhat stiff from staying out past midnight with friends and drinking a little too much. A fly buzzed near a sticky plate, and down the streets a dog barked. Through his mind certain thoughts passed and drifted into nothing. Just ten days ago he had finished the last of the Henry plays, which ended with the death of the good king and the rise of the house of York.

Pen and papers were kept near behind the large sacks of dry goods next his cot, but he was too lazy to reach for them. Instead he lay back, easing his body deeper into the straw mattress. Henslowe had been generous with the amount given for the history, and he had been able to send a quantity of money home with presents. If he continued this way he would perhaps no longer be poor, and for a moment he thought of what that might be like for him.

From below he heard a scraping of chairs and voices, and the playful banter as tables were erected for the supper. Above this rose the grocer's masterful voice, reviewing the list of foodstuffs: oyster pie, pullets stuffed with brawn, mutton in wine; from the tavern he had a dozen bottles of wine sent over. It would be a pleasure to see Jonson, who had just some days ago returned from the wars, though no one had heard from Marlowe in months, and he was not expected to come. Greene, who they heard was now living with a whore and spending his hours among thieves, had not answered their message. Still, a great many actors, writers, and friends from about the neighborhood would be there. With that William sat up decisively. Whatever good fortune came the way of John Heminges, the grocer deserved it, and this night brought the greatest indeed. Throwing on his ordinary garments, he hurried down the steps to carry in the kegs of ale and was soon stirring the pudding in the hearth wearing a large stained smock.

Evening came early and the light began to fade down Milk Street, and at six o'clock the bells sounded from the church of St. Mary le Bow that the workday was done. Shopkeepers took down their signs. In the rooms behind the store, a trestle table had been erected, surrounded by borrowed stools and benches. William hung bits of fabric for banners from the beams, having managed the pudding only slightly scalding his hand. When he climbed the stairs he took from its hook his new suit of brown embroidered with green metallic thread, and the soft linen shirt which had just been delivered from the seamstress. Slowly turning in front of the small mirror, he was much pleased.

Below he heard Rebecca arriving with her sister, who was also distractingly pretty, and their mother and father, who had the formality of wealthy merchants who knew all there was to know about court and city, and before whom a man dared not (as Heminges said) make a fart. Following them was the satirist Tom Nashe, who wrote tracts against the Puritans. The voices of actors with whom he had played roared from the street and then from the chamber below . . . dashing Dick Burbage the hero and his brother, Augustine Phillips, great-hearted, hefty Thomas Pope, who lived in Southwark, and the sly little clown Will Kempe, who could bite hard with his tongue when it pleased him, which it most often did.

"Thy servant, sir."

"Nay, I am thine."

"Oh pig, welcome."

As he perfumed his beard he could hear the sound of yet other men from the grocers' guild, with cries of "Thy servant! God give you a good evening." When William rushed down, he found Benjamin Jonson standing by the cheeses with a knife, absentmindedly consuming much of one. After they had greeted each other with joy, the bricklayer said gloomily, "I've bad news! 'Tis cried that poor Harry Hunks the blind bear is dead! *Requiescat in pace.* He was an unfeeling beast towards me, for all I loved him! By Satan's long tail, you look a worthy fellow . . . almost gentry, by my arse! They said hast scribbled thy way half through history, ha! Still, I have outwritten you with a song I've brought."

Meats and cheeses had been laid all along the boards, and all found places on benches or in the corners of the floor to sup. All the time the talk of the theater continued, until someone began to speak instead of court and patronage, and then the guilds, and then foreign lands. After carefully washing his hands in a bowl of water and drying them on a cloth, a lutenist tuned his instrument and sitting on the edge of the bench, said they would have Jonson's song.

The bricklayer's son stood beside him, his heavy hand on the musician's delicate shoulders. "'Tis a love song," he murmured. "I made it up one night in the wars when I thought I should die and never see your pissing faces more."

John Heminges, who sat behind Rebecca with both his large arms about her shoulders, nuzzled her neck and smiled. His eyes softened as Ben Jonson began to sing in his rough bass voice, marking time as he did so gravely with his large foot on the crinkly fresh rushes of the floor.

"Drink to me only with thine eyes
And I will pledge with mine;

Or leave a kiss within the cup,
　　And I'll not look for wine.
The thirst that from the soul doth rise
　　Doth ask a drink divine:
But might I of Jove's nectar sup,
　　I would not change for thine."

Then Jonson added, "I have said 'twas writ in a place near death. I have been near death and the hangman's rope and much, but I am here tonight at my bosom friend's betrothal, and God be praised, God be praised. If a time in the world did not bring us wisdom, we should not live to have a time in the world. Here endeth the lesson, amen. Silence for the song.

"I sent thee late a rosy wreath,
　　Not so much honoring thee,
As giving it a hope that there
　　It could not withered be.
But thou thereon didst only breathe,
　　And send'st it back to me:
Since when it grows, and smells, I swear,
　　Not of itself but thee."

"Now there's a lyric, Ben!" cried John when the last chord had died away. He rose and went unsteadily towards the bricklayer's son, drawing him into his arms and kissing his cheek several times. Then he cried, "Table to the wall, to the wall! We will have a dance and William and I shall dance a fiendish hard jig such as is the province of our clown Kempe, but for every step Kempe would take, we shall make three. This I swear as an honest man."

"And to his honesty I swear," cried William. "If I am my mother's son!"

The men cleared away the food to the other room and pushed up the tables, and then solemnly bade the women stand back to give room for the dancers. With great flourish and courtesy William and the grocer bowed deeply to each other and then the friends, who returned as graciously with curtseys and kisses. The lute and alto recorder struck up, and the dance began.

They danced together for a few moments and then William began to stir his feet more rapidly on the floor, which creaked below the low heels of his shoes; his single earring glittered in the candlelight of the early evening, and his high breath came and went in his throat.

"Oh sweet!" shouted the women with pleasure. "Why Jack, must go as rapidly! Can you not, Jack the betrothed man? Will you not haste to thy Becky's bed, master grocer?"

John was panting slightly for his heaviness, but William, more lithe, spun about and nodded to the musicians, who began the piece again in double time. His hair flew about his ears, and his eyes sparkled, and the women began to clap. "Oh, go faster!" they cried. "Oh, poor Jack's weary!"

"Ah well!" panted the grocer, who could not be unhappy this night. "I save my strength for the marriage bed, for I expect to wear the mattress thin. I have been a bachelor too long."

"Aye!" cried the friends, crowding closely together; in a blur of brilliant linen or light wool dresses, the women stood about modestly patting the stray hair which had escaped from their caps, and swaying seductively in these rooms which smelled of nutmeg and spices.

A grocer shouted, "Then Will, go faster."

"Well then, I shall."

At a nod the lutenist increased the speed once more, his nimble fingers flying, the recorder following, and someone else now having seized a small drum to keep the time. William ended in a spin, and careened purposefully into the arms of one of the girls, who shrieked and let him embrace her. He began to nibble from the tips of her fingers up her slashed sleeves to her shoulder while she cried out happily. When he looked up, Robin Greene was standing at the door.

There was something strangely dry about the small, red-bearded prolific author of plays, stories, and treatises in his double wool vest, shivering slightly and accusingly though the rooms were very warm. It seemed as if any moment a light breeze might take him away, leaving a few grains of dust behind. At his side was a heavy, bold whore far bigger than he with a bodice cut so low that the edges of her fat nipples could be seen. There was a reek about her of chamber pots and sewage, and she was dressed fantastically as if in rags dyed carelessly and stitched together. Near her the writer seemed a breath, and still that breath panted and sought life.

For a moment there was silence, and prim Rebecca and her sister drew slightly closer together, touching hands and leaning near their stern parents. Then John Heminges cried out in joy, and rushing forward at once, shouted out, "God's blessings! Hast been a time since we've seen thee! Come and rejoice with us this night! Give us the name of thy fair lady! Greet my bride for friendship's sake, and let us be merry!"

Greene turned towards Rebecca, carefully inclining his head as if afraid it might somehow tumble off and roll across the floor. Those who knew him came forward, though two or three shook their own heads in the corner at his companion, and laughed behind their hands while continuing to eat.

Jack cried, "Ah, come in!"

"I can stay but shortly."

"Then you will have wine. And you . . . mistress."

Still standing by the open door, shivering now and then as if some madness were inside him which shook and ruled him, Greene put out his hand for the goblet while his companion elegantly arranged her rags of skirts and, taking a knife from her girdle, cut an enormous slice of meat pie and began to eat it, licking the blade carefully with her great tongue. The small poet, however, did not drink his wine, but held it tentatively as a kind of offering which he was eager to give, and shook his head harshly at the proffered pointful of greasy mutton and crust.

The others had begun to talk again and some to laugh when his dry voice sounded once more. "Jack Heminges," he said, his glance moving about the room, "I drink, but do not stay, nor will I make merry, for I cannot. You know full well that there are those of this company who hate me and who have wronged me bitterly past what a man may endure."

John was speechless for a moment. "Wronged thee?" he asked when he found his voice. "Wronged thee, Robin? Who hath wronged thee?"

Screwing up his face and expanding his chest, the small writer shrieked out in a manner that brought silence to the whole room, "All you men of the theater and the pen! You say you wish me well, but hope in secret I will fail! Aye, you wits, you jeer at poor Greene!" His small burning eyes swept the faces of friends and stranger, and came to rest upon William, who was yet panting and holding the girl about the waist.

"Thou, Shakespeare!" he sneered, expanding his narrow chest again under the wool vests. "Why, you are a playwright of some reputation now, are you not? Men begin to speak of thee. And costly garments! Tailored to suit, and new, I might say."

Flushing slightly, William murmured, "What can you mean?"

"Ah, the innocent! You have the look of a man with coins in his purse, Shakespeare! And why so many? 'Tis an easy thing to sell the work of another for your own profit." Greene's voice rose suddenly to a shriek, and his red beard quivered as if pointing in accusation. "You have stolen my work, Shakespeare! Almost all of the Henry plays are mine, but credit was given thee. You have stolen the bread from my lips!"

John Heminges pushed his way to the center of the room, crying in the hearty tone which he employed upon the stage in his depiction of righteous priests, "Art mistook, Greene! William never stole a line of thine. Poor heart, the story's well known about the theater men! The notes lay untouched under thy bed in the dust. William made them new; they were given him fairly, and fairly he's done it. He has done it before my eyes on the grocery counter, this I swear on my hope of happiness in this life."

With a cry, Greene hurled the contents of his goblet. The red wine caught William across his shirt and fell in drops upon the skirts of the women, whose voices rose in anxious protest. He pushed the girl he had held from him, biting his lip under his mustache; so full of life was he yet from the dance that he did not entirely understand what was being said to him.

"Ah, by my arse has he done it, whoremongers!" Greene cried. "He comes from the country, where he sat at school with farmers' sons, and fancies himself better than those of us who are university men! Why, he could not have writ these plays. The words are mine!"

William came forward a few steps. "You had the chance to write the plays, but you did naught with them," he cried. "Why are you accusing me? Have I not ever been thy friend?" His voice cracked, a mixture of grief and rage slowly filling him.

Everyone began to shout, and in the midst the diminutive Nashe beat upon the one remaining upright table with the blunt side of a carving knife for silence until the pieces of crockery clattered against each other, while the large whore in her colorful clothes continued to eat as much as she could at the table, and stuff fruit tarts into her pockets.

Greene had his hand to his belt. "Aye," he cried out, his eyes sweeping all of them with contempt. "Aye, Shakespeare of the countryside or from what hole hast crept! You were but an actor, and a damn poor one, and now you've two plays on the boards and a new one to be rehearsed, 'tis said.

Where is thy education to do this? Every line of the play that hast merit has been stolen from me. I should have never trusted thee or given thee my heart."

"The words are mine!"

"Thou pisspot liar!"

With a cry, William thrust the other men aside and seized Greene by the doublet, whose rotting wool tore in his hand. He did not know if he forced Greene to the floor or if the red-bearded poet crumpled like dust, but they were struggling on the rushes. Someone shouted, "Ah, Christ, William! He'll draw his dagger . . . ah, Christ, William, watch!"

The whore, with a piercing shriek, rushed to her lover's side, but Greene shouted out, "Back, slut!" William had easily forced the other man's hands down, and like dust he now lay defeated. He turned his face and began to spit blood.

Heminges had fallen to his knees to separate them. "In God's mercy, William, loose him!" he shouted. "The man's too weak to harm thee! Jonson, give me your arm!" With some struggle and the blood of the coughing Greene splattering floor and garments, Jonson hauled the Stratford man up by the arm.

"Sweet Will, do not mind!" he roared. "Let Greene have his say! Thou art as honest a man as ever came through the gates of London. Christ's love, stand off, Will! Wilt harm him for his petty words?"

"Leave off, all of you!" Thrusting his hair back and looking at them all with fury and despair, William flung himself out of the door and ran down the street towards Cheapside. He rushed into a water carrier, dashing betwixt and between peddlers and the horses of men riding rapidly home this night. And as he went his own words of the tragic king from the last play stumbled through his mind: *O God! methinks it were a happy life, to be no better than a homely swain. . . .*

By this time he could hardly breathe, for in his haste he had flung open the creaking doors of three separate taverns and not discovered the man whom he sought. In the fourth, however, the hostess, who greeted him by name, said with a wary look that indeed he would find Christopher Marlowe in a private room beyond.

The poet was sitting alone at the end of a table with his head buried in his arms, and looked up bewildered as William came in as if surprised to find another person in this world but himself. For a moment they stared at each other in silence. William glanced with contempt at the curtained bed in the corner with its soiled red hangings. On the wall was a portrait of the Queen with one hand raised in blessing like some withering, white-painted saint. Bile rose in his throat, and he coughed bitterly into his arm.

When he caught his breath, he gasped, "I must speak with you. There's not a thing I would not have done for you, and now the turn's thine."

"Why sweet," said the poet playfully, "I did not expect you, for I've drunk the wine and have no more money." There was a sallowness about his face, and he passed his hand over his eyes several times as a sleepy child might do. He seemed like a child who needs to be put into bed, and the candle trimmed, and a kiss given.

But William spat, "I need no wine."

"Ah, I see! You've bathed in it, from the look of you! Speak, darling, if you have run so hard to see me, but I have little to give you, dear Will, not even kindliness." He leaned back, his face pale and thin; William saw in that moment, and heard the deep rattling cough, and then could bear to see no more.

Leaning forward, his clenched fists on the table and his hair hanging down before his face, he poured out all that had happened. Christopher listened carefully and for some time after the story was concluded remained silent. Raising his head, William demanded, "What can I do? Tell to me."

"Naught. Greene can write but little anymore. He lived as he chose, and it's sickened him, and if he does not choose otherwise, it will in the end take his life. His bitterness overwhelms him. But, Shakespeare, must let men live and die as they will. There's naught you can do about it. Neither Greene, nor our crazed bricklayer, nor myself."

William threw back his head. "We were friends!" he cried. "Can that mean nothing? Do you remember how we were? The five of us for a time as if we could not, would not, breathe without the other! I found you, and now you are all scattered . . . even honest Jack with his marriage! I found where I belonged, and now the place has crumbled, and you say there is nothing I can do, and I reply, I cannot bear this. I would rather never to have come than bear this thing."

Christopher leaned forward. "Aye!" he murmured. "I could have expected these words from thee, Shakespeare! We fools wish certainty in this earth . . . this most uncertain place of all, and we are sentient beings who know that even that shall be taken away from them. Where do we go when we die? Our souls disintegrate, our bodies to worms. You expect kindliness, but here each man grasps desperately as if we fled a burning, besieged city with such purloined goods as we could gather up in our arms! Do you seek kindness? That's found in small villages from which you hurried away, as did I, for their idea of it is to stifle a man. Ah, look at you!" He sat back with a mocking look about his mouth. "You come to me for comfort, and this is what you receive, but no man in the city would come to me for such. Am I a priest?"

William seized his friend's hands. "The hell with Jack's wife!" he murmured. "The hell with everything. Only let us return to what we were!"

"Ah, you fool, you fool! We can't! Perhaps we were never there at all, but only as you saw it! There's a courtesy in you and in your writing that will draw men, for we want to believe we can be there, and stay there."

"Why did you go off from us?"

"Time bears all things away."

"It need not be so."

"Oh, 'tis best! I shall not live to be an old fellow, Will! But then I should not like to be old. I like to be strong, and youthful, and find my way into whichever bed pleases me. I have no desire to sit by the fire mumbling into my soup—no, short is best. Poor Greene, old fleabitten bastard! Poor Greene!"

"What can I do?"

"Naught."

"Marlowe!"

"Shakespeare."

"Listen!"

"I have and answered."

"Not well enough."

"What wouldst have me say?"

With a cry, William buried his head in his arms on the table. "Ah, Christ's nails," he muttered, "'tis as if all the grief that ever was in the world sits in my breast tonight! Give me your hands again, Kit, damn you! We'll end alone, you and I, won't we? We'll end in a place where we call and no one comes—why? They are too busy and will forget us. I can see it now—for all my work I'll be a shilling-a-day actor. The plays pay little, and I'll never have enough money to be a sharer."

"Mayst."

"You dream, pig's ass. Ah God, God—my poor family! What will become of us, Kit?"

"Why, I shall in fact grow old to the degeneration I so bitterly long for, and thou wilt end a tavern keeper, reconciled to wife and family. And words will rule us. When we mount to heaven the gatekeeper will ask for proof of our worthiness, and we shall shake our purses upside down and out will fall naught but a rhyme or two, a few words . . . and mine unholy, and the saints will cry, what! Do they come with nothing more than this? If there is a heaven it will be this way . . . but mayhap the words will redeem us. I cannot say."

"Dost know me, Kit?"

"Without much thought, even so. Art pisspot drunk, coxcomb! Wilt weep with sentiment? Go home before the streets are too dangerous. Take light."

It was late when William crept home, and felt his way past the dirty platters and glasses through the shop and up the stairs. He had not reached the third one when he heard a groan, and a sigh, and a murmur, and then a creaking of bed ropes in the old rhythmic way. And he understood that John Heminges was there in secret with his beautiful Rebecca. Slowly like a dream, a few feathers which had escaped from the bed blew from the breeze of the open window across the floor, down the steps, and settled about William's shoes. In such ecstasy were the lovers that they did not know he stood there.

As quietly as possible he descended again and made a bed from some sacks in the back of the shop, clasping his arms about himself for warmth. He did not sleep, though, but lay staring into the darkness while above him the ceiling creaked now and then, and a few more feathers drifted down the stair.

THRICE WERE THE banns called for the wedding, for any man who wished to prevent to come forward. None came. John Heminges and Rebecca Knell were married in church; a celebration in the grocers' hall followed where men danced and sang until the sun began to rise.

"What, dost not dance, Will!" cried the grocer.

"Marry, I have danced every tune." Indeed he had, as if he would never stop, and when he sought a drink of ale his leg began to ache. The hall was too hot even in this early spring evening, and he walked out into the night and through the gates past the wide ditch outside the walls, and towards the orchards.

I do not wish to be here anymore, he said to himself. There is no longer any place for me. I must go home.

HENLEY AND WOOD STREETS

I N A RASH expenditure, he hired a horse to carry him.
As he began the first hours of the hundred-mile journey he had the mystical sensation that he was riding
back in time, and would presently when he crossed the
Stratford bridge see the little boy he had been, fishing pole over his wet
shirt, leaping on bare feet to meet him. At times his throat swelled with
emotion, and then he could not wait to be back home once more. The city
and all it contained appalled him; he thought of the crowds, the filth, the
noise of street costers bawling, the stink of men crammed so close together
that they read each other's dreams and mistook each other's wives. The
beggars bawling their hunger, the deranged weeping in the street, the
whores whipped in Bridewell; the willingness of men to steal your purse,
throw muckheaps before your door; the babble of other languages, and the
stink of the tiring room, where too many men making too little money in
a profession which had no honor snarled at each other, and then went on
to play noble men.

How could he ever have wanted such a thing, or thought it better than
his beautiful country town: the breeze in the willow trees by the water, the
barley fields, the very paths where still the dirt must retain the impression

of his boots as he ran off to meet friends by the bridge? He no longer thought so, and with a great shudder cast it away from him. He had been away so long he had ceased to count, and he thought, My children . . . my children! Then he was almost sick with excitement to see them.

He found the market smaller than he had remembered, and as he rode through it he pulled down his broad-brimmed hat with the drooping brown feather to remain unrecognized, ashamed as he was of his flushed face. Nothing had changed, everything was the same. Christ's nails! There was the grammar school where he had learned his Latin and subsequently in his own schoolmastering days had tried to instill a little of his love of books in smaller lads. Down that street past two or three houses was the tanner's house with its secretly incestuous father. There the market cross. . . . He wondered if the same baker still made hot buns with fruit in them at Eastertide and if boys still hunted in the woods for elves at midsummer. He paused and sent a prayer to Our Lord that nothing had changed at all.

He should join them now: once more on a Sabbath to wear brushed clothes and a plain collar (not ruffled hideously as in the city), to sing metrical settings of the psalms to the groaning of a bass viol; the exchange afterwards, the inquiries after neighbors' cows and sheep, orchards, wives, daughters. He was here the glover's son William, and need not struggle to be anything more.

Dismounting, he led the horse to his street and noticed that the scuffed spot on the door where he had kicked it some weeks before his departure had not been whitewashed these years. It was just the same, even the garden beyond, just a little older and dryer. The shop sign of a glove sewn with pearls had been faded by the passing seasons, and creaked a little on its chains. With this he took in his breath, and went inside the house.

His mother was crossing the kitchen, her apron full of turnips; she looked up at him irritably as if he were a tramp, and then gave a great cry and dropped the vegetables to the floor. He flung himself at her, pulling her soft, plump body against him.

"How comst! how comst!" she sputtered, weeping a little. "We have not seen thee these four years, not since they whitewashed the scene of the Resurrection in the town hall! Ah!"

Not trusting his voice at first, he held her against him so hard that she murmured a protest. Then he took her by the shoulder, and, sitting on the edge of the table, searched her face. There was the cap on her hair which she had saved market money to buy the year he left school, and the same pins which held it in place . . . but she was older, her face like a fine painted wall hanging that is here and there beginning to crack. Several times he kissed her hands. Then he swept up the turnips and emptied his full satchel to the table. "I've brought presents!" he cried. "See what's in this packet. Saffron!"

Modestly she replied, "Such expense! William!"

"Why, they never get such stuff here. Now look! Close thine eyes and take this in thy hands. Now, open!"

"Can it be silk hose?"

"Aye, dyed in such colors near Petticoat Lane!"

"Peaspod green," she said, shaking them out with a sigh so that they danced before her soft eyes. "Too good for me! I'll put them in the drawer for your daughters when they're married!"

"Promise wilt wear them!" he begged. "Nay, must not hide them in a drawer, sweet! For mercy's sake, do not put them there. Here's a book as well . . . how to fight against lice, fleas, rats, and other pestilences. I may have writ it myself, but can't recall." He looked about and breathing deeply to steady himself said, "Where are my children? And . . . Anne."

"Gone to Shottery for a christening."

"Ah," he said reflectively, sticking his fingers in his belt. Then, taking off his sword, he laid it on the table with the satchel still spilling its gifts. His mother pushed it tidily to one side and continued to prepare the turnips. William gazed down at the worn, yellowish linen of her cap with slowly rising disappointment; he had hoped she would sit down and ask him greedily for news of his friends, the plays, the grocery. But for the brief greeting and the offhandedly accepted presents, London did not exist to her. It could not exist, because she did not wish it.

He felt he had not the right to protest.

Instead he walked about the house, which seemed as small as the streets had as he had hurried down them. The children's toys, a jack-in-the-box and some dolls, were strewn about. A boat he had made, now partially smashed, had been carefully laid on a high shelf like a relic. Every time he thought he heard a door squeak his heart leaped and he murmured, My little ones have come! At last he came down and slouched by the hearth, staring at his mother. He wanted to hold her against him until there could be no further division between them.

"Art not glad to see me?"

"Oh aye," replied his mother with a sigh. "I am happy, but 'tis most unexpected . . . you'll find your father much changed. Ah, why didst go off? Hadst not gone to follow that Field lad!" Then she continued critically, "Your father reads thy letters to me. Who is this Italian Florio? A Catholic? Why, they are wicked people, darling! How can you sup with foreigners? Dost say thy prayers?" For a moment she ceased the sweeping back and forth of her work, and placing her hand on the side of his face, muttered reprovingly, "Christ love us, in ten years you'll have as scant hair as thy dad—'tis the wicked city air that chokes an honest man! And save my soul, what is that earring?"

His fingers flew to his ear as if to protect it; then he felt foolish. "I'll go out to meet the children," he said.

"Oh, they'll be here soon enough!"

"Then give me something to mend," and he was soon seated crosslegged on the floor examining a broken stool and the boat, tools and glue and nails neatly beside him.

After a time his father came in stiffly on his painful legs, as if he were an old sailor reluctantly beached on land. William embraced him with much emotion; he thought, Oh Christ, grant it me only and I will make it right for him! He knew the old man could scarcely control his delight in seeing him.

"Art well, Father?"

"Oh, well enough, well enough!" barked the glover. "Tell us of the city! What, shall he not tell of it, Mary?"

So William began to speak of Spanish leather traveling bags, Chinese embroidered silk, and enormous, fragile leaves of drying tobacco from three thousand miles away, all sold in the market stalls of Cheapside. Yes, he had met sailors who had been to the Americas; yes, a man black as ebony had come to one of the plays and flashed his bright teeth at the humor and he had also seen a Jew; no, not all men spoke to her Majesty kneeling, but often in ordinary conversation and made her laugh. No, he did not think she knew his name and most men claimed her still a virgin, though he did not know how they knew.

His mother's mouth pursed primly as she listened to these things, the grey eyes suspicious, hands curled in her lap, and a harsh sigh of disapproval now and then escaping from her lips; his father, however, leaned forward openmouthed, showing his strong teeth, nodding joyfully as if he had known these things all along. "Hath not Johnson's son Paul of this town traveled to London twice said much the same!" he cried, slapping his rough hands on his thighs, and looking about for confirmation.

Deftly William continued to search his mind for more things to amuse them which would not offend. He did not mention that a fellow player had been jailed for two weeks for brawling, or that he seldom set foot in a church, supposing that his friend Jack could settle things with the Lord for both of them.

In the middle of this the door from the street was flung open and his brothers and sister rushed across the floor and threw themselves in his arms, crying, "Sweet William! Bully lad! 'Twas the baker swore he saw you come!" For a moment he could hardly breathe for their welcome and shouting, "Cry you mercy!" held them at arms' length to see their faces. Handsome Gilbert the haberdasher who at twenty-five was yet unmarried; plump Joan who mewed at her infant and several times held it up insistently for William to kiss; and the two younger boys, who had rushed from school and trade, and who at once demanded to see what he carried in his bags.

Between holding them away and then against him so hard that his ribs ached with the pleasure, William cried, "But I must know every particular of your lives! How goes it with trade and with schooling—how goes it with Stratford?" That word trembled like a foreign thing on his lips and then broke forth with a smile. For the next few hours he was joyful with them, demonstrating formal swordplay as enacted in a recent drama, yet even as he cavorted and lifted his mother high in a fashionable dance, the words "my children" did not cease to beat in his head.

Towards the end of the afternoon when the light was fading outside the mullioned windows he saw them at the door and at once he left off dancing and became quite still. They were more beautiful than he recalled . . . my God, they were the jewels of the earth! There was the oldest, Susanna, with her wary little mouth and dark curls pulled back under her cap, and the freckled twins, Hamnet and Judith, who came in hand in hand. Quickly he approached them and then, near tears, knelt to touch their creamy soft faces and lips. "Why, how big you are!" he murmured. "How could you grow so and not wait for me? I thought of you as the same, but you're much more handsome! Come, kiss me . . . don't you know me?

Have you not had the sweets I sent and the drawings? There was one of me with such a frown. And why did I frown? Why, for wanting to see your faces!"

He felt the fragile bones of wrists, and the narrow chests under which were held so many dreams, none of which he knew. When he had asked them a thousand questions and made as much as he could of their shy, stunted answers, he took them up all at once on his back and went about the kitchen floor, through the rushes, pretending he was a horse and carrying them off to the city. Then seating himself by the hearth, he waited while they brought their treasures to show him: a clumsily half-embroidered pillow, a rock, a doll made of straw. Gathering the three children into his arms at once, he rubbed his mustache against their soft necks and tickled their round, warm bellies under the plain linen clothing until they squealed and shouted with joy.

His mother shook her ladle over the pot. "Hast come to stay? That I wish to know!" she murmured resentfully.

"By the Holy Rood!" said John Shakespeare. "Do not plague the lad."

"But I wish to know it!"

"Do not . . . plague him . . . Mary, I say!" The glover had half risen and made an angry gesture, but withdrew it and sat down muttering to himself about women and their ways. He drew his son into further conversation. Had he been to court? Did he know what was happening with land taxes or wars? Was it true they had a lottery in St. Paul's worth a fortune?

Towards dusk, William looked up and saw his wife standing in the doorway. She stood as quietly as if listening to something beyond her, and he could see her breath rising and falling under the grey bodice. For a moment he thought she listened for the echo of his footsteps from the hour he had gone away, and for the true reason of that going which she had never understood. She seemed to listen as if he were not here but yet far off. Then she turned to gaze at him as if reconciling the man before her to the one in her memory.

"'Tis I, dear," he murmured, gently disengaging himself from the children and rising to his feet.

"Oh, art come?" The voice was light and airy.

"Aye, lady."

"Of a whim?"

"Nay, more than that," he murmured, kissing her cheek. With awe he gazed at her stern profile, recalling how he had seen it bent over her prayer book in church when she seemed the most desirable woman in the world. Perhaps the fault had been his.

Oh, Anne, to whom I made a foolish vow, and whom I then abandoned! What have you done these years but sit at your loom, and wash the children's faces, teach them prayers perhaps? And lying in our bed alone, did you think of me? What have I done to your life? How can I ever make it up to you? Did you not ever deserve a better man, and might I, in the end, be he?

Darkness came, and the little town was silent; he heard once more the wind in the elms, in the rafters, in the chimney. As the wind filled the hollows of the house, repentance filled him until he felt he could bear no more, and yet no one said a word. His mother and father only sat about the hearth, she with her sewing as she had always done, though now with her shoulders more roundly bent, and he telling of the customers of that day. William could guess from how his father dwelt on each one that there were not many. Anne continued to sew, her beautiful back as upright as her marriage vows, which she—as her very bones seemed to declare—had kept faithfully even if he had not. Sitting near the hearth on the floor for the light, he puzzled over the broken boat. He would have to make it anew. And there was a scent over everything of old ashes, or dried flowers, or linen long folded in a cedar chest. He coughed.

"Dost whittle in London?" his father asked.

"Nay."

"Well, well—thy mother asked thee before: dost mean to stay?" The glover's shrunken lips compressed themselves in hope, gazing at his son in the same protective way he had all his life. William felt his heart cry out. Part of him wished to take those aging hands, kiss them, and kneel for his blessing.

With a dry mouth he only murmured, "I have thought to do so."

The clock struck nine, and they all knelt for prayers. "God be praised for bringing William once more to us!" John Shakespeare said triumphantly. "In the name of Christ, amen."

THEY WISHED EACH other a good night and, to save candles, felt their way up the steps. William urged his sleepy children to their cots, kissing their soft faces again and again, whispering promises in their ears of the places they should go in the morning. Then he went clumsily and with much strangeness into the bedchamber.

Anne was sitting on the bed in her nightshirt with narrow feet bare, brushing her long reddish-golden hair as she had done every night of her life. He stood by the door, and then she raised her eyes and said simply, "It's as it should be, William: art yet my husband."

He said, "I have longed for thee."

"And I for thee," she answered; he did not know if it was true or not, but at that moment for her sake and his he needed to believe it.

He came to her, pushing her back and untrussing his own shirt with his other hand. He felt the softness of her breasts and thighs beneath him, and the way she always lifted one leg slightly. His hand found the familiar crevice where the pelvic bones left off and he wanted to shout in his need. Creak went the ropes which held the straw-filled mattress, creak . . . he knew the sound traveled across the floor and gently shook the house.

Wind in the elms, and their movement together and she tossing her head back and forth in a manner almost severe. He wanted to please her and in the old way at her moment, gently placed his hand over her mouth so that the sound should not echo so greatly through the little rooms of his house.

They lay together and spoke of old things.

"Shouldst know this, William," she said. "Thy father sits at night and looks ahead with a mournful expression, and thy mother pretends not to notice. He longs for thee, Will, as I, thy lawful wife, do as well. Then there are of course the little ones, walking about the town as if their papa had died."

"I have not died."

"But still, day by day, you are not here."

"Anne, as I live," he replied hoarsely, "I am sorry for these things!"

"Then you will stay?"

"Would you not come to London with me?"

"Never! I could never go to such a place. Only say you will remain here, darling, only say it."

Then desperately he murmured, "Then yes, I will remain."

"Oh, God be praised!" she whispered fervently. "God be praised!" and she brought his head against her shoulder.

*   *   *

THE NEXT DAYS were spent in a flurry of welcome, as friends and kins-
men, some ancient and others come into this tidy world since his absence,
made their way down Henley Street to shake his hand and bid him well.
Never in that time could he go down the street without his children shyly
following. All about the countryside he went, carrying them on his shoulders when they tired, to show them the places he had known as a boy. A
shepherd grasped his hands, and in the inn were the same men about the
fire drinking from charred wood mugs. Jack Shakespeare's lad's returned,
they crowed. Cities are bad for any man—by the Rood, he's pale! That's
what cities do.

Behind him came the whispering. He's never going back again, came
his mother's voice; she and his wife sat like conspirators over their sewing,
pressing their lips together like women who have never allowed a harsh
word to escape them. He's never going back, praise Our Lord!

Standing in the parlor, William spent hours turning the pages of the
great Bible, recalling where the verses fell and how he had knelt on a stool
to reach it as a boy and solemnly touched the pages to experience the profusion of words. Then he walked to the garden to stroke the bark of the
apple tree and run his hands through the leaves like lace. The branches
quivered, leaves caressed his fingers, welcoming him like a lover. Above
him dipped the line of wash with white shirts like dancing souls between
earth and heaven. When he felt for Anne's body at night it was heavy,
limp, and welcoming, and in the end her arm lingered about him.

During those days he heard every story worth telling. They yet talked
of the rebellion of the northern earls of 1569, of the girl with child who
had drowned herself in the Avon and been buried in unhallowed ground.
The skins in the tanner's yard lay stretched upon their racks like tortured
saints from an old book of engravings. He creaked open the door of his
father's shop, and wondered if he could still fashion a gentleman's lace-
encrusted calfskin glove. The spring was full of flowers, and the fields and
cottages as beautiful as ever he had remembered them.

And yet he began to experience a strange sensation as if he could not
quite catch his breath. At first he wondered if he was ill. Then he had the
need more often to walk out alone, hands in his sword belt, head bent to
the dust of the road. Oh, I will be back, he told his children.

The truth began to turn itself over in his mind as he walked slowly,
hardly answering the greetings of the carters or town masters, barely

remembering to smile at them or, in the instance of the alderman, make his modest bow. He made his way to Clopton Bridge, looking back at church and town, and the words moved reluctantly from his lips as a whisper no louder than the soft wind in the trees.

I am not the man who once walked these streets, he said. I've changed. It has come slowly, imperceptibly, but it has shaped me to a way of thought far from this place where I was born. I need to play some role and hurl the speeches to the sky, to leap, and dance, and coming into the tavern, hear the shouting of my fellows, read everything and argue of more; I need courtly rooms and wretched alleys which hold the possibility of new friends. I have come to love the clatter of wagon wheels on cobbles, the thousand voices and the bells ringing over the whole ancient city, stone and thatch and steeple, and each distinctive soul. If I stay here I will make them happy, but I will give up all I am. Can I allow that? For what am I now but a theater man, sometime comrade to the odd and beautiful? What am I but a partaker and placater of tavern quarrels, and one who knows his whereabouts, however drunken, by the smell of the great river and the mounting of Paul's Cathedral like a benediction above us?

He began to sweat. He had lied to himself, and therefore to them, for he could not push away the knowledge that he could never again be the young man who had lived here. How could he speak of the things which enriched him: science, Italian writers, the whole world as far as Jerusalem that washed daily to the banks of the river Thames and left its glittering presence amid the muck and mud? They could not hear him here. Then lifting his face to the wind, he scented it as an animal sniffs a vague thing he distrusts which cannot be good, and he whispered haughtily, Who are these people?

Then all the sweetness of the May town with its gardens and heavy elms melted away from him, and the dull boy whom he could see walking by the banks with his hand groping for the breasts of his coy sweetheart became himself. Yet the boy was not, for if he were, he would one night pack a few books and a little linen and go off with a note of regret left under a candlestick on the old family wardrobe. The boy might stay, but William could not. Every man has his own path, though often not the one those who love him would wish.

Yet how to tell them? He woke each morning beside his again fretful wife, who had already begun to criticize him; he looked daily across the parlor to the door which seemed to stand between this place and all that was himself. How hard he tried to keep it from them, and yet how well they knew! His father began to avert his face from him, his mother hurried about in her tasks. Worse, he tried to keep it to himself, within his stomach, until he grew nauseous with the words he would not speak. Once coming down the steps and looking at them all below he turned to the wall to control his grief. Well, it was not them, but himself; it had always been that way. He understood it now. And it was still the same.

Finally, at the end of a warm day, he went into his father's shop and said, "I'm going now. I'm returning."

"Well, then go! Why do you linger?" cried the old glover.

"To say my duty to you."

"If you had any duty you would bide here. Nay, nay, do not touch me. Knowst my pain of all men, and yet you turn from me. . . ."

William whispered, "Sweet Lord," and passed his hand over his mouth. "I'll do well one day," he muttered, "and give much to thee and my little ones . . . this as Christ is my Savior I swear, this I shall do as I live."

His wife locked herself in her room, and he could not enter but heard her weeping, and the children clung to him on the steps, and only by promising them fantastical things could he break away, his heart pounding as if he were wanted for murder. Then he ran down the steps, kissed his mother and youngest brother, who was home from school. Looking up from the street, he saw his father gazing mournfully at him from the little chamber where he had long ago found the secret papers.

He hurried to the inn where he once again hired a horse and leaping up, began to push the beast into a gallop. In a flurry of dust the town receded from him, and he rode violently, gritting his teeth, digging his heels into the beast. Fields, orchards, inns, towns flew past, and perhaps some thought him a royal messenger in his haste, and that his stuffed satchels held precious letters of state rather than some quince jam and knit hose which his sister Joan, babe in her arms, had pressed upon him at the door. He did not know that he had been weeping for some time.

He had come to the top of the hill, and reining in the trembling nag, sat panting himself, looking about. For some time he remained there, the beast panting and pawing, for the rider could go neither forward nor back. A bitter cry burst from the depths of his belly, and he shouted, "Damn you all, then! What do you want of me? I can never in my life be what you'd have me!" It echoed across the fields over which the wind blew.

Bile stung his mouth. After a time he began again, but more slowly, his head bent forward, towards the city.

AFTER JACK MARRIED Rebecca, he went on much as he had done before, hurrying from his proud new grocery to some theater or private house with his lines from the part he was studying in a paper roll under his arm. He was up before dawn to shop for the store, for he did not trust his journeyman, and sometimes did not come home until two in the morning after a performance by candlelight at some mansion. William was close by when John Heminges, coming off the stage in heavy robes made hotter by the torchlight of the hall, fainted by the table of wigs and props.

Then from the rooms above the grocery came the first murmurings of quarrel: soft at first, apologetic in tone, they rose as the weeks went by— the wife's in sullen, tearful and anxious demand, the husband's in deep bluff denial. The child Susan stood at the bottom of the steps biting her fingernails or chewing on her apron strings.

The quarrel continued and soon had journeyed to the kitchen which lay behind the shop. Rebecca Heminges, her sloped nose in the air and her full bosom trembling, hurried about laying trenchers for the evening meal. "Well, what shall come of this, John?" she said. "Art more often ill than not! Must sell off the grocery and join the theater men, or leave the theater and be content here. No, I cannot bear it. I am as unhappy as I have ever been!" And with that she looked distractedly into all corners and with her apron to her face, ran from the door.

"Becky!" the husband shouted, breathlessly catching her in the street by the horsepost and seizing her arm.

"Leave off!"

"Where wilt go?"

"Home to my mother."

She ran down the street, and pulling his hair, he rushed back to the grocery and looked about at the bags, jars, barrels, and boxes as if they were to blame. "What she asks is not possible for me to give!" he shouted. "Sell off the grocery, leave this profession for that of the theater . . . madness! A living cannot be made in plays! Had I not been poor, mayhap my first wife would not have died. Now I just begin to do well again, and what would Becky have? She hath not seen the person she loved best . . . die of want."

The Stratford man walked around quietly, gazing at the stock and the painted sign above the door. "I think you must sell the grocery."

"Never as I live. For pity's sake, Will, go and bring her home!"

William walked over to Rebecca's mother's house, but the young wife had locked herself in her room and would not see him. The bells had rung that the day of work was ended and darkness had long since come when he returned. All the shops were shuttered and the heavy signs taken, but for that of the grocer Heminges. His door open to the warm February night, he sat by lantern light with a pile of papers beside him, and his head buried in his hands amid his shelves of jars and boxes.

"My children will go in rags!" he said.

"Nay, for truly I believe you'll do well. Now take up those papers."

"These?"

"Aye, the accounts and bills and such. Come!"

They went into the alley together. The wind had risen, and they opened the box and began to tear the papers and throw them into the wind. Bits flew up, clung to posts, landed on the extended upper stories of roofs, on chimneys, on firehooks. Pieces twisted up and then seemed to fly like a flock of birds down towards Cheapside to the bell tower of St. Mary le Bow, where come morning they would drift down to the churchyard when the first bells were rung. Then arm and arm, they went to fetch Rebecca home.

JACK HEMINGES WENT that very week to the grocer's hall to post notice that his shop was for sale, and it was quickly bought by a journeyman who had long had his eye on it. With this, they had to move once more. Rebecca had brought a dowry as well to the marriage, so between them they now had enough money to buy a house. They wanted to stay in Cheapside within the boundaries of the parish of St. Mary Aldermanbury, where Heminges had just been made a member of the vestry and she had many friends, and there was no thought at all but that William must go with them. He was finishing his first comedy about two sets of twins, and was so possessed by it he hardly noticed the move from one place to another. *This day, great Duke, she shut the doors upon me while she with harlots feasted in my house! . . . I never saw my father in my life.*

In the days just at Bartholomewtide when the annual fair was setting up outside the walls, they found the dwelling they wanted. It stood on Wood

Street just below Cripplegate and had three stories, a tiled roof, and a garden behind. The rooms were already furnished with some furniture of a century before, too heavy to move. William bought them as a wedding gift a wall hanging of David and Bathsheba painted on heavy cloth; thoughts of adultery filled him. He felt lately such an unfulfilled sensuality that he thought at times he would go mad.

In the small rooms of the grocery and now in the master chamber here he was painfully aware of the bolted sleeping-chamber door and the sighs and sometimes cries of passion which came from behind it . . . the outcry which is so much like pain and yet speaks of the most intense pleasure. Not for one day also could he put Rebecca from his mind. He had to love some woman, and none for a time did he fancy like her. Once he had come upstairs and saw through the open door of her chamber that she was standing naked but for the petticoat which had fallen to her knees, washing her arms and shoulders. Her large round breasts were uplifted, and she swayed slightly, and her belly was round and fertile from the child within. Desire which he had pushed aside rushed upon him, and he remained what seemed forever gazing covetously at her. Then he crept away, flushed with shame and lust. He felt as if he had stolen something from the man who was dearest to him in the world; he felt in his heart that he deserved whipping.

Thus some days later when he heard her mount to bed, he straightened his shoulders and walked slowly down to the parlor with its clean floor rushes and polished table. Jack was bending over the accounting books of the theater troupe, which he had just begun to keep, and William, sitting beside him, said, "I can't bide longer with thee, Jack."

Heminges pushed away his work at once. "Shakespeare, don't say it!"

"I must."

"This is madness!" Heminges's voice rang out in the masterly way of a man who has resolved much within himself. Rising, he went to the foot of the stairs to call Rebecca, who came down hastily with her hair loose and barefooted, her gown wrapped about her.

Her eyes grew wide when she heard the news, and hurrying across the room, she exclaimed, "Sweet Will, must never go from us!"

"I must, dear."

"But where shalt go?"

"I shall sleep in Holywell ruins."

"Dost jest! The rats will bite thee."

"I shall bite them back."

Not being able to bear their affection, he broke from them both and went out into the soft night towards Paul's Cathedral. The booksellers had long put up their stalls, and the sexton waddled towards him, key ring in hand, to lock up the churchyard gates. "Good night, sir!" he said. "God give you a good night!"

He walked for a time and then turned into the Mitre Tavern. There John found him some time later, and slid into the booth to look into his friend's face. "She's weeping," he said accusingly. "And I am nigh to doing it myself, which you know is not my way."

They took each other's arm, and walked to the gate, nodded to the sentry, and continued on past the wide ditch, leaving the houses which were built onto the wall like shadows guarding the ward behind them. Beyond it they continued to the fields, where the moon was full and the way clear. Then Heminges demanded again, "Why must go?"

"Why, Jack!" the Stratford man replied with forced lightness. "'Tis more of a complicated matter than I can say—God knoweth I would like to live as you do, but it cannot be—knowst—" He fell silent, unable to speak more words, but understood then that this man with whom he had shared most of his thoughts and troubles now knew this one as well.

Forgotten laundry moved sluggishly above them in the vagrant breezes, and something small and dark scurried down the path. He heard Jack's deep, sonorous voice in the darkness. "I am thy true friend," the grocer said seriously, "and as long as I have a roof it will always be thine. Know this as I live, Will, and as I hope for heaven."

HE STAYED IN the house in Wood Street some days more, for comfort and custom kept him, and then he went, his clothing and books in two boxes of medium size in a cart borrowed from the baker. He did not, of course, as threatened, sleep in Holywell Priory but lived with a few of the actors: the comedian Thomas Pope in Southwark, where the many children woke him, and then for a while he left the city and went to live near the courts in Westminster with a barrister friend who talked to him very much about law. In those days he made enough shillings from acting so that he was not quite as poor; the troupe toured now and then, and he finished his comedy. At night he would still often return to sup with John and

Rebecca. They had an infant now born of their secret coupling before the banns had been called. The child Susan always covered his face with kisses and sat upon his knee. Sometimes when he was alone with John they fell into silence, and he felt his friend's eyes upon him asking him to return, though they both knew he would not.

Then one day he discovered he could not find the play he had been reworking, nor his black hose, nor the stones his son had given him the last time he was in Stratford, and he knew he must find a place of his own to call home. He found a room on Bishopsgate Road within the walls. The floor was crooked, the bed sagged with its thin mattress, and the window looked upon a fellow who boiled bones in his yard.

PART HREE

EMILIA

T WAS STRANGE to him to be a bachelor alone, walk-
ing daily down Threadneedle with a bucket to fetch his
ale, trying to remember if he had taken his linen to the
laundress. He began many plays, finished one or two,
worked on another with a colleague, and threw away a great deal. And yet
every day when he woke he did not know if he would be gone from the
city forever by nightfall. Sometimes he dreamt he was in Stratford once
more, expecting to reach out his hand in the dark and touch the cherry-
wood chest, marked with his carved initials and Field's name, which had
always stood by his boyhood sleeping cot. If he had left things inside it, he
could not remember what they were.

It was the writer and translator John Florio with whom he spent many
evenings that season; Florio introduced him to the essays of Montaigne,
and also shared with the player his love of the classics. Often they sat
together discussing the infinite complexity of men, for Florio swore he
knew a thousand and no two were in any way alike. Yet it was Florio's her-
itage of the country of deep passions which most drew the player.

"Do you like Italians?" the translator said wryly when they were part-
ing one afternoon. "Well then, let me take you to sup with my cousins!

They're musicians about the court and countryside, and might amuse you if you wish to set your comedies in that land." Then the small, caustic, and meticulous man pulled down the side of his mouth and added wryly, "I call them cousins, though we share little blood if any. But all countrymen are cousins, aren't they? Especially when they want something from you."

The sun was descending in the west and glittering on the tops of steeples as they walked through Bishopsgate and turned to one of the small side streets named Petty France for the refugees who had made their home there. Even from the end of the street he heard the joyful music.

In a small parlor hung with cracking painted cloths, three bearded musicians were playing a dance on the viols, recorders, and drums, and in the midst of them, singing to their accompaniment in a low sweet voice, was a very small, dark-haired young woman. Clothed in a heavy green embroidered dress, its side borne out by the whalebone farthingale beneath, she swayed sensually among the floor rushes, a tambourine in her small hand.

He had been lost in thought of a new play, and at the moment she seemed not quite real but something that had come from the cracked paint of the wall hangings and stood before them. In spite of her grace, she bore her head a little stiffly from the heavy arrangement of braids and curls. He saw then that she must be even smaller than she seemed, for on her feet she wore chopines, the cork wedged shoes which made the wearer two or three inches taller and protected the gown from the dirt of streets and floors.

"Oh, an actor!" she murmured in a teasing voice when they were introduced, and he could not tell whether she was pleased or disappointed.

Supper was called, and the musicians and several women climbed about the benches around the table and began to eat ravenously, shouting at one another all the time. Outside the carts rolling from the city gate and the sound of one of the military companies marching with their pikes amid the monastery ruins of Holywell floated through the open window. William gazed at the musical instruments piled on chests and hanging from walls, and the heaps of dazzling clothing in which the musicians played. Music was stacked crookedly between several piles of books. Children crawled under the legs and pulled at the frayed ends of his doublet. "*Signore*, a penny!" they whined. "*Grazie, signore. . . .*" A green-eyed cat sat before the cask of bitter red wine and had to be nudged aside with a foot to allow the vintage to be drawn. He ate strange sauces and meats, and hard odorous cheeses.

After a time more room was made on the benches, and he found himself seated next to the dark-haired girl in the voluminous green dress. Her flesh was almost swarthy, and she gave off a full scent of perspiration, velvet, and hair oil. When she smiled her teeth were a little crooked.

The wine was heavy with sugar. For a moment they discussed it, and then, as they bent their heads over the platter of singed fowl, she said, "Thy name?"

"Will Shakespeare. And thine?"

"Emilia Bassano."

"Ah . . . then . . . you were born in Italy!"

"Nay! Here. My father came to be a musician and had me of an Englishwoman. Alas, he's no more! God took them both, alas, alas, and I bring flowers to their graves! God took them, and left me here to make my way as best as I can with my cousins and sing for my bread. These people . . ." She lowered her voice so that he had to lean closer to hear her. "These people would use me for their best interests—when a girl is pretty there's something to be made on it, do you not think so? Men look at her and think not of her but of her bosom. But this is the world, my friend. We cannot quarrel with the making of the world, for though we do it remains the same and leaves us but in tears. There!" She began to laugh, and then to talk freely of being taken as a child by musicians to sing sometimes in marketplaces for coins and that once in a while an old priest would give her an apple. Then they performed at great houses here and there, coming home in the darkest part of the night with her father in the cart, hemmed closely about with the instruments, awed by the impression of haughty ladies, and old courtiers with teeth blackened from too much sugar.

The talk turned to plays, which she saw whenever she could, and she began to imitate both the clown Will Kempe's hiss and drone and the young boys simpering as maids, and he laughed at her cleverness until his stomach hurt him. He drank the sweet wine and felt very happy.

"I like to be gay!" she exclaimed. "I would like never never to be sad!"

"Should not we all!"

"But more, I *demand* it, I will not have it otherwise. If the bird is not happy, it does not sing! What is thy name once more?"

"Shakespeare, but I'm called plain Will."

"Do you write tragedies and romances?"

"Only histories. I have thought for a tragedy or two but I have not yet writ a romance."

"Why, there can be nothing better! I do write poetry, but I should like to write plays as well. The good would be happy and the bad punished, yet they should all be romances."

Supper was finished, the tables cleared and upended against the wall. A few more men with instruments across their backs had come in, shouting in Italian. One of them rushed forward and pulled Emilia to her feet. He understood it to be a rehearsal, for they stopped often to demand repetition, and the girl's face turned from amused to sullen.

When he looked about, she had disappeared and Florio was gone as well. He thought to go home, but the emptiness of his own rooms rose up before him, and he drank more wine quickly, and began to be a little drunk. After a time an elderly woman, her hair severely pushed from her face, bid him be her dance partner. The music rose louder and faster, as did the laughter and the shouting. Only vaguely was he aware of another sound upstairs . . . it grew louder until he understood there was a quarrel. One voice was deep and angry, and the other flew into a fire of angry, high Italian.

One of the children had begun to whine, and the gaiety of the music had faded away as if the room had been swept; it happened as quickly as when a scene is changed in a play. He was in that stage of tipsiness when the room seemed now and then to be constructed in a crooked way, and he began to look for his satchel and cloak.

Suddenly Emilia Bassano was beside him, weeping terribly, crying, "I cannot stay here!" With her skirts sweeping the floor rushes and her arm over her face, she bumped into the door and flung herself through it into the night and the darkness of the streets surrounding Holywell.

He followed her clumsily. A cold winter wind blew from the fields, chasing with it all sensation of the crowded, smoky room with its pungent smell of unwashed children, burned fowl, the clothing which retained the sense of many roads, inns, carts, and houses where the musicians had traveled. It was the life of poverty where you lived only by giving pleasure to those who had the money to pay for it. Was this life not the same as his own?

William shivered. Above the spires of the church of St. Helen, the moon was now hidden and then revealed by the drifting clouds. Most of the small rushwicks before the doors of houses and taverns were already extinguished. "Emilia," he called wistfully.

As he moved slowly on the unpaved path, his eyes searching the alleys for which way she might have gone, the bell above him solemnly rang out the hour of ten. Approaching the priory ruins at the end of the street, he beheld a small dark shape seated on some old broken stones, her face in her hands, weeping bitterly.

Hurrying beside her, he whispered with great feeling, "Lady, what 'tis?"

"Naught—do not ask!"

"Mayhap I can be of help."

"I must never speak it! Should I mind for a disappointment? Is this not the way of life? Should we ever expect better?"

He did not know how to answer that, but drew the small, shivering body against his shoulders. The hair had been stiffened into its elaborate, courtly arrangement and the dress was heavily underlain with corsets, yet under all of this stuffing, silk, and iron he was acutely aware that there was a small, soft woman who seemed much finer than the raucous musicians who had but some half-hour before surrounded her.

Gradually her sobs ceased, and still she leaned against him in a distracted way. When she laid her hand on his doublet sleeve, he found to his astonishment that he was trembling.

"Art better then, peaspod?" he said.

"Aye—some . . . but they are vile, vile! I was raised in the household of a lady, for my father wanted better for me than these people—and now I am obliged to them—"

Something rustled, and then rushed near their feet into the bushes. With a cry she drew apart from him and began to look about in a suspicious way, making the sign of the cross three times over her bosom.

"Spirits!" she whispered. "I fear them, for I know they walk about here! Do you believe in spirits? Say!"

"Aye, and then again, nay."

"Oh, the dead, Will! The world's a very little place for the vast amount of the dead which envy us our lives—they envy me mine. Do you think truly a black cat can come at night and suck away the life of a child?" Her dark eyes were great in the moonlight, and she took him by the doublet sleeves in great earnest. "I am afraid, I am afraid!" she said, shaking him a little, and then buried her hands together in the folds of her heavy green velvet dress.

Purple clouds drifted across the sky, once more obscuring the moon, and still she sat motionless, head lowered, as if some grief was upon her. Kneeling impulsively by her side, he exclaimed, "But lady, the dead lie in their shrouds and seldom come to disturb us, and if they did I should beat them so that they would run away with bones rattling. Of what else art afraid?"

She could not help but smile. "I know not. Mayhap that I will one day be older, and lose all I have, which is my beauty. Oh, what am I without that! I weep sometimes for childish things, I know not why."

"For that alone?"

"For that principally."

He nodded sagely, and rubbed her small, cold hands with the practicality of a man used to care for others. "Oh, you are so lovely," he said, "that you will not lose that for centuries. I think me at this moment you will never lose it."

"Ah, you're sweet!" she murmured.

"And thou art shivering. Shall I take thee back?"

"Not yet, pray!"

They fell silent, and heard from down the street some of the musicians leaving. A horse whinnied. Then, touching her cheek, he said wistfully, "I would you remained here a time with me, sweet. What would I tell thee? Things I do not often or willingly say, I think. I have wept at times as well for reasons I did not know, but long after discovered them."

Solemnly she answered, "My father had some blood of the Jews in his body, and they say those people know things that others cannot . . . therefore I already know things of you that most men will never know. I know you are kind, and care more about others than yourself, a bad way to be in the world . . . one is swallowed up by such things. I know these things of you, and more."

"Oh, indeed! And when will you say them?"

"Mayhap another day."

"But how can I know on what day I shall see you? Or what hour?"

Emilia rose, and began to make her way through the broken stones to a lane from which he heard the flowing of a fountain. Following, he saw her kneel to splash water on her face. "There!" she said. "Now I am better! Now, William, my fair player! There are a thousand hours in this season to come! In which shall it be that you and I have leisure to tarry further together?"

She had come close to him and put her hands flat on his chest, and he bent to kiss her. Her lips were warm and full, and he was aware of water and perspiration and the heavy smell of the damp dress fabric. He kissed her again, feeling her little body pressing with much interest against him.

She murmured, "You're handsome enough to be a courtier! Some knight, some peer of the realm who appears in the crowd of an evening when we make our music and the torches smoke the room, and there are dried roses in the rushes, and the men and women are sweaty and perfumed, and handsome—and so they look at me as you do! Such eyes, William! Come, kiss again."

Once more he kissed her and brought his mouth down to the swell of her breasts over the bodice lacing, and she arched back, eyes closed with pleasure. "There!" she said seriously at last. "There, my dear! Have done! I like thee too much! Nay, I could have a fair passion for thee!"

Greedily he pressed his lips to her hand.

She murmured, "Will you come again?"

"I would rather stay this night."

"Oh, that's too soon! What must think of me?" Then he flushed in the darkness, for he had not thought anything but for his desire.

"Then at dawn," he murmured. "Shall I come at dawn? Emilia, wilt say why you wept?"

"Mayhap one day I will," she said. "But do not come tomorrow; 'tis too hasty! A week, perhaps more, to think on it—we both must think on it. Now bid me rest!"

He stood looking up at the dark windows for a time when she had gone inside. There was no music now. He was yet somewhat drunk, and feeling sick with the emotion of it and the wanting of her, walked home with shoulders bent. Robbers may have lurked, but they did not approach him. So deep in thought was he that he walked past his own house and had to turn back.

Inside the room he brought his fingers to his nose, for they were still fragrant with the scent of her hair oil, and then leaned against the wall in his sudden desperate rush of longing. To put aside women was to put aside some essential part of himself: he had always loved them, dreamed of them, woken sweaty with his sensuality, gone about the streets rank with his desire. Even as a boy it had been. Anne had been dark, but not so as this one, who was swarthy as if she had walked, centuries before, a proud and barefoot slave on the shores of the Mediterranean ripe for pleasure. Anne was plain English with her collars folded nearly in a scented box, with her flat feet and heavy walk . . . this one was storm clouds approaching from the sea.

He thought of her constantly over the next few days, counting the hours until he might hear from her, until terrible news came and drove all other concerns away.

ROBIN GREENE WAS dying. Bad living, foul drink, and whores had at last sickened him, said the actors, shaking their heads, and now he was ending his life in a room in Dowgate. At first William muttered, "The devil take him!" Then, as he removed the silver wig and heavy robes of the venerable bishop he had played that afternoon, his heart softened. Greene was scarcely more than thirty years! Could he truly be ending his days here?

Dark clouds had swept in from the north during the comedy, and by the time he left the theater he could feel the first drops of winter rain. Men with folded arms stared at him from fishermen's shops as he struggled upward on the muddy path, past silvery fish which shimmered on the rotting wood of shelves open to the street. A bit of netting tangled in his shoes; a wild dog scurried past him with its head low. In his mind as he went he thought of the first time he had seen Greene at Bartholomew Fair with his red beard as sharp as his tongue, and bits of poems and plays sticking from his pockets. Lyrical—not deep or startling, but sweetly lyrical.

> Weep not, my wanton, smile upon my knee;
> When thou art old there's grief enough for thee.

It was in an alley a few streets from the waterside that he saw the sign he sought swinging in the rain. He found a bitterly cold, dark room separated from the hall by only a curtain; rain was seeping through the edges of the board which covered the one window and across the sloping bare floorboards, which were naked but for stray clumps of rushes. A chamber pot, unemptied for some time, stood by the wall.

"Who's there?" called the sick man. "For Christ's sake, give me a little malmsey wine, a little drink." The voice was fragile, boyish and broken. "Oh, my stomach's burned! My heart's a shriveled thing . . . only a little wine. Who cometh? Speak thy name, for the love of God."

"'Tis Will."

"Ah! Thou darling! Come thou here, come closer . . ." Robin Greene seized the Stratford man greedily by the wet doublet, and burrowed his face into William's shirt like a child that seeks to suckle. "Nay!" he whined. "They do not come, they do not come, and soon it will be too late. For Christ's mercy, a little wine. "

William undid his packet and took out a bottle. It seemed a paltry thing to offer, but what of greater significance could he give? Certainly not words of consolation; he did not have any against something so terrible.

"That's right!" gasped the sick man, drinking. "No, wait . . . ah, I can't. Surely it's over that I can't drink wine. Hold me close . . . I shiver, I burn, I burn . . . my insides are on fire and I cannot cease to shiver."

"Hast had the doctor? Surely he will heal thee, Robin!"

"One came for mercy's sake, said I need only the undertaker. Said I have done this myself." He threw back his head, shivering, his thin, uncovered legs moving uncontrollably. "Where are the others? Will they come? Where are the times we've had? . . . More wine!"

William held his shoulders and helped him.

"I hate thee, my darling!" the sick man croaked. "Hate thee worse than before, for thou hast life. Go home, Will: the city's no good. Dost remember my wife, my poor wife? What will she do now, she who ever weeps for me? And my lad! Thy pardon, goodman, I will say no more." Arching up, he cried hoarsely, "Well, do they come? I remember once I waited four hours for Ben. Give me thy cloak to cover me!"

"Alas, it's wet through."

Greene began to gasp, and clung to William's hand. "'Tis coming . . . coming . . ." he cried. His eyes seemed to stand still in his head, and he arched his back so that the thin bony chest stood out like a ship's prow. "'Tis . . . oh, in Christ's mercy, forgive me my sins . . . now . . . now!" He shook so much that the blankets fell to the floor, his pale hairy leg quivering as if it had a life of its own, the thigh dancing, the bared scrotum wrinkled. "William, 'tis death . . . 'tis death . . . ah, the old lady in the corner!" he shrieked. "She hath come for me . . . save me . . . save me . . . nay, run, run for the love of heaven for a priest! Run, my friend!"

William tore down the steps and rushed into the street, where the rain still poured down roofs, the sides of houses, the shutters and posts, and in rivers down the muddy path. He ran first to the church, but the door was closed, and then round about to the rectory. His knock was unheard in the thunder, so he pulled open the door and came face to face with an elderly churchman who was eating thick soup with a large spoon, narrow feet in slippers and dressing gown tightly wrapped about him.

"There lieth a man . . ." William sputtered. He felt ashamed, as if his skin also stank of urine as he stood there entreating the priest; he was trembling and, to his surprise, weeping. He stood by while the parson slowly laced his hose and buttoned his coat and looked about for his prayer book, and then locked his door. The rain was falling more slowly now, and the sky was somewhat lighter though the streets were full of icy puddles which seeped into his boots.

"I shall take a chill," said the churchman peevishly.

"Goodman, must come! Canst not understand?"

He would have run ahead, but the man plodded on cursing the mud, and wiping the rain from his face. At the tenement steps he hesitated and with a frown took a stub of candle from his pocket, taking his time to light it. They had mounted a few steps when they heard a burst of brilliant, deep, masculine laughter from the room above. "Do they celebrate at this awesome moment?" demanded the priest. "Who is it laughs at this most terrible hour?"

The floor was yet wet, but two tallow candles wafted a stinking smoke through the small room. Ben Jonson, looking too large for the chamber, was unwrapping a capon from paper with a few other actors and prying a cork from a bottle. The bricklayer had been so solemn and religious of late his friends had not known him, and William felt his chest stiffen. What would he do? Give a sermon? . . . And then on what, a life of repentance or the joys of wine?

The sick man had left off his spasms and was half leaning from the bed watching them rationally. "Good fellows, good fellows," he croaked.

"Ah, here's Will!"

All eyes turned to the thin, disdainful priest, who shook his long coat to coax the water out of it. "What's this, a priest?" Jonson snorted at last. "Hast come to drink a draught with us, master? Art mistook. There are no dead men here, as canst see, for our friend's as merry as ever."

William looked from the visitors to the sick man, whose leg yet twitched, though the bed was now heaped with a heavy horse blanket, wherever it might have come from. He crossed to Greene and studied him, muttering, "Art yet burning with fever!"

The churchman peered angrily about. "I thought me the man was dead and left my good soup, I who have myself been in my sickbed three days this month! Dost play games with me, fellow?"

The sick man grinned, the spastic leg never ceasing nor the teeth from chattering. "Away," he muttered. "No winding sheets . . . my friends have come to drink with me."

"Then bad cess!" said the churchman, shaking his gown once more, and taking his candle. "Dost mock the ways of the Lord? And he needs confessing mayhap, and is in no state to have it. I come to shrive a dead man and find a living drunk, God help me. God help the young men of this age!"

Jonson leapt to the window and leaned out to watch the churchman go. "Ah, go off with thy sour face!" he bellowed. "Let me never see thee more! A fart of my arse to thee!" Then, turning to the bed, he said benevolently, "Come, fair Rob, sweet Rob!" Clutching Greene about the shoulder, he demanded in a paternal way, "What was this of dying? Say those words again and I'll clout thee down the stairs. Art a man in fair health. I myself shall cure thee. Look, friends hath come! Here's old stuttering Jack! Drink, Jack, to our friend's new health."

John Heminges was standing at the door, looking about the room with an appalled expression on his wide face; he bent to take up one of the tallow candles and, holding it before him, came closer to the sick poet. "Christ's wounds, this is no health, Ben!" he whispered. "Callst this health? . . . And on coming up I saw the priest go! Did he shrive him?"

"No, we sent him off."

"He ought be bled."

"Nay, he's healed! Friendship hath made him well."

"It can't be, he's bad."

"Jack, you are as dull a man as ever you have been!" cried the bricklayer. "One day without warning I shall fall dead myself of your company. He hath bid us dance and sing, and so we shall. What, Rob, shall we not dance for thee?" Still, his face was grim as he began the tavern song of the tinker who loved a lady.

William walked quietly to the window. The rain had stopped. Water dripped slowly from the house, and below the city seemed strangely purged and clean. From behind him he heard the sound of stomping, and understood that Jonson and his friends were dancing, taking hands and moving around in a circle. Then, hearing an unexpected sound, he turned.

Greene had tumbled from the bed to the floor. Struggling to grasp the cot's edge, he looked at them with beseeching eyes. His mouth moved spasmodically, but no words came. Then he fell to his side, shivered violently, and lay still.

Slowly the men began to creep forward. Jonson fell heavily to his knees and began to weep, his great shoulders shaking. "Will," he sobbed, "as we hope for heaven, fetch back the priest!"

William fled towards the rectory, and flung open the door. "Must come, he hath given up the ghost!" he gasped, and the little priest, trembling with indignation, made the sign of the cross and spat, "'Twas their bad ways hath done it."

Two days later they all stood together as their friend was laid in earth, and Jonson, whose new faith was deeply sincere, took the book from the priest and read out the words of the Resurrection.

WILLIAM GRIEVED LONG and silently. One of Greene's many pamphlets was published posthumously, damning the players and writers for their corrupt lives, and William was not exempt. For weeks he did not wish to see anyone, and even his fascination for the Italian girl turned to ashes. In his heart he knew that in spite of everything he would have sheltered Greene's life with his hands, as you shelter a weak flame on a windy night, walking hunched over the candle to protect it. He could not forget their times of joy.

Then during the playing of a tragedy at the Rose he unbalanced in a leap and fell hard to the stage; pain shot up his leg and thigh, and he found himself on the way home limping and furious. For two weeks another man took his roles. Only when he resumed his work, a fine wet mist flinging into his beard and filling his lungs, did he begin to long for life again as something worth having. Then he remembered the Italian girl had not sent for him.

But when he walked over to the musician's house outside Bishopsgate, a neighbor informed him they had gone away for a time, locking the doors. A few days following, however, when buying bread, he came across one of the lutenists, who told him that Emilia was employed as house musician by Henry Carey, Lord Hunsdon, in his house off the Strand. William felt the blood in his veins call to the Italian girl, and having perfumed his beard and pulled on new breeches and doublet embroidered about the sleeves with silver thread, he went to find her.

Past portraits of stiff-faced men and some suits of armor, he walked down the hall to painted double doors from behind which came the sound of virginals. She was seated before the instrument, her little fingers flying rapidly across the keys and her small yellow slippers tapping the floor in time. In the middle of a chord she stopped, the expression of her face mingled with confusion and pleasure. Then, breaking into a smile, she held out both her hands.

Hurrying across the room, he bent and kissed them. "Oh, do not cease to play!" he whispered passionately. "I love music to my soul! Go on, wilt? I will stand here and listen and hardly breathe but to keep good time to the melody."

"You speak well!"

"So I am told, though it seems but clumsy to me."

"So you will keep good time?"

Gazing at him mischievously, her breath fluttering in the hollow of the throat, she bowed her head and began to play once more, leaning a little closer to the music to see the notes of the faster passages as if she was short of sight. He sat back, lost in the pleasure of the brilliant scales. Sensuality filled him so he felt almost sick with its power.

Yet the second melody she began was the lament by Mr. Dowland for the great late clown Tarlton, and sadness began to seep into his flesh. The memory of the dead poet and the still present ache of his leg overcame his delight in this swarthy, fragrant girl, and for a moment he thought darkly that he had inherited not only his father's large brown eyes but his melancholy. He lowered his head to frown at the hem of her skirt, which swept the matting, and did not look up until he realized the melody had ceased.

"Will," she said gently, "art sad."

"I am in mourning for a friend."

"One you loved much?"

"Strangely I think so. He knew he had not fulfilled his promise here."

"Oh, I am sorry for this news! But do you think we have promises here?"

"I do, but most often I'm uncertain what mine are. We are selfish creatures, I think, Emilia, and love each other from that. But what else can we do? I aspire to heaven, but as hard as I try to climb towards it, I seem every day to fall back again. A petty grievance, a memory of some wrong done by another." He raised his eyes, and then his words fell away . . . oh by Christ's mercy, she was dark and lovely! For some days, in dreams and in waking, in the common acts of eating boiled cabbage or capon, in looking for his hose, had he not longed for her? And he thought greedily, but I am here and I live. . . .

"Emilia," he said formally, feeling joy stir within him.

"Oh, Will!" came the reply.

A plate of cakes made with figs and apples and a decanter of wine stood by, and he was glad to eat and drink, for he was uncertain now how he wished to begin. They spoke of small city matters, and the theater, and Italy, which fascinated him, and all the time there was a growing excitement through his body. Sweat formed under his arms.

She said suddenly with some strictness, "There is something I must tell thee." It was in the way a dame schoolmistress will correct a child who has misread a word of the Lord's Prayer from the hornbook.

Dazzled, he gazed at her pale yellow satin shoes and the light wool yellow stockings above, embroidered with birds up the calf. Here was all of life, and all of beauty. "Tell me only that you want me!" he cried. He stood, and taking her suddenly by the waist, urged her joyfully to the brown upholstered couch, murmuring in her ear what parts of her were made for love . . . elbow, arch of foot, the swell of her flesh above the soft blouse and tight bodice lacing. He would not have spoken so to a virgin, but he sensed she was not that . . . he did not know what she was, but that she was rich with experiences and sensations he had never touched, and he felt he must have them on his life.

Breath quivered in her throat under her necklace. He fell upon her as if famished. She raised her leg, and he sensed the heat of her and was wild with it and panting like a rushing buck through the forest, tearing branches, raising dust, trampling flowers.

"Thy beard bruises!" she panted between kisses. "It tickles."

"Let it . . . there!"

"Ah, Will!"

Then arching up, she said breathlessly, "You smell of wood . . . of dark, heavy trees . . . of forests . . . oh you are more than anyone could know . . . ah, touch me there!"

"Christ's wounds, lass! Too much lacing."

" . . . and you speak as they do in the country!"

"I am country-born, I hunted in forests, I am no city fellow. Curse these laces, lass, I will break them with my teeth!"

"Ah, thy beard tickles me. William!"

They were so close that he could hardly find the trusses of his own breeches, but still he had pulled away her drawers enough to open the space to the very secret crevices of her body. "Then lass, art mine!" he said between his teeth, and she answered, "Oh, could it be! Aye, thine alone, for not since we stood in the lane has there been a day when I have not recalled . . ."

There came at that moment a great banging at the doors; both were flung open, and a small old woman scurried in clapping her hands, screaming in Italian, and pushing William aside. Emilia leapt up and with trembling fingers, cursing under her breath, began to relace her bodice and tidy her hair.

William had rushed into a corner, hot and confused as when one is awaked from the loveliest dream with violence. In moments they heard heavy footsteps in the hall, and a sweet-faced man of some seventy years came into the room with his silver-handled walking stick. William knew him at once for the good soldier Henry Carey, Lord Hunsdon, the Queen's cousin, who was fond of the actors and had given them his protection. The dark curls of his wig stood out against the aged, pale face of a man who was no longer well.

His lordship put down his stick and opened his arms to Emilia, who came into them reluctantly, slightly turning her face when he made to kiss her lips. "Thy mouth, sweet!" came the gentle reproof. Then she turned and placed her lips, which must still taste of the player's kisses, against the old man's mouth.

William let out his stomach with a hard exhalation of air. He only wanted to take the girl by her soft arms in their slashed, multicolored sleeves and cry out, bewildered, What dost? What dost? Barely did he remember to remove his hat, and then he was strangely calm, regarding suddenly the room and what had occurred from outside.

Lord Carey let his hand respectfully linger on the waist and above the swell of skirt of Emilia Bassano, and then said with much courtesy, "You are one of the players, for I recall how you danced at my lord Essex's house some months past! Much pleasure do the actors give to me—aye, I cannot say what I would do in some moments of sadness had I not the playhouses! Welcome, welcome. We will sit awhile, and mayhap my Emilia shall play for us upon the virginals."

Bowing again, William took the indicated seat, also accepting from the servant, who gazed at him with scornful eyes, a pewter cup of ale. The young woman had curtseyed and gone to the instrument; with a complicated arrangement of skirts she seated herself and began to play. Lord Hunsdon began to beat time on his massive knee, nodding now and then. The notes passed by the player in the shock of what he had understood. After a time the lord's soft snores fell unevenly about the beats of the measure, making a discordant rhythm. His wig half slipped to the side.

By this time William had hurried from the room and down the hall in spite of the plaintive soft voice which called after him in her father's tongue, "*Caro mio, dove sei . . .*"

HE WAITED FOR a note from her, but it did not come. Then a few days later he walked to Florio to discuss the possibility of a play set in Padua and how it might be done. The greying, pointed beard and sharp face of the old bachelor, who could be scathingly critical of stupidity, seemed to understand much. With an amused look about the corner of his mouth, he drew from a portfolio on his desk a folded sheet of paper and held it out to the player.

"My young cousin," he said mildly, "had not thy street of dwelling, my friend. She gave this to me with tears in her eyes, for I think she's fonder of you than I have known her to be."

The paper was sealed with the crest of Lord Hunsdon in the wax, and said merely in a clear, beautiful hand, "Will you let me explain matters to thee? Thy friend, E. Bassano, in Christ's name."

More solemnly this time did he enter this house, sniffing everywhere the scent of the lord who owned it and somehow, inexplicably, the Italian girl. He found her in a very small chamber seated in a dark dress with no farthingale, and wearing a cross around her neck. Her face was plain as a peasant's, and with her thick hair hidden under a cap, she seemed like a nun waiting to be taken to the cloister. There was some sewing on her lap.

"You have much to learn in the way of the world," she said sadly, looking away at a small desk crammed with papers. "There he keeps much of the documents of state. He is an important, a good man. But naught of him, only of thee!"

Tears glimmered in her eyes as she glanced at William for a moment, and seeing his severe, bewildered look, she wiped them, and fingered the needle in the cloth. "I told you I have the sight from my father's people, the Venetian Jews! I see in you a man who so surely knows what he wishes the world to be that he cannot and will not see it for what 'tis. That makes you beautiful, but susceptible to so much that it would seem you should stay behind thy mother's apron strings."

William made a gesture of disgust and impatience, and then replaced his hands on his knee. His sword tip touched the floor, and his earring glittered.

She said, "Shall I go on?"

"Do."

"Only if you listen."

"Well, then I shall."

Beginning to make small, meticulous stitches, she said, "Lord Hunsdon is my protector. My father placed me, as I told you, in an English house which gave me fine manners, but when I was fifteen the master began to pinch me on the stair and thrust his hand into my bosom, and the mistress, blaming me, made me go. My father was then dead, so I fell into the hands of my cousins for a time, until my lord took me under his protection. I would have great use for virtue of the common sort, my dear, had virtue any use for me."

William tore at the rolled edges of his new velvet hat and murmured darkly, "And what of that? What can that mean?"

"This, sweet. Women fade quickly, and must make the best of things while they are young. I am hoping one day he will marry me. He gives me dresses and jewelry, and rooms in his house."

"Ah!" William said. The hat's delicate black feather came away in his hand, and he threw it to the floor.

Gravely she leaned forward, the needle daintily piercing the fabric in what looked like a plainly made smock for the small child of a servant or some parish woman. "I tell falsehoods when I must, but to you I'll speak truth. He has me to his bed, but it has been some seasons since he could do more than stroke me. I have no lover but this, and am honorable enough not to take one, though I confess, William, I burn, for I am still young! I am still young!" Then, rising as if a widow greeting those who had come to console her in her loss, she hurried across the expanse of room which seemed to separate them and gave him the tips of her fingers.

He did not know what to do but kiss them, and found them so soft. He pressed the hand against his cheek, feeling her delicate ring scratch against his cheek and beard. She was so little and alone.

"Now," she said with great formality as if she were twice her age and the owner of a great house, "I have spoken the truth. If you still wish to visit with me now and then and drink a cup of wine, you may do so, for you know I like thee well, William. And what in life can be perfect, my dear? For I am told that you yourself are a married man. Is it not so?"

Nodding with shame, he leapt up with his hat and would have gone, but turned in a kind of despair and saw her waiting by the arras curtains with the sewing slack in her hand. "Well, I will come again," he murmured as if the words burned him.

"I do not give favors easily."

With a hoarseness he answered, "I shall make you wish to give them to me as you have never given them to any man before."

MAY CAME, AND he ran wildly through the fields with his arms outstretched to embrace the spring with Emilia. She came often in dresses embroidered with little flowers, or a hat with ribbons which she seldom wore on her hair but hung down her back. By a stream they took off their shoes, waded, and splashed each other. They read poems aloud, he some early verses for a long poem he hoped to complete.

> Affection is a coal that must be cool'd;
> Else, suffer'd, it will set the heart on fire.

They held each other in the field, in laundry sheds, in a boathouse where they climbed into a ferry whose once gay green striped awnings were faded and its cushions gnawed by rats. She despised rats, snakes, spiders. He brought his face close to hers until her large eyes lost focus, and searching under her lace-trimmed linen petticoats, he touched again her flesh. He felt the life under her belly and in the moist folds between her thighs, and she untrussed his breeches for the full swelling of him and sighed. More she would not permit of herself or him, for she said love was these days a thing taken cheaply: had for pennies, it was as easily thrown away. Theirs should last forever. She knew an astronomer, she confided, who had all her trust, and he would draw the charts to name the time and place when they should truly belong to each other.

Entranced, sometimes furious, sometimes beseeching, he could only nod and agree with her. He carried away with him the scent of her hair oil and the place between her legs on his fingers, and went to sleep with his hand to his nose. His fellows began to laugh and tease him for his distractedness, which he bore with good grace, and yet he would not tell them the name of the lady.

In the woods one day they found the body of a dead child, a little boy, not more than three years old. He was half covered with leaves and dirt, and slightly shriveled, as if he had lain there a long time. The body was naked and bruised, and the hair stuck with dried blood. Emilia began to cry, kneeling and covering her face and rocking back and forth.

Shaken, he thought, Should it be one of mine . . . Hamnet, or Judith! Christ, hath it been these three weeks since I have writ to my father of them?

Yet drawing Emilia against him, he whispered, "What 'tis?"

"Naught, naught!—do not ask!"

Later they came across a schoolmaster and told him to report it to the constable. They could almost not bear to leave the child there, and they strewed the stiff little body with flowers before going home.

SHE WAS, HE understood from her great sense of drama, from the land of masques, intrigue, the first great theatrical tradition. Sometimes it irked him, other times he loved it. Always when they kissed until they were panting, lips made tender and bruised, she would stand on her toes and whisper in his ear, "The soothsayer hath said soon, soon! Not this week, for my courses flow, but he hath read the charts and said it will not be a long delay."

Then she sent for him, and said, come. Beloved, *carissimo*, come to me this night when the moon has risen one hour, and softly up the stairs and bring all thy desire, for I am ready for thee.

*   *   *

THE OLD WOMAN must have been sleeping in the back hall, for when he knocked, the door creaked open at once, and, cocking her head, she looked suspiciously up at him. She scratched the palm of her hand, and waited half leaning on the door, and he found two pennies to give to her.

"My mistress is waiting," she said.

A rushlight in a rounded dish was thrust into his hand, and her knuckles pressed into the small of his back to direct him up the damp back stair. Up and up he climbed, past the first floor, startled by the sudden shriek of a small monkey, and then up as instructed to the second landing. A hall of several doors lay before him, but from beneath one came the faintest firelight, and to this he hurried. If death had waited behind that door he would have gone.

It was a dusty room, hung about with rare French wall tapestries of unicorns and ladies. There was a dressing table and mirror, and wardrobes, and towards the wall an enormous bed on which a heavy fur cover was flung, and many pillows. Emilia was standing before the table with a candle in her hand, barefoot and wearing only a white simple chemise, with her rich hair loose and hanging to her thighs. Putting down his wicklight, he came towards her.

She put her arms around his neck, and he swept her to him, kissing her loose hair and her neck and her mouth. Then he carried her to the bed, hurling some of his clothes about the room. Under the chemise she was naked, and arching up, she pressed her soft belly and small breasts against his body. She called him many tender names in her father's language, many of which he did not understand, and some he did and would have been puzzled by had he thought of them . . . *mio amor, mio piccolo bambino, caro caro fiore* . . . my love, my little child, beloved beloved flower! She kissed him all over, until they both cried out and muffled their faces in each other's hair and shoulders.

The night was hot and still, and the courtyard below very dark. From the river they heard the complaining of ferrymen, and the ever-present lapping of the water against the dock steps. They teased, whispered, nuzzled, and spoke of many things. With a shudder, she said, "Oh, dost remember the child?"

Lust arose again. He wanted to grapple with her, wrestle with her, hold her arms until he felt the very bone within them. He wanted the bone itself, and to kiss her inside to her very viscera and heart. Later when they had slept a little and awoke to the mystery of each other and stroked each other again, he found within the sheets her satin corset, and saw by the candles that one piece of bone was working through the shimmering cloth, as if a bone through skin.

Then they were hungry and ate cold meat pie sitting crosslegged and naked on the bed, the mutton fat encasing their fingers and the pastry falling in crumbs, sharing one goblet of wine. He would have embraced her again, but was exhausted and frowned at his failure, and began to think of darker things. "Emilia!" he said sternly. "Say again—the old man does not have thee!"

With scorn she replied, "He cannot! Do you think him handsome, strong, potent as you? Hearty country fellow, you could please a room of wenches! He gave me a home, and pretty things, and honored me—my cousins would beat me. He gave me kindness and pretty things, and I gave him myself. What else had I to give? I am a woman! There is no profession I could train for and no one to pay for the training. I am only a musician."

"And lovely!" he said, touching her hair.

"Oh, William! I've seldom met a man as true and gentle as you—but come closer, and let me tell you more of my story, though it makes me weep. I was fifteen years old when one of my cousins took me in a barn outside the walls, where he found me in tears for my dead father. Oh, for months he had gazed at me with dewy eyes the way boys do when they are warm with wanting. I was then with my other cousins, who would not give me food to eat when I did not play my music well. His name was Eduardo, and we were to run off and be gypsies, and dance and sing about the world together. We would run away and be married near the docks, where they do not inquire into anything, and return to sunny Italy, away from this vile, damp city. Oh, I was so innocent, my dear! I think I have not been innocent again until I met you."

He stroked her hair, which was tangled here and there from the combs and oils and perfumes and curling. Some he wound about his wrist, other strands braided into several parts, some passed over his lips, and all the time he murmured passionately, "Poor love, with no one to protect you. Dost not know I shall protect you from this time forth?"

"He left me, William! I think he went for a soldier after a time; I don't know. I would not eat, I could not sleep. My hair, my lovely hair, began to fall away, and they had physicians in who bled me, but no one knew. Then Lord Hunsdon, who had always been kind to my father, one day bid me come, and for some time did not touch me . . . he waited, but I knew it would come. A midwife gave me a little bit of sheep's blood, and I cried out at the right moment when he thrust inside me, and after quickly, quickly drew the packet out and dabbed my hand in it and rubbed it between my legs. Poor lamb! he cooed. I've hurt thee, poor lamb! Oh, my lord, for love of you, 'twas worth the pain, for God knowth we women are born to suffer, yes, we suffer for the sins of the world! This was my answer."

William felt dazed. He had made so many braids of her hair that his fingers ached, and he began to kiss her shoulder

She was sobbing. "Oh, oh!" she wept. "How often I have prayed for the Blessed Mother to help me. For this Eduardo I would have been a different woman. I would have known poverty, and bent my back over the washing tub."

"Was there—a child—"

But she only wiped her face with her hair and gazed at him with wet, happy eyes. "But all this with thee," she said, "is past."

He began to kiss her once more, thrusting her down, tasting the salt and sweat of her underarms, and the round warmth of her belly, putting his tongue between the dark, thick hairs of her most private flesh. With his love he wished to wipe away the trace of any other from her lovely body, and indeed after when he looked down at her, truly exhausted, he saw with some satisfaction that she was marked with him and would be his forever.

"*Caro!*" she scolded sleepily into his ear, gently bringing her palm against his buttocks in reproof. "What hast done with my hair? 'Twill take an hour or more for Alicia to put it right again! Wicked oaf!"

SOMETIMES HE GREW morose. "Suppose, Emilia," he said, "that you were in Hunsdon's house on the Strand and I in my rooms near the gate, and that a great earthquake shook the city and split it and my half was broken off, and the whole of it swept out to the river and the sea . . . I calling thy name above the wind, you not answering. I had such a dream, Emilia, and even as I shouted above the wind, I heard from the city, though it was now some hundreds of miles away, the sound of music, and knew there was a dance and you were dancing there in canary-yellow slippers with all the young men from the court."

"Oh, the folly of thy brain!" she said crossly.

"Nay, not folly—aye, I dreamed such a thing and woke in the darkness with nothing but the sweat of wanting you, and the rind of cheese from my dinner to greet me. Some poor soul retching into the gutters below, cursing the world, echoing what was in my heart, darling, to have you here with the old man's stroking, and me there. Then I wondered if life is always and only a sorrow! Is this all we can expect, is this all any mortal can have, even the Queen herself, who mayhap sits in virgin chambers and lusts over young lovers she will ever forbid herself to have?"

"Will, why must talk of such matters? You press my arm so hard it will leave a mark!"

"There, I'll kiss it! What wilt? Remember I am acrobat, actor, musician. I can sing a song, rant through a speech, and tear my hair! In addition I can play the clown, though I will not do it here. Emilia, Emilia, read me your poems!"

"Will you laugh at my efforts?"

"Nay, I shall not on my life!"

She bent her head closer to the papers, which trembled as she read, as did her voice. "Why, they're good poems," he said sincerely.

"And what do you write?"

"Remaking a tragedy called *Titus Andronicus*. Silly stuff, but the towns-folk like such things. Men baked into pies like mutton! Oh, I could wish you such a pie, Emilia, for myself alone to devour."

"Now you are silly again," she said happily.

STILL, THERE WAS always with her the terror that she would one day be old, and at times it possessed her so that she would stand rigid with fear, and be unable to respond to him. When they passed ugly old women her face would become almost pale. They evoked an anger and a fury in her, as if they had failed, and in such, betrayed the whole of their sex. In this she sometimes shrieked at the servant who waited upon her and kept her secrets and other times covered the wrinkled, resentful face with kisses of remorse, and thrust upon her hair ribbons or combs for which the servant had no use. Emilia had no money, but she had things: she had dresses, and stomachers, and embroidered stockings, and books. The old man did not trust her to give her money.

William felt it strange. Weeks before he had been a contented man, willing to drink until he slept, honest in friendship and work but in other things not particular for niceties. He had cared for friends and occasionally himself, but now all revolved about her, and he finished his tragedy quickly to resume his hours at her side. Did she frown? Did she turn her face when he went to kiss her or open her mouth to receive his tongue? He could tell by the feel of her breasts how much she was his, and in the act of lovemaking he won her once more and triumphed with his cry and the outpouring of his seed.

Sometimes he looked at her darkly, resenting his bondage. Lord Hunsdon was often away, and William would come up the back stairs and knock three times at her door. With a cry she received him, covering him with kisses. He was astonished at her passion. In this sumptuous sleeping chamber with its dark red hangings which seemed to be made for adulterous love, he found a world he had not known before. His blood quickened with danger: Hunsdon was the actors' patron, and if he should hear news of this liaison, how might not the men suffer? These thoughts he pushed away in the violence of his desire.

Once in the middle of the night after they had quarreled slightly, he woke to find the room illuminated with many candles and she standing naked before the large mirror. Slowly she turned, her hand passing across the small high breasts, and then backwards to her shapely buttocks. Stunned by the beauty of it, he forbade himself to breathe. For a moment he saw himself as a hunched, grinning beggar who looks at beauty through a crack in the wall and licks his lips and should be whipped for it. Then that image passed in the wonder and imagery of her, and the innocence of his beholding.

For the candles glittered against the dusky warmth of her skin, which spoke to him of the olive groves of the country from which her ancestors had come, and the ancient hills full of ruins from the crumpled empire, and an earth so rich and old that it spoke the very history of all mankind. This was her history: emperors, coliseums, more. Then as she stood there turning thoughtfully this way and that to admire the upturn of a nipple, or raised one arm above her head so that the dark, curling hairs beneath it also caught the light, she seemed almost a saint.

After a time his eyes moved from her naked, turning body to the image reflected in the large, round mirror: there were the glittering candle flames, and the shadowy, succulent flesh of the foreign girl. Yet beyond in the mirror was also the large bed with its heavy half-drawn hangings, its rumpled coverings, its pillows half fallen to the floor, and himself. Through his half-sleeping state he saw a handsome man with well-shaped bare shoulders and chest, and such tenderness as seemed somehow obscene. For a moment he did not know it to be himself, and then startled, stirred as if to turn away.

The bed creaked.

He held his breath, worried that she might have heard him and the private reverie of her devotions be disturbed. Later she would come to bed, her nipples and warm patch of hair between her legs sticky with his seed pressed against his back, and they would sleep soundly until dawn came as an invader through the curtains now closed against the world, as the barbarians did once over the hills of Rome. The scent of the waxy, perfumed guttered candles would linger in the dusty air, her nightdress where it had fallen in the rushes like the remains of virtue. But now there was this.

He was exhausted with loving her: no sooner did he spill himself between her warm thighs than he wanted her more than ever before. It seemed she was all he had ever wanted. It was true Lord Hunsdon would come home, and for a time they would have to find a place, a secret way. His chest filled with anger at the thought, and then he could bear to feel no more. With his head on his bare arms, he remained watching until what he beheld seemed to meld, and girl and mirror and candles, plans and hopes and future, and all else folded away into sleep.

THE LORD OF SOUTHAMPTON

E WAS SLEEPING some hours past dawn a few weeks later when the message came, brought by a boy in livery who tied his horse to one of the posts on the wide, dirty, shop-filled avenue of Bishopsgate and mounted the steps. If not for the bit of paper nailed to his door on which the player had scratched *W. Shakespeare his room*, the lad might never have found him, but as it was he knocked briskly on the scuffed paneling and called out respectfully, "A letter from the most gracious Countess of Southampton for the player Shakespeare if he be within!"

William had been dreaming he was in the chamber of French tapestries with Emilia crawling about, looking under the bed for her slippers embroidered with birds in red thread. He stumbled from the sheets wearing only a sleeping shirt to his knees, and struck back the wood bar from its iron casing. "I am Shakespeare," he muttered in a gruff voice, rubbing his unshaven cheek. "Wouldst?"

"This letter then is yours."

"My lady of Southampton? I have heard her name, but why hath she writ to me?"

"I know not, fellow, but shall wait below with my horse for your reply."

The player walked reflectively in his bare feet through the scattered, dry floor rushes to the window. He had not been asleep before dawn, and now he had no idea what o'clock it was, for he had pawned his watch yesterday. Then he had drunk with Jonson, which he had sworn not to do, and now by the light he reckoned it near the dinner hour of eleven, and he must be at the theater by one for the performance. For a moment he could not remember what they were performing that day, hoping only that his parts were not large. They had given six different plays that week alone; still, this one he had written, and therefore ought to know it.

Breaking the blob of green sealing wax and shaking his head to clear it, he began to read. After a time he raised his eyes to the table past the hardened lump of bread to the letters which had recently come so many miles from his father and his son, a request for payment from a physician who had treated his cough, and some small coins. His now sharp eyes took in the entire room, and he sat down on the stool and reread the letter. It was a request for a dozen sonnets to be delivered by a specific date.

He had never written a sonnet in his life, but to this moment had reworked or created anew some five or six plays, plus those uncountable number of treatises written when he first came to London on subjects of little interest to him. He had just sent money home and paid many bills and had little left. More than money, he was intrigued with the commission, yet once again his mind returned to the fee. He wondered if it would be paid in advance, in which case he would also retrieve his watch. He could also buy a present for Emilia, though what he could give her was paltry compared to her protector's largess.

He threw himself down on the bed with his arms under his head to gaze at the water stain on the ceiling, which seemed sometimes to be very like the hooked profile of Elizabeth, the now much aged but still sharp-minded virgin Queen. Many thoughts passed through his mind. In the end he leapt up, scribbled a formal reply that he would attend the Countess of Southampton at her leisure the next morning, and signed his name with a great flourish. He whistled as he opened the window, and let the note drift like something borne by the wind which may land where he could not say.

DRURY HOUSE, ON a tree-lined walk past meadows away from the main Strand, which crossed between the cities of Westminster and London, was one of the new great houses which had been built during the reign of the Tudor kings and queens. It had been a time of the greatest prosperity since the wily Harry Tudor had rightfully wrested the crown from Richard III on Bosworth Field. Never had the mighty lords of the land risen as quickly, and yet did not quarrel with their sovereign but gathered about her like walls enclosing a great garden.

The usher took him down a hall and into a small room and there left him. With much interest, William looked about at the heavily worked wall hangings with their armorial or mythological designs, the fantastically embroidered rug which covered the table with its pattern of daisies, long twirling vine stems, acorns, and leaves, and the blue Venetian glass bowl upon it. The whole room with its thick cushions and hangings and rugs seemed to be embroidered with silk on linen or velvet. On top of the mantel was a delicate silver vase commemorating the defeat of the Armada and engraved both with Minerva vanquishing the snake and the motto *A thousand shall fall beside thee, and ten thousand at thy right hand, O Elizabeth, Queen!* By the vase, a hairless monkey studied him, and from the corner a tall clock ticked the minutes in a ponderous way.

His mind worked quickly, absorbing much of what he had seen. Then he turned, for the door had opened. A gracious woman of not yet forty years came towards him, wearing a high starched, gathered neck ruff of many yards, decorated with seed pearls. She wore at her belt an embroidered sweet bag which would contain the usual fragrant herbs. Nodding at his bow, she spoke his name.

"Word has come to me that you are a poet of discretion and sensitivity," she said. "I believe I can entrust you with a secret to explain what I need from you."

The words somewhat astonished him, but he bowed gravely.

"I must also trust in your originality," she continued, walking to the writing desk, on which were several oval miniatures, and taking one into her hands. "They cannot be simply sonnets, but must be writ with a specific matter in mind. I am a mother of one son, whom I love more than anyone else in the world. I have spoiled him mayhap, kept him close to me, and the Queen is much of the same mind as myself. He is eighteen years of age and hath been an earl since my husband died many years ago. His guardian, Lord Burghley, wishes him to marry his granddaughter. 'Tis an excellent marriage, but I am afraid my son is somewhat free of spirit, and wishes to remain single."

"So the poems are to be . . ."

"An argument to him to marry."

He wanted to shake his head violently and then, spreading his arms, to cry out, But one cannot persuade someone to marry who doesn't wish to . . . and why would any fellow wish it at eighteen when all the world's before him? Even for all the gold in Christendom, I would not do it!

For a moment, memories of his own youth rushed through his mind; scowling, he folded his arms across his chest. He felt a curious empathy for the young man, yet at the same time he understood the practicality of the matter. He was flattered to be asked to write when there were so many more famous poets about the city (there was Edmund Spenser, Tom Lodge, George Peele, Tom Campion, and the elusive Marlowe), and he needed the coins. He bowed and kissed her cold hand.

As he was leaving he heard music, and turning for a moment, glanced inside a wainscoted study. In the corner by the light of the rainy day the beautiful young Southampton was playing the lute. His hair fell in curls over his shoulder. For a moment he looked up as if expecting a lover, or his own future.

The player saw it all clearly in that moment: the richness of the room, the languor and resentment of the boy. It melded somehow with the richness of the food he had seen carried down the hall and the white ringed hand of the countess. Then he was on the street again, walking towards the Strand with its taverns and shops and traffic, whistling "Bonnie Sweet Robin Is All My Joy."

IT WAS FROM the edge of the platform in the house off the Strand where the actors were playing that night and had now come to make their last dance that William thought he saw the young Earl of Southampton standing much entranced with his attendants. His proper name was Henry Wriothesley, pronounced Risley, as his friends, it was said, called him in school—that or Harry. As soon as the comedy was applauded, William hurried down to look at him more closely. He was directed to a supper room, where centerpieces of mythical gods carved from hard, glittery ice sat next to silver platters with embossed replications of saints' lives which held ripe fruit. Great vases of fall flowers drooped in the warmth of the chamber, leaving a thick scent of leaves and forests: the floor rushes, newly strewn, were soft under their feet.

"Where is my lord of Southampton?"

"He returned to his studies."

Yet William had managed to obtain in his rapid way a further impression of the boy to whom he was to write the poems: gracefully tall and lithe, hand on sword hilt, ribbons bound about lovelocks the color of tarnished gold, and a little angry. Someone laughed and said, "Oh, Southampton! Why, the talk in the city was all of him two years ago, for he for ran off to France at sixteen to serve under Lord Essex, whom he met in school, and whom he idolizes. Queen had him brought back by the ear, so to speak. He hasn't a penny, for his guardian won't give him money for the price of a harlot until he agrees to marry his granddaughter. Half the poets in the city hope he'll be their patron, for he loves verse."

William went home and began his first sonnet.

> From fairest flowers we desire increase
> That thereby beauty's rose might never die . . .

When he had finished it he read it over thrice, much pleased. Outside the small window he heard the chimes toll midnight as he sprinkled sand on the ink and then shook the paper gently back and forth.

IT WAS RAINING that October day a week later as he ran up the Strand, the wide sloped brim of his velvet hat heavy with water, splashing in the great puddles. Alehouse keepers gazed out through the downpour before their red wicker lattice, and a drenched cat fled. High chest heaving, William rushed up the path towards the crenellated Drury House with its dozens of windows and formal gardens and gave his name to the steward. The lackey turned up his chin at the dripping visitor. The lady Countess, he said, was away for the day, but the young master had mentioned that if the poet should come he would himself receive him.

Storm had darkened the room where Henry Wriothesley, Earl of Southampton, was writing alone at his desk. Tree branches scratched at the windowpanes, and all within seemed dulled by the dark grey weather as if it somehow were a prison cell, and the lackey had thrown a great bolt behind them so that the poet and the young man could not escape. Even the rare Chinese bowl filled with rose petals which sat upon the table held no light.

Henry Wriothesley was dressed in black doublet and hose, the golden hair bound back. He seemed in that moment very young and alone, and the heavy piles of paper before him too much for his comprehension, though he had a reputation as a scholar both at Cambridge and in the law temples, which he still attended. Rising, he said with shy eagerness, "Ah, come in, come in! I do know you, player, for I believe you're also the poet who wrote the history of the quarrel between the houses of York and Lancaster, and poor Harry the King! By the saints, those were such days!" He spoke onward rapidly and with some deference, as he might to an elder. "My lord Essex and I lay awake at school at times and talked about them. There's something satisfactory to the act of conquering, but how can we do so with a Queen who both wants and does not want peace?"

Then as if he had said too much, he bit his lip, flung back his head, and exclaimed, "Will you not sit down? I am pleased to meet thee, Master Shakespeare, for I have been a half-dozen times to thy plays, and would like to have a copy of them. They are not printed yet?"

Bowing slightly, William replied, "No, good my lord, for fear they'd be stolen by other playing troupes."

Henry Wriothesley scraped his own chair closer, flung himself into it, and leaning with his elbows on the table, gazed with great interest at his damp guest. "Aye," he said passionately. "Is this not the way of life that men take things wrongfully from another? Countries, women, plays . . . in my case, they take hope, pride, all. I despise my guardian and his attempts to make me marry, but I will not despise your poems which encourage me to do so. You are merely doing a service; I shall take them in that light." Leaning back, he said in a charming way, "I do not mind being scolded like a school lad in verse by the man who hath made me weep over the death of our brave Talbot."

William murmured his thanks; not wishing to dampen the embroidered cushions, he sat forward slightly, studying the young man before him. Those about the city called Wriothesley beautiful, and he was indeed, in the way of very young, masculine men when they balance for a short time on the edge of youth. His skin was smooth and fair, a few soft hairs on the upper lip all the sign of a beard. There was a flush in his cheeks of easy embarrassment, as if he were too modest to acknowledge that he owned all about him. The hands were slender and strong, and looked as if they could wield a sword with determination.

"Have you brought more verses? Give them here!" Southampton strode to the desk, put up the oil in the lantern (for the room was yet very dark), and read them quickly. Then with a mischievous smile, he raised his face and said, "But you do not demand personally that I obey these things?"

"No, my lord."

"Then we shall have this secret between us. You're wet with the rain! Move closer to the fire and I will send for mulled wine, and you shall tell me more of the War of the Roses. Which house, Plantagenet or York, had the greatest claim of right to the throne, thinkst? Did York deserve to have his youngest son die? The boy was innocent, and yet they killed him, poor little Rutland! I can see these things from the view of the people as well as the throne, for my grandfather was humbly born." On he spoke of the history of the last century with great intensity. The lackey came in with wine and veal pie made with sage and currants, and for some time they discussed the ways of men and kings. Southampton seemed much drawn to his grandfather and bragged of him; his eyes glittered when he talked of warriors and fighters. He wanted, he said, nothing more than to go to war, and his hands clenched when they spoke of it, and he jumped up and strode about the room.

"But you know Marlowe?" he asked.

"My lord, I do."

"Oh, there's a wild one!" He began to laugh, and then a knock came at the door. The two attendants who stood there were sent sharply away, but only minutes after, two beautiful young women in heavy satin gowns floated curtseying into the chamber; in musical voices, they declared they had a message for the Earl from the lady Countess, his mother, who would shortly return. At first the Earl made to kiss them, and when they flushed, shaking their heads, he said sullenly, "Bid her wait, send her my duty and my love! Say one of my poets attends me this hour."

He but plays with them, William thought as he sat by the fire. He plays with them as someone will try out a dance step and after some minutes be bored with it, and leave off for some other amusement before the music is done. He smiled slightly, hearing the soft clop of their chopines as they retreated across the floor rushes.

The young man threw the bolt of the door and once again flung himself into a chair by the player, taking up another cake and looking at it for a time. "How wondrous to be an actor and portray so many feelings of men!" he murmured. "To be one man and then another, instead of always the same one. I should like that."

With his delicate fingers moving over the embossed design on the silver cup he held, William answered, "Aye, my lord! Yet even a player when he goes home at the day's end is himself."

"A pox on that then! Doth nothing remain?"

"Oh well, mayhap. I have fancied myself many things, and in my writing still more."

"To be a king?"

"In some way, mayhap."

"Does your trade please you?"

He had made out the embossed design to be the Southampton crest, and slowly stroked it as he replied. "I believe it does. At times very much. At other times, 'tis hard and I would like to lie and sleep . . . aye, to sleep a long time, and forget the things I've left undone! I am a lazy man, as my father used to say at times when I would lie abed reading. 'Will, great lout, arise! The clock's struck eight and the day half done, arise!' " He laughed, and putting down the cup, lightly slapped his palms upon his now dryer wool hose.

The boy demanded passionately, "Is now one of the times it pleases you to play upon the boards?"

"Mayhap—I cannot say." His own words startled him, for it was as if a man, long contentedly married, were to be asked of a sudden, "Art pleased to have a wife?" and find himself murmuring, "Nay, I know not." He gazed at the fire irons with their handles of a bare-breasted woman and said with some confusion, "'Tis a complicated matter, to be fond of or to despise your trade! A man finds something he can do not too badly, or is apprenticed to this or that, or falls into a trade by birth! 'Tis thereafter melded to him, and he perhaps becomes what he does. Have I answered you, my lord?"

The young man burst out, "Say on."

Suddenly feeling very much the glover's son, and remembering the muck of his own street and the man boiling bones in the yard, William murmured, "As you will, my lord. I do not know in the end if I have much of interest to say. I am a simple man with some gift of words, that is all."

"Oh, I do not find you simple!" cried the Earl fastidiously. "I do not find you simple in the least, for I don't care for simple people! But then who is that way, truly? We are all so complex! I have one understanding of myself, and then I appear in ways that I could never expect. I have one understanding, for instance, of my mother, and she another. We see two different people. But you are not simple, Shakespeare! Stay a time, and give me a game of chess."

The board was brought and the marble pieces neatly stacked, though one pawn was missing and Southampton broke off one of his doublet buttons in its place. "I lost it, I know not where," he said.

The rain fell now softer as they bent their heads over the board by the light of three candles. In the end the Earl cried with some disgust, "You have let me take your Queen! Darst not do such! For the love of Christ who died for us, do not placate me—I am coddled so I shall soon be a pudding or cheese!" He sprang up as if the afternoon had been spoiled, folded his arms over his chest, and after a time looked up with a humble smile.

"I have a hasty temper," he said.

"My lord, I as well."

"May I ask something of you?"

"Oh, ask as you will."

"Do you have a love?"

"My lord, I have."

"Is she fair?"

"No, dark and bewitching."

"Ah! There's sport, as my men say. . . ." They laughed roughly, and if the Earl thought to carry the matter further, he did not. When they made to part he said amiably, "Will you send more poems?"

"I shall."

"When will come the next?"

"This very week."

"I shall write in thanks to you." The Earl smiled, and threw his voice low again so that he sounded surprisingly gruff. "I am your servant," he said playfully.

William gathered up the chess pieces and then, placing his hand over his heart, bowed slightly. "My lord," he replied.

WITHIN THE NEXT few weeks he brought over several more poems, and was twice entertained with the Earl's retainers when the talk was all of hunting and war, and once spent an hour alone with his lordship and another time found him gone out, the servants did not know where. Still, brief letters began to come now and then, slipped under the door and written in the boy's own hand, and gracefully sealed. William found them when he came in from rehearsal or a visit to the laundress.

My dear Shakespeare,

I am sorry to have been at my fencing when you came. My mother keeps me home and I am dull today. My guardian calls and lectures us both, and clears his throat. Thank you for the manuscript of the three Harry plays, which delight me. I hope the money was sufficient for the copying. We have the new sonnets, and the one that beginneth "When I do count the clock . . ." hath particularly pleased me. I would like to send you something for yourself, but am kept so short by Lord B. In all good faith and Christ's mercy,

S.

My dear Shakespeare,

Woke with a flux today. I want only to be at war and have fenced for an hour. Will you write perhaps sometime a comedy to be performed privately at my house, something about men sworn to adjure the society of the other sex? It would be fine merriment. Hast told me thy lady hath dark hair, so must make the lady of that coloring! Do: it will make me laugh.

My dear Shakespeare,

Went gambling last night in her Majesty's privy chamber and lost all I had and am melancholy. Nay, I have found one gold sovereign and here enclose it for what? Ale, cheese! Mayhap I shall disguise myself as a groom and go with thee. I take my rapier and thrust at curtains and shadows. Marlowe was here last night, and spoke of you as shy. What, are you so? I like you better for it. Write me a love poem, will you do that? That would be amusing.

I am going to my estates this week and hope to ride there before snow comes. I leave my mother and all, and just go. Come with me.

THE ESTATES OF Titchfield were towards the southern coast, and in a mad and precipitate gesture, Southampton forbade any of his retainers to come. In the cold grey of the December morning he walked with the player towards the stables, and selected two strong horses, and thus they

turned from the city past the old grocery shop and the bear garden. It
began to snow as they went on, both dressed in plain brown suits, heavy
woolen hose, and thick cloaks for the coldest weather; they wore also
swords, and the Earl had a pistol against robbers. Every now and then he
touched it, and then looked over his shoulder angrily as if he expected to
be followed, and then with a sweet shrug, began to breathe more easily.

"I cannot bear the lot of them," he proclaimed.

Arriving at farmlands and directing the horses towards the southwest,
they marked how the snow was tumbling to the fields and barren trees, the
thatched houses, and the occasional old stone manor as far as they could
see. They stopped in an inn for refreshment and to feed the beasts, and
went on. The wind blew from the sea far away, and the snow settled on
their thick gloves, and on the crevices of their sword hilts. Though they
told no man in stable or inn of the rank of the younger traveler, hosts and
boys responded with a certain wary deference.

For hours they talked of every manner of thing, and still the snow fell.
Then Wriothesley said eagerly, "Tell me of thy life, tell me everything."

"A long time to say it all, my lord."

"Begin then. . . . "

Village after village they passed, and still the snow fell without ceasing,
and for a time, when night began to come, they thought they had taken the
wrong turn and had no idea which way to go. Through the smell of frozen
wood and earth came the scent of a fire. William's heart spilled open, and
he spoke of things he had not remembered in years and knew his words
were heard by the intensely listening profile of his companion. The player
thought, He's deep and pure, and I believe I am beginning to know him as
none of his retainers or those relatives of his so high at court have ever
begun to do. Strange how he listens! Yet if he knew my thoughts, he might
rush up and away, like a bird. He must not know them.

With this some reserve came into his voice, and Southampton looked
over at him with some disappointment, and gradually ceased to speak as
well.

They turned off from the main road because the Earl swore he knew the
way, and then they were lost once more. Dismounting, they led the horses,
feeling their way through the forest, stumbling now and then in the snow;
the Earl cursed like a soldier, and outdoing each other in curses, they soon
were friendly again as if nothing had occurred. How delicate is friendship,

William thought. Like the life of a man, seemingly sturdy, and yet one unexpected sickness or knife's thrust can waste him to naught. You want with friendship to cup it securely within your hands, and yet there, without light or freedom, it withers. Then can anything last securely in all this mortal earth but a dingy faith in some eternal being, or perhaps our longing to have some importance to one another?

The lantern flame made shadows of dark trees, but they did not see low branches until they fell into one, and once William felt his leg go under him, and hoped it would not hurt him much. At last they came into a clearing and saw the shape of the great house, gates, and walled gardens, which had once been an abbey, before them. "I am master here!" cried Southampton, and cupping his mouth, shouted.

Men with flaming torches hurried towards them. "Hallo, my lord!" they cried anxiously. "What, can it be you indeed, worship? Good my lord, dear my lord, we have prepared nothing! You come without warning! We have not even time to gather holly berries to deck the hall!" They spoke in the scolding yet deferential way servants address a lord who used to come to them for comfort or sweets, and who has suddenly grown. They parted with many bows before their master, murmuring his name and flinging wide the door.

In the cold great hall with its armor and banners, his lordship's voice echoed imperiously to the musician's gallery. "My man and I are famished and near dead with cold! Bring the robes lined with fur that were my grandfather's, and make good the fire in the dining hall. We will have meat and bread and whatever food you have."

With his shoulder he thrust open doors into a smaller, wood-paneled hall which, after a bowing boy hurried about lighting torches in their wall brackets from one length to the other, showed grave and ugly portraits on wood and canvas of dead relatives. Southampton himself, his wet things half stripped away, began the fire. There was a long table with a shabby rug upon it, and the old rushes on the floor stank of dog and rancid scraps. Within minutes they were both enveloped in fur-lined robes, seated in great chairs whose upholstery had been half devoured by mice, their feet on stools before the blazing fire.

"Here silent monks gathered for dull prayers!" the lord said with some awe, pausing as he hurled off his wet hose to the grate. "They read tales of fasting, scourging, martyrdom with arrows and by grilling over a gridiron like roast mutton without thyme. This abbey was given my grandfather, the poor monks turned to the snow to beg, and now it's come to me. I wonder if they think of me at times. I, a sensual, life-loving man who believes not only in virtue but in joy as well. And thus we come here, I the lord of this windswept manor, and you as in times of old as my bard. Sing me a song, player Will, while we wait for our repast! Sing me of . . . valor! Art a poet—tell me of Henry that was at Agincourt."

He flung back his lovelocks boyishly, impatiently, and then cried out in a voice of scorn, "For we have no Henrys now upon the throne, but a crooked old lady with a crooked soul who seduces manhood, and eats and spits it out and ne'er opens her legs one jot but sayth, 'Marry, nay! Marry, nay!'" The Earl's voice rose to imitate her bark, and he lifted a sleeve of the fur to cover his face. "'Marry I shall, marry I shan't'! Marry, a fart on her marries and her barrenness and her use of men and of me." With that he leapt up and reaching high, took the picture of the young virgin Elizabeth, thought to put it in the fire, but turned it instead with its visage to the wall.

"There's my father's face looking down at us," he said with some awe, lowering his voice and pointing to a portrait of a kindly-looking man in his middle years. "And he loved her . . . but I say, a piss on her." He poured out the warm wine which had come and raised his glass to the ancestral portraits.

"Well and for that," returned William, drinking, "a piss on her."

"Drink to that, and to the downfall of tyrants in petticoats!"

"To their end!" cried the player. He gazed at Southampton, who had begun to stride up and down manfully, frowning at everything, the long dressing gown stirring up the dust in the rushes. Though London was many miles over snowy roads, he suspected the Earl could even now hear the scratch of his mother's pen as she wrote to him, "Dear sweet heart, to run off so suddenly! What means this, my Harry? Thy guardian is most displeased." Even now it seemed the Earl walked quickly to escape the thought.

Wiping his mouth, the lovelocks now drying in a frizzy way, the long legs bare under the dressing gown, the young lord began to speak again. "Shakespeare, listen! I believe you are my friend. Would you truly have them mortgage me at eighteen years to a bride, a bride all cosseted in whalebone stays and farthingale, to make another of me? Do you think I should make another of me? Do you think it true? Christ's wounds, I want to show forth the one I am without another." He drank again and said angrily, "Poet, thou hast pleaded falsely."

"I pleaded thy mother's plea."

"For coins!"

William leaned forward with his arms out and then, bending over, became the crafty beggar at the gate. "Oh, a coin or two, good master!" he whined. "A half penny . . . mercy . . . oh, I die for lack of sustenance! Knowst I am but a poor player, and must beg at Christ's gate for succor . . . good my lord, alms, alms, and do not spurn me!"

The Earl burst into laughter, leapt up, and flung open his arms. "Christ, pisspot!" he cried. "Oh thou devil, whoreson! You shall have all the food when they send it up from the kitchen. Why hath it not come? In Henry's day they whipped the scullions for slowness. I would not do such a thing, wanting to be loved. Aye, I want love and never have enough of it, but more, I want respect. . . ." His voice had grown bewildered, and then he began to stride up and down the chamber again, and from the end of it, his voice echoing, shouted, "Amuse me while we wait for our meat! Act something else . . . be . . . I know, the Archbishop."

"Wait . . . now . . ." Pompously William began to walk, chin up in the air, while the boy beat upon the table in his joy.

"Ah, that's the old fellow, I have sat through enough of his sermons! And now, someone else . . . the Queen!"

"The Queen!" William leapt on the table and, thinking for a moment, suddenly bent his back and began to wag his finger and speak in a low, seductive, reproving, elderly voice. "Sooouthampton! Boy! Wilt not do as thou art told! Bad fellow—wilt go to wars! Bad! There, I shall lock thee in thy chamber, wicked boy . . . Sooouthampton!"

The Earl threw himself into the rushes, tearing them up and throwing them over his head. Bits of foul straw, dust, and long-crumpled flowers fell down about him into his hair as he sat crosslegged, rocking with laughter. "Oh, God's love, I have disturbed a nation of fleas!" he cried. "Ah, my stomach! Nay, come here, master player, no more. I shall . . . die. . . ."

William leapt from the table and with a sweep of the robe, bowed low, and the Earl caught him, pulled him down, and pushing his face in the rushes, held him there. Gasping, the player protested, "I cry thee mercy, my lord! I cannot breathe. . . ."

"To demand I marry—"

"Mercy! I retract it all!" Released, he knelt beside the Earl, whose hair was covered with dried rushes, and slowly diverted his features and voice until it once more bore an uncanny resemblance to the aged virgin Queen's. "Slovenly!" he began again in the scolding voice of the old sovereign. "Shalt be locked in thy chamber, given no chance to mount my maids! How many of my maids have you mounted this morn before dinner, Sooouthampton!"

"Ah, God's wounds! Cease, for the love of Mary, cease!"

With a low creak, the doors opened, and three servants entered with trays. Southampton stood, and summoning his dignity, began to brush off his robe. Outside the wind had risen, and was blowing the snow about in heaps. He hurried out the door and to another, which when he opened it let the bitter gusts fly across the old straw, stirring their robes, their hair, the arras curtains, and the leaves of the dried flowers which had been left in a vase on the serving table. Gravely the servants bowed themselves out. The Earl cried then, "Come, guest! Let's sit not on benches but upon the table as if we were ourselves edibles, as we will one day be food for worms, and there discourse on life and love."

For a time they ate as if they could never bear to stop, hacking slices from the cinder-covered mutton and scooping the prunes and apples and fowl cooked in a pie with their hands. All the time the wind howled, and the flames leapt up.

"What songs," Southampton said breathlessly, "would minstrels sing here if this had been a castle rather than an abbey? Would the warriors come and, seeing me, take me with them as I so heartily desire they would do? Take the lad to war as he so heartily desireth to go, kick away mother and guardian and riches and all, and let him go in plain clothing, a man to the wars!" He drank more wine and then said more sadly, "In thy plays we can fancy ourselves anything! I would be an actor! I would be Talbot, dead for England."

"Was he the better for it, my lord?"

"His soul was. For what do most men but eat and drink and, sodden, take their rest? Are we fools to think a man is something more? Nay, nay—now I speak seriously. But first I must wear flowers. I have a fancy to it." He was somewhat drunk, and began to look about as if for flowers.

William leaned closer: even as he did so he knew that were he not also a little drunk he would not dare. "Are you sad?" he said gently.

"I am sad and will wear rosemary for remembrance in my hair," replied Southampton, breaking in a youthful voice into the old song of infidelity.

"By Gis and by St. Charity,
Alack and fie for shame
Young men will do't if they come to't
By cock, they are to blame.

"Quote she, 'Before you tumbled me,
You promised me to wed,'
'So would I have done by yonder sun,
And thou hadst not come to my bed.'

The Earl leapt down, ran to the walls, and took down two heavy broadswords. "Now we must fight!" he cried. "We must fight as the men of old when they were true men, as my namesake and great ancestor Harry the Fifth did at Agincourt. . . . Come, have at thee! They are rusty with the blood of the dead. Let us hold them in living hands." Taking one in both hands, he swung it. "Nay, take shields as well, take shields! You must defend yourself from me, player!"

With a cry they rushed each other, the player deftly allowing himself to be knocked backwards, then springing gracefully to his feet. Again and again they made at each other, now knocking one wine decanter and the plate of meat to the rushes, and the dogs, which had been let in, growled and barked at their long robes. These they cast aside, and fought on in their breeches until they could not breathe anymore, and Southampton leaned panting against the table.

"My heart beats so!" he cried. "How can a heart beat so within the chest of a man and not burst it forth? You're strong, though no longer young— why cannot we be the same years exactly! But you're already seven and twenty; it seems a great age."

They sat once more about the table, half pulling on the robes over their sweating bodies. "We needed fire before," the boy said, as if puzzled by his weariness. "And now we are in a heat from our passions. Soon it will be four and twenty hours since we left the city, and not have rested. Alas, though! I'm weary, too weary to bed, sweet Will, so we must stay up all night. Wilt bide with me?"

"My lord, I will."

"A piss on 'my lord' . . . Harry, as my friends call me!"

"A piss on that: hast said it."

"But you must say my name."

"Harry then, dear my lord."

The Earl held out the cup and leaned forward, putting his hand unsteadily on the player's shoulder. "More wine! Tell me everything. I have never yet lived, I know nothing. Oh, Christ! I am eighteen years and have not bedded a woman. No one knows this but thee: say you will not reveal it. Swear on thy life!"

Quietly William answered, "I shall tell naught ever, ever, that you have revealed to me. Nothing could ever make me say a secret of yours, my lord of Southampton."

Southampton thrust back his hair, and then, hanging his head so that the long face could not be seen, murmured wistfully in an almost inaudible voice, "Tell me how it is with your mistress . . . when you are together naked, how 'tis."

"How 'tis?" replied the player incredulously.

"Even so."

"You wish in truth to know this?"

"I do."

The player nodded, and with some gravity proceeded to elucidate upon the construction of women and the particular aspects of coupling, all the time leaning forward and gesticulating minutely with his hands, which made shadows on the wall. Then he concluded generously, "The truth must be, dear Harry, that each time it is different and with each particular damsel! Have we fought, are we tender, am I weary of my own thoughts, is she dull with hers? Ask the same, what 'tis like to speak to a friend? Why, in each speaking 'tis different even in each time. If she were thine, it would also be a different matter. But it's sweet. I know nothing sweeter than when she opens her body to me and is mine alone."

The Earl's face was also in shadows, but his breath deep and steady as he listened. Then he murmured, "I think of it sometimes, and then not again, but when I go to do it, I turn away with a sickness in my stomach, fearing I shall lose all I have. She'll be with child, and I bound to her forever—I who do not wish to be bound to anyone."

Rubbing his face sleepily, he looked up at last and yawned. "How much I like your poems!" he murmured. "Yet more than them, I like to be here alone with thee where no one knows we have come. You began to tell me something when we were riding before, and we broke it off when we turned roads. Our heavenly selves . . ."

"All of life consists of the struggle between our baser and our heavenly selves."

"Where does friendship come in that?"

"What is heavenly."

"Tell me some of the poems."

William shook his head slowly. "Nay, I am too drunk to remember any clearly, but in the morn if you give me pen and ink I shall write another."

"It is that simple for you?"

"Nothing is simpler."

"Sing me a song then."

"Oh, here's a fine one—

> "Whoso to marry a minion wife
> Hath good chance and hap,
> Must love her and cherish her all his life,
> And dandle her in his lap."

They mounted singing up the creaking step, one of the servants standing below rubbing his eyes resentfully, for he had yet to cover the fire and let the dogs into the yard. At the door of his bedchamber Southampton hesitated, and they listened to the wind rattling the roof and tile.

"Motley," Southampton said, "I'm fond on thee. You shall be my poet and I thy patron." He threw one arm around the player's neck. "God send thee sweet rest!"

William made his way up the steps, found his own room, and pulling close the heavy dusty bedcurtains, made himself a nest of blanket, sheet, and pillows in the bed which had been warmed by some servant but a little time before. Stretching his feet, he discovered a hot brick well wrapped in thick cloth. Then turning to his side, his hand under his cheek, he gazed into the dark, dusty hangings.

Dreams were strange. The snow had melted, and he walking on a road alone in the breeches and coat of his boyhood when there was heard the cries of a coachman and with a great holocaust of dust there came a carriage, its runaway horses with nostrils dilated and eyes bulging. And

William knew that Southampton was inside, and ran forward. He seized the horse by the halter, was dragged, choked with dust, struggled up, yanked, forced the two beasts to halt, though he heard his arm snap, and feared it broken. Then he flung open the door.

No one was inside but a small servant with bright eyes who never ceased to sew together a neat border on the slashing of a scarlet brocade doublet sleeve. Oh, the young master's not here, he said with pursed lips. Oh, he has gone gaming or a-playing of tennis! Why have you run so, fellow? Oh, close the door, close the door.

"His lordship left at dawn," the servant announced when William arose the next morning. "His attendants and his guardian's men came and needed him at once. He bade me say you might follow or remain as you like. Only let me know when the horse is to be made ready. He left this purse as well for your needs, and desired me to give my thanks, to send a man to accompany you, and to say he will send for you presently."

Thus William returned to the city, but no letters came from the young nobleman of Drury House. After some weeks he wondered if a messenger had arrived, and finding him not at home gone away, so he wrote his name on a larger scrap of paper and stuck it on the door. Still no word was sent, and the player fretted. It was like a deep conversation begun, one of the deepest of your life, when the person with whom you are speaking rises and excuses himself, saying, "Wait here . . ." and then does not return. Ashes from the fire settle in the wine cup, the bread grows hard, the tavern keeper puts up the shutters. The words he would say dried on his lips. He was beginning to write the history of Richard who killed the princes in the tower, and put much of his confusion into it.

There is a strange occurrence that comes now and then into the lives of strong people when they feel with a terrible anguish that everything that they have done, felt, been to this moment has been wrong and that they have seen a perfection, and cannot obtain it; that everything they have ever done to this point has been of little value. He thought then of his mother, whose grave dignified face when raised in the hope of affection reminded him of the countenance of the skilled embroideress who was attached to Drury House and always seemed to be on her knees measuring the span of a window cushion. Like her and any other of his social standing, William Shakespeare was able to be no more than his lordship's servant. Had he ever fancied himself more? By some heavenly decision or a more mundane path of human fate some generations before, Southampton's lot had been cast among the highest-born of the land and his own among actors and tradesmen. The pride of his heart cried out against such an absurd separation.

His lordship had a fascination for commoner things, desiring tales of tavern life, the world of seamen who set out in their boats hours before dawn, of blacksmiths, of farmers; of streets, alleys, of not the life of theater which the audience saw, but the true one of camaraderie and discipline. He was much moved by the story of a Warwickshire shepherd who at the age of six and ninety still drove out his sheep each morn. He wanted to know of couples, copulating in poverty, whose rank cottage spilled with fifteen dirty children. William drew in his breath and grimaced when he recalled the stories he had told. Did this nobleman in his silks find a poetry in the relentless work which destroyed all dreams but of the bravest man? Did he suppose the brown flesh of gleaning pauper women was as soft as that of those wellborn young women who for a betrothal contract or even the hint of one would be more than happy to copulate with him?

Scorn rose, and he curled his lip as he went about his work; it passed into wistfulness once more. He thought of many things in those days, of his childhood and of the years since he had come to the city.

He recalled the sea.

He had seen those vast waters for the first time a few autumns before at Dover as they surged towards foreign shores. The players had come to tour, and he had left them in the inn and gone out to walk alone. Stripping off shoes and hose, he had wandered for some time along the edge of the tide, kneeling now and then to pick up rare shells, once arcane housing for creatures whose bodies were no more. He had taken up this one and that, seizing the prettiest, and then as he held it in his hand, noticing the light move from it. It was only an empty carapace, slightly broken, in his palm, whose lines were delineated with the wetness.

As he walked he had reviewed much of his life from its earliest days, distracted now and then by a shell or two. When at last he returned to the inn, where the other players wondered what kept him so late, he had left the shells on a rock behind him, keeping only the memory of them. The next day they were gone, for the sea had claimed them. He was astonished at the childish sadness he felt at this, which he would not for his honor express to anyone.

He walked through London with such thoughts as these until, in spite of the crowds that moved about him, he felt himself the only one left in all the world. He only knew he had in the past months gained something ineffably precious, and now, uncertain if it remained his, he did not know how he could bear to be without it.

Yet in all of this he was extraordinarily busy trying to understand how he could earn his bread, for plague in the city had again closed the doors of the theaters. He could write plays, but no one needed to buy them. There was but one trade he knew, and now it had been taken from him, and the letters home were full of excuses and little else. Bad enough to be treated at times like a vagabond in his work, asked to show his papers from the protector of the troupe which certified his honesty, bad enough that that protector was the man with whom he shared his mistress! Sometimes he walked over to watch Jonson carefully laying his bricks, and they sat upon the unfinished wine cellars eating bread and discussing the vagaries of life, for Benjamin had married a sweet, honest girl and was very happy. Once he went with some shame to borrow money from John Heminges, who in his careful husbandry always had some tucked away, and to pour out his frustrations. What had they all chosen? What were they to do? They toured briefly, and returned with little more than they had before.

His consolation in those months was to wander over evenings that cold winter when he was in the city to spend the night in the arms of the Italian girl, where her small erect breasts and warm thighs became a place to lose himself. It was now Emilia's custom to fasten a yellow silk handkerchief to her window frame when Lord Hunsdon was not at home to let the player know he might hurry to her warm bed. He had begun to write of lovers in Verona, based on an old play which she liked very much, and they lay together with the snow rushing against the window, leaving ice on the little yellow silk, and read her verses here and there.

> O, speak again, bright angel! for thou art
> As glorious to this night, being o'er my head,
> As is the wingèd messenger of heaven . . .

They drew the bedcurtains and placed a candle holder carefully on the sheet before them, drank wine, and talked of the warm cities of Italy. They had become accustomed to each other, she to his travels, touring, and sometimes dark moods, he to her petty and greater untruths, her vanity and suspicious nature. Thus he told her less and less of what was in his heart, nor did he ever mention to her the name of the young nobleman to whom he felt a closeness he had never felt in his life before, and from whom he now was apart. He did not understand that he was gradually withdrawing from his friends; once John mentioned it, and he shrugged moodily and said it could not be.

Of late he felt he was becoming, under the jester and good fellow, a much quieter man. Perhaps the ghosts of the evicted monks in the country house in the snow had come into his soul, and bade him keep his peace.

APRIL SAW THE delivery of the last of the short sequence of sonnets to Drury House. No one was home to receive them, but an usher gave him a small bag of coins and wished him good day. Early spring brought no warmth, and a servant swept the walk with a scratch of broom, chasing away one errant leaf that tossed up and scattered back.

He looked back at the great house, whose windows glittered darkly, and if someone watched from within he could not be seen. His heart was very heavy. Still, why should he deserve more? The young lord was the darling of the court and praised by many poets, all far better known than himself. William walked away through the noise and mud of the city.

Yet though the theaters looked to open again and he had begun a long lyrical poem on the loves of Venus and Adonis, he found himself that day unable to concentrate on the romantic speech of the eager goddess and her young lover, who preferred the hunt. Pushing aside the rough pages, he sat with hands open at the table, gazing towards the creaking window shutters, vaguely hearing the sounds of carts and carriages and peddlers from Bishopsgate below as if they were centuries from him. With a sudden movement he took a clean paper, and digging the quill's nub into the page until it was dented, began a letter.

My lord, I trust you have received the sonnets and must confess I have writ more but these from my own private soul, and not for hire. Thus you have stayed in my mind. But have I offended you that you do not send for me? Only let me know in what way I have done so, for more than any gold you can send, you yourself are dear to me. Believe that truly, for it is the truth as I am honest.

In all duty,
your lordship's servant,
W. Shakespeare

He sent it by a wet, ragged lad and was arriving at the theater shortly past noon that very day when the boy returned with the damp reply stuffed in his shirt.

Come if you will. Southampton.

EARLY SPRING SUN was shining through the receiving room of Drury House, glittering on the silk and silver threads in the armorial hangings and on the curling daisies of the embroidered table rug. From the corner ticked the pendulum of the tall clock, as if no time had passed at all since the player had last heard his footsteps whisper on the floor mats. The desk was laden with many papers, and the chair pushed back as if the young Southampton had leapt up at the sound of the opening doors. He now stood by the window with his back to the room, the deep gold hair tangled about the collar of his full, sweeping dressing gown, which gave him the air of an impatient, wealthy abbot.

When he turned, his beautiful face was lightly flushed as if he had been woken from an uneasy sleep. With his hands in the belt of the gown, he narrowed his eyes and inclined his head slightly at the player's bow.

"God give you a good day, Shakespeare."

"And you, my lord. I hope you have been well."

"God gives me good health." Then as if with embarrassment he muttered, "I meant to send for thee."

"I am your servant, my lord, and await your pleasure."

The Earl's pale face seemed to darken, and he thrust back his hair. "Why did I not send?" he muttered. "I am like that of times. Art dear to me. The truth is, I find you both strange and somehow bitter to the taste like radishes, bitter and sharp and then again so sweet it startles me and I know not what to make of it! I go to the theater with my men and see you play this role and that. You're a clever man, not a great actor as Burbage or Alleyn, but somehow wiser. I read the Henry plays yet again, and wish myself within them." He hesitated and then added, "I have at times longed to be here with you."

William felt his heart constrict in his chest, but he only bowed. The confused resentment of the months of silence following their closeness rushed upon him, and he pushed them back.

The young man continued a little uneasily. "Such as it is—I think all people who are dear come to have a certain power over us, and I felt mayhap you did—that 'twas more yours than mine. When thy letter came, I looked for a sonnet—none was sent. I was disappointed, I know not why."

Though the player's words were unfailingly polite, he could not entirely disguise his resentment. "My lord has many poets," he said. "Each one is hungry and hopes for a patron, and flatters you for this cause. We all flatter you, but truly this is the way of society. There is no harm in it, only at times for some, a little pain."

The young man looked up at once, murmuring, "And to whom cometh this pain?"

"To the one who feels sincerely."

"Have you flattered me as well?"

"Mayhap."

"Have you said things never meant?"

With his voice lower, and gazing at the pattern of flowers in the brocaded table rug, the player answered roughly, "No, my lord," and then bit his tongue. He would at that moment have liked to leave the room, but could think of no excuse to do it.

Southampton threw down the tassel with which he had been playing and, standing, cried, "I thank the saints for that! We had some merry times! Why did I cease to send for you? I don't know. Why did you write such a letter to me?"

"I cannot answer that."

"But Shakespeare! I freely give the right."

The player grimaced again, and walked to the mantel to study the silver vase upon it with its engraving of Minerva and its praise of the aging sovereign . . . *O Elizabeth, Queen!* "I cannot tell you what I do not know," he said with difficulty. "Will you ask of falconry or hunting the deer at dawn? Or the sweetness of stolen deer meat? Of the things I cared for as a lad? That I could tell you well. Will you ask of faith in others like a banner singed and torn and yet lifted high and run with by some stupid lad who knows no bet-

ter but that this is honor and he will uphold it until he falls? I am a country man, my lord, a glover's son. Why do you ask of me more? Of the com-
plexities of my heart, and when I would be loyal and when betray, I know
little. I do not know, or mayhap would not look, for mayhap what's within
my heart would put me to shame. I do not write lines for some player now,
but must speak myself, and that is a burningly private matter!"

He felt Southampton looking at him deeply. "Do you feel things you
cannot express?" said the lord. "I think rather it is 'will not.' No man is as
clever with words as thee. I have been in your company too much not to
know it! And yet you hide behind it."

Drawing in a deep, sharp breath, William answered, "I must: my throat
burns with shyness, with reluctance to speak words concerning my own
heart. Where I am from, dear my lord, it is not manly to speak overmuch.
We live and feel deeply, though we are silent concerning much; we die,
and the memory of us is soon gone. I am my father's son, a little stern,
mayhap a little dull. I cannot allow myself to know all that I feel and
desire, for I would disapprove of it, and 'tis difficult to live in the same
body with a man whose company you frown upon. I stand here not as Will
the man who writes fine speeches, but as a Will I do not know. He is a
stranger to me, my lord, and I am almost a little afraid of him, for I do not
know what he will do to disgrace me."

Southampton came towards him and stood close, biting his lip and
looking this way and that, the slender chest moving under the long, cler-
ical gown. He burst out, "I have known no man like thee, Will."

"Nor I thee, my lord . . . or shall I say 'Harry,' as you have asked me once
to do."

"Ah, do not . . ."

"Pray, my lord," answered William, compressing his lips once before
speaking. "Do you not wish me to call you so?"

"No, call me by my name."

"Then what? What is the matter I should not?"

"Do not praise me because I am thy patron."

"I never will do so."

"Swear on thy life."

"My lord, I thus swear."

Confronting him, yet arms crossed over his chest to protect himself, the
Earl demanded, sticking forth his chin as a boy challenges another behind

the schoolyard, "Then why did you write?"

"Why? Thy company's dear, and missing it, I do not know where I stand. I had a life without it, dear my lord, and now to be without it seems such a deprivation that it hurts me to my soul."

"But I do not know what I want of thee!" cried the Earl. "I do not know what I want or can have. . . ." He took the player by the sleeves as if to entreat something of him, and then, bending suddenly, kissed him fully on the lips. William's eyes darkened. Unthinking, he put up his hands as if to defend himself, and found he was shaking so he could not speak.

The Earl folded his arms across his chest once more. "Well, so it is, and I have missed thee as well," he murmured. "I have a strange love for thee, I know not from where it comes. I want thy stories and thy wisdom and cannot quite put thee from my heart."

Suddenly striding to the window, he stared out into the gardens. "I am used to servants," he said resentfully, "and yet you are somewhat more, but how you came to be that, I do not know." Then, passing his hand over his mouth, he cried violently, "I want something to die for, I truly do! I want to go away to war and die young in honor. Ah, God, why am I so many men in one flesh? For one of them would go away just with you, and I know not why. We must go away, we must go to war together! We must live and die for each other the way men did in days of old."

As if he could bear no more, he walked quickly to the table, took from the rug his sword, uncovered it, and balancing it on his knee, began to rub at the blade with a soft cloth. "My father said a man must polish his own sword," he murmured. "Wait, before I have forgot! Take this, 'tis money and thine. Take it and let us not think of it again! You have need of it . . . take it, take it!"

William did not move, though his lips still burned with the kiss and his throat remained as hot and dry as if the cinders of it had singed him. "Then hear another poem to thee," he said. "I would not have sent it." Leaning against the heavy broad table near the bowl of rose petals, he took out some sheets from his doublet. For a time he hesitated, and then, look-ing away to the large windows which opened to the yard below, began to speak with great simplicity.

> "When, in disgrace with fortune and men's eyes,
> I all alone beweep my outcast state

> And trouble deaf heaven with my bootless cries,
> And look upon myself, and curse my fate,
> Wishing me like to one more rich in hope,
> Featur'd like him, like him with friend possess'd,
> Desiring this man's art, and that man's scope,
> With what I most enjoy contented least . . ."

Southampton did not look up but continued to polish his sword; the long hair fell down over his dark, frowning face as from below came the barking of dogs, and the laughing of a servant girl.

> ". . . Yet in these thoughts myself almost despising,
> Haply I think on thee, and then my state,
> Like to the lark at break of day arising
> From sullen earth, sings hymns at heaven's gate;
> For thy sweet love remember'd such wealth brings
> That then I scorn to change my state with kings."

The young Earl was silent for some moments when the poem was done, almost as if he expected more. Then he put down the sword. "I am not worth that, but I do thank thee, William," he murmured, standing clumsily. Walking across the room, he took the player's arms as if to congratulate him.

William replied nothing, but raising Southampton's right hand, kissed the palm of it thoughtfully, then bowed and left the room.

THEY DID NOT see each other for some time. Southampton fell into some minor disgrace at court and went to France, and William reluctantly packed his things to tour again. The small company of men and boys took a much abbreviated version of the Henry plays, each actor taking upon himself so many roles that he now and then rushed as the wrong character into the wrong scene, or began to speak in a broad French accent when he was to portray an English churchman. Each evening there was a reckoning of the sum which had been taken at the door. He finished the first half of the Richard play by the inn's kitchen fire one night with the singing of crickets in the high grass beyond the stone walls. *Deform'd, unfinish'd, sent before my time into this breathing world, scarce half made up, and that so lamely and unfashionable that dogs bark at me, as I halt by them . . .* The kitchen maid, standing with a great pot in her hands, winked as he looked up; he stared at her. Later he would wake many a night with the words on his lips.

May had come, and once he slept in a field rather than endure the filth of another cheap inn. Lying on his back under the trees, he began to consider what the Earl had once lightly told him, that his youth was gone. His mind passed from his children to Southampton, who must be even now being entertained in some glittering Parisian home, joining the men at gambling, which he loved to do. The young man wrote but once, and that briefly, and William wondered if Southampton had now wearied of his poetry, preferring Marlowe's more fiery lines. If he should be cast away! What did he have? His life, with all its variety, seemed strangely empty, as if his soul had left it. He did not think of the kiss, which confused him, and which he could not understand.

He had come home again and was sitting in his room on a sunny June afternoon mending one of his hose when two of the actors hurried up the stairs, hardly able to speak for their tears. Marlowe was dead.

William hurried at once to Drury House, running up the stairs to the Earl's sleeping chamber, where he found Southampton lying facedown on his bed. "The fool, the fool!" the Earl whispered. "A tavern fight! But didn't we know it would be like this?" Leaping up, he began to stride up and down the room, and when he passed the table in his agitation his swinging arm swept a glass of Venetian blue to the floor.

William walked slowly down to the river: tears clawed at his throat, and dried again. He stood hunched and staring over the dirty water at the theater across the way. Picking up a rough stave, he beat it against a part of the crumbling wall, the last of which fronted the Thames from the oldest days. The world could die for all he cared, but for a few he loved most dearly: one of those had been Christopher, and now he should never be able to tell him.

Not knowing what else to do, he returned to his work. In his room, stiff parchment, torn from the accounting book of some defunct monastery, was bound with string about the individual packets for unfinished plays. Each packet held notes and history, on which were scribbled such words as "But was there no kindliness in Richard's heart at all?" or "See Tom Morley for the serenade melody by Midsummer." Still another bit of parchment contained the growing number of sonnets which were his private world. He was often too busy to see Emilia.

Months passed until the first frost came to the city. He was finishing the comedy he had promised to the Earl; at times he found it tedious and at others laughed aloud, throwing down his pen in joy. Sometimes he did not wish to work on it, and other times could not keep from the pages. It told the story of several young men of good birth who made a vow to abjure the company of women and live an abstemious life of study for three years' time. The aspiration is not realized, for they each fall in love and thus betray the others and submit to the ways of all men. It was to be a private performance, with much of their secret wit bound within the lines. He called it *Love's Labour's Lost*, and it was to be performed at Drury House on Twelfth Night.

SMOKE OF THE perfumer still lingered above the rushes of the principal rooms when the actors, musicians, prop masters, and boys arrived hours early to erect their platform. Two nearby chambers were given them to dress, and soon the chests and benches were covered with wigs and costumes, gloves, feathered hats, farthingales, and stomachers. A cracked mirror stood alone to the side, and as the hour grew near to ten of the night when the play would begin, the general fluster of things undone which proceeds every performance increased like rising voices.

Instructing, cajoling, and sometimes shouting, being asked every question from entrances to repetitions of a dance step to the tilt of a hat, William rushed among them. Someone had forgot the music to a song, and it was agreed to substitute another. In a corner men and boys counted under their breath, rehearsing the final dance in the diminutive space. He was to play Berowne himself, the third courtier who abjures love and pleasure for three years, and stood muttering his lines with a frown on his face as another actor laced the stuffed silver-embroidered slashed sleeves to his doublet.

Through the slightly opened door, he could look into the hall. It was no longer dim and empty with its unoccupied chairs and benches, but now glittered with uncountable numbers of candles while the sound of feminine laughter like the tinkling of small bells rose up to the high ceilings. This was not the ordinary audience come to stand about in all weathers in the open theaters, but was composed of the dignitaries of the court, who were here as much to be beheld as to see the play. Clusters of women perfumed like flowers wandered about greeting each other, moving sideways at times to accommodate their heavy farthingales; each wore her family's fortune in gowns and jewels, each had her bosom exposed to the depth of crevice and her hair wound up with pins and fragrant oils. Men from the law temples or the courts had perfumed their beards and boasted heavy velvet suits embroidered with gold thread, the breeches and arms of the doublet thickly stuffed with bombast. Servants moved among them with deference, offering trays of sweetened wine, of pastries, of meat tarts flavored with rosemary.

His stomach tightened: it must not fail to go well.

Emilia had also come with friends, wearing a golden yellow kirtle and dress, and pearls woven here and there into her thick, high hair. On elevated chopines she tripped about the room, her white bosom bare and glimmering in the candlelight. She seemed a jewel among shoddier pieces as she stopped to embrace one woman or another, and a thrill moved through William, for though no one knew it, she was in truth but his alone.

The trumpet blew, and the acting men and beautiful young boys with bodices stuffed with bunched fabric to make them shapely gathered about the door. Then the musicians struck up the dance, and with a cry the players entered, carrying torches before them. The audience had drawn about on benches or chairs, or stood muttering softly and laughing to each other over the words as the first scenes passed by with the prince and his courtiers forswearing love. As soon as William left the stage he hurried about the tiring room encouraging the boys to let their voices ring out, noticing the faulty tuning of an instrument, a poorly gartered pair of silk hose. Scene followed scene. The foreign princess and her ladies captivated the hearts of the men; the clown and schoolmaster and pastor had their scenes as they also wrestled with the predicament of love.

He was everywhere; not once did he stop for a drink of ale.

Love was proclaimed triumphant, the final dance was given, the actors made their bows, and from various parts of the room came a few voices calling for the poet. In his long curly wig and white doublet embroidered with silver, William emerged to acknowledge the men who had proclaimed his name. He did not know whether it was the candles or his pride made his face burn so, or the understanding that Southampton, whom he had not seen in a long time, had hurried to the platform's edge to clap and shout.

The Earl caught his arm as he stepped from the stage. "Well done!" he whispered. "How cleverly you worked in our friends, good Florio and others—I laughed until I ached."

The whisper of approval was such a benediction that William felt flushed as with a fever, yet seeing so many men about them, he lowered his voice and murmured only, "My lord is kind."

"Come, I must have private words with you!"

Drawing the player into a passageway down which servants hurried with trays of wine and sweets, the Earl began to shake him playfully, and then, pushing him against the paneled wall, whispered impetuously in his ear, "Ah, you very devil! I have this night found out which lady's thine—the swarthy little foreigner with full bosom and dark hair! And now I have the reason I have not seen you—'tis because of her!" The young man's voice was sulky, and when William looked more closely he saw to his amazement that there was genuine hurt in his eyes.

He replied quietly, "My lord, I must protest! Hast not seen me because you did not send for me."

"But what a lady you've chosen, Shakespeare! All the city knows she's mistress to her Majesty's soldier cousin. You devil! Then you don't mind to share her . . ."

At that moment several men came by to speak to the Earl, who began to punch them roguishly in the arm; their voices rose in shouts. William could hear his fellows retreating to remove their costumes. He was disappointed that an intimate conversation had been so abruptly broken away, and when Southampton returned to him distracted, he was suddenly sick of all the house and its titled guests who snubbed him, and only wanted to be away where he could consider whether he had succeeded or not. The Earl began to talk of his anger at the Queen, which had been aroused by something said to him; he thrust back his hair and then, leaning against the wall, lowered his voice and began to drift into other thoughts as if he had forgotten both the play and the lady. He was somewhat drunk, though only the beautiful eyes revealed it, or a slight stumbling on a word or two.

From the other room came the burst of laughter of some remaining guests, and the sounds of chairs and other small furnishings which had decorated the platform stage being taken away. With a slight bow, William said, "The players have need of me, my lord, and I must bid you good night."

"Ah!" cried the young man. "That's not charitable! In the name of mercy, must stay with me until the guests are gone. My mother's here, and I cannot bear it. Wait! We will find some tavern and go disguised; we shall be two German travelers who cannot wrap their tongues about English! Come!"

William shook his head and replied, "That must be on the morrow, for none knows the work to be done as I do." He did not add, But you will not send for me then. . . . He was increasingly sad, and did not wish to reveal it.

But the Earl cried out, "Ah, Shakespeare! Would you did not go now! No man is free in life, is he? You are freer than ever I shall be, I swear it. Good night, you pisspot!"

William slowly walked through the emptying hall, smiling wryly at the few remaining compliments, and once in the tiring room again, began wearily to remove the silver embroidered white satin costume and the wig and headdress, and to rub the rouge from his face and lips with a cloth. Had he expected more honor, or that thanks would linger? His head ached, and he had no wish now but to go home alone to his bed with his inexplicable discontentment and bury it within his pillow.

Yet no soon had they all boarded the rocking ferry at the docks to ride downstream to a wharf closer to their own streets than he remembered Emilia Bassano's coy glance at him, and suddenly more than solitude he wanted the solace of her soft body. "Come, I must go off!" he murmured, climbing over John Heminges. "Do move thy knees, Jack, so I do not overturn us."

"Where do you go, pray?"

"Here and there." By the wherry's lantern, he gazed at his friend, concealing what expression he could in his face and voice, understanding how much the man knew him. Do what he might, say what he would, the damnable man knew him. He thought of the seasons they had spent together in the grocery shop on the south side, the poverty and the parsimony. At times they had wept before each other: what greater intimacy could there be? And he looked down at John's hand, which lightly held his arm, to steady him or restrain him he could not say.

With emotions heavy enough to burst through doublet and cloak, he gazed away at the dark river water and said with a forced laugh, "We do go different ways, Jack! What we want's not always the same. Should it be? You the family man, I in my own way free."

He felt the hand on his arm tighten a little, and his friend's cold mustache brush against his ear. "William, do you go to the musician Bassano?

She's our patron's mistress! Should he find you out, you may be set upon by his men, or imprisoned, and we may find ourselves forbidden to play. 'Tis unlike you to be so careless."

"He'll not find out."

"So say you, goodman."

With a jerk, William pulled his arm away and stood up. Leaping gracefully to the wharf, he swept off his hat and made a bow to the small wherry of actors. Then he untied the rope, hurled it to the ferryman, and watched it pull away into the sound of oar scooping deep water. The lantern threw but faint light upon the river, and after a time the wherry seemed to meld into the darkness and to have gone as thoroughly as if it had never existed, as if actors and props had somehow been taken into another world and he left in this one with his uncomfortable desires, standing on a wet wharf alone with the empty warehouses about him.

Hurriedly he began to mount the familiar moonlit streets towards the west to the house of Lord Hunsdon and his lady, such as she was. Oh, Emilia! Swarthy and untruthful, fascinating and leaving him wanting so often that he returned again and again to find within her arms something he began to suspect would never be there! There was the beauty of her, the woman men sighed over and she was his alone; that flattered and aroused him. He, the country lad, to have won and kept such a beauty! Hunsdon, their protector, who could not take her, was of little consequence, he thought scornfully. The man with all his money would have writhed to understand that he was of such little consequence at all.

Thus he came through the back orchard to the little courtyard with its water fountain and statuary, and whistled under his breath with joy at the limp yellow silk handkerchief which dangled from the window, announcing that he might with impunity mount up to her. She had given him a key to come after the old woman was asleep, and this he fit to the lock, and slipped inside, feeling his way up the dark steps. As he went he recalled the sound of the several people who had clapped, and how they had called for him, and his heart swelled with pride.

The room was perfectly dark, and smelled of guttered candles, and the dust of the tapestries, and somehow the perfume of her swarthy little body. He could barely make out the great skirts of her evening dress embroidered with brown roses which had been flung over a chair, and the tangle of a white silk stocking which lay in the rushes before it. Silently he began to walk across the floor, his shoes bending the dry grass with a slight crinkle of sound, his groin warm with anticipation of her touch.

Then he became quite still. With his finger against the covered buttons of his doublet under which his heart had begun to beat a little faster, he listened. The bed creaked, and there was a murmur and then another . . . then a soft laugh, only the laughter was not hers. It was a male voice, and he thought, God's wounds, 'tis my lord Chamberlain! Jack was right and now there'll be the devil to pay!

He would have left, quietly, sick and trembling, had he not heard the low laughter again, for it was not that of an old man at his pleasure, but of someone far younger.

Without moving, as he had listened in the woods when hunting, he put up his head and sniffed at the air. Then he reached in his pocket and struck his flint, lighting the little candle he always kept about him. The sound, however soft, and the low light cut through the dusty air of the chamber. There was a sudden silence from behind the bed hangings.

In one moment he had yanked back the curtain. The dim candle fell unevenly on Emilia's naked breasts and next to her another body, masculine, with much wider shoulders. With strength he did not know he had he pulled them both up, and looked into the face of Henry Wriothesley.

With a shout, William turned and knocked everything from the dressing table; the candle fell to the rushes, and the weeping Emilia dropped to her knees, snatched at it, and smothered the flame with her hands. It was the last he saw of her that night, on her knees with the faint burning smell of a few of the rushes rising in the night and her hair covering her face like a curtain. Him he could not remember at all, but as something painfully slender, white, vulnerable, and damned whom he had dared not touch any more than you will reach to touch a ghost which hurries past you from where you cannot say.

HE COULD NOT go home to the emptiness of the room, to the half-written scenes of love in the Verona play, and the beginnings of sonnets and the letters from him and the notes from her with her poetry, and the presence of both of them who meant so much to him. Instead he walked, pausing now and then in his very exhaustion, to the Theater outside the city walls. The watchman nodded pleasantly, expressing little surprise at the early arrival, for William was known for his diligence. He shut himself in the tiring room, and with his back to the door, gazed stupidly at the costumes. The memory of what he had found returned, and he groaned and drove his fist against the door until the knuckles were scraped and bloodied.

Dawn had not yet crept over the steeples of the city when he heard the sound of a horse, a command given the watchman, and someone trying the door against which he had remained standing, startled by the pain of his bruised hands, gazing stupidly about him at all the familiar things and seeing nothing. Then he unbolted the latch and stepped aside. Without looking, he could feel the shy, furious breath of the young nobleman behind him.

The Earl cried, "I looked for your at your lodgings and everywhere else. Will you not listen, Shakespeare?"

"I will not."

"I am not entirely at fault."

"Indeed, my lord?"

"At least hear my words."

"Can I prevent them?"

"I merely approached to kiss her hand, for we'd seen each other before but never spoken. This was when the musicians were playing an interlude before you came on once more in your part. And then when you were dancing on the boards we stood close, and she asked me to come to her that night. I said I would not for your honor, that she wronged you to ask, and still I could not put her from my mind. Later when the play was done, I begged you not to leave me because I knew myself tempted, because I had never yet—but you did leave, Shakespeare! Did I not ask you to stay?"

"She asked you."

"Aye, plainly. Oh, it was so much of nothing, this bedding! 'Tis sport, but next to friendship . . ."

He attempted to take William's arm, but the player with a shout broke from him. Throwing his voice into the mellow tones of the countryside, he said scathingly, "Do you dare come here?"

"I did not mean you to know!" came the reply.

"Would it be less harm to have kept it secret?" William answered. Turning to take hold of some of the thick costumes which hung from heavy wood racks, he began to pull one down, and then another and more, taking the bulk of their thick brocade and stuffing, their painted fleurs-de-lys and cloth of gold, and with all his strength hurling them to the floor between them as if a barricade which could never be breached.

"Do you see this, my lord?" he cried. "Look here, look here! Here are kings, here are bishops . . . here's a crown, and here a mitre, painted cloth, cleverly dyed, cleverly ornamented though this cloth is no more gold than I am a wise old fellow to trust a friend. These are costumes of roles, and are of themselves empty. . . ." Violently he threw down another, and kicked the pile aside. "Here is emptiness, my lord . . . but before you myself, a man who grieves! A man who grieves that you whom he loves so betrayed him! Are you so protected that you know not right from wrong, or that if you stab me I will not bleed? Do you not know that, Southampton?"

The flushed young man had come forward with his hands humbly extended as if to stop the tirade of words. William moved his own hand to push him away. "I beg thy pardon with all my heart!" Southampton gasped. "I thought you did not mind to share her. She's free enough, being Hunsdon's whore and before that, God only knows . . ."

"My lord, be silent!" At that moment William would have struck him; he could think only of the box of staves and dulled swords some feet from his hand, and how he could have taken one up with the swiftest, easiest gesture.

There was some time before either moved. Then Southampton's voice broke and he swallowed several times, and angrily turned away. "I have wounded you deeply," he said, and began to weep. "My God, my God, I have wounded you, Shakespeare!"

The player, dazed by exhaustion and feeling, stood stunned. For a moment he wished he had never seen the young man, and could go away. Then, as if in answer, compassion and love began to rise within his chest; it had nowhere to go, for it squeezed his ribs until they felt to crack and crumble.

Southampton had sunk to the floor with his arm over his face. For a time William remained standing with his arms folded across his chest. Then with a murmur he knelt and laid his hand on Wriothesley's shoulder, and then touched the wet face. He felt a shock of bitterness rush through him, and then astonishment. He wanted to shout, Yes, weep! but will your tears return me my honor?

And yet as he raised his hand to wipe away the tears that spilled childishly down the smooth face, he found himself trembling so hard that he thought he might break apart, and be who he was no more. Surely it was not possible for a body to remain whole and yet keep within its breast such contradictions of emotion.

Southampton repeated, "I have wounded thee."

"Hast deeply," came the gruff reply.

"Christ's mercy, I am sorry for it. But told me thyself . . ."

"Told what, pray?"

"That you feel towards her, in so many words you have told me . . . but it can't matter, she can't matter at all. Ah, Christ's mercy! Take my hand! I say let the girl be damned! Let's go on as we were. Come, we will hunt, we'll play at bowls. What do you wish? It shall be yours. . . ."

Not daring to trust his voice, William did not answer, but gazing at the face which gradually sought to find its pride again, felt such tenderness he wondered once more if he might break apart. No, he could not live, not with such things in his heart. Yet in spite of his bitterness he wished to give something to this young man as one brings garlands to that which can at least from time to time achieve perfection, and that was his forgiveness. For a moment his chest swelled with wisdom. A strange sort of joy began to arise, a triumph over his baser self. He took the slender hand and clasped it firmly. Henry Wriothesley looked at him with his pale face exhausted from grief. "Then it is all right between us?" he murmured. "For this I humbly thank God. . . ."

HE STAYED FROM Emilia for a week and then went for his lust, and in the end bedded her long and passionately. In between were her tears of regret, stammering that she had not known what she did, that she had given in in a moment of weakness, that she deserved William to leave her forever, that he was her only darling.

Kissing his mustache, lips, and small beard again and again, she murmured, "I've sinned indeed. I will light candles to the saints in secret, for I have sinned."

"Then you will have naught more to do with him!"

"By Christ's love, I swear it."

"Can I trust you, sweet?"

"What, do you not see my tears?"

"Are there others than me?"

His voice rose with jealousy, but she wrapped her dressing gown about her body and cried in a saintly way, "Oh, never! . . . What do you think of me?" The tears glimmered in her beautiful eyes, and she shook her hair like a penitent about her. Still he left with some suspicion, swearing silently as he hurried down the back steps that he would not come again to Emilia Bassano, and even as he did so he knew he lied.

The winter moved on in this uneasiness: in one hour he forgave entirely and the next felt his wounds. Overburdened with tenderness and anger, he wrote sonnets, sending a few, keeping most within their cracking parchment binding. The Earl was away for a time, and William was on tour, so they did not see each other but once, when they rode in the forest, speaking of little, for too many subjects were too painful to touch. Only after a time did he understand that the nobleman and the Italian girl were lovers again. At first he was so stunned that he could feel nothing, and then, in the place where was that nothing, newer and deeper emotions began to grow.

SENSUALITY LIKE THE smell of earth in the spring, lifting earth and feeling it sift through his fingers: leaves, flowers, bits of wood. He knew it first in the warmth of the womb about him as he lay coiled, waiting to be born. Did his small body arch when some hands released him from swaddling clothes, and the cool air touched him, and did he cry out to lose that touch and be bound in rough cloths again? All his life he craved both to be bound and to be free, and struggled between these things.

The awareness of himself: whose were the hands that had first touched him and let him know that most individual of things, I am myself, and thus wakened his longing for others? I am myself, and yet what am I without others? He must have known these thoughts before he could find words, nursing at his mother's breasts until his belly was full and warm, and he slept.

After a time these sensations mingled with further ones about him. The cry of the night owl, the heat of fire, the creak of the ropes of the parental marriage bed, the whisper of wind through the woods near his childhood house, the taste of cool, firm apples. He had climbed those trees and looked down over his world.

Memories which had not passed his mind in years caught him, full of the clean sweat of boyhood in the age before he truly knew what it meant to take upon himself another's grief. He was twelve years old, running through the scattered weeds and sticks of the forest to bathe in the stream with young Dick Field and an idiot girl who lived with her grandfather nearby. The three of them stripped, curious, greedy. She was older than they, barely formed breasts rising from her ribs; the first woman, it was told to him from the pulpit, had been made from the rib of man. Fantastical as it was, he somehow believed it to be so.

They were naked, the three of them. Field's flat chest and belly and the delicate penis with a drop of water balancing from it seemed to reflect William's own body. The two boys had crashed through the woods, scraping themselves on thorns and branches, whooping like savages, rolling in the leaves. After them limped the grinning girl, crying like a sick cat for them to wait for her. She came through the trees with the sun behind her like something holy, and if they had had any inclination to touch her, it dried within their chests. If he felt anything else, he did not know it. He and Field cut their thumbs and mingled the blood that day, saying, Forever.

Everywhere on the higher branches birds, their feathers glittering in the sun, seemed to call him. At night, the cry of the owl spoke to him alone. Loving best always what he could not quite touch, hiding above his brother in the apple tree.

William, where are you?

He could not remember the face of the blacksmith's wife whom he desired so much, only that she smelled of the fire and soap, and he could never look directly at her when they passed in market for that he wanted her.

Late-afternoon sun glimmering on water which was rushing somewhere beneath a bridge and himself leaning on his stomach over the stone railing to watch it, setting forth one of his boats which one day bobbed off and they could not catch it, no matter how they hurried along the bank. "Where's the boat, Shakespeare?" demanded Field. "Dolt, ass!" They walked miles and never found it, and did not speak for three days until they grudgingly forgave each other and made another. But where does the water go? he asked his father that night. My lad, to the sea! But how does it come back again? Oh, in circles, sweet . . . everything goes round and round forever. But how can water, being the same substance, be both salt and pure? Why hath it been so created?

Will can make up anything, his sister said. If we were not here, he could pretend us—that's what Will can do!

Going off to tramp the woods with his friends, speaking secret words backwards, a world that no one knew but themselves. Coming to the common after to find girls about the maypole, skirts flying over their bare calves, dirt flying up from their bare feet. Oh their bare thighs! He wrote a song about it, verses and verses.

Will can make up anything. Oh God.

And then what had occurred? These rough passions subdued in propriety, and his wild feelings tucked like the folded papers in a lawyer's portfolio. No time to run about the woods. And here he was, Master Shakespeare the player.

Why, here was Master Shakespeare, now near thirty years of age. A little heavier of foot, of belly perhaps, and assigned increasingly the somber, fatherly roles. Inside he had not changed, or had he? What could anyone know of him? Now and then his name was put out as having writ a play, yet mostly what he earned was not enough, and he seemed always to struggle up a hill, and then fall halfway down again. Still when he walked about the city on certain days, he could now and then hear one apprentice turn to another and whisper, Master Shakespeare the player!—as if he were a personage of some importance. He shook his head wryly at the words. To what estate had he come? Poverty always nipped at his heels, and hunger pressed out against his belt. No sooner did a good London season begin than the plagues came, closing the doors; he had not recovered yet from that. But for the small amounts his patron sent to him he might have had nothing.

And yet this patron who held out his hand so tenderly to aid him was the Italian girl's lover; he did not need to know by finding a brooch, a bit of lacing, or the very scent of the man between her sheets and legs. He did not need to ask what meant her sometimes downcast eyes or looking faraway, and then how heartily Southampton greeted him on their few occasions together and then gazed off, a defiant flush coming to his pale cheeks. Then sometime later in the evening flinging his arms about the player too roughly, as if in some way he wished to hurt him. The long hand on his arm declared, Oh, this little matter shall not come between us! The rough chuckle of all things sensual . . . women are but sport, Will!

And knowst (the young nobleman's eyes repeated silently, threateningly, and then again with the greatest charm)—knowst, Will! Dost not love her. I do not flout thee, my friend! We but make good sport! If I had defiled your wife, it would be one matter, but this girl who will go with any man another. Can you not see it? And dost not love her. . . .

Ah, but did he? Love was purity, was it not? A covenant of comfort between man and wife, two pairs of worn slippers under a bed, the looks of agreement across a room—he had always known what love between man and woman should be and vaguely hoped for it, and yet he had roughly torn the first chance of love, and found this one past mending. Then so be it! Must he go wishing after things, and never letting them be as they were? And though he did not have all he wanted with her, he yet had his pact with Southampton. They had not spoken of it, but it was there, and strangely, this sealed it. Only speaking with his dark eyes, and those but scarcely raised, he had spoken the words to this young nobleman: I give my heart to you in exchange for yours. *Give me thee for me.*

And somehow, in spite of the pain, the Italian girl was binding them day by day into a new closeness. He did not understand it, but it was so. As a navigator studies his maps, he traced with his eyes the path on her naked body where the glittering boy had let trail his hand, knowing full well that the map led not only to her, but to himself. If he lost it, he might never find his way back again. Yet (and he never could have expected it, nor could he have explained it even to himself), he felt it of great importance to protect Southampton's innocence from her. Oh, he knew her, his Emilia! She did not love the infatuated young man, but gathered him to her for his lands and titles, for that he was adored by some of the greatest in the land. She did not love him, and she did not know him, as he did both. Thus under his breath he repeated the covenant once more, *thee for me.*

All else could be damned if he had that. Did it matter if Henry, forgiven for his sensual fault, slipped shortly thereafter into transgression again? It stung at first, it enraged, and then he drank the bitter draught. Life was imperfect, and in the end he must be faithful to what mattered most, and that was that nothing must come between Henry Wriothesley and himself. *That God forbid that made me first your slave, I should in thought control your times of pleasure . . .*

During this time, he continued to write. Some weeks he wrote well, other times not much at all. Once he wondered if a time would occur when the words would not come when he called. Then and again while working he found strange depths of himself like an ancient cracking chest, whose leather hinges have rotted away, and when you reach down into them the very papers crumble in your hand. Love letters, notes of rebuttal, a testament of faith. Was this his true being, which he thought he had left Stratford to find? These ever surprising, crumbling, and unexpected feelings within himself? Loving where he would not, serving where he resented it. The inner self full of shameful things which seemed forever separate from the outer man who lived by resolution.

Sometimes when he had spent a joyful evening with Emilia, the girl would suddenly press her hands together as in prayer, and then in a rising voice of accusation, cry out, "What do you think, what do you think? I wish you would not do it, William, for I know you do not think of me . . . ." And then he rose from the swarthy fragrance of her mouth and thighs, washed face and beard, and went out dressed to the streets where the sun shone on the cobbles. Then he knew himself in all the plainness of his worn boots, mended hose, and insufferable emotions. He was Master Shakespeare memorizing yet another role, and then hurrying home to find, he hoped, a letter from his son.

AT THE END of the bitter winter the men toured again. Frost crept over the land and into his bones; frost gathered in his beard, and his legs were so stiff that they did not wish to go forward. The apprentice boys were chilled to the bone, hung their heads, and whined to leave firesides to struggle forth on foot, horse, and cart to the next town. William had made friends with one of them, and gave him his woolen vest and second pair of gloves. They were walking beside the cart going somewhere, and everyone was angry for the cold and there was hunger in the land.

Back in London one day, he passed a bookseller's at Paul's and noticed one of his plays printed in the small form of unbound quarto. How odd to see the words he had spoken so passionately on the stage in print! He had also finished his second poem dedicated to Southampton telling of the rape of Lucrece. How effuse was the dedication: *What I have done is yours; what I have to do is yours; being part in all I have, devoted yours. Were my worth greater, my duty would show greater* . . . It was a poem of violence and ravishment, and he now wondered why he had written such a thing. Still the Earl had sent a present of the greatest generosity by a goldsmith's boy, and thus the great dread of want began to subside from William. Tradesmen greeted him more unctuously; he and John had become sharers that winter with the acting troupe of the Lord Strange's Men.

During a stage fight that spring, he was wounded. It had been a complicated duel almost like a dance, yet in the crucial moment his mind wandered. Panic crossed John Heminges's eyes as he hissed, "Go left, go left, damn thee!" William stumbled, and the blade, though somewhat dulled, sliced through the fine full linen of his sleeve. The audience applauded.

Red drops of his blood lay like a path across the plain scrubbed boards of the tiring room as his fellows, confused and apologetic, swabbed the long shallow cut. Heminges, however, said sharply, "Twice more of that and you shall be selling apples like the cripple at the gate."

"We had planned to turn right."

"Left! Are you not thinking?" John's two apprentices stood by gaping; the younger had torn some cloth from an old shirt, and mutely held it out. There was consternation that Master Shakespeare could be wounded. He felt the kindness of everyone as an unbearable heaviness, and turned away, inexplicably wanting to weep.

As he walked out with John after, the theater rising behind them, the grocer looked at him simply and said, "I believe you've come to be ashamed to be an actor, ashamed of us and what we are making here."

William drew in his breath sharply, his upper lip raised in a haughty way. Yes, it was true! The very common, daily life he had known these past years of theater and street repelled him, as well as the men with whom he had shared it.

They were standing by the military practice grounds with their well-scored archery targets, and a few broken arrows left in the high grass. The former grocer shook his head. "Never mind it, then," he muttered. "Sometimes two close friends will grow in different ways. I feel to say damn thee to hell, Shakespeare, but my heart's too heavy to do it."

William remained looking after him. He understood clearly as he stood there that he was no longer close to the actors; he was in fact close to no one, not even himself. Aware of the pain of his wound, he swore slightly and walked off with hunched shoulders, thinking he must somehow mend his life, and not knowing how to do it.

IT MUST BEGIN by breaking with Emilia: with great effort day by day he began to wrest away small bits of himself which he had shared with her—his silliness, his philosophy, which he felt to be increasingly like his father's—as you rush into a burning house, and come away singed yet with something precious clasped against your body. Yet what he wrested seemed when he woke the next morning to be returned again. He went humbly, furiously, lustily to her rooms, and was sometimes sent off with hard words. "No, you do not love me!" Tears spilled from her eyes, and against all his will he could not help the compassion which flooded him. Sometimes he despised her, and then worse himself. He had walked too long down paths he would not go until he began to wonder who he was indeed, and bitterly he cried out against the lust which bound him to her.

Yes, both of them, he cried. I shall break from both of them! Resolutions made in the clarity of the summer morning fell from him when night came and loneliness once more enveloped him. Once more he made his resolution, but coming home after a few days' absence from her arms, would find, slipped under his door, a letter in her hand. With some rouge left on his face from his performance as if he had been slapped, he would stand in the dim light reading her seductive words, and resolution melted in him as if it had never been.

For three months he went away on tour and did not return. It was the most difficult time for him, his nights sleepless with wanting her body and some word from Southampton. He thrashed as he slept and cried out so that he woke his fellows. When he returned to the city he did not even go to his rooms but yet in his mud-stained traveling clothes and hose he had not changed in a week and with his satchel over his shoulder with its books and writing, he hurried to her house.

She was at her dressing table when he threw open her door, and stood up at once with a cry. "Hold me, comfort me!" she gasped, running across the room to him. "God forgive me my sins! Nothing worse could have occurred. I'm with child, and my lord Chamberlain is putting me away by marrying me to the musician Lanier, a stupid man! I thought to go to have the baby taken from me, but last night the Virgin appeared to me in a dream and told me I would be damned if I did so." Several times she made the sign of the cross. "I am alone, alone!" she gasped. "I have always been alone."

For a moment he was stunned to silence. Then, putting down his satchel and cloak, he said wearily, "Emilia, I have been away a time. Is it Henry's child you bear?"

"Nay, he has not been near, I swear it!"

"Then who is the father?"

"For mercy's sake, do not ask!"

"Is it the Lord Chamberlain's, Emilia?" he cried, taking her by the shoulders. "Have you told me false about him? What other lies have you told me?"

With a shriek she pushed him away, tearing down her hair and beating her fists violently against her breasts; her face had a sallow, worn quality for a moment, like that of an older woman who looks enviously from her wash basket to the pretty girls in satin rushing across the court and knows she will never be like them again. Sobbing, she began to walk up and down the room. "Do you know what it is like to be a woman?" she gasped. "With us life takes away daily all that we're valued for and all that's worth having! Is this not enough that I shall be married like chattel? I was poor and fatherless, and you blame me!"

She began to strike her breasts again, and gently he came to her and restrained her hands. She trembled then, and struggled with him, and he looked into her face, which once more was that of the angry, passionate Italian enchantress, the daughter of centuries. "Perhaps the babe's thine!" she gasped. "Perhaps it is his . . . aye, 'tis the truth that it may be his. My courses are not regular, and I do not know. Oh, you judge me as does he, and how dare you do it, William . . . you who have a lawfully wedded wife! Still, though it be to my ruination, I will not murder the unborn child within me. It will be mine, no one else's. Mayhap it will one day love me as I would wish to be loved."

Still gasping now and then with a soft sob, she put her hands gently on his chest as if to plead with him, or put some space between them. "Oh, William!" she murmured reproachfully. "Oh my player, my sweet love! Knowst how dearly I have loved thee, truly, truly, and if you were free, I should be your good and loyal wife. And knowst my bitter unhappiness. Hence I beg you, if you have ever loved me or wished me well . . . speak to my lord of Southampton for me! I had hoped . . . yes, I must confess it to you! . . . that he would one day marry me, and he calls me such sweet names that that hope is not entirely extinguished. He could defy his wretched mother if he wished. Oh, William, beloved! Have you ever wished me well? Then do this thing. A musician's daughter does not marry into such a family, though she be more clever than many a lady, but mayhap . . . wouldst ask him . . . to think on it . . . beloved William." Her voice died away.

Astonished, he raised his eyes with a frown to look into her beautiful face, which was now swollen with tears, though hope glimmered in her bright dark eyes. "You wish me to ask him to *marry* thee, Emilia?" he murmured.

"I do."

"He will not do so."

SOUTHAMPTON DID NOT reply to the message. That early fall the Italian girl was wedded to the musician Lanier, and went to live with him in half a dark house within the city walls.

THE LOVERS

E WAS MORE exhausted that early winter than he could ever recall before, sick with the cold and the wind which seemed to have embedded itself inside of him. Was he growing old? He was just past thirty, but the life he led was hard. He walked or rode on tour for a dozen hours, coughing into his arm, sometimes with rain lashing his face and seeping into every garment which he wore. They rose at four of the morn to rehearse, played at two and sometimes when they could again at night. Other times they were for hire to walk in great processions, or as mourners in somber black behind the casket of some personage. Once he was a satyr in some welcoming ceremony, wearing very little. They did these things or had nothing, and then the actors looked lean and anxious; there was that dull silence as if they would never do anything else again. His knee troubled him more these days, and he was gradually moving to roles which required less movement. He danced but seldom.

In a locked cupboard in John Heminges's house were the only complete copies of each of the plays he had written. Sometimes he felt his soul was caught behind that latch.

One December day he ferried to Marlowe's grave in Deptford and sat before it, head on his knees, for a long time. He had by now written more plays than the dead poet. Greene was also a memory, only a comedy or two of his holding the fancy of the fickle city audiences, and his little wife and son had disappeared, no one knew where. He now and then saw the large whore about the streets. At least he had some friendship again with Field, who had printed both his long narrative poems.

He was these days sometimes bright and jocular with his fellows as if to excuse his former removal and then again silent. At times he remained motionless for seconds on the stage, his speech ended, gazing up at the clouds which seemed to blow ever northward from where he had come. More and more he stood apart from his own life, observing himself.

He stayed away from the Italian girl for a time after her marriage, but her flesh called to him and he went once more to her arms. That afternoon he found a silver button on the floor, and picking it up, recognized it to be the same as the one Southampton had broken off from his doublet that day long ago when he had first spent the afternoon with him, and they had played at chess.

He came to her, because she begged him, the night she miscarried of the child. Then for weeks he went no more. I shall leave them to each other, he thought with some bitterness. I must, or lose my mind.

THROUGH THE DULLNESS of his thoughts one day when he was coming home with his dinner wrapped in paper, and a copy of Chaucer's *Troilus and Criseyde* under his arm, came the remembrance that Southampton had turned one and twenty years and thus entered into his majority and the management of his own estates. He may have remembered the date, or he may have heard someone speaking of it when they played some nights before at Gray's Inn. With the wind blowing hard from the river, he hurried up his steps, unlocked his door, and began to look about for the letter. Beloved friend, it said. To the devil with my guardian! Come and drink wine with me to my freedom. In Christ's name, come!

The eve set for the celebration was this very one. William, through duty and what he construed as old affection, clothed himself warmly and set out on the long walk through the city and beyond once more.

The receiving room of Drury House was brilliant with innumerable candles, whose flames reflected in the wine goblets and the silver threads of curtain and chair embroidery. He had heard music as he came down the hall, and when he turned to the corner of the room he saw the Italian musicians. Between them stood Emilia Bassano singing one of her Venetian melodies.

She was even more beautiful that night than he had remembered, and at once his heart was full of many things he had sworn he would not feel again. As he watched her laughing and curtseying to the guests who moved about with their wine, he sensed a strange, wild despair beneath her gaiety. What did she here? Was she no more than a paid singer as in her humble beginnings when she traveled with her father, or had she come as guest and sang for her own amusement? And yet he did not trust himself to approach her, but remained by the window seat watching her dance and shake the tambourine.

With a curtsey to yet another guest, she broke from her cousins and hurried across the room to him. "Hast kept away!" she whispered, caressing his cheek with her cold little hand. "How I have mourned for you! You make your Emilia very unhappy when you keep away from her. Do you not miss me, sweet Will? Hast another love?"

"Nay," he murmured uncomfortably, hoping she would not know what denial and rebellion had been in his heart; he wanted her suddenly very much, and must smooth over his absences and neglect. Selfishly he wondered what penance he must pay, what small matter of compliment or other he must give before she would open her arms to him and let him forget all within them.

She had returned to her singing, beating the tambourine with the heel of her hand, her voice a little hoarse and raucous. He moved even deeper into the window seat to watch the men who admired her, and the women who gazed at her critically. No one spoke to him at all, and after a time he began to drink sugared wine deliberately, feeling with each mouthful a new part of his body falling away to inebriation. When he had enough he would have the courage to rise up and go away, however unsteadily; perhaps he would have the courage not even to say goodbye. To become involved with her again was madness . . . what, would he never be free? Could he not even rule himself?

Southampton had suddenly come in with some guests from Paris. It was not only his clothing, the deep burgundy doublet whose sleeves were slashed to reveal the scarlet silk of the blouse and the rings on his hands, that made him glitter, but there was an astonishing happiness about him that could almost not be contained in the slender body. This handsome figure, gold chain on his chest, was in every movement aware that he was one and twenty years and all the world must know it. The world did not consist, of course, of the strange shores across oceans known as the New World, nor the Indies or the Holy Land, but only the court of little England, with its supplicant courtiers and aged sovereign.

For the next few hours, men of varying importance and women exquisitely gowned came by carriage and departed again, hurrying up to the young nobleman to curtsey, or grasp his shoulder with approval and well wishes. The Earl was wild with gaiety, kissing the women passionately on the lips and whispering into their ears so that they burst into laughter. For a while William from his corner wondered if the Queen herself would enter, her stubborn, wilting body dragging about dresses encrusted with jewels, her white hair under a wig. He remembered how he had imitated her that snowy night for Southampton's amusement and smiled. Only one time did the young lord glance in the direction of his player, and then he but raised the corner of his mouth. Never had they greeted each other in public as warmly and naturally as they did when alone, and William only knew this moment how much it had always troubled him. Not to clasp hands, throw an arm about the shoulder! He shook his head.

The evening had begun to grow late, and the musicians made effusive bows and cries of pleasure as they were paid, saying, Your lordship's servant, your lordship's servant! God keep you, worship! They bent over the Earl's hand with its heavy rings, the strings on their instruments quivering. Emilia seemed to be drifting out with them, and William rose unsteadily to his feet and with as much control as possible walked to follow and speak his intentions, for he now felt it an urgency that he spend the night in her arms.

She was standing by the open door; a few flakes of snow had drifted in to her rich burgundy overdress and her dark hair, and glistened slightly as if she had been suddenly arrayed in diamonds.

"What, will you stay?" he murmured, kissing her neck. "Shall we not go away together, Emilia, and say ten thousand pisses upon this place?"

"Aye, leave off . . . not now . . ."

"Let me take you home."

"You are drunk, William!"

"I shall beat your husband to amuse you, I shall strangle him with his untuned lute strings. There, lady! Shall I lift you about until you're dizzy for your amusement? Kiss me! Dost prefer me drunk or sober?"

"Nay, better drunk, for sober art too serious!" she laughed, stroking his face and beard. "Later, I promise." Quickly she put his hand to her breast and gave him a brave, sweet smile.

The candles were burning low, though several men still stayed about talking near the table. Now more like a lady than an itinerant musician, Emilia walked towards them, tucking a strand of her long hair under her cap which had come undone in his fumbled embrace. Between the guests she fluttered, turning gracefully to smile at this one and that, chattering in Italian and French, blushing when a French phrase escaped her, putting her hand against her bosom, crying, "Oh forgive! What can a poor Italian girl do?"

From outside they heard the faint strains of singing. The Earl shouted happily, "By the Lord's mercy, every guild hath sent its lads to carol this eve!" and began a few songs he knew, urging others to join him and swinging his goblet to keep time so that drops of red wine dribbled across the floor. Happiness still glistened about him as the snow had for those moments on Emilia's dress. He stood with parted lips looking towards his future, and, affectionate and charming, flung his arms around this guest and that, protesting the night was too early and they should not go.

"Peace on earth!" cried Emilia to all of them. "Christmastide! In Italy they sing in the streets. I remember it as a child! In this one season of the world, we must all love each other. But what do I know of things, being but a poor Italian girl and an orphan? What do I know, gentles?"

One by one the visitors departed to carriages in the snow, until the last kissed her hand, held it too hard and long, and leaning over, touched the hollow of her neck. She cried out delicately. "Signore, I beg you . . ." and he laughed coarsely and, giving his hand to the Earl, called after his friends and went from the door. Southampton followed them and after a time returned. The servants were clearing away the dishes, and Emilia was leaning wearily against a chair as if she had given her best performance and could do no more.

William rose uncomfortably. "I must also be gone," he said, for he felt if she would not come with him, he would go home sullenly alone.

But Southampton stepped before him and cried, "Shall you leave me too, sweet Will my poet? I am one and twenty years old this night, and we must celebrate! Are you not happy for me? My guardian, Lord Burghley, had the kindness not to come this night! Oh yes, I would have thrust him down the steps by his lace collar, saying, 'You have mistook my door, sir!' My attendants would have stayed, but them I sent off. No, I have had enough of their 'my lords.' Ah, if my old and ugly guardian had come we would have beaten him, would we not, Will?"

Still standing, the player answered, "My lord, I cannot stay."

"By Christ's mercy, I say you shall," cried the Earl, flinging his arm roughly about him. "From friendship, not from deference to me . . . from mercy if you will. The three of us together! By my salvation, should we not be friends? All of us. . . ."

Snow was still falling outside the windows, and the carols of Christmas sung by groups of guild members to the strains of the city band hung in the air as Southampton and the girl moved closer together. William stood very erect, though he was unsteady with drink, watching them both with a terrible dark pain in his heart. For a moment he thought to draw his sword and whip it across the shoulders of this insolent, unthinking young man. "Oh sing, my black-eyed Emilia!" the Earl cried.

A lute remained in the corner, and taking it up, the Italian girl began to sing in a tired, coarse voice:

> "There is a lady sweet and kind
> 'Twas never face so pleased my mind,
> I did but see her passing by
> And yet I love her til I die!"

Watching her across the room, William felt his body begin to ache from the length of wanting her and his repressed fury. Madness to have come! Should he not this evening depart quietly and leave her alone with this dear cruel Earl who stood apart, slowly unbuttoning the embroidered doublet, his stomach slightly thrust forward in weariness, and drinking the last of someone's wine? As the player sat on the window seat he saw the two of them draw together, the young man bending to kiss the Italian girl, his fingers searching her bodice for the nipple of her breast. He sat in a daze of sorrow and disillusionment until he looked away, stood suddenly, and made to go.

Within seconds she was standing beside him, having taken his hands.

"Will," she said eagerly, "come up! Come up with us."

Compressing his lips, he shook his head, but still she tugged at his hand. "Come!" she said. "I love you, I want you to . . ." She came into focus with her sweet, childish smile, and he reached up to touch her hair, which was now half unpinned, and then the exposed right nipple. It seemed to call to him intimately, and he claimed it as his.

"Madness," he muttered, but let himself be pulled. "What are you doing, sweet? . . . Wait, I can but stand . . . well then, have your way." He gazed at Southampton, who had stripped off his doublet and stood with shirt unlaced, the hat yet tied across his shoulders. With a deft motion, the Earl undid the strings and tossed the hat across the room, where it settled on the head of a statue of a monarch.

"God's blessings, Majesty!" he said.

"What king is it?"

"Whatever one, be damned!"

"Will shall make a play of him with clowns. *Now is the winter of our discontent made glorious summer by this sun of York . . .*" Together they joined arms and began to go up.

"Oh Will, art not steady!" she giggled.

"He holds his pen steadier than his legs."

"My pen hath drunk but ink . . . now may pen and body drink thee."

"Thou jester!"

"What is o'clock?"

"Past midnight."

The sleeping chamber had been prepared by servants, for new candles glistened in silver holders and dried herbs and flowers had been strewn on the thick linen sheets of the bed, which was half hidden behind heavy thick green hangings. He had been here once before when he had found the Earl prostrate with grief over Christopher Marlowe's death, but now at night with the snow falling softly outside, it was a place of warmth and secrecy. Everything was of the richest color, from the hairbrush worked in lacy silver and red enamel to the Turkish rugs new to this country and laid not upon the table but on the floor. He took off his shoes, feeling the luxury of the softness. Emilia's scent was swarthy and a kind of musk. He was dizzy with sensation and desire, and in the strangest way, much calmer. He suddenly felt he had come to a place where he had been long expected and would be richly welcomed.

The bolt of the door was slid.

Walking languidly to the dressing table, the Italian girl began to untruss the first laces of the heavy dress which sat atop her kirtle. At once William crossed to her and unlaced the other side. Next came the saffron kirtle, now a little worn at the edges yet embroidered with leaves and birds. Henry, laughing, stumbled close and pricked his finger on one of her pins. With a soft curse, he stripped off his own shirt, hurling it to the floor, and then knelt to tug at the leather strands which held the heavy clumsy farthingale. "Here's the trouble with her, and I have it every time," he muttered. "But Will's best at these things. What do I know if not from him of women or of life?"

"I've taught thee . . . naught . . . Harry," was the emotional answer from the player, full of gratitude for the thanks.

"Aye, hast!" said the Earl devoutly, drunkenly. "That we must all love one another . . . and we have always done so and shall. Why, were it not for thee, Shakespeare!"

"Oh peace!" murmured William.

The farthingale creaked slightly as he let it drop upon the Turkish rug and helped her step from its center. Next their fingers moved to unfasten the satin corset which had bitten into her flesh over her plain linen shift. Barefoot, she shook out her hair so that it tumbled down past her thighs and then held out her arms, first to one man and then the other, with a sweet, childish smile on her face. She had never looked so contented and so sweet.

With one sweep, William lifted her and carried her to the bed. Even as he kissed and bit her he kept one hand to loosen his doublet buttons and untruss his breeches. They too dropped to the floor. He knew nothing but his desire, though he had somehow partially drawn the bed hangings. "Stay off!" he shouted, his voice unclear in the direction he felt the Earl stood. Again and again his body thrust into hers, and the bed ropes creaked and pulled. Feathers floated up, the room smelled of warm candles and the moisture between her legs.

Someone was shouting, and he knew it to be himself. The cries came from a place so deep in him that he had never known it before, and he thrust and thrust inside her until he had spent himself entirely. He rolled from her to the side with his arm over his eyes and heard the bed creak, and her sigh and the murmurs of his friend, whose boyish grunts and rough bawdy language seemed an echo of his own. Jealousy rose up, and a violence which frightened him, for he had always thought himself a gentle man. He wanted to leap up and push his friend off the girl and beat him with his sword, yet even in those furious thoughts, he was sweaty and aroused again. Oh, well done, Harry, he thought. He smiled for a moment and felt happiness flood him again.

The bed creaked violently. Jolted and almost sick with excitement, he knelt to place his hand on her tangled loose hair as she tossed her head back and forth. He touched her lips, feeling her sharp little teeth close on his finger, and then the cool shoulder of the young Earl.

After, he took her again, and felt her exhaustion beneath him. Under her sighs was pretense. He understood somehow she was frightened, and was irritated with her, for he himself felt so happy.

They slept, and woke. He woke once, and then again. The candle had burned out, and from the bed hangings he dimly made out the shining satin-covered farthingale like white bones upon the floor, and the glistening of her necklace upon the table, and the dull glint of the Earl's sword and his own.

AGAIN AND AGAIN they returned to the chambers that winter when men froze to death in unheated rooms, and children without licenses begged for food on the streets. Yet even though he saw these things they did not exist for him once he came into the chamber with the Turkish carpet, the bed strewn with herbs and dried flowers, and the three of them. Hands clasped, her sighing. Nothing else: no beggars with rags bound against frozen feet, no wars, no bills to pay and lines to learn, no unwanted child stretching insidiously under the faintly rounded belly of the Italian girl, for she was made once again not for motherhood but for men's desires. Emilia fell asleep, naked to the waist, and he lay beside her leaning on his elbow and gazed at the Earl, whose shoulders and chest, with its few scattered pale hairs, seemed as if they had just been formed, so youthful were they.

"Why, you must sleep, Harry!" he said gently.

The very world had ceased to turn, if turn it did as the new science said it must be, and they stood upon it. Time did not flow, but curled near the hearth. Many nights that winter he came there, or if he could not go, his soul went and left his body sleepless. Every night riding through the white drifts of the empty city streets to be welcomed without question by the guards, to hear her play the lute and make a harmony to her songs. What Emilia's husband thought they never knew, for she never mentioned him, though someone said he had come to the theater looking for work, a market basket with a small quantity of food within it on his arm and a lute of poor quality strapped over his shoulder.

He wrote nothing. The ink dried in the glass container, the paper curled at the edges, a play was substituted for the one which he had promised to his fellows.

Sometimes their secret life seemed a strange, dark thing. Other times they played hide and seek in the dusty house that was far too big, and once she hid so well behind a curtain of another empty sleeping chamber that they spent an hour hurrying through the rooms with low-burning lanterns, imploring her name.

Oh Emilia! *Cara, dove sei?*

They ran through the rooms like children, whispering, throwing open cupboards, hurling dank pillows at each other and caps and nightshirts of people long dead, discovering by candlelight miniature portraits of worthy citizens they had never known. "That's my grandmother," Southampton said when they found a new one in a drawer, and put it carefully in his dressing-gown pocket. They found a viol with three strings, which Emilia tried to play. Softly they whispered, so that their voices would not carry to the chambers of the house where slept the lady Countess, but sometimes their laughter rang out. They found in a wardrobe heavily embroidered clothes so old that they were full of holes, and also flat, soft, pointed shoes whose toes were so long that they had to be fastened about the ankle. In these clothes they draped themselves, becoming the warring kings of two centuries before who fought to control France and England. Another time they draped themselves in creamy white linen sheets and played Romans, with Southampton wearing a wreath of holly leaves in his hair and declaring he must be off to the forum.

Still other nights they sat on the bed and spoke about things they never thought to mention before. The Earl sang a song his grandmother had taught him. Emilia spoke of her first new dress, and how she had never stained or torn it until she outgrew it at last. William most often preferred to amuse them and once more made them laugh.

If he had lost something of himself he did not recognize it, as you will not know until a time after that you have dropped something precious, sometimes until years after. He was stupidly, blissfully happy, for there was a safety in it. He woke, sometimes so dazed that he could not tell which arm was his, which leg, which belly. He was always so tired, he the writer who no longer wrote. He tried again and again, and finally tried no more, glad that he did not have to return to his own rooms and see the papers dusty on the table by the window.

And there was Southampton: the strong white arm across under his head, the pale buttocks, the intimacy, the terrible, dark, startling intimacy of waking and hearing his breath. Sometimes he sat up and looked across at the sleeping boy, his heart such a confused mixture of feelings he could not begin to separate them.

Once having had no sleep in two days he woke uncertain for a moment where he could be. The curtains were partially open and the moon had risen, and in that white pure light he could see that Southampton had knelt above him, and was looking at him with the deepest tenderness he had ever seen on his face; he seemed as beautiful as the statue of an unclothed Greek. He bent his head and the golden hair moved across William's arm. Then he kissed his mouth. William lay as if stunned.

He moved his throat to say "Do not," but no word came. In the midst of their embrace he cried out in resentment, falling, crying out, striking out to be free, and the murmurs he heard were of consolation. His body opened, his seed spilled. He pulled the young man against him, gasping for breath against the naked shoulder which somehow smelled of leaves and the woods after rain.

I DO NOT know what I want from you, Henry Wriothesley had said; I do not know what I can have. Thus they had touched each other. William, waking alone the next morning in the great bed, remembered it all at once. And what was he to think about it? Had it been a dream? Was it offensive, was it sweet? Was it a comfort perhaps, that he had touched him at last and been touched by him, the young god?

They had embraced, and after hid their faces against each other's shoulders and hair. And strangely the young man had wept silently for a long time, his back shuddering, and William had whispered gently in his ear all the soft things he might say to his child. Strange, mysterious how it was, and yet how could it not have come to this? Christ's mercy, define us love! For he had loved this young man, this Harry Wriothesley whom the world called the honorable lord of Southampton, so much that it had sometimes seemed to burst these past few years through his very chest. He had loved him as friend, brother, child, and idol. Touching him, he had found his breath human and warm. He had smelled also of sweat, and then of sex and soldiers' barracks, this boy who would go to war.

I do not know what I want of you. Those were the words that had been spoken to him, and William in turn repeated them as he lay in that large bed alone with the earliest grey light of a winter morning creeping across the now dulled colors of the carpet. How peculiar that without knowing it he had wished to find a room like this all his life—a chamber of warm fire and feather quilting, of trays of wine and food, of all the comforts, apart from his daily world, a chamber where things within it might be done to never trouble the conscience. A room truly of the mind, locked away, so precious and secret that it must only tremble on the edge of existence in this ordinary world. And oh the sweet ferocity of what he had been given, the unexpected welling up later of his trembling grief and of the boy's! Were people supposed to grieve after love? Perhaps if it truly tore them asunder, flung aside flesh, muscle, and rib and reached into the very heart. I do not know what I want of you—he understood nothing; he dared not try to understand, wanting only to feel and afraid of that.

At last he rose, dressed, and walked downstairs. In the library Southampton was seated with his secretary, his head bent over some papers; he did not look up. William walked home to gather his things, for he had a rehearsal and a performance that day.

HE SAID HE would not return, yet he did.

He came after his work was done, which was already late, and as he hurried down the hall heard Emilia singing once more. She was sitting on the floor by Southampton's chair, and the young lord caressed her hair, but when William came in, he raised his eyes and looked at him for a time in silence with parted lips.

For a long time they remained there, talking of matters that seemed important then and which they would forget soon after, and at last mounted up together. The girl fell asleep so heavily that he wondered if something had been slipped in her wine, and then understood it had been indeed. Turning on his side, he looked with the greatest gentleness and wonder at Southampton. Then everything in his soul cried out.

They came together, the Earl's mouth against his chest, and he aroused to a passion he had never in his life conceived. Cursing under his breath, he urged Henry down and kissed him, closing his teeth over the slight mustache. He kissed him as if he would drink his soul, and found himself gasping. His chest was so tight he thought he would die, and all he wished was to consume Southampton, to devour the flesh of his thighs, the handsome shoulders and neck, the arms and the pungent, perfumed hair beneath them. He wished to tear him open and thrust his arm inside him and to hold forever after, in his own hands, the essence of this illusive boy who meant . . . oh God! . . . what to him? This stranger, this beloved stranger. *Thee for me.* He had wanted nothing more than that and he had never wanted to take less.

He felt from him first laughter, the body then tensing as if to strike, and at last absolute giving. Unwilling to release each other, they slipped to the soft thick rugs, pulling one of the heavy coverlets with them, moving under it and then throwing it off. In the darkness Henry's teeth were white and shining as a small ferret's; he stifled his shouting in William's arm. That became the steady rising breath and then the panting of someone who runs as if for his life. His voice very low, he whimpered again and opened his dark startled eyes, winding his arms around William's back, shooting up his seed in a gush of white like the substance from milkweed on hot summer days. Then he lay on his side for a time, his hand to his lips.

"I want to be so many things and have not the courage," the Earl murmured. "In truth, I have not the courage to die for anything, or perhaps not even to truly live."

"You will have all you need when you need it," was the gentle answer. "I swear to it, you shall have it!" In a heap of covers and with a deep sigh, Southampton fell asleep with his head on the player's shoulder, clasping his hand so that the warm gold of his ring pressed against William's palm.

THE MAN FROM Stratford said he would not return and yet he did; he felt he could not draw breath, and yet it did not matter. Sometimes he looked with some guilt across the parlor as Emilia put down her goblet once more and murmured that she was yet again inexplicably sleepy. He did not know what he did with his days, what roles he played, what battle scenes he planned. Then he could remember nothing, not his lines and barely the names of his fellow actors, and sent word to John Heminges that he was ill and another man must take his roles.

He had ceased to live in any place but this chamber where he could touch that youthful, warm body and make it cry out in longing, passion, resentment, pleasure, and pain . . . pain for his own withdrawal, the pain of the younger man giving himself in a way he longed for and yet which shamed him. And still he wondered how we give ourselves in lovemaking. Sometimes the mere trembling and spilling of seed (that most often of all and least complicated), but other times with the soul torn open so that you stagger, bloody and half from this world, with tears in the eyes towards the other who has become everything.

Later he would understand that it was a week or perhaps a little more in which the girl slept in dreams of wine and laudanum and he gazed at Southampton as if to find within his embrace his own soul. In his memory it would remain years and years, centuries, to stand ever apart from time.

Once Emilia, insufficiently drugged, sleepily awoke, and they both spoke to her with great gentleness, calling her such sweet names that she looked at them in bewildered wonderment. Yes, he understood he had loved her, even through his deep disappointment, and he wanted her still. His longing for Southampton was a different matter. He cried out in the pain of that longing which had possessed him for so long, and returned again for more. He wanted to caress and hurt, and after that to comfort. And the Earl would push him fiercely away, the rings of his fingers flashing, and then the strange tears which came again and again. And then in the morning they would part: Henry Wriothesley to the court and his poet to walk about the city.

Up and down the poet wandered, to the fields and beyond, to the ruins of monasteries, to look at other men as they were real and he now a ghost who existed only when night fell. Once he passed his own theater and heard his company, and the musicians playing for the clowns to come. Then he could not bear it. He did not belong there anymore, but neither did he belong where each night his feet led him.

On that night when they had embraced once more, the Earl fell into a restless sleep, but William, who had slept little more than hours in the past nights, could not close his eyes but lay staring into the dark with one arm thrown protectively about the young lord and the other tangled in the hair of the Italian girl. Somewhere down the lane a cat cried pitifully. He was sensitive to the faintest creak of the bed ropes, even his own blood in his veins. Disengaging himself with utmost care so as not to wake them, he walked slowly towards the dressing table.

Thus he saw his own reflection by the fast-guttering candles, a fairly handsome man with a high masculine chest, advancing towards himself as towards someone he had known a long time but of whose reception he was uncertain. Puzzled, he passed his hand over his sternum as if trying to feel his soul. As he stood there gazing into the glass he vaguely made out the bed, but those within it were now the ones obscured in shadow. Then it all darkened, and he saw nothing, but covered his face with his hands.

Slowly as if drunken he began to feel for his clothes, and had just found his boot when he heard the low voice from the bed murmuring, "Where do you go?"

"I must go home."

There was silence from the darkness, and then Southampton said quietly, "I would wish it not to be. I think you'd wish to end this matter between us, Shakespeare. It is odd that it should end when I do not know how ever it begun."

"It was on my part from longing, I believe."

"For what?"

"For what you are, to touch it . . . I cannot dare think you longed for me as well. But it must end, my lord, for it cannot stay."

The young man stirred. "Why?" he murmured achingly.

"Because I have lost myself. But do not fret. The night's cold; cover you both. Good night, dear Harry."

PUTTING UP HIS cloak and hood, the player went out into the empty streets. At once the wind clawed at his garments, whipping them up, hurling them from his body, slapping his face. He was shivering so he could not think, nor did he know where he went but from street to street, past all the taverns and closed bookstalls and shops which he knew, and everything silent as if all the world had died and he alone remained.

Past silent warehouses he went and windmills which had ceased to turn, and streets where no man stirred, and sleeping beggars, and once a quarrel. This street he had walked one night years before when coming home after he had seen the bear die for men's amusement with Christopher Marlowe. The poet was dust, and what did that mean? He had told William with a smile, I am not a man like you. In Christ's name, what was he like then? Who was he?

Dawn was just creeping over the housetops in the coldest hour of the day when he felt his way up the steps to his own room and slept for a longer time than he had ever before.

WORD CAME SOME days later that Henry Wriothesley was called by the Queen to attend her in progression from house to house across the countryside, and he went. No letters were sent: each time he heard boots on the stair, William flung open his door, but no messenger greeted him.

He went for pity to visit the Italian girl, and listened patiently while she tore at her handkerchief and asked when Southampton would return. A few times she tried to entice him to her bed, but he shook his head. There was in him a strange distaste for lust, the depths of which he began slowly to understand. He knew himself incapable of embrace.

He understood slowly, because with the beginnings of understanding came an emptiness which greeted him at dawn and lay down at night beside his bed; he did not know where to run from it. It was as if you came into your beloved house and found it empty—not a chair remained, only on one shelf a book which did not interest you, and a broken window. Then came grief.

Grief rising from the chest, choking the breath, wanting to stop the heart, wanting to stop the mind. It was done for the three of them, and the secret paths which led to each other would grow over, never to be found again. The worst was that he alone had done it, and he knew it well, for when finally there came a brief message from Southampton, saying the poet was missed, he did not answer.

Then when he thought he was beginning to recover, grief came once more, so painful it could not keep him in his room, but flung him into the street, running, stumbling, wanting to shout. What had been the very center of his life was fading away. What is there to replace such a thing? His beautiful young god was mortal and fallible, and the girl they had both loved in their own ways was no better than she should be. Of this he had played a part. How darkly, strangely, and insufficiently she reached out for love as if it were garments easily changed, secure in her falsehoods to herself that her youth should last forever. Poor beautiful Emilia! And to make these both more than they were, for he could never accept them as they were, was to end himself.

He lay in bed two days with a fever, and his landlady, who thought he had a plague, would have sent for his friends, but he forbade her. Then for the next months he saw no man but for his work, but remained alone, and in all that time the soot of city fires which made their way past the wood shutters gently covered the bound portfolios on his writing desk by the window.

THE ROOM ON BISHOPSGATE

URING THAT TIME in which he noticed little but
the tumbling, half-finished, and painful thoughts in
his head, soft breezes were beginning to blow from the
fields through the winding streets of the city. One day
he removed his second wool jerkin and felt the fresh wind for a moment
touch his bare neck. Then he bundled again, shivering defensively. When
he came home from marching in yet another procession with the coins
paid in his pocket, he noticed the unaccustomed disarray of the room for
the first time, as if he had come into the place of a stranger. A little kitten
whom he had found starving and taken home for company was asleep on
his ordinary brown doublet, and had left there a fine dusting of pale gold
hair. Tenderly he scooped it up with one hand, and looked about for a place
to put it. Every corner was full of papers, and when the little creature had
been placed among them she amused herself by chasing a mouse, and scattering what was left of the order.

Kneeling in exasperation to push them roughly back into place, his fin-
gers touched the broken seal of a letter, and he saw Southampton's crest.
There was only this one, which had come when the Earl had returned from
France, and he had not answered. Even if it had meant he would be cast

into starvation or go for a farm laborer, he could not have replied. And yet as he knelt there he knew it was so much unfinished business. The kitten batted his fingers. Then he was seated crosslegged on the floor, quickly perusing this bill and that note, crumpling some into the brazier, smoothing others more tenderly.

Under it all was one of his common portfolios made of old vellum, and when he opened it he drew in his breath sharply, for there in neat order were all the sonnets he had ever written for his patron. Slowly he turned the pages, feeling nausea, impatience, indignity, confusion, and devotion, and all the untidy array of things which had so possessed him until he had no longer known who he was.

For three days they remained in the corner on the floor, the kitten batting at the string which bound them, until on the fourth morning when the cool spring air woke him, he leapt up, threw open the shutters, and gazed down the street. Below the man who boiled bones looked up, and touched his cap. If he leaned to the left, he could have a glimpse of the street itself over the rooftops, the heavy dull reds of shop signs, the worn thatch and scuffed brick of roofs much marked by bird droppings and soot, and over it all came the soft wind of early spring once more, saying come!

The clock had just struck seven of the morn as he washed in the basin with fresh water from the street pump, trimmed his beard, and dressed carefully as if for his wedding. Then, taking the parcel under his arm, he locked his door and hurried down the steps to the street. If he had thought where he was going he might have turned back, but his mind was so full of many things that only his feet directed him. Even as he knew the stone turrets of the house on Drury Lane were within his sight, he kept his eyes to the path. The gardeners were at work, and the embroideress was arriving with her basket of silken threads.

The servant, however, was a new one who did not know him and haughtily made him wait in a lesser chamber while he hurried doubtfully off to announce the caller to his lordship. Then William might have left and was about to do so when the man came back and held open the door that the player might pass into the parlor.

Though the sun was now mounting into the heavens, the room was yet curiously dark, for heavy curtains were almost closed against the yard below, from which rose the sound of boys exercising the horses. They were heavy draperies, meant to divide the chamber from the more tawdry world of London's taverns and shops which lay but streets away in one direction and the fields of high grass and beginnings of farmlands which lay in the other. There was the same embroidered rug on the table, and on the mantel the great vase with its engraved words, *O Elizabeth, Queen!* though in this light the salutation was dull.

In that corner by that chair, Emilia had set her lute; it seemed a very long time ago.

As he looked about at everything, his heart was so full that he could not begin to sort out the feelings within it. Then the curtains parted and Southampton came into the room—he came in a sort of light as if he bore within his slender body part of the very sun. Embarrassment and joy filled his handsome face, and he took both the player's hands in his own and shook them heartily as soldiers greet one another.

"Why, Shakespeare!" he cried. "Why, damn thee, scamp! I wrote twice, nay more . . . much for me, and you did not reply! Then I saw you play one of Jonson's comedies, but could not come round to greet you. I could have ordered your presence as patron, I suppose." He frowned, and laughed in a slight embarrassed way as if caught in a lie, and concluded, "And now you come! But embrace me! What, have we become such strangers that we do not embrace?"

William said clumsily, "How are you, my lord?"

"Harry . . . hast forgot?"

"Well then . . . Harry."

"How do I? My blessed mother plans to remarry, and I shall move to my own dwelling. You can imagine I'm eager for that! Goodbye, house where I was a child! What times we had, didn't we, Shakespeare! And what will come now, who can say? But you must have wine, and we must talk . . . there's much to speak of. Be seated, pray be seated. Why do you stand there as if you wish to go away again at once when you've just come?"

Wine was poured, but the goblet was one he had not seen before, and then when he looked about, the room itself no longer seemed as he remembered it. Something had changed; he did not know what for certain. Slowly he raised his head to listen to the outpouring of news about court and women. Still he knew that the young man was uncomfortable for all his easiness of speech, for he leapt up then and again to walk about the room, speaking as if to the curtains and table rugs rather than to the poet. Once he opened the curtains, and the sun came spilling across the room.

"I'm at court now much more! Aye! There's one of the Queen's ladies-in-waiting whom I am determined to steal." Southampton turned with his old, glittering smile. "But that's the way of the world!" Striding forward now, he seated himself by William, and looking at him at first severely, put his hand tentatively on his arm.

"I knew you to be well," he said, "for I inquired. But a friend of mine who heard your play that night in this house asked if the man Shakespeare has gone away or died of a pestilence. For he said there's been no new play from his pen these many months."

William thought quietly, I could not write them, for I had gone away from myself . . . but you can't know this. How could I have ever expected you to know it? And yet whose fault was it what occurred between us? Perhaps what we wanted from each other could not be upon this earth.

He said, "I have come to give you the sonnets which I wrote for you, the ones your mother commissioned and then many others. Many you have not seen before, because I wrote them in grief and resentment, and was ashamed of them. They belong, after all, to you." He held out the packet.

"But sonnets should be lovely, not painful."

"Perhaps, but this is how they came to me."

The young man stood up and, walking to the window, drew the curtains a little and began to read. He stood there turning the pages with many emotions passing his face. "How deeply you feel things!" he murmured. "I have never met a man who felt as deeply as you do! I have never absolutely understood it, nor do I wish to I think . . . it cannot be comfortable to feel like that."

William looked away. "Do as you like with them, burn them perhaps. Yes, perhaps you should burn them, for they say more of me than I'd wish most people to know."

"William."

"My lord."

"I've said once that men in my position are praised in verse for what they can give. Was it but this?"

"You know 'twas not like that with me."

"Why?"

The player closed his eyes for a moment. "We do not choose when and to whom we give our hearts," he said. "Of all life's mysteries, this must be one of the greatest. What in the end is love? I speak not of lust, my lord, but love as best we know it. It must be a sort of extending outward towards another, and yet we do it to the very edge of our lives. To gain what and why? I do not know. The approval of the beloved? His affection or hers? Why does it sometimes seem worth all life to have?"

The Earl thrust the pages roughly back into the packet and looked for the string, and seeing that William had risen, cried out suddenly, "Ah, do not go! Stay to sup!"

"You are more than kind, but my work calls me," was the player's answer. He did not say, I do not love you anymore. He could not bear to say the words to himself for the cry of loss which must rise to his lips. Nor did he say, I wanted to give you everything I ever was, but you did not want it, and worse you did not even know how much was there for you, nor will you ever.

But Southampton had not noticed the silence, or if he did he felt it best to walk up and down the room. "Emilia wrote to me," he said offhandedly. "Her husband does badly, and she asked me for a pension or at least a gift. She hopes the man will be knighted one day. Ha! It can't be, for he's a fool! I sent her something, and did not answer again, but if she is in trouble I would, of course—but of you, William! What will you do?"

Barely finding his voice, he replied, "I do not know; it does not matter."

They spoke for a moment more, and then the player, bowing slightly, left the room. It was good that he knew the way so well, for the tears which had filled his eyes and blurred his vision, and under his breath he yet repeated, Burn the sonnets if you will . . . burn them. Let me go to my death in silence.

LATER HE COULD remember nothing of the day, of the usual problems of performance, how he got on and off the stage, or what he played. From time to time rushing across his mind came the thought that Southampton must be urged to burn the poems, and he would repeat the injunction and find his throat swollen with tears which he had to force away for his next speech. One of the apprentices ran after him with a problem, and John Heminges asked him for supper. Still as he hurried home through the city gates, he repeated the words which had been in his mind all day: Burn them.

Now the last of the pale golden light of the afternoon lingered in his room. Raising his dull face, he stared at the sunlight on the floor and at his writing table, as if he had never seen it before. For a moment he wanted to cry out again, Burn it all, burn it all. . . . Ah, God, the way writing was with him! Not a pretty craft as it had been with Robin Greene, but breathless and tender and torn from all he knew. Even the impossible comedies grew from that. How could he ever put on paper such intimacy? It was not the fashion of men of his part of the world to speak such things. Then he could not bear the thought he had done so, and wanted to hurry down to the boy on the corner to send another message to Southampton: do not keep the sonnets, burn them. For a moment tears came, and he wished to hurl everything into the fire. The actors owned the rights to the plays he had given them, but he need do no more; those half-finished ones with his own life embedded within the lines he would destroy.

And yet he did not. He knew even then that what he wanted more than anything was to write again. It was not merely to earn money to buy bread, but something that he knew he could not live without, something that held and protected him. And standing in the small room, he cried out, Lord, what have you made me? For writing, he suddenly understood, was more than a craft to him, something which had grown from happenstance and now seemed a heaven he had lost.

He knew that in these past months he had lost something it was terrible to lose, and that was his soul. Yet in the strange way life comes to be, he understood that everything would come as it always had into the writing and be purged. And he thought, Dearest Christ in heaven! Everything has formed me for what I am today.

Christopher Marlowe told me I was hidden; I was mayhap, but all that was hidden within me has emerged, and though it has torn me, and I bleed, I live. I must be this way, the manner of man I am. And Jack has known me, for that day when he had lost his money and felt he might never get on in life, and we sat by the stream and watched the little girl play, he said, There comes a time when you must know what you are at heart, and return to it.

There was Stratford and his father and mother, and sister Joan, now grown, now a prudent housewife. In the summer and fall they made up preserves, shelves upon shelves; they killed calf and pig and salted meat, and so the circle of the earth went round and round. And ah God, how much he loved them! His poor father with remorse which had seeped into a happy life and warped it, his mother and his wife who had never let themselves know joy for fear of losing it. But he was not them—he was himself. In the end he was not his father, nor his friends, nor any man but himself, and that was a comfort. He could do that no better than he could, but as poorly as he did it, he could do that better than anyone else. If he had had a mirror to look into he knew he would see his own face as he had not done in some time.

Slowly he began to clear away the shirts and hose, bills and kitten from the table to find the papers underneath. There were the beginnings of the play on John Lackland, the wretched younger brother who made such a poor king. *Aye, marry, now my soul hath elbowroom; it would not out at windows, nor at doors. . . . I am a scribbled form, drawn with a pen upon a parchment, and against this fire do I shrink up.*

It was all there, the ink, the sand for blotting, the bit of wax for sealing letters. Clearing a saucepan from the stool, he cautiously sat down before the piles of paper, found a little ink in a glass jar, and took up his pen. And then it came like words long unspoken, this story of the dissatisfied king who could not love.

The bread lay untasted on the shelf; he was thirsty but he did not reach for the ale. Dusk began to descend over the shabby roofs and chimneys of the city, and the air grew cooler, and though he was shivering he did not cease to pull on his extra wool jerkin. His body cramped, yet he moved still closer to his work.

And thus as darkness came he continued to bend over the page, shoulders hunched, until he could no longer see the words he wrote, though still in his mind they did not cease.

HISTORICAL NOTES

———◆•◆•◆———

About this book and the historical Shakespeare:

This novel covers the period in Shakespeare's life through the creation of his earliest plays, the so-called apprenticeship years, and concludes in 1595 when he was
almost thirty-one.

Thousands of books have been written over the past three centuries about this
greatest of all writers, drawing from contemporary records of baptism, marriage,
and death and documents of property and litigation. There are also the writings
of his colleagues—from Ben Jonson, who commented that he "lov'd the man, and
do honour his memory (this side of idolatry) as much as any," to his fellow actors,
who swore there could be no man as courteous, gentle, and worthy as he.

In the writing of this novel I have employed these generally accepted and/or
documented facts: William Shakespeare was born in Stratford in 1564, at eighteen he impregnated a woman several years older than he named Anne Hathaway
and married her. His father was a glover and may have secretly been a Catholic.
William came to London sometime after 1587 and became after a time a successful actor and playwright; in his early career he wrote two long poems dedicated to
his patron, the Earl of Southampton, for whom it is also suspected he wrote his
sonnets. Upon his retirement following 1610 he removed to Stratford and there
died on his fifty-second birthday in the year 1616. That his was an unhappy mar-

riage has been a conjecture of long standing, and I took it as dramatic license. He had three children, and lost his son young.

According to his early biographer John Aubrey, who received all his information secondhand, Shakespeare was a well-favored man, and the several references in the sonnets to his lameness are generally interpreted to mean his poverty; tradition has it, though, that as he grew older he played more stationary roles, and in view of this, I have given him a now and then troublesome knee. Of those who claim that someone else wrote the plays, the least said the better. Anecdotes of the period reveal he liked women very much indeed, but biographer Aubrey claimed that Shakespeare was a temperate man, and if invited to any kind of debauchery, would reply he could not come.

As I have said, the period of this book continues only through the early, apprentice phase of his work. The great plays—*Hamlet, King Lear, Julius Caesar*—were yet to come and with them the full expanse of the English theater. He had in those beginning years a very long and hard struggle with poverty and obscurity, which has never been fully appreciated for its difficulties. He could not see that he would one day be a prosperous gentleman, nor could he envision the pontifical marble busts in his likeness that would decorate many a library in the centuries following his death. Perhaps he would have laughed with astonishment.

Some facts and dates of Shakespeare's life have been slightly altered and others filled in by dramatic imagination. Those "lost years" from 1585 or so to about 1593 still puzzle scholars as they consider how he could have earned his bread before his first minor successes in the theater. Tradition has it he was schoolmaster and perhaps clerk of law; some say he minded horses outside the playhouse. That he could have written any of the thousands of treatises on many subjects sold by booksellers in their stalls is a matter of conjecture, but he must have had a scrappy time for some years and done what he could for bread.

As a writer I have taken great interest in following the path of the slowly emerging artist, always an individual matter and one of much personal struggle. I believe Shakespeare was in his youth a charming man who moved with grace, danced, was much drawn to music and laughter, and was deeply sensual. It is no wonder his colleagues loved him so much. Even after four hundred years, his works speak to us of his astonishing empathy for his fellow men.

The story of the sonnets and their love triangle:

"Anything more truly intimate has never been written," commented the Elizabethan historian A. L. Rowse of the 154 sonnets very likely composed in the years 1591–1595 by Shakespeare to the young lord of Southampton, his patron. Some of the poems were addressed to or concerned Shakespeare's dark-eyed mistress, with whom the two men were subsequently involved, to the poet's confusion and pain. I am convinced the sonnets were private, the first group being commissioned by the Earl's mother or guardian to put forth argument in poetic form to persuade the young man to marry, and the rest continuing in an astonishingly personal way to express devotion, resentment, subservience, older wisdom, regret, and passion as the relationship between poet and patron grew. I believe that they were never meant to be published, and their one edition, full of errors, was quickly suppressed. It is pure fortune that we have them today.

The self-sacrificing, romantic love of the poet for the young lord on whom he depended for patronage, and even more for his affection, has never been absolutely demystified, perhaps because it cannot be. Something so complicated in the human heart cannot be unequivocally laid plain and bare, nor does it make it easier that they were written by one man who was by nature strongly heterosexual to another. With Dr. Rowse I do believe that the love triangle between the poet, his mistress, and his patron was the great crisis of Shakespeare's life, absolutely changing him and pushing him directly from his youthful work towards the depths of feeling and character of the mature plays.

Of the identity of the Dark Lady of the Sonnets, there is rather more dispute. I have chosen for this novel the Italian musician Emilia Bassano, of whom I speak further later in these notes. Other possibilities are Mistress Davenant, an innkeeper's wife, whose son, later a successful theatrical entrepreneur, claimed to be Shakespeare's illegitimate progeny; the Queen's lady-in-waiting Mary Fitton, though she had a fair complexion; Lucy Morgan, also lady-in-waiting, who subsequently kept a brothel; and the sister of the ill-fated Earl of Essex, Penelope Rich.

Of the historical characters in the book:

JOHN SHAKESPEARE, 1530?–1601. He was a respected glover and alderman who eventually fell from economic and political favor in his town of Stratford; it is not known why, though some papers supposedly found two centuries ago indicated that he was a secret Catholic. Gradually he lost land and money. That he suffered from a depressive melancholy is my own interpretation, drawn from his son's interest in the depleting quality of melancholy.

MARY ARDEN SHAKESPEARE, 1540?–1608. The daughter of a gentleman farmer, she married John Shakespeare of Stratford around 1557; five of her eight children lived to adulthood.

ANNE HATHAWAY SHAKESPEARE, 1556–1623. The daughter of a farmer in Shottery, she was eight years older than William Shakespeare. Pregnancy forced her into marriage with him. She subsequently had three children: Susanna and the twins Hamnet and Judith. Because of his but brief mention of her in his will and the fact that he did not live with her for twenty years but in London it has long been assumed that the marriage was an unhappy one.

BEN JONSON, 1572–1637. He was a brawling, brilliant man. His first profession, after that of his stepfather, was bricklayer, though he had been educated under the great historian Camden at Westminster School; he subsequently became one of the three most famous playwrights of the period, living on into great age and sickness, yet surrounded by young poets who adulated him and were known as "the tribe of Ben." His monument in Westminster Abbey reads "O rare Ben Jonson!" and can still be seen. For dramatic purposes, I have made him a few years older in this novel than he would have been in 1587.

CHRISTOPHER MARLOWE, 1564–1593. The enigmatic poet blazed into London in his early twenties with his bloody, haunting, gorgeously written plays. Kit, as he was often called, numbered among his friends members of the nobility, scientists, poets, and cutthroats; he was arrested several times for fighting and left a mixed reputation both as a heretic and, as one poet called him, "Morley, darling of the Muses" or "kind Kit." Apparent in his writing is his sexual preference for boys or men. He died in a tavern brawl in 1593 at the age of twenty-nine; his three killers were acquitted of his murder.

ROBERT GREENE, 1558–1592. This lyrical playwright burned himself out after several romantic comedies and novels, deserting his wife and child and spending the last years of his life among whores and criminals. His last work, a tract against the theater, vilified many of his former colleagues and accused Shakespeare of plagiarism.

JOHN HEMINGES, ?–1630. Heminges, a grocer who became the informal dean of all London actors in his old age and the greatest shareholder of the Globe Theater, was one of Shakespeare's closest friends. He had thirteen children with his beloved wife, Rebecca, and collected Shakespeare's plays after the playwright's death; otherwise many of them would be lost to us today. A monument is erected to him near the Guildhall in London.

PHILIP HENSLOWE, ?–1616. The son of a gamekeeper, he made money in pawnshops, as a dyer, in real estate, and in brothels before turning his entrepreneurial sight towards the theater. Subsequently he owned the Rose, Fortune, and Hope playhouses. His famous accounting book, the best document we have on the daily workings of the Elizabethan theater, remains today in Dulwich College, which his actor son-in-law Edward Alleyn subsequently founded.

THE EARL OF SOUTHAMPTON, 1573–1624. At the age of nineteen, when the young Henry Wriothesley became Shakespeare's patron, he was the most beautiful and admired young nobleman in the land. Subsequently, he followed his idol Lord Essex to war and came to disaster with him in 1599 when they both rebelled against the Queen; at first sentenced to death for treason, he was imprisoned in the Tower until her death in 1603. He later went on to become a conservative peer of the realm and a patron of the colony in Virginia.

EMILIA BASSANO, 1570–1654. The Bassano family were Venetian musicians, many of whom came to the musical London court in the 1580s to seek their fortunes. Emilia was the illegitimate daughter of an English mother and half-Jewish Italian father. Brought up for a time in the household of the Countess of Kent, she was the mistress of the elderly Lord Chamberlain until he married her off at her pregnancy to a commoner. A beautiful girl with somewhat easy morals, she lived to be quite old and to publish her own book of poetry. It is likely that she was a potent influence on Shakespeare's fascination for things Italian, and some believe that in the later years of his writing he fashioned the character of Cleopatra from her capricious disposition. Her likely identification as the enigmatic and long obscure Dark Lady of the Sonnets was brought forth by Dr. Rowse only in the last twenty years.

Of the London Shakespeare knew:

The London to which Shakespeare came in the late years of the sixteenth century had much of the medieval about it with its thatched and tile roofs, half-timbered houses, and some hundred stone parish churches. A hundred thousand souls from merchants to beggars and scholars to thieves were crammed within the city walls, whose streets, mostly unpaved, led to lanes and alleys so small and numerous that some were but a few steps in length, and there was hardly a man (save the great Elizabethan topographer John Stow, whose book *The Survey of London* was printed in 1598) who knew them all. A few theaters had recently been constructed outside the city walls (and hence out of the jurisdiction of certain Puritan city fathers), or across the river on the south side near the bear gardens and cockpits. Though its sanitation system was primitive and odorous, the city was sweetened by an endless number of gardens full of herbs, trees, and flowers. Swans floated on the Thames, which was crossed only by London Bridge or by ferry. The original Globe Theater would not be built until 1599.

It has been a little more than four hundred years since the young Shakespeare first made his way down those streets, and much of what he knew has been lost to us because of fire, war, and the relentless progression of civilization. Still, certain original sections of the city walls remain, as do some of the ancient churches. A short walk west from the old city along Fleet Street will bring you to Middle Temple and its great oak hammerbeam hall, which often saw the performances of plays. The London Museum has many invaluable exhibitions of the period, from the very garments of Queen Bess to a hoard of pretty Elizabethan jewelry found under a street, and the reconstructed Globe Theater is a fine replica of such outdoor, thatched playhouses as Shakespeare would have known. If you travel on the Thames by boat and look at it rising on the south side, you will feel perhaps a little of the wonder he experienced when, as a country boy, he came to this great city with some hope in his heart that he might one day be an actor and a writer of plays.

The sonnets:

In 1591 the Earl of Southampton, Shakespeare's patron, to whom many scholars believe the sonnets were written, was eighteen years old, beautiful, spoiled, and the last of his line. His mother wished him to marry quickly, and the proposed match—to the granddaughter of the Queen's minister Lord Burghley—was one of the most advantageous in England. The first seventeen sonnets were written to encourage him to this marriage. Shakespeare was a new writer at the time, with probably very little money in his pocket, and would have been glad to have the commission.

II

When forty winters shall besiege thy brow,
And dig deep trenches in thy beauty's field,
Thy youth's proud livery, so gaz'd on now,
Will be a tatter'd weed, of small worth held.
Then being ask'd where all thy beauty lies,
Where all the treasure of thy lusty days,
To say, within thine own deep-sunken eyes,
Were an all-eating shame, and thriftless praise.
How much more praise deserv'd thy beauty's use,
If thou couldst answer, "This fair child of mine

Shall sum my count, and make my old excuse,"
Proving his beauty by succession thine!
    This were to be new made when thou art old,
    And see thy blood warm when thou feel'st it cold.

Early in the book of sonnets, Shakespeare abandons the plea for the Earl to sire children to allow his beauty to live on; now the theme is that Southampton's beauty will never fade because of the poet's praise of it. Some singular closeness must have occurred by this time between the near-penniless writer and the pampered nobleman to account for the affectionate tone of the following.

XVIII

Shall I compare thee to a summer's day?
Thou art more lovely and more temperate.
Rough winds do shake the darling buds of May,
And summer's lease hath all too short a date:
Sometimes too hot the eye of heaven shines,
And often is his gold complexion dimm'd;
And every fair from fair sometimes declines,
By chance, or nature's changing course, untrimm'd;
But thy eternal summer shall not fade,
Nor lose possession of that fair thou ow'st;
Nor shall Death brag thou wander'st in his shade,
When in eternal lines to time thou grow'st.
    So long as men can breathe, or eyes can see,
    So long lives this, and this gives life to thee.

While the poet's closeness with his patron continued to grow, Shakespeare still had to tour the countryside as an actor, an insecure profession of low social esteem of which he was often ashamed ("made myself a motley to the view") and which exhausted him.

CX

Alas, 'tis true I have gone here and there
And made myself a motley to the view,
Gor'd mine own thoughts, sold cheap what is most dear,
Made old offenses of affections new.
Most true it is that I have look'd on truth
Askance and strangely; but, by all above,

These blenches gave my heart another youth,
And worse essays prov'd thee my best of love.
Now all is done, have what shall have no end;
Mine appetite I never more will grind
On newer proof, to try an older friend,
A god in love, to whom I am confin'd.
    Then give me welcome, next my heaven the best,
    Even to thy pure and most loving breast.

It must be noted that close friendship between men in the Renaissance was often spoken in terms of love. But whatever their personal relationship, the poet is aware that because of the discrepancies in their social situations, it can never be publicly acknowledged.

XXXVI

Let me confess that we two must be twain,
Although our undivided loves are one.
So shall these blots that do with me remain,
Without thy help, by me be borne alone.
In our two loves there is but one respect,
Though in our lives a separable spite,
Which though it alter not love's sole effect,
Yet it doth steal sweet hours from love's delight.
I may not evermore acknowledge thee,
Lest my bewailed guilt should do thee shame;
Nor thou with public kindness honour me,
Unless thou take that honour from thy name.
    But do not so; I love thee in such sort,
    As thou being mine, mine is thy good report.

Yet the relationship is not equal, for whatever the Earl feels for his poet, he is accustomed to treat all of lower social station as servant, and makes little exception for Shakespeare. The word "will" in the next-to-last line of the sonnet below was both a play on the poet's name and the Elizabethan slang for pleasure or sexuality.

LVII

Being your slave, what should I do but tend
Upon the hours and times of your desire?

I have no precious time at all to spend,
Nor services to do, till you require.
Nor dare I chide the world-without-end hour
Whilst I, my sovereign, watch the clock for you,
Not think the bitterness of absence sour
When you have bid your servant once adieu;
Nor dare I question with my jealous thought
Where you may be, or your affairs suppose,
But, like a sad slave, stay and think of nought
Save, where you are how happy you make those.
    So true a fool is love, that in your will,
    Though you do anything, he thinks no ill.

Somewhere in the relationship the Earl sharply hurt his sensitive poet; perhaps it was the first time Shakespeare understood that his patron was involved with Shakespeare's dark-eyed mistress.

XXXIV

Why didst thou promise such a beauteous day,
And make me travel forth without my cloak,
To let base clouds o'ertake me in my way,
Hiding thy bravery in their rotten smoke?
'Tis not enough that through the cloud thou break,
To dry the rain on my storm-beaten face,
For no man well of such a salve can speak
That heals the wound, and cures not the disgrace,
Nor can thy shame give physic to my grief;
Though thou repent, yet I have still the loss.
Th'offender's sorrow lends but weak relief
To him that bears the strong offence's cross.
    Ah, but these tears are pearls which thy love sheds,
    And they are rich, and ransom all ill deeds.

The following sensual poem gives an astonishingly frank portrayal of Shakespeare's love life with his mistress, so frank that it has been called one of the "gross" sonnets by those who prefer to conceive the living poet as above such matters. In it, he shakes his head over how far his intellectual self is divided from his physical urges.

CLI

Love is too young to know what conscience is;
Yet who knows not conscience is born of love?
Then, gentle cheater, urge not my amiss,
Less guilty of my faults thy sweet self prove.
For thou betraying me, I do betray
My nobler part to my gross body's treason;
My soul doth tell my body that he may
Triumph in love; flesh stays no farther reason,
But rising at thy name doth point out thee
As his triumphant prize. Proud of this pride,
He is contented thy poor drudge to be,
To stand in thy affairs, fall by thy side.
    No want of conscience hold it that I call
    Her "love" for whose dear love I rise and fall.

The poet is desperately torn between the dishonor of the love triangle and his
tender, protective stance to his rival, and tries to reconcile it in literary terms.

XLII

That thou hast her, it is not all my grief,
And yet it may be said I lov'd her dearly;
That she hath thee, is of my wailing chief,
A loss in love that touches me more nearly.
Loving offenders, thus I will excuse ye:
Thou dost love her because thou know'st I love her,
And for my sake even so doth she abuse me,
Suff'ring my friend for my sake to approve her.
If I lose thee, my loss is my love's gain,
And losing her, my friend hath found that loss;
Both find each other, and I lose both twain,
And both for my sake lay on me this cross.
    But here's the joy; my friend and I are one;
    Sweet flattery! then she loves but me alone.

In the following sonnet he seems resigned to the strange, unhappy situation,
the bewildering mixture of "comfort and despair" from which he cannot shake
loose. Here "hell" is Elizabethan for the female sexual parts.

CXLIV

Two loves I have of comfort and despair,
Which like two spirits do suggest me still;
The better angel is a man right fair,
The worser spirit a woman colour'd ill.
To win me soon to hell, my female evil
Tempteth my better angel from my side,
And would corrupt my saint to be a devil,
Wooing his purity with her foul pride.
And whether that my angel be turn'd fiend,
Suspect I may, yet not directly tell;
But being both from me, both to each friend,
I guess one angel in another's hell.
    Yet this shall I ne'er know, but live in doubt,
    Till my bad angel fire my good one out.

Now the poet cries out bitterly against the power his sexuality has over him, which binds him to a woman who is not faithful.

CXXIX

Th'expense of spirit in a waste of shame
Is lust in action, and till action lust
Is perjur'd, murd'rous, bloody, full of blame,
Savage, extreme, rude, cruel, not to trust,
Enjoy'd no sooner but despised straight,
Past reason hunted, and no sooner had,
Past reason hated, as a swallowed bait,
On purpose laid to make the taker mad,
Mad in pursuit and in possession so,
Had, having, and in quest to have, extreme,
A bliss in proof, and prov'd, a very woe,
Before, a joy propos'd; behind a dream.
    All this the world well knows, yet none knows well
    To shun the heaven that leads men to this hell.

Through the sonnets we return time and again to the assertion that though the poet will find but a common grave, his words will make the young Earl immortal against the ravages of time. Over four hundred years after they were privately and passionately written, the poems continue to be read with much awe and delight—though it is, of course, the poet himself and not the man he praised who has achieved immortality.

LXXXI

Or shall I live your epitaph to make,
Or you survive when I in earth am rotten.
From hence your memory death cannot take,
Although in me each part will be forgotten.
Your name from hence immortal life shall have,
Though I, once gone, to all the world must die.
The earth can yield me but a common grave,
When you entombed in men's eyes shall lie.
Your monument shall be my gentle verse,
Which eyes not yet created shall o'er-read,
And tongues to be your being shall rehearse,
When all the breathers of this world are dead.
    You still shall live—such virtue hath my pen—
    Where breath most breathes, even in the mouths of men.

ACKNOWLEDGMENTS

Many people contributed to the writing of this book. I am most indebted to Dr. A. L. Rowse for his several suggestions and encouragement of the project (particularly to carry it through to the story of the sonnets), and for his lifelong work on the Elizabethans and Shakespeare, whose gentle creative character he delineated so remarkably. His work on the sonnets, now sadly out of print, was invaluable. Also a true guide and inspiration was the remarkable *The Book Known as Q* by Robert Giroux, as well as the writing of Professor Stanley Wells. Peter Quennell's work was influential, particularly in his delineation of the poet's slow growth, and the remarkable classic study by Caroline Spurgeon, *Shakespeare's Imagery*, helped bring the poet into greater clarity in the many facets of his character. Any errors of history and all imaginative leaps of the novelist are my responsibility alone and blame cannot be laid to any of the above respected scholars.

I owe a great debt to the New York Public Library for its comprehensive research facilities, in whose Arents Collection I was able to hold in my hands many original volumes from the sixteenth century, and to the English-Speaking Union for sending me to England, where I first walked about Stratford and saw the streets where Shakespeare was a boy. Much of my London research was facilitated by the remarkable London Museum; many a precious research book was bought in the Guildhall bookstore (including a cherished period map) and many a fascinating detail learned in touring the site of the new Globe Theater and its museum, for which I am grateful to its late director, Sam Wanamaker, and his assistants. But as I have been studying the Elizabethans and Shakespeare since childhood, I can no longer list all my sources; they murmur in my memory like songs I have always known, but cannot remember first hearing. When I was a child their world was realer to me than my own, and perhaps in some ways it still remains so.

I most deeply thank my husband, Russell O'Neal Clay, for his unfailing support during this project as well as excellent editorial suggestions. Friends and colleagues who read the work in draft and made insightful comments which strengthened it include Elsa and Sol Rael, Katherine Kirkpatrick, Peggy Harrington, Judith Ackerman, and Phylis Ravel.

I would like to thank my writing group, Katherine Kirkpatrick, Elsa Rael, Ruth Henderson, Isabelle Holland, Judith Lindbergh, and Casey Kelly, and its extended members, Shelby Evans and Peggy Harrington, as well as Madeleine L'Engle, who has been a mentor and often a mother to me. Members of my church, St. Thomas Fifth Avenue, have stood behind my work with an unfailing enthusiasm. I am grateful to parishioners (particularly my dear friend Ellen Beschler), musicians, and clergy: the Reverend Dr. John Andrew, the Reverend Gary Fertig, the Reverend Richard Alton and his wife, Barbara, and the Reverend David Sellery and his wife, Christine. Many thanks to the sisters of the Community of the Holy Spirit and to my employer, the Manpower Demonstration Research Corporation, especially Patt Pontevolpe, Judy Greissman, Betsy Dossett, Jim Healy, and Judy Gueron, for their willingness to adjust my schedule for the needs of this book and for understanding when my mind was now and then in another century. Friends who encourage my work and advise me in it are more numerous than can be listed, but I wish particularly to put down the names of Bruce Bawer, Chris Davenport, the McGaugley/Whitehead families, and Renée Pachter Cafiero and Christine Emmert, with whom I read aloud much of Shakespeare in my teens.

Many thanks to my family for their constant interest and support. To my younger son, Jesse Cowell, and his friend Grace Egan; my older son, James Nordstrom, and his wife, Jessica; and my stepsons, Jeremy, Benjamin, and Christopher. To my parents, Viraja (who particularly encouraged this book) and James Mathieu, and to my mother- and father-in-law, Genia and John Head; and to my sister Gabrielle, my sister Jennie, her husband, Gerald, and my nephew David.

Finally, I would like to acknowledge my agent, Donald Maass, his assistant, Jennifer Jackson, and my publisher, W. W. Norton. My thanks to the first editor on this book, Mary Cunnane, for whose artistic advice I am most grateful, and to the second editor, Patricia Chui, who cheerfully "inherited" it and has seen it expertly through from manuscript to publication; also to Nicole Wan, to Nicole Hala, and to the whole superb staff and consultants of the company, so many of whom have contributed to this work. With all my heart, gentles, I extend to you my most gracious thanks.